BORN TO
BE BADGER

BORN TO
BE BADGER

SHELLY
LAURENSTON

KENSINGTON
PUBLISHING CORP.

www.kensingtonbooks.com

KENSINGTON BOOKS are published by
Kensington Publishing Corp.
119 West 40th Street
New York, NY 10018

Special book excerpts or customized printings can also be created to fit specific needs. For details, write or phone the office of the Kensington Sales Manager: Kensington Publishing Corp., 119 West 40th Street, New York, NY 10018. Attn. Sales Department. Phone: 1-800-221-2647.

The K with book logo Reg US Pat. & TM Off.

ISBN: 978-1-4967-3019-0 (ebook)

ISBN: 978-1-4967-3017-6

First Kensington Trade Paperback Printing: December 2023

10 9 8 7 6 5 4 3 2 1

Printed in the United States of America

To Mom.
I miss you, lady.

Prologue

"I'm a bad mother."

Kerrick "Kerry" Jackson gazed at his wife as they quietly indulged in a late-night gallon of rum raisin ice cream in their dark kitchen. They were keeping their voices low due to the five teenage girls sleeping upstairs in their only daughter's bedroom. They also kept the lights out through the house, but they could see each other fine in the darkness with only the glow from the microwave and the timer on their electric stove. He adored how the blinking light from the stove that she never bothered to set to the right time highlighted his wife's black hair with that one big white streak down the middle, her mane half in dreads and half in wild curls, piled on top of her head in a ridiculously messy topknot. And her dark eyes peering at him from beneath those white lashes that everyone at the high school thought she'd dyed just so she could be the "edgy mom." But Ayda Lepstein-Jackson didn't dye anything. All that white-and-black hair was completely natural, including the white eyebrow over her left eye.

"Why would you ever say that?" he asked her.

"Because we should have gone to the game."

"You keep saying that, but Tock made it very clear she didn't want us there."

"Was it clear, though?" Ayda asked, her brow furrowing, skin bunching in the center of her forehead where, according to her, she'd accidentally slammed into a telephone pole when she was nine. The entire area had swelled and the skin had broken right in the center. There was no obvious scar, but when she frowned, it puckered up again the way the swelling once did.

"Was it clear?" he repeated. "She looked directly at us and said, 'I don't want you there.' I'm not sure she could have been any clearer. Our daughter's not known for being vague."

"Our daughter and her team won a nationwide basketball championship, and all those other parents were there in Chicago . . . but not us."

"Maybe those kids needed their parents there. But our girl does not. We didn't *need* to be there for her or for her friends." The four other teammates sleeping upstairs with their daughter at this very moment. A tighter crew he'd never known. "Even little Cass's parents didn't go. I know for a fact they're in France . . . *checking out* the Louvre." He raised a knowing brow at his wife, but she only frowned in confusion.

Not bothering to clarify, Kerry ate another spoonful of ice cream and admitted to his wife, "I think we all know the girls had additional plans for that championship besides winning it, and they simply didn't want their families there screwing up their timing. You know how our Tock is about time."

His wife gazed at him, her tongue in the midst of licking her spoon. Slowly, she put the spoon down. "What additional plans?" She gave a little gasp. "A boy?" she asked, eyes wide. "Or a man?" She gasped again, going on before her husband could get a word in. "Oh, my God. Is she involved with a grown man? Wait . . . is it a criminal? Has she made friends with a criminal?"

"What?"

"Is she having unprotected sex with a criminal and he just got out of prison and lured her to Chicago to have unprotected sex with our minor daughter? Is that what you're telling me?"

For a few seconds, Kerry could do nothing but gawk at his wife. He loved her. He really did. Had since the moment he'd met her. But, in a word, she was *nuts*. Nutty nuts, as one of his cousins called her. But he actually loved her nutty nuts-ness. It made their married life . . . interesting.

"No," he finally told her, briefly glancing up at the ceiling when he heard what sounded like one of the girls getting out of bed . . . or falling out. "That's *not* what I'm saying. At all. I don't even know how you got there."

"She's a beautiful girl. What criminal wouldn't want her?"

Kerry shook his head to stop himself from laughing and dipped his spoon into the gallon of ice cream.

"Our daughter," he promised his wife, "has not been lured by anyone. Nor will she ever be lured by anyone."

"Then why wouldn't she want us there with all the other parents?"

"You didn't notice the extra duffel bags all five girls brought back with them from this trip?" Kerry asked.

Ayda blinked. "What?" When he gave a small shrug, she immediately shook her head. "No. No, no, no. Are you telling me they were"—she lowered her voice even more—"*stealing?*"

"Why are you whispering? You know who we are; what we are. Did you expect our daughter to be any different?"

"My family does not steal, Kerry."

He couldn't help but snort. "Are you kidding? Your family may steal files or nuclear secrets or warheads, but they're still stealing. And that's in our daughter's blood. Like the white stripe in her hair and the fact that she snaps at random people on the street when she feels they've gotten within seven feet of her without her express permission. It's what makes us . . . *us*. Why would you expect any different from our girl?"

"Because I do! I have worked *hard* to ensure our daughter does not involve herself in any of that. No thieving. No lying. No conning. And absolutely *no* geopolitics that can destroy nations. I won't tolerate it!"

Kerry dropped his spoon into the gallon ice cream container and took her hand. "Baby, you can't deny what our daughter is."

"I'm not denying what *all* of us are. I'm simply working to ensure that—"

"She ignores her instincts?"

"No. That she finds a . . . better path."

He blew out a breath and told his wife, "Baby, our daughter—

Emily 'Tock' Lepstein-Jackson—is, and always will be . . . a honey badger."

"Being a honey badger doesn't mean she has to be—"

"Rude? Mean? Dangerously unstable? Of course, it does. Because it's in our blood like your Uncle Ishmael's giant fore-head and my grandmother being able to run marathons back in the day even though one leg is shorter than the other. Our baby is what she is. And what she is, is a snarling, snapping, seventeen-year-old thief who has a very good eye for jewelry, fine art, and kitchen cabinets where she and her badger friends can spend the night. You can't change that."

"*I* changed. I'm pleasant—"

"But it's a struggle."

"—I don't steal—"

"But we all know you want to. Especially when something's shiny."

"—and I go out of my way to do the right thing."

"So does your daughter. That's why she almost got expelled three weeks ago for attacking that football player who got handsy with some tenth grader she doesn't know."

Ayda shook her head. "I had to do some fast talking with the principal on that one."

"Fast talking or lots of threatening?"

"Combination. But she was right!" Ayda suddenly announced. "What he did was not okay and I fully support her protecting the sisterhood." She looked out the sliding glass doors and gave a little sigh. "But . . . still . . ."

"Stop," he ordered. "She's fine. She'll always be fine. So she probably robbed some mall jewelry store and took all their tacky wedding rings and those low-quality tennis bracelets worthless husbands buy their wives when they clearly have nothing but contempt for them."

"That seems a little harsh."

"I would *never* waste my talents on getting that sort of thing for you. *You* get only the best of what I can get off the black market or steal from the quality jewelers. Just like my daddy does for my mom."

She tried to hide her smile but he still saw it. And loved it.

"Our baby," he went on, "is only testing her skills. She and her little friends plotting a heist from a mall store is just healthy teens scratching an instinctual itch."

She scrunched up her nose in that way he absolutely adored. "You can't really believe that."

"Of course, I do. That's how I got started. At one of those chain jewelry stores where most people buy their wedding rings for second and third marriages. Besides, how cute were they? All trying to pretend that the bags were filled with nothing more than stuff they bought at the game. Let them have their moment. It will build their confidence."

After staring at him, her mouth hanging open, Ayda asked, "You really think this is helpful?"

"This is helpful. And I am helping. I'm helping *you*. Because the one thing you don't want to do is get on the wrong side of our daughter, which is what you're about to do. Tock can be mean. My Aunt Lucille won't even speak to her anymore. Said she is Satan's minion."

Ayda pulled her hand from his and began to rub her forehead. "Our daughter is too young to be pulling heists with her friends. She doesn't know how dangerous they can turn. I could easily still be doing time in South Africa because of that heist that went bad."

"First off, it wasn't a heist, sweetie. You took over a diamond mine and started a military rebellion. Didn't they make you their queen?"

"No!" she lashed back. "They made me the 'goddess of our enemies' blood,' which was an honor, I'll have you know."

"And your mother was the one who got you out of the country and the reason we can't visit some of my cousins." He shook his head. "South Africa does not want you back, baby."

"I am aware. And I don't want any of that for our daughter."

He frowned. "She wants to go to South Africa?"

Ayda slammed her fists on the table. "Goddamnit, Kerry!"

A loud thud outside the glass doors startled them out of the fight they were about to indulge in, and they looked over to see a man lying facedown on their lawn.

"Who the fuck is that?" Ayda wanted to know.

"I have no—"

Another body hit the ground, followed by two more. A few seconds later, Tock and her four honey badger teammates silently landed beside the men, each dropping from the second-story landing.

"What in the world . . . ?" Ayda softly gasped.

For varying reasons, none of the girls had returned to their homes after the team bus arrived at the school to drop them off. While the full-human teammates had gone off with the team captain for a huge celebration party at her parents' house, Tock and her friends had come back to the house for steaks and shrimp and fresh, still-scrambling scorpions; locally sourced, of course.

After the dinner and a few hours of TV, all five girls had gone to bed. Kerry had assumed that was it. They wouldn't hear from the girls until morning. Or, if they were acting like normal teenagers, maybe they'd sneak out to smoke some weed or drink a beer or two. That was truly all he'd expected.

He now realized, though . . . he should have known better. Because, at the end of the day, Tock and all her friends weren't like him and his siblings. Or Ayda and her family. They weren't just honey badger shifters. They were honey badgers. In their hearts. In their blood. In their souls. They couldn't switch off the honey badger inside them to easily assimilate with full-humans. Many other shifters didn't even know their kind still existed.

Their families could blend into any gathering without trouble or concern. They could live for years . . . decades . . . among full-humans without a hint that, at a Sunday family meal, they all indulged in slabs of grilled cottonmouth snake in barbeque sauce along with poison-laced wines. But there were badgers that didn't assimilate. They didn't bother. Because they didn't care. He now realized that was his daughter and her friends . . . these girls were true honey badgers. Mean, vicious, snarling honey badgers that no one should ever sneak up on. Or try to kill while they were having a sleepover at a friend's house.

Too stunned to do anything to help his child, Kerry instead studied the men on the ground. He knew Chicago gangsters when he saw them. Gangsters who were in his house because his child had not stolen from some mall store. She'd plotted and planned and executed a heist from someone much more dangerous. Someone who'd send henchmen to get his stuff back from little girls, even if they had to kill everyone in the house to do so.

Kerry was awed. He bet the heist timing had been impeccable.

When it came to time, his daughter was always impeccable.

What foolish, foolish men these were. They thought nothing of sneaking into a suburban house in the middle of Wisconsin to get their boss's stuff back. How hard could it be, they'd probably reasoned, grabbing jewels back from little girls?

But Tock and her friends . . . he almost laughed.

The girls were still dressed in their bedclothes for the overnight stay at the Lepstein-Jackson house. Tock in Kerry's old college football jersey, even though she had no interest in the sport. Mads in her Chicago Bulls basketball tank that was so long it reached past her knees and had the name "Jordan" emblazoned on the back. Little Cass Gonzalez—whom the other girls now called "Streep" for her ability to cry on cue whenever she was accused of stealing something from the teachers' lounge at their high school—wore a Hello Kitty nightshirt, Hello Kitty socks, and a Hello Kitty headband to hold back her long brown hair. Gong Zhao had on what Kerry could only call a silk negligee with matching silk robe cinched at the waist by a matching silk belt. It seemed a little mature for a girl barely seventeen, but Gong—nicknamed Nelle for some reason—never wore typical teen clothing. Everything in her wardrobe was designer, including what she was currently wearing. And why a seventeen-year-old had a Lacroix negligee and robe, Kerry really didn't know. Max MacKilligan, smiling as always, had on a pair of running shorts and a cut-off T-shirt with the singer Pink on the front.

There were, however, some additions to their sleep outfits that hadn't been there before they'd headed off to bed.

Like gold and platinum necklaces inlaid with diamonds. Ruby and emerald rings on their fingers. Thick platinum bracelets on their wrists and—for the smaller ones—around their biceps. And at least two wore tiaras that he was almost positive once belonged to a European royal family.

"Is that one of the Dutch royal jewels?" his wife asked, her voice filled with awe as she gestured to Gong's neck.

"Yeah. I think so." Whatever place they'd broken into was probably a regular jewelry store for the world to see but, underneath or on another floor, laundered stolen jewelry for high bidders. That's what his kid had gone after.

Kerry didn't know which confused and concerned him more: how his daughter and her friends had found out about this place in Chicago, or how the people in Chicago had found out about his daughter and her friends so quickly. No one, absolutely no one, would expect a bunch of teen girls to break into a place like that. A smash-and-grab, maybe, but a planned assault in the middle of the night with no alarms going off and no cops arriving until the manager came in the next morning to open up? That was a job for old-timers who had been jewelry thieves for decades. That one last job before retirement. Not a starter job for five girls who were still in high school.

Tock signaled to the girls and they began to move. Kerry was only able to glance quickly at an equally shocked Ayda. The seventeen-year-olds had hand signals to communicate silently, as if they were combat trained. They didn't do that sort of thing on the court. They yelled at one another when they wanted to make a certain move during a game. But when they had bodies to deal with in the middle of the night . . .

Kerry gave a short shake of his head. He knew his girl was special but *damn!*

Cass grabbed an arm and was about to start dragging a body away when her gaze locked on Kerry and Ayda. She let out a strange little "eep" that they could easily hear despite the glass doors.

"What?" Mads whispered.

Cass simply motioned to Kerry and Ayda with a jerk of her chin and all the girls faced them. Stared. Their eyes glinting in the darkness like any other night-seeing animal.

For a moment, Kerry thought the girls would just run off, leaving the bodies behind. He wouldn't blame them. It was a normal adolescent reaction to being caught with dead bodies.

Of course, he reminded himself, these were not "normal" adolescents. Not even normal adolescent honey badgers. That was clear when little Max MacKilligan raised her arm in the air, waved, and yelled while grinning, "Hi, Mr. and Mrs. Jackson! Beautiful night, huh?"

Kerry had no reply. He was not sure he was supposed to reply. Because that would be weird.

But he had to let that thought go as he saw his precious daughter begin to slowly walk toward the glass doors; the frown she had on her face grew deeper and darker the closer she got.

"Oh, my God," he heard his wife whisper, "she's going to kill us both."

He thought Ayda might be right when Tock reached the doors and stood there, glaring at them both. In that moment, Kerry truly believed his daughter was actually contemplating killing them. Not because she wanted to or hated them, but because they'd seen too much. A terrifying decision but, if he wanted to be honest, very logical. And his daughter was always logical.

He held his breath as she slowly lifted her hand and abruptly jabbed at the glass.

"Is that *my* rum raisin?" she demanded loudly.

Kerry and Ayda both looked down at the ice cream they'd been eating and then at each other. They were at a loss, but Tock was waiting for an answer.

After clearing her throat, Ayda softly replied, "It's rum raisin."

"So *my* rum raisin," his daughter insisted, annoyed. "All the rum raisin in this house is mine. You know that, Ma."

His wife blinked a few times before replying, "I . . . uh . . . guess that's true. You do love rum raisin."

"Are you going to replace it?" his child wanted to know, finally sounding like a true teenager.

"There's more in the freezer in the garage," Kerry told her.

"You sure?" Tock demanded.

"I always make sure there's rum raisin in the house, baby. I know how you are," he added.

"I'm going to be really mad if there isn't. I was planning to eat it for breakfast."

"That's not breakfast," he told her.

"It is for me. Don't try and control me, Dad," she whined.

Then, with that, she turned away and motioned to the bodies.

Without another word, the girls reached down and grabbed arms or legs. Cass and Gong took one body; Tock and Max took another. Mads hefted a large male onto her shoulder, then grabbed the leg of the last. Tock also reached down and took a leg and, together, the girls walked off with their prey.

When they disappeared into the trees behind the house, Ayda looked at him with an expression that could only be called . . . tense.

"Before you panic," he began, ignoring her raised eyebrows and wide eyes, "I'm sure they're just going to bury those bodies on hyena territory. You know . . . because we all bury our bodies on hyena territory."

The fingers on her left hand began to tap on the wood table. Not a good sign. His wife was much more frightening when she became silent. Chatty, hysterical Ayda could be reasoned with. But silent, finger-tapping, *glaring* Ayda could not.

"Okay," he continued. "I'm guessing you're *not* worried about where they're planning to bury the bodies."

Fingers tapped.

"Or how your daughter and her friends quietly killed four armed gangsters in our house without our even knowing . . ."

Fingers continued to tap.

"Or how those gangsters knew it was Tock and her friends in the first place."

Still those fingers tapped.

"Instead, I'm guessing that you are trying to figure out how your *mother* is involved in all this."

The tapping immediately stopped and her fingers curled into a fist. Kerry leaned back in the chair.

"Yeah," he said on a long sigh, "that's what I figured."

Chapter 1

Eleven years later . . .

First the bump; from behind. Then the mumbled apology. Lastly, a piece of paper shoved into her left hand.

Emily "Tock" Lepstein-Jackson kept walking through the crowd, not looking at the man who'd bumped into her. Instead, she waited until she reached a porta potty. She didn't go in. She couldn't do that. She went around it and stopped between the porta potty and the six-foot security fence to look at the piece of paper in her hand.

This sort of thing hadn't happened in a while, because she wasn't working for anyone. Well, she wasn't working for any government. She did work for the shifter nation. That's where her true loyalty lay. Governments were changeable entities— one day a democratic paradise, the next a totalitarian nightmare. She didn't want to end up on the wrong side of history, so she gave her loyalty to the one group that hadn't changed in thousands of years. Shifters. Their only goal was to keep their kind safe and able to thrive. They never wanted to be science experiments. They didn't want to be hunted for trophies. They didn't want to be sex toys for those who thought they were "exotic." And they definitely didn't want to end up as steaks on some full-human's dinner plate.

That was a belief system Tock could get behind. And an employer who didn't sneakily shove pieces of paper into her hand in the middle of a street party thrown in honor of her teammate Mads's grandmother. She was in Detroit with her four teammates and some big cats to relax. To eat amazing food, to get in a little street ball, maybe to flirt a bit with the local cutie pies. Not to be part of some covert operation that could get her—

"Shit."

Tock crumpled the paper, pulled out a lighter she only used for this sort of thing because she didn't smoke, and set the paper on fire. She held it between her thumb and forefinger until it had burned down to the tiniest scrap. Her fingers hurt a little from the flame, but they'd heal soon enough.

She dropped the remaining scrap and came around the porta potty, pulling out her phone and sending a quick text to her teammates: **Gotta run. See you back in Manhattan. Won't miss practice.**

The last line was specifically for her teammate Mads. She knew that would be Mads's first question. Their pro shifter team, the Wisconsin Butchers, was headed to the finals, and her friend wouldn't let anything get between them and possibly winning this year's championship. Because when it came to basketball, Mads was a little . . . obsessive. She'd always been that way, though. Since the day Tock had met her. The girl loved basketball. It made sense when Tock thought about it. Basketball was Mads's "safe space." A place no one could touch her. Literally. The girl practically had wings on her feet. No matter how horrible Mads's family was to her—and they had always been fucking horrible—they couldn't say anything to make her feel insecure about basketball. Because Mads was that good.

Of course, Tock wasn't a bad ball player either. She just didn't take it as seriously as Mads did. Tock did like winning, though. She was very good at winning. She even had a little "we beat your ass" dance.

She really shouldn't put herself at risk—which meant possibly risking the championship—but she knew that there were times in life when you couldn't ignore a request. Even when you really wanted to.

Away from the street party, Tock quickly found the car that was waiting for her. All the information she needed had been on that slip of paper: the car she would drive to the airport about an hour away; the private jet she'd take back to the East Coast; and an inkling of what she'd be doing once she got there.

She slipped her hand under the back left wheel well of the car until she could feel the key stuck to the metal. Pulling it out, she wirelessly unlocked the door and started the engine.

Tock walked to the driver's side door and opened it.

"Where ya going?"

Startled, she glanced up at the big cat leaning against the passenger side of the car while he ate a Jamaican beef patty out of a greasy paper bag.

"What are you doing?" she snapped. "Why are you following me?"

She was at least a mile from the party. He had to have been following her!

He shrugged. "Just curious." While still eating, he held out the greasy paper bag to her. "Patty? They're really good. I've already had, like, eight."

"Cats," Tock sighed.

Shay Malone watched the honey badger. She was glaring at him, but he wasn't sure why. He hadn't really done anything. He was just curious whether she was stealing this really nice car. A brand-new Mercedes-Benz that easily cost over a hundred grand was not something someone just picked up as a rental. And who left the key under the tire?

People up to no good. That was who.

And honey badgers were always up to no good, weren't they? At least from what he'd seen so far.

Tock leaned across the roof of the car and snarled, "Go. *Away.*"

"Are you stealing this car?" he asked. "That is so not cool."

"No."

"I know it's a rich person's car but that doesn't mean you can just take it. That's wrong. Stealing is wrong."

"I'm not stealing anything."

"If you're not stealing, what are you doing?"

"I have to take care of something. Alone."

"Okay. I'll just tell Mads that you drove off in a car that's not yours and you keep whispering. In the middle of Detroit."

Tock immediately glanced at the watch on her wrist. It was a big watch and looked very expensive. Maybe a boyfriend's watch. He didn't know. He'd never asked.

"Fine." She glared at him. "Get in."

Luckily, the car was a sedan and not a small, two-door nothing that his legs could barely fit in, much less his shoulders.

Once inside, with the doors and windows closed, Tock said, "I have to go help someone. I'm not stealing anything. This car was left for me."

"Wait . . . *should* I get Mads and the oth—"

"*No.*" She closed her eyes again and let out a breath. "I don't want them involved."

"Why not?"

"That's my business. Now get out."

Shay thought a few seconds before replying, "Nah."

"What do you mean, 'nah'?"

"I mean, nah. I'm not going anywhere. If you're not going to have your friends backing you up, you should at least have me. I'm helpful."

"I don't need your help."

"Either *I* go or I get Mads. And when she hears you're doing something dangerous alone so close to the championships . . ."

Tock gripped the steering wheel with both hands and began taking in breaths through her nose and blowing them out through her mouth.

"What are you doing?" he asked.

"It's a calming technique that will hopefully prevent me from beating you to death."

What was disturbing was how calmly she made that statement. Only her gripping hands and red knuckles told him how pissed she was at the moment.

"I'm just trying to—"

"Stop saying you're trying to help. You're just being a pain in the ass."

Shay didn't say anything. He simply stared at her until she turned her head, her eyes going wide.

"Are you about to cry?" she asked.

"No." And he wasn't. "But my feelings are hurt."

"Cats don't have feelings."

"Yes, we do. And you've hurt mine. But I've made a commitment—I'm going with you. Despite your cruel words. That were so hurtful to me."

She began to say something, stopped, let out a long sigh, and finally pulled away from the curb.

When they hit a stoplight, he held the bag of beef patties under her nose.

"Want one?" he asked.

The way she glared at him. Glared at him so hard. They sat there long after the light had turned green. They didn't move until the drivers behind them began to lean on their horns and yell curses out their windows.

That glare . . . he honestly didn't know if he should laugh or find a way to hide under the wheel well like a confused kitten.

He was relieved he didn't have to make the decision one way or the other when she finally began to drive the car forward and held her right hand out so he could put a patty in her palm.

Tracey Rutowski swung out the doors of the Gucci store on Old Bond Street. It was early morning and she had appointments all day at the Royal Academy of Arts in the hopes of finding the next Michelangelo or Monet. Or, even better, the next Mapplethorpe or Basquiat. But first she had to check out a nearby empty storefront to see if it would work for her newest gallery.

She stopped at the black SUV waiting for her and handed over the Gucci-branded shopping bag that held her new black purse. It would go into her closet with all her other black purses and backpacks and clutches; black jeans; and black T-shirts and sweaters. It was her signature style. Black.

The feline standing by the driver's-side door took the bag, his nose twitching when he looked at it.

"What?"

"More shit you won't do anything with but spend a lot of money on?" he replied before rudely tossing it into the open car door.

"You're always so negative."

"I'm a realist. And you're a hoarder."

"I am *not* a hoarder." She glanced away before adding, "I just like pretty things. Just be glad I purchased it and I'm not running down the street with Gucci security chasing behind me."

"You mean like last time?"

"That was not Gucci . . . that was Harry Winston and I was just keeping my skills on point. Now stay here," she continued. "I just have to go check a building about a block away. After that we'll be—"

"Really?" he cut in . . . with that *tone*. "You *have* to do this *right* now?"

Neil Jeffers had been her bodyguard, driver, assistant, and friend since they'd met all those years ago when they were both way too young to be doing what they were doing. But it had bonded them. Like war buddies, except Neil was still a feline; which meant he was "dick-y" on principle. Just to irritate her.

"Patrice wants me to take a look. It'll take five min—"

"Twenty. It'll take twenty minutes. And I thought Patrice was on vacation."

"She is, but she never stops working. We both know that. And once I get this done, we can go." When he rolled his eyes, "What? *What?*"

"Nothing. Go, go. Keep everyone waiting, like no one has anything better to do but wait for you."

"Why the feline sarcasm?"

"There's no sarcasm. We all just *looooooove* waiting on you. It's the most amazing part of our day."

"Sarcasm," she accused before turning away from him and heading down the street until she reached the empty storefront her Realtor, Patrice, had texted her about.

Patrice often found Tracey the best locations for her galleries, no matter what country they were in. They'd worked together since the '90s, when Patrice had located that burntout building in the Bronx for Tracey's first show of local young artists. Most of them were people of color with strong political opinions that they clearly expressed in their work. The event was a huge success, bringing in some very wealthy, pretentious art investors and critics as well as people Tracey actually wanted to impress. But then the NYPD showed up and it turned into a horrible riot . . .

Okay. Maybe *she* caused the riot. But the cops had made her mad.

In the end, though, that little felony on her record didn't stop her career. In fact, over the last three decades, she'd gone from edgy, rebel art procurer to ruling establishment art procurer.

At this moment, she had galleries in Paris, Rome, Toledo, Manhattan, Los Angeles, São Paulo, Lagos, Johannesburg, and Sydney. She also handled private procurements for billionaires upon request. She was supposed to have opened a gallery in Hong Kong a few years back but she'd been banned from entering China since the late '80s so . . . yeah . . . no gallery in Hong Kong. Or Tokyo. Or Seoul, for that matter. East Asia had pretty much banned her, but every couple of years she still attempted to make her way in. It wasn't as if she didn't bring a lot of money with her. But gee . . . you steal a few Ming Dynasty items by tunneling into a few unknown tombs with your claws and honey badger skills, and everybody gets mad at you! She was young! A teen! You'd think they'd let it go. Especially once she'd returned what she'd taken.

And yes, Tracey already had a gallery in London, but she'd always wanted to get her gallery onto Old Bond Street. A near-impossible task for an American like her, unless you knew someone who knew someone who knew someone who had connections with Buckingham Palace.

A place she'd also been banned from entering since the late '80s.

Her reputation with Parliament wasn't much better, but at least they hadn't cut her off like the Crown. Because who knew when they'd need her and her sunny disposition to help out MI6 again? Not that they'd asked for that help, but she'd given it willingly anyway. Whether they'd wanted it or not.

Tracey knocked on the big wooden door. When no one answered, she pulled on the wooden handle. The door silently opened and she stepped inside.

"Hello?" she called out. "Anyone here?"

She stepped farther in, her attention focused on the building's layout. Walls would have to be knocked down as this had been a clothing store previously. But the high ceilings were great, and she loved the natural light that . . .

Tracey's nose twitched as a very specific scent hit her . . . offensive on every level.

Hyenas. Fucking hyenas.

She hated when Neil was right. She should have gone right to her meetings instead. She didn't even have her gun on her. She'd left it in the car so she could go into Gucci without problems. She'd forgotten to grab it before coming here.

She wasn't surprised this was a setup. It wouldn't be the first time she'd been ambushed. Or the fifteenth time. But she was surprised when the hyena who emerged from the shadows wasn't a Romanian female with muscles the size of cantaloupes. Tracey had taken a Matisse right out from under the talentless bitch and she knew it was an affront that would not go unchallenged.

This, however . . . she never saw coming.

"Freja?" she asked. It had been years since she'd seen the mean She-beast. "Freja Galendotter?"

The hyena smiled. "Hello, Tracey."

More hyenas moved in from the shadows she'd so appreciated when she'd first walked in. They surrounded Tracey but kept their distance. Because they were all male. Not a female hyena among them except Freja. And she knew why.

"That's right." Tracey couldn't control her wide grin. "I'd heard my niece kicked your ass. Tore your entire Clan apart with the help of a few lion males." She kissed her fingers like a French chef. "Sensational."

Freja's expression hardened into one full of rage and hatred. Not so much for Tracey—they really didn't know each other well, despite years of threats between them—but for Mads, the daughter Freja hated because she hadn't turned out to be some super beast. A combination of hyena and Tracey's idiot brother had produced what most mixes with badger produced: a regular ol' honey badger. Just like her father. Honey badger genes always ruled supreme when it came to shifters. None of those coydogs or ligers or bear-cats. No matter what you or your family was, if you mated with a honey badger . . . you got a honey badger. And the Galendotters never let her poor niece forget it.

Tracey's mom had offered to take the poor kid into the family, but Freja was such a vindictive sociopath that she refused. She kept the kid she hated just so she could make Tracey's brother miserable. Because he hadn't given her what she wanted: some freakish child she could use to torment her enemies.

Freja also made it clear that if any of the Rutowskis attempted to take the kid, she'd kill Mads herself. Cut her throat right in front of them. At the time, Tracey believed that threat. Why? Because Freja's own mother and the females of that clan would do whatever they were ordered. If that meant killing a kid, they would do it. Without even a question.

But that was before Mads had finally fought back and wiped out her mother's clan. This attack must be Freja's last-ditch effort to turn her fate around. To once again become one of the most feared hyena clans in the States. By killing her daughter's family.

"So let me guess," Tracey said. "Mads destroyed your Clan and now you want revenge? My God!" she blurted out. "What did my brother ever see in you? You are *so* mundane."

"I'm not here because of Mads. I'm here for you. You've got so much money on your head, I'll win my Clan back. That's why I'm here."

"You expect me to believe that this has nothing to do with my niece?"

"I don't have to do anything about her. She and her friends and all you worthless vermin . . . all of you will be getting what you deserve, and I won't have to lift a finger."

Tracey frowned. "What the fuck does that mean?"

"You really should be worrying about yourself right now."

"Because of you?" Tracey snorted. "Oh, please."

Freja sneered. "I should have taken you out a long time ago."

"So you're a bounty hunter now?"

"As much money as they're offering for you?"

"Is this bounty out of Germany?" Tracey asked. The Romanian female was out of Germany.

"No."

"Rome?" She lowered her voice. "The Pope?"

"What?" the hyena snapped, surprised at her question. "*No.*"

"Sierra Leone?"

"Would you stop? You're pissing me off!"

"From what my brother says, that's not hard."

The hyena pulled a gun from the back of her jeans waistband, pointing it directly at Tracey's head.

"A gun?" Tracey said, smiling. "How edgy."

"I know all about you. I'm not taking any chances."

"You? You know about *me?*"

"Yeah. I know. Badgers. Tough to kill."

"No. Not about the honey badgers. I mean about *me.* Maybe my brother told you? About my past."

"You were a whore?" Freja asked drily.

"Besides that . . ." Tracey lowered her voice. "About my involvement with different governments? About the accidental military coup in Mexico?" She gave a little grimace. "That unfortunate thing with Margaret Thatcher?" She lowered her voice even more. "About Gorbachev?"

"*What?* What are you talking about? You sound insane."

"So . . . my brother never told you anything. About me. Huh."

Pete didn't want to be here. He didn't want to have this crowbar in his hand. He didn't want to be in a foreign country!

But he didn't have much choice. It sucked to be a hyena male. Especially if you were born into a clan that had such mean females running it.

He was only sixteen. Too young to set off on his own. At least that's what his mother had said before telling him she and his sisters were leaving to join another clan and he might as well stay part of Freja's. She'd dumped him like so much trash and now here he was. About to see a middle-aged woman shot to death for . . . what? Existing? And was the gun necessary? He'd been raised to believe that his kind didn't need weapons. They didn't need to fight. But now his aunt was about to kill a middle-aged lady with gray in the roots of her black-and-white hair and lines around her eyes. He didn't want to hurt her. He didn't want to hurt anyone! He just wanted to go. Anywhere.

But before he could scream that out, he heard something pop and the uncle standing next to him went down screaming. He saw that his uncle's leg didn't look right seconds before a baseball bat slammed into the back of his uncle's shoulders. He crashed to the ground, sobbing in pain.

Pete looked at the woman now standing beside him. She was a short, brown-skinned Latina with thick, black hair that was a messy mix of braids dyed purple and curls. There was a tiny heart tattoo under her right eye, a bigger tattoo on her right hand that said something in Spanish. She had on loose, worn blue jeans, splattered with blood . . . and some paint, he guessed, since blood wasn't usually blue, green, and purple; a black tank top with the Motörhead logo on the front; and a double silver chain necklace with an eagle charm and a feather charm.

She barely glanced at him, but then he heard her ask, "How old are you?"

"Si-si-si . . ." He swallowed, tried again. "Sixteen."

She motioned behind her with a jerk of her head. "Get over there," she ordered. "Stay out of the way. Don't do anything stupid."

"Yes, ma'am," he muttered before quickly moving to the far wall. When he turned back, he saw a cousin's head snap around from the swing of that bat. A different woman had struck the blow that sent his cousin reeling, though. This lady didn't have dark hair with white streaks. She was blond, her hair in a thick braid down her back. And she wore more expensive-looking clothes than the other ladies: a tight black skirt, white silk blouse, and very high heels that she twisted and turned around in without ever slipping or falling on her butt. She simply ducked another cousin's punches before slamming the front of the bat into his gut and then pulled back and swung, cracking his cousin in the head. He went down hard and didn't move, but he was still breathing.

Done, the woman tossed the bat to yet another middle-aged lady, who easily caught it. She flipped the bat in her hands, spun her body around for momentum and swung, sending an uncle flying across the empty store. Swung again, and a cousin crashed into a nearby pillar.

This woman had on a white sleeveless T-shirt, a sleeveless denim jacket, gray jeans, and work boots with big heels. Her hair was chin length on one side and shaved down to the skull on the other. The remaining hair barely covered an old tattoo that Pete couldn't quite make out.

As all these new women attacked and battered his cousins and uncles, they moved forward until they'd knocked out or so damaged the male members of his family that none of them could move from the floor they were lying on.

Finally, the women stood beside the first woman he'd seen, but his aunt still had her gun pointed at that woman's head. Yet that woman hadn't moved. She hadn't looked away. She'd done nothing but stand there and stare down his Aunt Freja.

Pete didn't understand. Who were these women? And where had they come from? His uncles and cousins had searched the place before lying in wait for the first woman to show up. They hadn't seen anyone in the store. Hadn't smelled anyone. And yet here they all were. All staring down his aunt.

He knew all the women were supposed to be honey badgers but the only thing he and his uncles and cousins had been told was to make sure they didn't get their claws on a gun or knife because badgers didn't fight fair. Due to their small size, they felt it was their right to even the odds when going up against bigger predators. Meaning his Aunt Freja felt justified using a weapon on this lone badger. Fuck shifter honor, apparently. Pete was sure Aunt Freja never expected backup for the honey badger female or for these additional badgers to be so damn mean and handy with one simple baseball bat.

It was easy for these women, too. This was not a battle to end all battles between honey badger and hyena. This was a near-decimation that took less than two minutes and had left his aunt completely alone. No backup. No protection. His uncles simply too damaged to move. His aunt might count him on her side, but Pete didn't want her to count him. He couldn't get his feet to move. Not even to run away. All he could do was gawk and tremble. Not a pretty sight when one was considered an apex predator.

Focused on his aunt, the first woman said, "If you think you're fast enough, you can take the sho—"

His aunt took the shot. It should have blown the woman's head off. It didn't. Because she moved. So fast, Pete barely saw her move. One second, she was standing in front of his aunt, about five or six feet away with her friends beside her. The next, her friends had scattered and the woman had spun around, facing the same direction as Freja, and with both palms on the hand holding the gun.

Without releasing Freja's hand, the woman somehow managed to take the gun apart. She didn't break the weapon into pieces the way a grizzly would. Or break Aunt Freja's hand the way a grizzly definitely would. But somehow, she took the gun apart; pieces of it dropped to the ground at their feet until his aunt held nothing but the ammo-less frame.

With no useful weapon, Freja used her free hand to grab the back of the woman's head. The woman lifted her arm, bent it, and brought it back, burying the elbow in the middle of Aunt Freja's face. She did it so hard that his aunt's nose wasn't simply broken; half of it was buried deep into her skull. He wasn't sure she could breathe out of it anymore.

As the woman stepped away, his aunt slid to the floor, both hands over her face. When the woman reached her friends, the four of them pulled out their own guns and aimed them at Freja. Pete was going to cry out, hoping to stop them, but the woman said something first.

"What the hell are you guys doing?"

The blonde glanced between Freja and the woman. "We kill her now. Yes?" She had a heavy Eastern European accent and was pretty, now that he could see her clearly.

"No. We're not killing her."

"We're not?" the brown-skinned Latina asked. "Why?"

"I promised Mads I wouldn't kill her mother."

"You mean when she was ten?"

"Yes! I made a promise."

"You promised me her *soul*," the blonde growled.

"Oh, my God." The woman faced the blonde. "Is this about your ancestors again?"

"The year was eight-fifty-six—

"*Seriously?*"

"—and life in Rus was hard, but not for honey badger. But then the Galendotters raided my people's village. Nearly wiped all of my ancestors out. But we survived and vowed revenge. And honey badgers . . . we never forget. We never forgive."

"I'm not letting you kill her because of a more than thousand-year-old grudge."

"What kind of badger are you?"

"One that keeps promises to her sweet and sensitive niece."

The woman dug her phone out of her black jeans with one hand and motioned to Pete with the other.

"Come here, sweetie," she said kindly and, with no other options, he finally managed to move. Toward her. He couldn't believe she'd even noticed him. He wasn't crazy about the idea of standing next to her, but she didn't hurt him or even threaten him. Simply put her arm around his shoulder and walked him to the door.

"I'm going to give you a number to call," she told him, real kindness in her voice. "The man who answers helps orphan shifters. He'll get you a place to stay and some food and figure out what you want to do next so you don't have to go back to any of Freja's foolishness if you don't want to. Okay?"

He nodded, not sure what else to do.

"You have a phone, right?" she asked when they were out-side; a black SUV idled on the street right in front of the empty store. He sensed it was there for her and her friends.

Pete pulled his phone out and in seconds she'd sent him the number where he could find help. He prayed she wasn't lying, but he had no other option but to trust her.

"Now if you don't want to go back in there . . . and I wouldn't if I were you"—she turned him away from all her blood-splattered friends—"you should just walk down the street and make the call. Okay? My friend will send someone really nice to pick you up if he can't. Okay?"

He nodded. "Yes, ma'am. Thank you."

"Good luck, sweetie," she said.

As he was walking away, wondering what the hell was going to happen to him—and also wildly relieved he had been given some kind of weird permission from a honey badger not to go back into that empty store to take care of his broken family—he heard the badger speaking into her own phone. He slowed his step to listen, making sure she wasn't calling someone to come get rid of him. But she wasn't.

"It's me," he heard her say.

As she reached the waiting SUV, he heard a man from inside the vehicle yell, "I knew this would happen! Why don't you ever listen to me?"

"My niece is in trouble," the woman said into the phone, ignoring the man who'd yelled. "And if my niece is in trouble, so's your granddaughter."

Chapter 2

She didn't speak to him. Not during the drive to the airport. Not when they were getting on the private jet. Not when they took off and headed . . . somewhere. She didn't say anything. But she did keep checking two things: her phone and her watch. He didn't understand why she needed to check her watch when she could easily see the time on her phone. Then again, her nickname was Tock. From things Mads and the other badgers had said, the woman was big on keeping time. Maybe looking at her watch was just a habit. Habits were hard to break.

About an hour into the flight, she disappeared into the bathroom, and when she returned, she was dressed in a tight black T-shirt and leggings and thick black boots. She put on a black tactical vest and began loading several weapons: four guns with what he could only describe as a shitload of extra magazines; and six knives of varying sizes that she slipped into sheaths cleverly sewn into her clothes.

"That's a lot of weaponry," he noted.

"Is it?"

"Well . . . for me, it's a lot. I don't really know anything about guns or knives." He lifted his hands. "I just use my claws." He unleashed them, watching his fingers change so that the short human nails instantly disappeared and the tiger claws exploded from the tips. His claws were over four inches. Longer than those of full-blood Amur tigers, but that was typical of shifter cats as they tended to have longer claws and fangs than their full-blooded cousins, and were often larger and weighed more. It made sense. Big shifters breeding with other big shifters often led to even bigger cubs and pups.

"See?" Shay asked, holding his claws up for her.

She glanced up, frowned, and went back to loading her weapons.

Realizing she had no interest in holding a conversation with him, Shay looked around for something else to do. He noticed a stray looped thread coming from the fancy leather seat next to his fancy leather seat. Curious whether he could catch the tiny loop, he reached one of his claws out toward it . . .

Once Tock finished loading her guns and putting them away in the appropriate holsters, she glanced at her watch. The current time matched her estimates, which always made her more relaxed; allowing her to finally lean back in her seat and take a few minutes to mentally prepare for—

"*What did you do?*" she demanded, sitting up straight.

The cat looked at her; blinked. He didn't try to untangle his claws from the threads he'd pulled out of the open seat beside him. Nor did he attempt to hide the strips of leather that had fallen to the jet floor, leaving nothing but a half-undone seat in the middle of the private jet that she did not own.

After examining his handy work, he shrugged. "I just wanted to see if—"

"Forget I asked," she cut in. Tock was in no mood to hear cat logic. "Just untangle yourself and stop touching things."

He retracted his claws and the giant, loose ball of thread dropped onto the seat. But as soon as he relaxed, she watched his gaze search for something new to tear apart. The cat was a menace!

Desperate, she reached into her travel bag and pulled out a magazine.

"Here," she ordered, forcing the magazine into his hand. "Read this."

"Mechanics?" he said out loud, reading the magazine title. "Like cars?" he asked, hopefully.

"No. Like physics."

The hope drained from his face and he glanced at the cover. "I can't think of anything more boring."

"Physics is not boring."

"Isn't it, though?" He gazed at the cover for a long moment before unleashing one claw and slowly dragged it across the pristine cover. The magazine was three months old but it was still pristine because that's how Tock kept her things. Pristine! Clean! Intact!

Annoyed and desperate, she reached over and snatched the magazine from his hands. But when she looked at it, she saw that his single claw had torn right through half the pages.

"Dammit!"

"You shouldn't have snatched it!" he complained.

"What is wrong with you?" she wanted to know.

"Nothing, actually. Just sitting here. Enjoying life."

"And making my life miserable."

"That happens sometimes when you hang around cats."

"I am only hanging around you because you insisted."

"I just want to—"

"If you say 'help' one. More. Time."

He blinked, then said, "Assist?"

Tock bared a fang, but before she could bite his claw off, a door at the back of the plane opened. She relaxed into her seat and prepared herself for the next annoyance in her life.

"Emmy."

The cat's eyebrows went up and Tock knew he was trying not to laugh.

"Do not call me Emmy," Tock growled.

"We're cousins. I can call you what I want."

"Not if you want to keep your face—"

"Hi!" the cat loudly announced, making both badgers glare at him. Most badgers weren't fans of loud, annoying noises. "I'm Shay Malone."

Her cousin looked the cat over for a good ten seconds before turning back to Tock and asking, "What is *that* doing here?"

"I brought him." She made it sound as if she'd done so willingly, but that was because she didn't need to get into another fight with one of her cousins.

"Why?"

"Because I wanted to."

"Why didn't you bring your little friends instead?"

Tock's left eye twitched a bit at her cousin's tone. "Because my *teammates* were busy, and you know *why* I didn't bring them."

"Whatever." She handed Tock a plain, gray folder with pockets. "Have this memorized by the time you leave the jet. At the appropriate time, a vehicle will be waiting for you outside the hanger. You know what to do." She glanced at the cat again, sniffed, and returned to the back of the plane, shutting the door to the private cabin firmly behind her.

Letting out a long sigh, Tock opened the folder. That's when she heard the cat say, "She seems fun."

Smirking, she looked up, expecting to see the cat also smirking or outright laughing. But he wasn't. And she realized he was serious.

"Maybe not friendly," he added. "But . . . yeah . . . fun."

"My cousin," Tock slowly explained, "is third in command of the shifter division of a very dangerous organization. Trust me when I say, she's *not* fun."

"I bet she's more fun than you."

Pissed at the very idea he'd say such a thing out loud, Tock lifted her right hand and unleashed her claws. She was about to slash them across the cat's stupid face when he suddenly pressed his giant cat paw against her much smaller badger one.

"Look at that!" he enthused. "The size difference. Fascinating, isn't it? But look how long your claws are, considering the size and all. Do you ever paint them? I know a tigon that paints her claws the colors of her favorite football and hockey teams. Do you ever do that?"

It was in that moment Tock thought about putting a bullet in the cat's head and ending this situation right here and now. She could easily dispose of the body and, after a shower with good soap and extra-strength shampoo for her hair, she was sure his brothers would never know that Tock had been with Shay Malone in the last few minutes of his life.

But no. She would not do that. Why? Because she wasn't her grandmother. Either one of them. One was a descendent of Caribbean pirates who had quietly but firmly owned the seas, and the other was from a very long line of Polish Jews that were always on the side of any resistance. Both were from matriarchal families that had no patience for weakness. Tock, however, had promised herself she wouldn't just remove people who got in her way or simply annoyed her. Life was too short to be that angry all the time.

So, after letting out a very long, slow breath, Tock refocused on the papers her cousin had handed her and began to read. Moments before she exited the jet, she would set these same papers on fire to get rid of evidence, and do her best not to do the same to the cat sitting across from her, who was busy focusing his attention on a new piece of thread he'd just found on his own seat.

"Nice building," Shay noted, looking the office building over from his spot in the passenger seat of the black SUV. "It's kind of weird, though, being out here in the middle of the night."

Once they'd landed at the private airport, they'd waited on the plane for hours. It had been a long and boring wait because Tock wouldn't talk to him. She'd spent her time going through those papers her cousin had given her as well as a small notebook she carried in one of her many pockets. Unable to get a conversation started, he just watched videos on his phone. He ended up having to use his ear buds, though, because she'd snapped at him when the Marvel heroes got a little too loud for her. Who didn't want to listen to superheroes destroy entire cities in an attack that no full-human could ever hope to survive?

He heard Tock sigh at his comment about the building. "I thought you were the quiet one."

"Quiet? I guess I can be. If I have nothing to say. But if I do—"

With a small growl, she got out of the vehicle. He followed, closing the door behind him.

"What are you doing?" she asked, when she reached his side of the SUV.

"Going with you."

"No. Absolutely not."

"Yeah, but—"

"In exactly five minutes, you will switch to the driver's side of the vehicle and start it. You will be ready to drive away from here when I return. Do you understand?"

That seemed reasonable to him, so he replied, "Yeah. Sure."

"Let me see your watch."

Grinning, Shay held his arm out for her.

"What is that?"

"My Gumby watch."

"That looks like a kid's watch."

"It is. My dad gave it to me when I was six. I keep changing the band because, ya know . . . I got bigger."

"Is there a timer on it?"

"On a Gumby wristwatch? No."

Another sigh. "Gimme your phone."

He pulled his cell phone from his back pocket and handed it to her.

"Unlock it, Einstein."

"Oh. Yeah." He used his thumb and she immediately took the phone back once it opened.

She spent a few seconds looking through his apps before announcing, "You don't have a timer app on your phone?"

"What do I need that for?"

"I don't know. For football practice?"

"The coach and Keane tell me what to do and I do it. Then they tell me when to stop, and I stop. What do I need a timer for?"

"Oh, my God," she muttered before he watched her download a free timer app and set it up, after glancing at her own ridiculous timepiece. It looked like something a three-star general in the Navy would use.

She handed his phone back to him. "It's on vibrate, so pay attention. When it goes off, get in the car and start it. Understand?"

"Yes. What about security?"

"There isn't any except the guy at the front desk inside."

"Are you going to kill him?"

"No."

"I'll be really mad if you kill him."

"I'm not going to kill him."

"Promise?"

"Oh, my God," she muttered again before turning away and disappearing around the right side of the building.

Tock began to climb the side of the building, using nothing but her hands and feet. She wore gloves to protect her palms and climbing shoes for her feet. She'd been "free soloing" since she was three, when her father found her climbing the side of the house to get inside the room where they kept the family safe. She needed some cash to buy a watch. She loved how the little arms on watches moved and how the device kept one apprised of each second, minute, and hour of the day. Her parents thought her love of time was "cute," so they'd purchased her a Mickey Mouse watch, which she simply found insulting. She wanted a *real* watch. Not some ridiculous kiddy watch. So, while her parents were unloading groceries for a big family party, she'd decided to scale the side of their house, get into the room with the safe, break it open, take some money out, and buy herself a *good* watch. A proper watch.

It never occurred to Tock that her parents might be angry. She just knew what she wanted. So she began scaling. She was halfway up when her father caught her.

"What the hell are you doing?" he'd demanded. Once he got her down, he'd told her, "You never steal from family, baby. If you want something from one of us, you ask."

She'd held out her arm to silently explain that she *had* asked. She made sure her face expressed the disdain she felt because she wanted to let him know that she had asked and *this* was what she'd received.

Her father had smirked. "Got it. Got it."

And he did. Despite her mother's disgust at "catering to a three-year-old's whims," he'd taken his daughter away from the family party in their backyard and driven her to a special watchmaker. There he'd had a watch put together just for her, one that wasn't too big for her little wrist but still had the kind of information she wanted and was sturdy. As she outgrew one watch, he'd get her a new one. She never had to ask again. He always knew exactly what she needed and when.

Despite that, though, she still kept learning to climb. She didn't like ropes and all the gear mountain climbers used. She liked just using her hands and feet. Her ability had gotten better with age and surprisingly helped with her basketball skills. And if she ever slipped, she always had her claws to catch her.

She usually free soloed for fun. Sometimes when she needed a break from her teammates, she decided to climb a tall structure in the middle of nowhere. Or when she needed a little extra cash and decided to take something sparkly from a New York condo or a piece of art that should really be in a museum.

Yet every skill she taught herself or had been taught, her grandmother found a way to use. Most of the time, Tock just said no when orders came in. But her grandmother knew that Tock would never turn down a job if her family was in trouble. So here Tock was. In Maine, of all places. Climbing the side of a building.

Well, at least it wasn't the middle of a Maine winter. Free soloing was a real test when everything was covered in snow and ice.

Tock reached the fifth floor and used a glass cutter to make a hole in the window that allowed her to slip inside the building.

She silently landed on the floor in a crouch, placed the glass circle carefully to the side, and took a moment to get her breath and her bearings.

Turning her head, she listened for any noise. Sniffed the air, checked for scents. In the end, it was a sound that caught her. Tock locked on a target a few offices away, pulled her .40-caliber Sig Sauer, and moved.

Shay stared at his cell phone, watching the timer tick down. He knew he could put the phone back in his pocket and wait until it started vibrating, but he didn't trust that. He'd promised Tock that he would be helpful and helpful meant paying attention and following her orders. It was why he was such a good football player.

So he watched the timer and waited, his back against the wall of the building. Near the glass doors, but not in front of them so the security guy wouldn't see him. His gaze was focused on the phone but his ears twitched at sounds coming from the other side of the building. Someone was trying to remain quiet but he could still hear them.

He opened his mouth, stuck out his tongue, and breathed in. The scent of multiple full-human males—some of whom had not bathed recently . . . ew—and gun oil filled his senses. He immediately dropped his phone, shifted to tiger, shook off his clothes, and did what he did best.

Tock knew exactly which door she needed to go to. It had been in the packet of info her cousin had given her. But she followed the sounds she'd locked on until she reached the right door. She didn't move in. Because there should be a scent. Actually, there should many scents. And one of them should be from what her grandmother had always called "our secret weapon." The secret weapon of all honey badgers. Effective on full-humans and shifters alike . . . except wolves. Because wolves were nasty animals that loved a strong anal scent. They might not want to marry you if you were forced to unleash it, but they also didn't pass out or choke to death. A few had even been known to roll around in it like the disgusting beasts they were.

That was the scent she should be locked on now, but all

she could smell was full-humans, gun oil, and . . . nothing. No honey badger scent or the scent of an unleashed anal sack. If one of her young cousins was trapped in a room with a bunch of full-human agents and, for some reason, she couldn't fight her way out, she would definitely unleash her anal sack. It was what her kind did when they had no choice. Or when they were just being dicks. But either way . . . it should have filled this floor with its horrific odor. Bodies should be lying around, dead or choking to death.

Now, her cousin could already be dead, but then Tock would smell dead honey badger. But she didn't smell honey badger at all.

Tock shook her head. Nope. She didn't like this. Something wasn't right.

She started to take a step back when she caught the scent of full-human male coming up behind her.

Her weapon raised, she turned just as a metal pipe slammed against her head with such force, all she could do was fall to the floor and hope that she hadn't lost an eye where the side of her head had been caved in.

"Where'd he go?" one of his men asked. But he didn't have an answer. He knew what he'd seen. A man standing with his back against the wall, staring at his phone. He'd come with the woman, and the plan was to knock out all stragglers. Or, if said stragglers put up any kind of fight, kill them and dump the body in a lake about ten minutes away.

He checked the SUV, but the man wasn't in there. It wasn't like the guy could hide behind the seats either. Dude was *massive*. At first, he'd thought the guy was part of the wall. He was that wide. Not fat. It was his shoulders and chest that were wide. And layered in muscle. He wondered what the guy's workout was. Steroids, maybe. Couldn't be the regular steroids that illegally floated around his gym. They all used those, but none of those drugs could make anyone that big. Must be something new on the black market. Once this job was done, he'd have to find them for himself.

Of course, a guy that size, they would definitely have to kill him once they found him. No way that whatever 'roids this guy was on would make him calm and rational. Or easy to put down. They'd have to be ready.

"He's not over there either," one of his men said, gesturing around the building with his elbow while gripping his automatic rifle in his hands.

He nodded. "We need to find—"

The screaming startled him. And by the time he turned around, all he saw was the feet of one of his men disappearing into the shadows of the upper building. As if something had dragged him *up* the building wall.

But . . . that was impossible . . . right?

No, no. The big guy probably had rope or whatever. Climbing gear. A guy like that probably climbed mountains for fun.

He took a step forward but immediately stopped when his teammate's body hit the ground . . . everything from his nose up was gone.

He and his men took a step back and began firing into the darkness. They couldn't see anything but that didn't matter.

Until another one of his men was suddenly yanked back into the darkness of the right side of the building. They heard their teammate's screams but before any of them could attempt to help, his body was tossed out into the small bit of light that came from the building.

He gawked down at the body. It had been torn apart in less than ten seconds. He and his men passed silent glances before they all backed away, turned, and took off toward their van.

There was no amount of money worth this kind of crazy.

Shay stayed feline and ran around the building, tracking Tock's scent. He found where it stopped on the ground and quickly realized it went up.

So that's what he did. He launched his eight-hundred-pound body vertically, using his claws to grab the wall long enough to launch his body up again until he reached a window with an opening cut into it. He tried to fit through it but his cat head was too big. He briefly shifted back to human but . . . again . . . his head couldn't quite get completely through without wiggling, and forget about his shoulders. Those were a definite no-go.

Instead, he just shifted back to tiger and shoved his massive body inside; glass broke all around him. He knew the advantage of surprise was blown, but he didn't care. As a natural ambush hunter, he knew a friggin' ambush when he saw one.

And Tock was in the middle of an ambush without her usual backup of psychotic honey badgers.

He shook the glass off his fur and headed toward the door. He briefly paused, though, when he heard grunting and thuds.

Now running, he hit the closed door with all his weight and took it down. He stood on the splintered wood and watched while Tock repeatedly stabbed a man in the neck, her entire body on top of his shoulders, legs around his neck.

Another man came toward her and she stopped stabbing long enough to slash the second man's throat, then slash again. This time straight across his face, ripping him open from forehead to underneath the jaw before burying her knife into the throat of the victim she was currently riding like a horse.

Both men dropped and she expertly landed on her feet.

Shay shifted back to human. "Outside—"

She held up her gloved hand. "I know. Ambush. They're here for me."

He thought about asking her why, but he probably didn't want to know. Something else was wrong. He could feel it.

"Are you okay?"

She shook her head and he reared back a bit when her left eye wobbled, meaning it was not firmly in its socket. He wanted to scream and cover her face with his hand, race her to the hospital. But a honey badger wouldn't appreciate any of that. And honey badgers were weird anyway when it came to healing. Few even got the fever that helped all other shifters heal naturally. Instead . . . they just sort of pulled themselves back together. Or, even stranger, didn't seem to notice any damage. He clearly remembered watching Max MacKilligan dig a bullet out of her shoulder with her claws. There was blood and some grunting, but within a few hours, she was completely healed and her arm worked fine. She wasn't even affected by blood loss.

See? Weird.

Still . . . Tock didn't look right even for a honey badger.

Shay heard cracking sounds and he watched in horror as the broken bones around her eye snapped into place, securing the eyeball. He thought she was out of trouble until Tock gestured with her right hand to a spot over her shoulder. "Get this out for me, would you?"

She turned and he saw a big syringe hanging from her spine. He cringed and quickly grabbed it, but a simple tug didn't pull it from her back. He pulled hard again and again until it finally came out, leaving a small hole in the skin and a milky white substance leaking down onto the floor.

"Uh . . . Tock?"

"Yeah." She turned and faced him, gazing at the syringe in his hand. "I know."

"You know what?"

She didn't answer right away, still staring at the syringe. But finally she looked up at him and said, "This doesn't feel right."

"Of course not. Someone shoved something into your spine."

"Yeah, but poisons. I'm a badger. But . . . this is different. Something's different."

He didn't understand what she was trying to say. Tock wasn't a big talker but she was always clear in her communication.

Maybe she was just freaked out. He didn't blame her.

"What's different?" he urged. "Tell me. I'll fix it."

She didn't respond, though. She simply dropped to her knees, then forward, crashing into his legs.

"Tock? Tock." He lowered her to the ground, crouching beside her. "Tock? Talk to me."

But it seemed she couldn't. Her eyes were wide open and her body was rigid. He'd found her and her badger friends passed out on his floor before. Filled with poison from some snake or whatever that they'd all willingly eaten. At the time, he'd thought they were all dead. They hadn't been breathing and their hearts had stopped for a time, but no. They weren't dead. They were just honey badgers high on snake poison.

But this situation was different. This time her heart was beating. Her breathing was steady. He could hear both. Yet she seemed . . . frozen. Stuck. Her muscles rigid. Her eyes unblinking.

The elevator *ding*ed and the doors slid open, revealing five armed men. Not the ones he'd already dealt with in the parking lot because these guys had recently bathed and used body spray.

The men were about to exit when they saw a naked, bloody Shay crouching beside their prey. They paused, confusion on the parts of their faces he could see—everything around the eyes and bridge of the nose was covered by balaclavas.

Shay roared. The loud sound startled the men. They began firing but he'd already flipped up and by the time he'd punched his way inside the wall, he was tiger again.

He moved easily through the darkness until he reached the elevator. He shifted briefly to open the hatch in the hall ceiling, and shifted back so that he could jump down without making a sound despite his massive cat size.

The men had already moved into the hallway, their heads turning this way and that, searching for him. They didn't know what they'd seen, but they were smart enough to know they'd seen something.

Shay low-crawled up to the one closest to him before going up on his haunches and slamming his front paws against the man's back. Not only knocking him into the man ahead of him—putting both on the floor—but snapping the first one's spine and crushing his ribs.

The rest of the men turned toward him and away from Tock. Shay swatted his paw one way and the arm holding an automatic rifle flew. He bit down on a shoulder and forced another man to his back. He lifted his back legs up at the same moment and unleashed his back claws so that he tore open a chest and, moments later, pulled the balaclava off a face. All in one move. When his back legs had landed again, he readjusted his maw from the shoulder to the jaw. Then he spun around, using the screaming man he held to knock down the remaining prey. He crushed the jaw between his fangs—mostly to stop the annoying screaming but also . . . why not?—while lifting a front paw and slamming it against the other man's face. His claws tore off skin, muscle, and bone, leaving nothing but a half-empty skull.

With all the new attackers finished off, he took a step toward Tock. But he heard the *ding* of the elevator again and spun around to face it, standing over her body. Ready to kill whatever came through that door.

Hackles up. Fangs bared. Bloody drool pouring from his mouth and onto poor Tock, Shay readied himself for whatever might come through that elevator door. He lowered the front of his body so he could easily launch himself into the fray.

The elevator door opened but no one came out. Not immediately.

Then he saw the tip of a silencer move slowly around the edge of the door, and he unleashed a roar in warning. The silencer froze, then lowered and *she* suddenly appeared in the hallway.

She reminded him of his community college English professor. Older. Straight white hair cut so it dropped across her right eye. Not tall but between the high heels and her erect bearing, she *seemed* tall. Dark brown eyes simply gawked at him as her perfectly manicured hand gripped her weapon.

"Huh," she said, still gawking at him. "She did bring a cat with her. Such a strange girl, my granddaughter."

Tock couldn't move. She felt . . . frozen. She could still see, but couldn't blink. Could breathe, but couldn't speak. Could hear, but couldn't move her head. She was stuck. And it was horrifying.

She didn't understand. She'd been hit, at some point in her life, with nearly every natural poison and a lot of manufactured ones. More than once, in fact. That included the most lethal snake poisons and even Ricin once. That had been truly unpleasant. Then there'd been the arsenic, cyanide, and that damn ghost pepper Max had slipped into her burrito. Tock had had them all and—if she were affected in any way—it was just to be knocked out for a while. Sometimes her heart stopped, but it always started again. Same thing with her breathing.

Whatever was happening now, however, was so different. For the first time in her life, she felt defeated. Like she'd never move again. She would always feel this way. Trapped in this body. She wanted to scream, but she couldn't.

Through eyes that couldn't blink, she could see the destruction the tiger brought down on the mercenaries—as long as the action happened over her head. But she couldn't duck or join in. She couldn't even cheer him on. She could only watch as bodies and body parts flew by.

But then she heard it. Heard that voice. That goddamn voice!

And sure enough . . . her grandmother—whom they all called Savta—leaned into her eye-view and gazed down at her with obvious disdain.

"I leave you alone," she admonished Tock in her Israeli accent, "one minute. Two. And next we know, you are on floor like dead body." She paused, then added, "It is your mother's fault. She made you weak after I warned her not to."

Unable to walk away or even roll her eyes, rage built up inside Tock and, before she knew it, she growled. A reaction that made her grandmother look a little surprised. She was never surprised. So why was she surprised now? Something was wrong, very wrong, and Tock wanted to know what the hell was going on. And she wanted to know now.

"You just walk into trouble and think you can always get out," Savta continued, pretending that Tock's growl hadn't taken her by surprise. "But look at you now . . . on the ground. Stuck there like a log."

Hearing her grandmother chastise her for doing a job she was only on *because* of her grandmother, had rage building again inside Tock.

"Hey, Emmy!" called her cousin Uri, born and raised in the States like Tock but also with dual citizenship. He annoyingly pushed his face beside their grandmother's so Tock could see him. "Bad day?"

Rage building.

"Why is she on the floor?" Uri's sister Shira wanted to know from the other side of Tock. "*Why are you on the floor?*" she practically yelled in Tock's face.

And building.

"Is she dead?" Shira asked her brother. Then she yelled at Tock, "*Are you dead?*"

"She's not dead," her grandmother replied. "I think it's that new poison."

New poison? There was a *new* poison that worked on honey badgers and no one had told Tock? No one?

"New poison?" Uri asked.

"Do you not read the encrypted newsletter Savta sends out?"

"I'm sorry," Uri snapped back at his sister. "I've been busy saving the world. I don't have time to run around reading newsletters like I'm part of a club run by our grandmother. No offense, Savta."

"I understand," her grandmother soothed, petting Uri's big badger shoulders.

"Of *course* you understand him," Shira snapped back. "He has a penis."

"Disgusting child!"

"Sister!"

Shira waved their grandmother and her sibling away. "We all know you are nice to the boys, Savta. And yet you treat the girls like they are naturally stupid and thickheaded. Who knew a uterus was such a handicap?"

"Ewww," another cousin announced from outside Tock's eyeline. "She's drooling." She leaned in and practically yelled, "*Do you think you can stop drooling?* It's really grossing me out."

"I don't think she can stop drooling," Shira said. "She's been poisoned. She might be dying." Shira looked down at Tock and loudly asked, "*Are you dying? Tell us if you're dying.*"

And *snap*.

Using every bit of will she had, Tock raised her arm and grabbed Shira by the throat, doing her best to strangle the life from her even as the rest of Tock's body was unable to move.

She didn't care. She might be dying, but she'd make sure she didn't go alone into the next world. Nope! She was dragging her idiot cousin with her!

Shira slapped at her arm and her other cousins attempted to pull Tock's hand off, but Tock used all the power she had left to end Shira.

Her grandmother rolled her eyes before motioning to someone just outside of Tock's limited view.

Then, Shay was there. He was human and leaning over her so he could look her right in the eyes.

"Let her go, Tock. I have to get you to a hospital."

"Will a hospital help?" Uri asked. "She looks pretty far—"

With one big hand, Shay sent Uri flying out of Tock's sight, which she greatly appreciated. So she relaxed her hand and dropped her arm.

Without waiting, Shay picked her up and started walking.

"Where are you taking her?" Tock heard her grandmother ask the cat.

"Away," he said to her family before adding, "from all of you."

"Why would you need to do that?" her grandmother asked drily. "We're delightful."

Chapter 3

Once the elevator doors closed and they were heading down to the first floor, Shay looked into Tock's eyes. She still couldn't blink, so her eyes were wide open and looking right at him, but she didn't appear terrified so much as pissed off. Whether that anger was directed at her family or at the ones who had done this to her, he couldn't say. He didn't know her well enough.

He knew honey badgers, though. Not only from his recent dealings with Tock and her teammates but from his own little sister. Keane might want to pretend that Natalie was "only half badger" but she really wasn't. She was *all* badger. In every way. Which meant that from the time she'd been born, she showed no fear. Even when she lost her hearing completely, she didn't seem to care or notice or cry about it. She just learned sign language and how to read lips and, when necessary, used her loss of one sense to get what she wanted from those she called "too stupid to be worth treating with respect."

Shay actually found it funny when his sister manipulated people by suddenly being unable to read lips or speak or acting lost and terrified. True, he'd made her give the million dollars' worth of diamonds back to the dealer after fooling him into thinking she was having a breakdown in the middle of his store; when he went to call 911, she'd swiped the diamonds from the counter while another customer attempted to help her. She'd almost swallowed them before Shay gripped her hand and made her drop the damn things. She didn't even want that stuff. She never wanted diamonds or pearls or any jewelry to wear. It had just been something she could do and, in the moment, he'd laughed. But he refused to let his sister become an outright thief. The Malones had enough felons in their family.

Despite all his knowledge of badgers, he still felt as if his heart had been ripped out of his chest when he stared down at Tock's face and saw tears leaking from her eyes. Logic told him that the tears were simply protecting her from dry eye because she couldn't blink; but with her in his arms, unable to move, she seemed so vulnerable. Honey badgers never seemed vulnerable. Despite their tiny size and big mouths. He wanted to wipe her tears and kiss her forehead, but he knew better. Tock was not a woman who would appreciate being tended to like a wounded fawn.

So, instead, he simply said, "Don't worry. We're going to get you better." That's what he said out loud. Inside, he thought, *I will never let anything happen to you until you can rip throats from necks again.*

The elevator *ding*ed when they hit the first floor, and the doors slid open. That's when he looked away from Tock and into the face of an armed man he did not know.

Shay roared but when the man didn't back away or start shooting, he quickly realized he was dealing with another badger cousin.

"Found them!" he yelled to someone. Of course, "found them" seemed inaccurate because he had done nothing but stand in front of an elevator while it came down. It should have been, "Here they are."

Shay didn't have time to point that out, though, as the badger gripped his shoulder and pulled him out of the elevator with Tock still held tight in his arms.

"With me, with me," the badger ordered, pushing Shay toward the front doors. "We have transport outside."

And they did. An actual helicopter, waiting on the lawn in front of the building. A nice one, too.

The helicopter door was opened from the inside and the

female who had been on the private jet with them motioned him forward.

"Come on!" she yelled over the engine noise.

Scrunching down as far as he could so the top of his head wasn't taken off by the rotating blades, Shay got into the copter. He had settled into a seat with Tock in his arms but she was quickly removed by someone else, and the clothes he'd left behind on the ground were shoved into his now-empty arms.

"Put something on," the female complained. "No one wants to see your big tiger dick."

Lovely.

While Shay struggled into his clothes without being able to stand up, he looked over his shoulder to see IVs being put into Tock's arms and blood being drawn. They'd also closed her eyes.

"Stop worrying," the female ordered him. "We're pretty sure she'll be fine."

"Pretty sure?" he barked back.

"What? You want absolutes in this life?" She sniffed. "There are none. Better get used to it, kitty cat."

Yeah. He was positive now. As the helicopter took off while another landed to retrieve the rest of the badgers they'd left behind, Shay felt positive he hated these people.

Once her cousins closed her eyes, Tock couldn't see anything. But it was a relief not to have them stuck open. That had been particularly unpleasant. Of course, now she could only guess what was happening around and to her from the prodding hands and annoyed voices.

Then again . . . her family always sounded annoyed. As if everything they were doing for you was sooo much work and sooo much trouble. They'd do it . . . for you . . . but it was a lot of work so you really should appreciate all of it! They didn't do that just to family members either. President of a country, prime minister, richest person in the world, ten-year-old whose ball rolled under a car—everyone, to Tock's family, was an equal opportunity annoyance.

"Aa-sha, how much longer do we have to wait?" she heard a distant cousin complain.

"Listen to you. Our cousin could be dying! And you complain about being forced to wait."

"*You* were just complaining five minutes ago!"

"I'm *hungry*! Do you want me to starve to death?"

Tock tried again to move parts of her body as she'd done with her arm. She figured she must be annoyed enough by now. But no. She couldn't move anything.

She'd be more freaked out except that she could still feel that big cat hand on her. Sometimes he had his hand on her shoulder, against her forearm, or brushing her hair from her face after someone took out her ponytail to sew up a small cut in her head. Someone had asked him to leave. More than once. But his answer was always the same: "No." And one really couldn't move a tiger if they didn't want to be moved.

So Shay remained even when they reached the shifter medical facility, and Tock's family came and went. Along with medical staff made up of cats, dogs, and a couple of bears. Yet they didn't seem to know how to fix her either.

After a while, Tock began to panic. Was she going to be like this forever? Trapped in her own body? Waiting for death?

Before Tock could really spiral into suicidal ideation, someone was prying open her eyelids.

"Hi, Tock. It's me . . . Stevie."

Fuck! Why was Stevie MacKilligan here? Who had brought her here? What was Tock's grandmother thinking?

There were two things she knew *never* to do when it came to the MacKilligan sisters. One: Never say, "I dare you" to Max MacKilligan. Because not only would she take the dare, but she would make sure to destroy everything in a ten-mile radius while performing the dare. The second thing . . . ? Never. Fuck. With. Stevie!

Not because Stevie was a problem. She wasn't. No matter what Max said. In fact, Stevie was a very sweet, soft-spoken genius who made Albert Einstein seem kind of slow. But Stevie was protected. She had to be because all sorts of people wanted to use her genius for their own evil goals. If you messed with Stevie, you had to deal with Charlie MacKilligan.

And no one wanted to deal with Charlie MacKilligan.

Half wolf, half honey badger, Charlie was Max's eldest sister and a very atypical shifter because she couldn't shift. She could unleash claws and fangs, but that was it. She never shifted fully into wolf or honey badger or something in between. But what she lacked in shifting ability, she more than made up for with massive strength, brutal determination, and an obsessive focus on protecting her siblings.

Tock, Mads, Nelle, and Streep did their best to avoid Charlie. Four females who weren't scared of much, they'd learned early to be scared of the slightly older hybrid. Not because she'd ever hurt them but because there was just something about her . . . something terrifying. Predators knew predators and did their best to avoid them. At least that's what the smart predators did. Sure, a Kamchatka brown bear could fight a Siberian tiger in the wild, but why would he? Wasn't life hard enough without having to pry the massive jaws of a fellow predator from one's throat? Wild animals knew that and shifters knew that.

And when honey badgers found someone to be scared of . . . they listened to their instincts.

Since the first time they'd seen Charlie MacKilligan interrogate her sister over why she'd been thrown off a school bus on her first day of junior high, they'd all known they were dealing with someone—some*thing*—very dangerous.

Although when it came to Max, Charlie's biggest job was to keep the troublemaker in line; when it came to Stevie, her job was keeping her sister *safe*. Keeping her from being used. Keeping her from becoming obsessive and possibly mentally snapping from the pressure to perform. Keeping her from accidentally destroying the world with a random physics equation.

Anyone who tried to get around Charlie so they could use Stevie was merely asking for a knife to the chest. It would not be the first time.

Which was why panic really set in when Charlie's angry face appeared right next to Stevie's.

She'd never admit it out loud, but Tock would kind of miss her grandmother . . .

Shay felt better seeing somewhat familiar faces. Keane had problems dealing with "the sisters" as he called them, but not Shay. Stevie was sweet and friendly, trying her best to make them all get along for his kid sister's sake.

And Charlie . . . ?

Well, he couldn't think of better protection for Tock among all these strangers. Family or not.

Of course, Charlie did look particularly pissed. And she only said one thing when she entered the room:

"Where's Mira Lepstein?"

Shay didn't know that name but something told him it was the grandmother.

"She wasn't with us when we got here." He motioned to the nonmedical personnel in the room. "This is Tock's family."

Moving only her eyes, Charlie looked down at Tock. "What's wrong with her?"

"Someone poisoned her, but I don't know what they used."

Stevie shrugged. "Neither do we, but I've been trying to find out." She walked around the bed, studying Tock. "It's man-made and they've been modifying it—making it stronger and more specific."

"So it's for shifters," he stated.

"It's for *honey badger* shifters," she replied. "It's for our kind."

"Who'd want to kill honey badgers specifically?"

Lips pursed, Charlie turned her angry graze over to a male lion standing in the corner, writing in a chart.

It took the cat a moment to notice, but when he did, he snorted and said, "Oh, puhleeze. Get over yourselves."

"If we were going to destroy anyone, it would be hyenas," the lion male went on. He glanced off, eyes narrowing. "We *hate* them."

"Full-humans?" one of Tock's family asked.

"If you mean inside the government, or *any* government,

doubtful." Stevie shrugged. "Our people are *everywhere*. They'd let one of our organizations know about anything like that. But outside the government . . . ? Maybe."

"Maybe one of our kind knows but is like him about hyenas."

They all looked at the lion male again and he tossed his hands up in exasperation. "Seriously? Look, I may bite the heads off hyenas when they get on my nerves, but I'd never *lower* myself to poisoning them or you. We are *lions*. Proud. Beautiful. Amazing hair." He motioned to Tock's family. "Besides, the only shifters I know that do hinky shit are the honey badgers."

"We fight to survive," Charlie coldly explained. "So if that means putting a bullet in your head . . . we'll do it. And it's not our fault if you're not faster than a bullet. Or a knife. Or a club. Or snake venom powerful enough to take down a herd of rhino. But that being said, we'd never poison each other."

"Why not?"

"It's tacky," the badgers all said as if that answer was somehow obvious.

Shay shook his head and said, "Look, I appreciate all this, and I know it's important to find out who is doing this, but right this moment, we need to help Tock."

"Who?" the lion asked.

"Your patient," Shay spit out between gritted teeth.

"Oh. Yeah." He nodded. "No. We've got nothin'."

"What does that mean?"

"We have no idea how to treat this poison."

"You can't leave her like this."

She was just lying there. Eyes closed. It was breaking his heart.

"We've had subjects that have regained full movement in three days."

"The latest victims are taking six days," Stevie explained to the lion from behind Charlie. She'd probably moved there because the lion had talked about biting off heads. She was easily frightened. Despite being half tiger and half honey badger, she had none of the savage bravery that both her species possessed. It was as if in combining, the two had cancelled each other out.

"Every time they use this poison," Stevie continued, "it's been stronger and stronger."

"And you still don't know what it is?" one of Tock's cousins demanded.

Before Stevie could reply, Charlie gave a low snarl and warned, "Watch how you talk to my sister."

The badger took a step forward, clearly not enjoying that warning from a hybrid. Especially since honey badgers didn't usually get hybrids, no matter who or what they bred with. But the MacKilligan sisters, including his own baby sis, were different. So very different. Not only from the breeds of their parents but from one another.

Another cousin stopped her angry relative and said something in a language Shay didn't understand. With a nod, the badger took a step back, but Charlie was still tense and ready for a fight. Then again, from what Shay had seen in the short time he'd known her, she was *always* tense and ready for a fight.

"There is something I can try—" Stevie began.

"Then do it," Shay said.

She glanced off, appearing uncomfortable. "I don't know if it'll work. It's really just a guess, and I haven't had time to try it out on any random test subjects to make sure I'm right. So if it goes wrong, it'll go *very* wrong and—"

"Just try it!" they all barked except Charlie. She just gave a louder warning growl, and Shay lifted his hands, palms out, and added, "Please, Stevie?"

She blew out a breath, nodded. "Okay."

Stevie pulled a backpack like the one he used to have in high school off her shoulders and dug inside. She took out a slim, long, silver case and used a code on the keypad to unlock it. When she produced a very large syringe with a very large and scary-looking needle, Shay began to doubt his insistence on subjecting Tock to this treatment. He'd only said "try it" because he knew Tock could handle most things. Like all honey badgers. More important, he knew how brilliant and ethical Stevie was. She wouldn't try something that she knew *wouldn't* work. Especially on a friend of her own sister's.

But that ridiculous needle . . . And what was that stuff in the syringe?

Stevie went over to the tray beside the lion. While staying as far away from the big cat as she could and watching him with panicked eyes, she pulled on nitrile gloves, took an alcohol wipe from its packaging, and moved over to Tock.

She pushed the blanket off Tock's leg and moved the gown away from her thigh. Then, after sterilizing the area with the wipe, she took a very deep, long breath, briefly closed her eyes, and after muttering something he couldn't understand, pushed the needle into Tock. She pushed hard because she had to get through that thick badger skin. The same thing happened any time his mother had taken their baby sister to the doctor for vaccines.

Shay was sure he'd heard a whimper come from Tock, and he brushed his fingers against her cheeks, hoping to soothe her. To let her know she wasn't alone with these insane people.

Stevie pushed the plunger down on the syringe, waited a few seconds, then pulled the needle out.

"Okay. That should do it."

"What did you give her?" one of the cousins asked. A question they should have asked a few seconds before, Shay abruptly realized.

"A mixture of forty-seven poisons from some of the deadliest snakes, scorpions, and spiders known to man."

There was a stunned silence for a long moment before the room exploded with the rage of all those honey badgers.

"You did *what*?"

"Neither I nor the medical center will be responsible for any of this!"

"Oh, my God!"

"You'll pay for this, MacKilligan!"

"We'll need to get the family together as soon as possible for the funeral."

"No problem. I know a good rabbi."

"Tock, you've always had the worst friends. The worst!"

"I am *not* telling Savta we allowed this on our watch."

The explosion of panic ended, though, when they all realized that Stevie had launched herself onto the ceiling and was walking on it until she reached a vent to crawl into. A few seconds later, she reappeared on the other side of the room's glass window, staring inside.

Charlie moved in front of the glass doors and folded her arms over her chest. The expression she wore was a direct challenge to anyone in the room who wanted to get past her to Stevie.

Not liking the tension in the room, Shay readied himself to grab Tock and evacuate her any way he could.

Then the explosion. Not from any of them. Or some device attached to the building. But from Tock.

Suddenly, screaming the entire time, Tock sat up. Every muscle in her body was distended, straining against the flesh. Veins popping. He could only see the whites of her eyes, and her fangs and claws were out. She thrashed on the bed for a few seconds, then flipped off and landed on the floor.

That's when everything stopped.

Stevie pushed her way back into the room, muttering under her breath, "Don't kill me. Don't kill me. Don't kill me," to everyone else as she made her way to Tock's side.

Shay already had his arms under Tock when Stevie crouched next to him. "Get her on the bed," she ordered, and he did as she said.

She pressed her fingers against Tock's neck, placed her ear against Tock's chest, then announced, "Her heart's stopped. Perfect."

"You killed our cousin," someone said. "Our grandmother is gonna be pissed."

"Perfect?" Shay repeated. "How is this *perfect*?"

"Wait . . ." Stevie said. And they did. But there was nothing. No sound. No movement. Not even a dying gasp. Nothing.

Horrified, Shay leaned over Tock's inert form on the bed. But with surprising strength, Stevie yanked him back. He didn't know why until he looked at the bed and didn't see Tock but just a slash of fresh blood across the white sheets. He only had a moment to wonder where she was and why she was bleeding, when Stevie pressed her hand against his neck and told someone, "Dammit. I think she nicked his artery."

What? Nicked whose artery? Not his. He'd been—

Shay was on the floor and didn't know why. That lion male and Stevie were hovering over him, twin expressions of panic on their faces.

"I think it was more than a nick," the big cat told Stevie, and Shay wondered where all that blood on the pair came from before he blacked out completely.

She was traveling through the ceiling of some building she didn't know. She was in full flight mode, which was weird. Honey badgers didn't really do the flight part of fight or flight. They mostly just fought and backed up. Fought and backed up. Until their enemy wisely retreated. But everything inside her was telling her to move, move, move! So she did.

As she did, though, she could hear yelling from beneath her. Could hear the word "Tock!" yelled over and over again. She just didn't know why. Were they counting down to something? Did they need a clock? And why not "tick-tock"? Who just said "tock"?

Since she had no idea what was going on, she kept moving. On all fours. Through the ceiling until she found a duct that had fresh air coming in. She went for that, slamming her body into the metal until she forced it out. She dropped onto the ground and took off running. She heard lots of people coming after her. Then she sensed some were in front of her. She stopped. Backed up. Turned and ran the other way. But there were more there. She stopped. Backed up, and tried a different direction.

It didn't work. She was surrounded. She bared her fangs and hissed in warning. That's when she realized she was in her honey badger form. But that was okay. There were a few people staring at her. Moving in.

She'd take them all on.

She charged forward, ready to destroy, when a person she didn't know tossed a live king cobra in front of her.

The snake was pissed, rearing up; its neck flap spread in warning, and that's when she realized how hungry she was. She could not care less about these people surrounding her. All she knew was that she wanted to eat.

She changed direction and threw herself at the snake. It bit into her neck, injecting poison into her veins while it wrapped its long body around her. But she was too hungry to care. She just grabbed it by the head with her two front claws and pulled until she'd torn its jaw from the rest of it. She fell asleep after that.

But when she woke up again, she began eating. She was just so damn hungry.

She was covered in cobra blood and had half its face stuffed in her mouth when one of the people she didn't know crouched close to her. She hoped he didn't expect her to share any of her snake with him. She didn't share on principle. Only her teammates got that kind of special treatment.

"How ya doin', cousin?" the male asked with a smile. "I have to say you're looking much better."

Not appreciating that comment on her looks, she angrily hissed at the male, flecks of blood hitting him in the face. Then she released her anal glands so she could enjoy her meal in peace, but these others . . . they only laughed and appeared relieved. Still, no one left so she could eat by herself.

Disgusted at such rudeness, she went back to her meal. Just let them try to get the cobra from her. She'd show them. She'd show them all.

Because, God! It was just so *rude*!

Chapter 4

Mads stared at her teammate. Actually, they all stared at her. Gawked, really. How could they not? Tock was in a rage. Pacing back and forth, ranting and raving. At least . . . Mads guessed it was ranting and raving. She wasn't really sure.

"What's happening?" Nelle finally asked.

"I think she's yelling at us," Max guessed.

"Ranting and raving," Mads corrected.

"Really? Are we sure?"

"No," Mads admitted. "We're not sure."

How could they be sure when Tock was in her honey badger form during all this?

All that was coming out of her blood-covered mouth were squeaks and hisses and growls. But the way she kept stopping to look at them from time to time, Mads felt pretty sure that Tock thought she was talking to her teammates and that they understood her perfectly.

When they were all in their honey badger form and needed to communicate something, it really just took a look or a quick hiss. Maybe a soft bark in warning. And immediately they knew what the other was trying to say. But it wasn't like a family cartoon where dogs and cats and badgers could chat with one another. At least not for them. Maybe for full badgers. Maybe they had complete conversations like in a Bugs Bunny cartoon. Maybe all those squeaks and hisses and growls made sense to fellow full badgers. Mads didn't know. All she did know was that when she was human and Tock was badger . . .

her teammate could be saying nuclear weapons were about to drop where Mads was standing and Mads would take the hit because she had no idea what was going on. None.

"Should we say something to her?" Nelle wanted to know.

"Like what?"

"I have no idea."

Streep crouched down, and Tock stopped in front of her. "Honey," she gently began, "we're trying to understand you, but—"

Tock's snarling hiss was so brutal that Streep stumbled away from her, then lashed out with her own snarling hiss and a flash of fangs. Something they rarely saw from her. She was a sweet badger. A rarity among their kind.

The door to the waiting room flew open and Keane Malone stormed in.

"Where is she?" he demanded. "Where's the bitch who nearly killed my brother?"

As one, they all pointed at Tock and, after a quick blink, the anger faded from his always angry–looking face before he finally admitted, "I can't yell at her when she's like that."

But, apparently, she could yell at him, charging forward and hissing, nipping at his big feet.

"What is she doing?"

"She's warning you not to fuck with her."

"Yeah, well, you can tell her—aaaaaaah!" he screamed when Tock ran up his body and started to attack his throat and face. "*Get her off me! Get her off me!*"

Was he kidding? Mads wasn't going near Tock when she was like this. She needed her teammate healthy and ready for the upcoming championship. The last thing she was going to do was get into a badger fight that might injure them both. None of them would. Nope. Keane was on his own. But he was being kind of a dick anyway, so he sort of deserved it.

Finn was standing over his brother's inert form when he saw something strange out of the corner of his eye. He looked, but there was nothing to see, so he turned back to his big brother. He called Shay his big brother not just because he was older than Finn by a couple of years, but because he was his *big* brother. Keane might be the tallest of them, but Shay was the widest. Like a bus. It was his crazy big shoulders. He had trouble going through doors sometimes. He tended to "loom" behind people without meaning to; when they turned to find this giant man standing behind them, it led to panicked screaming and running away. Something that always hurt Shay's feelings.

Although he talked much less than their eldest brother, Shay was definitely the most sensitive of their family. Especially for a cat. He cared about people. And things. Like dogs. He cared about dogs. Even Finn didn't get that. Why care about something that could take care of itself and tended to run in packs when left on the streets? The family had three "outside dogs" at their house in Queens, but for all the Malones except Shay, the canines were there simply to protect the house when they weren't home. Finn didn't even know their names. Wait . . . did they have names? Probably. Shay was the kind who'd name a dog or house cat. He was friendly to everybody. Even when they'd first come face-to-face with Mads and her friends, he was the one who felt they should be kind to them. Finn just wanted to keep things polite because their baby sister was half badger. Keane, however, still tried to pretend his sister was tiger only, so he was rude to any honey badger he met. But not Shay. He wanted to hang out at the MacKilligan house. He wanted to chat with Charlie MacKilligan about dog stuff. He cared about the trio as his baby sister's half-sisters.

It was the caring side of Shay that had gotten him into this trouble. He'd gone off with Tock Lepstein to keep an eye on her because he knew if something happened, Mads was going to be . . . well . . . mad. Not only because their basketball team had made it into the championships, which would be coming up soon, but because—although she'd probably never admit it—Mads and Tock were best friends. They all called each other teammates but the relationship was more than that. For all five of them, but especially for Mads and Tock. They'd been looking out for each other since they were thirteen. Finn had always known that if he had a relationship with Mads, he would always have to make room for Tock. She'd be around somewhere. Showing up to their dinner out, sitting in seats behind him at the movies, or asleep in his kitchen cabinets—all his honey gone.

Normally, he wouldn't want anyone sleeping in his cabinets. He wouldn't want anyone around that much at all. But if he wanted Mads around, he'd have to accept Tock, too. Yeah. He knew he'd fallen hard for Mads Galendotter. A woman whose entire life seemed to revolve around basketball. The most boring of games. She sometimes compared that boring game to football. As if there was any comparison! One was a sport of strength, power, grace, rigid rules, and the innate ability to withstand major head trauma. The other was for tall freaks who could jump. In theory, neither Mads nor her friends should be able to play basketball in the shifter pros. They were honey badgers playing against She-bears, the big She-cats, and She-wolves.

Not only taller breeds but wider. Especially the bears. Those females had miles-long shoulders and legs. They might look like they loped and lumbered around, but nope. They could move like lightning down the court and knock smaller players out of the way with ease. But Mads and her friends were honey badgers. What they lacked in size, they more than made up for in brute viciousness. Finn had to admit . . . he did love watching Mads play. That ball was hers, and she wasn't giving it up to anyone once she had it. And if she didn't have it, she was going to get it.

He just didn't know what was going to happen when the season was over. The championships were in New York but her team, the Butchers, was from Wisconsin. She'd need to be in Wisconsin for practices and whatnot. He would never ask her to quit the team or, even worse, quit basketball altogether. Not only because it was clearly her calling in life, but because it was how she made money legally. Because when these honey badgers weren't playing basketball, they were stealing. They stole a lot. Badgers loved stealing and breaking into shit. And they would steal anything, from ancient art to the finest jewelry to cars to clothes off the rack to farm equipment to the steak off your plate—a situation that had nearly led to bloodshed between Keane and Max MacKilligan. In his defense, though, he'd been really hungry that day.

Not wanting to spend years of his life visiting Mads in prison, Finn would really prefer she play basketball. She loved it and it was legal. Even if the full-human world didn't know any of these teams existed or had their own arenas and worldwide fans who cheered with growls and howls.

It was the same for Finn and his brothers. They could have been professional bone-breakers like most Malones. Or they could have gone into hockey . . . also like most Malones. But football seemed to be their thing. They'd started with pee-wee football and when they hit junior high, they joined school teams. All three of them were offered full scholarships to college, but by then their dad had been killed and they had to stay home and take care of their mom, baby brother, and baby sister. Their team coach had been devastated each time one of the brothers made the decision, and he always asked the same thing: How could they just give up football and a chance at a college education? But they weren't giving up anything except eventually being part of the NFL—something that would never last because of all those blood tests that got more and more invasive as the years went by. Well, not only that. It was also Keane. His brutality on the field was legendary in the shifter league; Finn couldn't imagine what would have happened if his big brother had gone pro with full-humans. As it was, none of them were sure he'd make it out of high school football without killing someone on the field. The man needed someone he could hit with all the force he could muster, someone who would get up again. Like Alaskan bears. Keane loved playing against Alaskan bears.

But they were part of the New York Crushers and had no intention of leaving. Not with their youngest brother still late on his growth spurt and college coming up in the fall; and their baby sister now part of their half-sisters' lives. They had to stick around to make sure everything went according to plan. Their youngest siblings weren't going to suffer like they did when their father was killed. They wouldn't lose everything. They had a chance, and Keane, Shay, and Finn were going to make sure they both got what they deserved.

Finn continued to gaze down at his brother. He was pale but a specialist had been called in to deal with his wounded artery. The shifter world had lots of artery specialists on the medical side of things. It was the first area every predator went for when there was a fight.

The fever had also taken hold but they'd given Shay medication to control it. So he wouldn't be running around the hospital, trying to fuck any non-related female whose scent he'd caught. But just seeing him lying there was upsetting. Shay didn't make a lot of noise, but you always knew he was around. He was a presence in his own, quiet way. Right now, the room seemed empty.

Finn heard something smash against one of the glass windows that surrounded the hospital room and looked over to see Keane flinging something off his head. A huge honey badger hit the window but didn't fall to the ground. It used the power of the throw to shove itself off and back at Keane. Wrapping itself around his brother's skull.

Screaming, Keane tried to pry the badger off, but it was holding on with all its claws. Blood had already begun to leak down Keane's forehead, and he was starting to get hysterical.

Finn let out a sigh. He'd tried to stop Keane when he'd stormed out after seeing their brother and hearing what had happened from some woman they didn't know. She'd had an accent and was extremely pretty, but she was also badger and her explanation had not been kindly told. Unless they were up to something, badgers were brutally straightforward about . . . well . . . everything. Keane had not responded well to any of it.

And now he had a badger on his head.

With one last glance at Shay, Finn moved across the room and opened the glass door.

"*Get it off! Get it off!*" his brother begged.

Finn knew it wasn't Mads attacking his brother. She had lighter fur, which got even paler when she was human. She liked to say it was the Viking in her that gave her that blondish fur. But it could be any of her teammates. He had no idea. The hospital was currently filled with honey badgers. And Keane, when angry—and he was almost always angry—could make a Benedictine nun aggressive as any of the nuns in their Catholic high school could attest.

Taking a breath, Finn reached out and attempted to grab hold of the fighting badger. But as soon as it felt fingers brush against its fur, it spiraled around, slashed at him—nearly taking his eye out—dropped to the ground, and ran into Shay's room. It kicked the door closed with its back feet and by the time Finn and Keane made it into the room, it was standing on the bed facing them. Its back legs were on Shay's chest, the front legs on his knees. When they moved toward it, the badger hissed so viciously that they immediately backed up, which was just weird. Amur tigers didn't really back up for anybody. They didn't have to. But seeing that angry badger face, Finn kind of understood why lions avoided these guys in the wild.

They were nuts.

After a beat, Keane tried to step forward again, but his motion unleashed another hiss that had Finn remembering he really should update his will.

"I think," Finn suggested, "we leave."

"Are you nuts? Do you want it to finish the job it started?"

Finn frowned. "Are you saying that's Tock?"

"Yes. And she's insane."

Actually, she was the most rational of Mads's group. It was why he liked Tock so much. But, more importantly, he understood Tock. So he immediately relaxed.

"Maybe she's just pissed you keep calling her 'it.' And she's clearly protecting him," he told Keane.

"What?"

"She's protecting him. Look."

"She's the one that almost killed him."

"That was an accident. She didn't do it on purpose."

"I don't care. She should suffer."

"She was poisoned. Then poisoned again by Stevie. Then she ate something that poisoned her—"

"I'm pretty sure she enjoyed that last part."

"I think she's suffered enough, don't you?" He glanced over at the hospital bed that his brother lay in. Tock—appearing more like a weirdly shaped, medium-sized dog than a badger—stood on top of him, still hysterically hissing at them, attempting to warn them away from Shay.

Finn couldn't imagine his brother being any safer.

"Let's go. We should find out what the hell is going on, anyway."

"Going on with what?"

"The badgers."

Keane shrugged. "I don't care what's going on with them."

"And that's probably why your wounds are still bleeding."

"Were you ever going to tell the other badgers in the world that our kind is under threat? Or just let us all die from some unknown poison like we're diplomats in a foreign country?"

"Awesome burn, Sis!" burst from the other side of the room and Nelle briefly closed her eyes to keep from laughing. Some days she really wished she could just gag Max. Of course, she'd tried that once but the little psycho just chewed through the leather.

"And my sister's right," Max went on. "We're all out here at risk, and you guys aren't warning anyone."

"We've been working on an antidote," one of Tock's cousins explained, "but our supposed *experts* are having trouble figuring out what kind of drug it is."

"Hey!" Stevie sat up in her chair, glaring across the room. "Is that directed at *me*? Tock is alive and attacking people because *I* fixed the problem!"

"You took a gamble with my cousin's life. You could have killed her!"

"Do you really think I'd use something on Tock without having tested it at least once?"

Charlie's eyes narrowed. "Tested it on who?"

"It's *whom*," Stevie corrected, which meant she was about to lie. Nelle had been studying Max's baby sister ever since she'd met her. She found the nervous genius absolutely fascinating. Especially when Stevie thought no one was watching. Just the other day . . . she'd had a verbal spat with a squirrel before it chased her back into the house. See? Who needed television or social media when you had a MacKilligan to watch?

"*Stevie?*" Charlie pushed.

"Rats, okay? I used rats. Like all scientists that don't care about animals."

"Rats *die* from rat poison that you can get at any grocery store. Meaning that we both know they couldn't handle a snake poison of any kind much less the deadliest ones in the known world. So on *whom* did you test it?"

"Well . . ."

Charlie slammed her fist on the end table next to her, cracking it in the middle.

"*Max!*" she bellowed.

"How is this my fault?" Max immediately wanted to know.

"Because you allowed yourself to be a test dummy yet again!"

"I was bored and she needed answers. I was trying to help."

"I thought you didn't know what was going on," one of the cousins annoyingly pointed out.

"I didn't," she said with a shrug. "Stevie just asked whether I'd mind if she shot me up with a few combinations—"

"*A few?*"

"—of snake poison," she continued, ignoring Charlie's further bellowing, "and I said sure."

The panther that Max had been dating for a little while now turned to look at her and asked what all of them were thinking. "Why the fuck would you do that?"

"I told you. I was bored."

"Max," Charlie sighed out, "how many times do I have to tell you not to let Stevie test shit on you?"

"But I need her," Stevie argued. "She's incredibly resilient."

"Yeah," Max agreed. "I'm . . . that. Super that. And, after twelve or thirteen years, I've only died, like, three times."

"Actually, it was four. But I always brought her back," Stevie quickly added when Charlie's eyes grew wide. "You know all my labs are equipped with defibrillators and—"

"And that stuff they use on meth addicts when they O.D."

Stevie nodded at Max's contribution. "Exactly."

Charlie abruptly stood, her chair loudly scraping the ground. "I'm going home now," she announced. "Because if I don't . . . I'm going to kill everyone in this room, including *you two*." She pointed at her sisters, who reared back. Max in mock shock and Stevie in real shock. "And I will feel *no* remorse about any of it. So to avoid that . . . I'm taking my Black ass home, and I'm going to take a couple of Xanax when I get there. I can do that now, because I have a prescription. My psychiatrist strongly felt I needed something extra on days that my family *pisses me the fuck off*!" She cleared her throat, calm once again. "We'll talk more tomorrow when I don't want to stab all of you in the eyes."

In silence, they watched Charlie walk out of the room and disappear around a corner.

See? Now that was entertainment.

Which was why, all those years ago when she'd met Max and the others on that school bus, she'd known that she was very lucky. She hadn't been in the States long, and she'd been having trouble making friends. She'd only met full-human pups and if they weren't put off by what a teacher once called her "snooty Hong Kong accent" or advanced education, they were just bigots who didn't like Asians. That was fine. Bigots were everywhere. But a few times people weren't bigots—they just hadn't liked *her*. She didn't understand why, though. She was always polite. Damn near nice. And yet . . . parents didn't want their kids playing with her. Or didn't seem comfortable when she went to their awful birthday parties with the clowns and water guns.

But once she'd met Max, Tock, Streep, and Mads, she'd finally understood what the problem was: full-humans sucked and honey badgers were awesome. She'd been waiting all her life to meet honey badgers who weren't related to her by blood; since she had, she'd never been happier. True, she still had to deal with her family—her father didn't count because she thought he'd hung the moon—but her teammates had always given her an escape. All four of them were so ridiculous and took such risks, how could she be anything *but* entertained?

The room was silent a few seconds more after Charlie left, until one of Tock's cousins turned to Stevie and asked, "What made you think all that poison was going to help Emmy?"

"Who?"

"She means Tock," Max said.

"Oh! Right. Uh . . . that theory was based on my research on how this substance interacts with our bodies. Honey badgers are very aggressive. Instinctually. And, it turns out, so are our cells. When we are hit with most any toxin, our bodies see it as a threat and react accordingly, immediately getting into a fight with anything not supposed to be there. But with this new toxin, that instinctual reaction does not occur. Our cells don't see the toxin as a threat so they don't fight, even while this thing is tearing us apart from the inside out. So I thought maybe if we used something our bodies automatically react to, it would prompt the cells to push anything out that didn't belong there, whether perceived as a threat or not."

She let out a breath. "But what worries me is that every time they change the structure of this thing—and they keep changing it, trying to make the toxin stronger—it gets worse for us. I'm concerned that this product will hit a point where our bodies will no longer be able to fight, no matter what we do. In fact, I think it will actually be able to kill us."

"In other words," another cousin said, "we are running out of time to find out where this is coming from and put a stop to it."

"Exactly. As strong as we are as a species, we're not immortal, and we're not indestructible. We're just . . ."

"Hardheaded?" another cousin questioned.

Stevie nodded. "Well . . . yes."

"Why are *we* here?"

The question was offensive in its coldness and every badger eye in the room turned to look at the giant Amur tiger who'd asked it.

Keane Malone. Uncontrollable feline rage stuffed into a half-Mongolian, half–Irish Traveler body with nothing but vengeance and football on his mind. Six foot eight and at least three hundred and fifty pounds, Keane was avoided by nearly everyone. Even Nelle's fellow teammates avoided him as much as possible. They liked Shay and Finn well enough, but Keane was considered persona non grata ever since he'd lashed out at Max when she'd offered him delicious Danish and he'd practically spit the kind gesture back in her face. Considering Max was not known for bouts of kindness, his rude response was a true affront to all of them.

Nelle understood his rage, though. She couldn't imagine how angry she'd be if someone had murdered her father. Of course, if someone murdered Mae, her sister, she wouldn't care. But that was Mae's fault. She was an asshole.

"You're here because your brother is stalking our cousin?" suggested another of Tock's cousins, this one wearing a skull-cap.

"My brother was helping your sister—"

"Cousin."

"—which personally I think was wrong. He should have let her die writhing on the floor."

Tock's relatives snarled in response but Nelle quickly rubbed her nose to stop from smiling. Keane was just so . . . cranky! Who had the time to always be so unpleasant? Who *wanted* to be that unpleasant? She knew honey badgers in their nineties who were less caustic! And that knowledge made her want to laugh. He was a ninety-year-old man in a thirtysomething's body.

A giant, perfect body that she did love to watch from a distance. Although she couldn't imagine spending any real time around the cat. Who wanted to spend precious moments of their far-too-short lives with a cranky cat?

Besides Max MacKilligan, that is. Although the captain of their basketball team did seem happy with her new jaguar boyfriend. Then again, knowing Max, that was probably because all she really did was torture the poor guy who'd stumbled into her life not so long ago. Zezé Vargas had no idea what he was getting into when he fell for Max MacKilligan.

"The only reason you're here, *cat*," an older badger explained to Keane, "is because your brother decided to insert himself into the situation. In future, if any of you want to avoid such an experience, mind your own business."

Not surprisingly, Keane didn't like that sentiment at all. With fangs exploding from his gums, he took an angry step forward. Finn quickly caught his arm and pulled him toward the door. A very wise cat, that Finn. Because every one of Tock's cousins and uncles and aunts went for a hidden weapon secreted somewhere on their person. Nelle recognized the move. Unlike the rest of her teammates' families, Tock's matriarchal relatives were not thieves. They knew how to steal, of course—they were still badgers. But that wasn't the family "business." Their skills weren't defensive . . . they were predatory.

Because if Tock's family snuck into a building or into someone's room, it wasn't to steal a guy's Rembrandt. It was because the guy was doing something so morally reprehensible, it had been judged that he could not go on. And Tock's family were some of the people who dealt with that particular issue, led by their matriarch, Mira Malka-Lepstein. And while Tock and all her cousins called Mira "Savta"—Grandmother in Hebrew— there were entire networks of scumbags in the world who called the She-badger "Grandmother Death." A very fitting name from what Nelle had heard over the years.

Sadly, Tock's mother hated that name. Hated the way Mira lived and had trained her children and grandchildren to live. Of course, Tock's mom, Ayda, was a pacifist, or what Mira had apparently once called a "hippy with no redeeming value, trying to make the woman who gave her life feel bad."

The biggest problem between them was that Tock was not a pacifist. She was anything but a pacifist. Also allegedly said by her grandmother, Tock was "a vicious little badger that knows how to break a man," which was supposedly the reason Mira Malka-Lepstein had a special place for Tock in that cold badger heart of hers. Something that did not sit well at all with Tock's mom, who wanted more for her daughter than a lifetime of checking her home for listening devices and assuming any man coming out of the shadows was trying to assassinate her.

So the two—mother and grandmother—did the sort of passive-aggressive family fighting over Tock that Nelle found fascinating. It was so full-human in its subtlety. Because there was nothing passive aggressive about Nelle's clan. They were more aggressive-aggressive. Meaning that if Nelle had to toss her sister out the window to get her point across, then that's what she had to do . . . and had done. More than once. And why her mother would then state in no uncertain terms, "This is why your sister hates you. You understand that, yes?"

Yes. That she understood. Direct, clear, concise. Downright brutal in its clarity.

And brutality was something Nelle could always respect.

"You need to calm down."

"They're pissing me off."

"Everyone pisses you off. That doesn't mean you shouldn't calm the fuck down."

Keane understood what his brother Finn was saying, but he was just so angry.

He really hadn't thought much about it when his brother had texted that he was going off with Tock. Thought maybe they were hooking up. He could understand it. Tock was pretty and had the kind of long legs his brother loved on a woman. If Shay wanted to distract himself for a little while with a honey badger, who was Keane to question? But if he'd known that idiot was going off with a honey badger on some kind of crazy "secret agent assignment," he would have yanked his dumb ass back before he'd made it out of Michigan.

Now, yes, it was true he'd been working with the honey badgers to find out who'd killed his father, but so what? He'd do anything to not only find the assholes behind his father's death but to rain down the kind of vengeance his kind was known for. He wouldn't stop until his father's killers were in their graves or their remains had been spread across the Eastern Seaboard. Either scenario would suit him. And if that meant working with and spending time with the most difficult and annoying species known to man, then fine.

That didn't mean, however, he was willing to lose any more family to this vendetta he had against his father's murderers. He wouldn't lose his brothers or sister over that. Not now, not ever.

So seeing Shay lying there . . .

"You need to breathe," his brother flatly warned, and Keane realized his fangs were sliding out of his gums again.

Deciding Finn was right for once, Keane took a few deep breaths. He did need to calm down if he was going to deal with all these new badgers and the doctors and nurses who, for some reason, seemed to be made up mostly of lions and snow leopards, which was just weird. All he truly cared about right now was Shay's health and safety; the last thing he needed was to be kicked out of this hospital because he couldn't keep himself from biting off the heads of a few honey badgers who had managed to piss him off.

Keane stood in the hallway, away from the room with all the badgers—so that he didn't have to see their stupid faces and get angry all over again—with Finn standing silently beside him. Just when he thought his anger was finally under control, he heard the *ding* of an elevator. An older female walked out, a phone glued to her ear. She spoke in a language he didn't know and looked around at the different rooms before turning and heading away from him and Finn. Keane didn't think much about it until he saw Charlie MacKilligan slip out of a doorway to follow her. Still nothing noteworthy except he could see Charlie was carrying a pump-action shotgun.

Eyes wide, he glanced at Finn and, without saying a word to each other, they both ran down the long hallway after the insane honey badger who was genetically related to their baby sister. They were cats and fast so they caught up quickly, before

Charlie could do anything. Keane wrapped his arms around her waist at the same time Finn tried to yank the gun from her hands. When he couldn't get it loose, Keane spun away and went in the opposite direction with Charlie clasped tight against his chest.

"Hi," he heard Finn say to the female who had just turned around. "If you're looking for the honey badgers, they're in the opposite direction."

The female's high heels clicked on the floor as she passed Keane. Her eyes, dark and suspicious, were looking at him so hard, he could do nothing but turn again with Charlie still clasped against him so the She-badger wouldn't spot her or her weapon.

Thankfully, Charlie didn't put up a fight. He played football with her now, and she was the strongest, meanest fighter he'd ever seen. He was not in the mood to get his ass kicked by a tiny, rabid animal if he could help it.

When they heard a door close somewhere down the hall-way, Keane dropped the crazy female and pushed her away from him.

"Are you insane?" he wanted to know.

"According to my therapist, I just need to focus on what's important. And what's important is putting that bitch out of my misery."

Finn grabbed the shotgun again and tried to pull it from her. His brother was using both hands; Charlie held on with only one. It was sad. After about ten seconds, Charlie finally told Finn, "You know you won't get it from me unless I give it to you."

"I am aware of your freakish strength," Finn said. "But I'd appreciate if you'd just give it to me. Please."

She released the weapon and Finn let out a long breath. "I swear," he muttered. "You two."

"What does that mean?" Keane wanted to know. "Unlike her, I don't use guns. I simply tear the spine from *my* enemies."

"And I like to avoid too much mess," Charlie announced.

"How is a shotgun less messy?"

"Angle of the weapon."

"Really?" Keane nodded. "I didn't know that."

"Stevie says it's all about physics."

"Could both of you stop it?" Finn snapped. "When I was hoping you two would eventually get along, I didn't want it to be over the way people should cleanly die for pissing you off."

"I told that old bitch to leave my sisters alone and she didn't listen to me," Charlie argued.

"See?" Keane said, nodding again, "I totally get that."

Finn briefly closed his eyes, which meant he was really getting annoyed. He tried to hide it but his feline temper was no better than Keane's.

"I understand you are both upset, but Stevie *and* Shay are both adults who can make their own decisions. Stevie wanted to help. Good for her! It seems the help is greatly needed. And Shay is going to be okay. You can yell at him when he's better," he said to Keane.

"Good. Because I will."

"Until then," Finn went on, "don't attack little old ladies in hallways."

"She is *not* a little old lady," Charlie corrected. "She is a honey badger that has destroyed entire governments with her schemes. She may remind you of your grandmothers but she'll tear your throat out as soon as you look at you."

"I don't deny that, but she'd probably do it some place private. Not in the middle of a shifter-only hospital. We do have rules, you know."

Charlie blinked. "We do?"

"Yes," both males said together.

"You mean they'd call the cops? They'd rat me out?"

Keane always forgot that the MacKilligans didn't have much experience with the global shifter world. They, like most honey badgers, spent more time in the full-human world. One reason was because that's where most of Stevie's early work had been done. But it was also because they'd never had the overall shifter experience as Keane and his family had. They weren't born in shifter-only hospitals. They didn't go to shifter-only summer camps or shifter-only vacation spots. According to his baby sister, the MacKilligan girls didn't have anything close to that life until they were forced to move in with Charlie's grandfather after her mother was killed. He was wolf and even though he accepted his granddaughter and her half-sisters, the rest of his pack were extremely uncomfortable with having three honey badgers around.

Glancing at Charlie, Keane realized he might have more in common with her than just his baby sister. They'd both lost a parent at a young age. They'd both been forced to grow up way too fast because of that loss. And, now, the most important thing to both of them was protecting the family they had left.

He still wished his sister was spending most of her time at his house with the rest of the family, but he also began to feel a little better about her living with Charlie. He wished he could say the same about living with Stevie and Max, but he didn't want anyone experimenting on her and he didn't want Max teaching her to be a sociopath. He had enough to worry about these days without those concerns.

"If you kill a shifter in a direct challenge with claws and fangs, you'll be protected," Keane explained. "But if you shoot a shifter in the back without warning . . . you're going to jail, Charlie. And then there will be no one but *Max* to protect Stevie. And that stuffed toy Stevie calls a boyfriend."

"Don't pick on her panda. She loves him, and he's good for her, but I see your point." She shrugged. "Okay. I'll wait to kill her."

Keane nodded. "Good plan."

Finn, eyes wide, snapped, "No, it's not!"

Mira stared into the room where her granddaughter slept on top of a feline. She was still in her badger form and was snoring. The feline, recovering from a neck wound, was under a medically induced sleep and would not be shifting any time soon, not until his body was done healing.

When Mira had sent her grandchild on this assignment, it never occurred to her Emily was in any true danger. At least no more danger than she would be on any other rescue mission assigned by her grandmother. Rescuing one of her many cousins was something Emily had done quite a few times over the years, for both sides of her family. This should have been a simple smash-and-grab . . . except with people.

But then that call had come from Tracey Rutowski. As soon as Mira had gotten that warning, she knew her grandchild was in danger, and she'd moved accordingly; but by then things were already in motion and it was too late to pull Emily out of harm's way.

So here her grandchild was. Hurt. Recovering. And who knew if she'd sustained any long-term damage. The doctors certainly didn't know yet. Neither did the MacKilligan girl who had pumped her grandchild up with so much venom, Emily could wake up babbling about dancing pink polar bears like Mira's Uncle Jakub. He used to drink Polish vodka with Vipera Berus venom. Of course, so did all her other uncles and aunts, but Jakub drank it all day and into the night. Just sipped, sipped, sipped until the low-potency venom eventually damaged his brain. After that, he used to see pink polar bears that liked to dance. Sometimes her uncle would join in. It made for interesting Shabbats, but she did not want the same for any of her grandchildren. Especially Emily. A brain like hers needed to be protected because it would do great things one day when she stopped wasting her time on dumb American sports and worthless friends.

But those were thoughts for another day. Right now . . . Mira had to admit something to herself. Unlike pacts between warring countries and taking down dictators, she finally had to accept that she couldn't handle this situation on her own. Because now civilians were being harmed. True, it was just an oversized house cat but it was the principle of the thing. She had no desire to harm the undeserving. Mira kept her ire for those who had earned it. House cat or not.

Which meant only one thing . . .

Letting out a long sigh, she hit redial on her phone and waited.

"What?" was the reply she got, and she rolled her eyes at the massive disrespect.

"You were right," Mira grudgingly admitted. "And I think you should get involved."

"Me?" was the response, and Mira could easily imagine the smirk on that face when the question was followed up with, "Or me and my *friendsssss*?" She drew the *S* out on "friends" so that the word sounded like it was coming from an actual asp.

Mira gritted her fangs—because they were out now, in annoyance—and said, "Yes. You and your"—she let out a sigh—"friends."

"Hey, guys," Tracey Rutowski yelled away from her phone, "she wants all of us!"

And the annoying, undisciplined badgers drunkenly cheered back, "Friendsssssssss!"

Unable to tolerate another moment, Mira ended the call and snarled so viciously, her half-conscious granddaughter on the other side of that thick, protective medical glass raised her badger head and hissed back.

Chapter 5

When Shay opened his eyes he knew three things . . .
It was morning.

He'd almost died.

And someone's head was resting on his penis.

If he hadn't almost died, he would simply go back to sleep and be just fine with someone sleeping on his dick. But this was weird because he *had* almost died. He could see all the hospital equipment, smell all the shifter breeds that were roaming around, and feel the wound that was still healing on his neck. This was not a time when he would go out and get himself a girlfriend. Maybe the fever had gotten the better of him, but he didn't think so. Shifter nurses didn't let their feverish patients run around hospitals trying to fuck each other. So then what the hell?

Carefully, aware he didn't want to undo the work that had been done on his throat, Shay lifted his head just enough so he could view the end of the bed . . . but all he saw was an amazing bare ass. Just resting there. Within touching distance of his hand, but he knew better. Shifter females were like any full-blood predator. They didn't like to be touched without their explicit permission, and a guy was taking his life in his claws if he tried anything else.

The problem at the moment was that the owner of that perfect ass was waking up and rubbing her face against the very thin sheet covering his dick.

Closing his eyes, he tried to get control of the one uncontrollable thing about him, but nope. It got hard. Because she wouldn't stop rubbing her face against it or growling.

The growling! It was definitely the growling.

Unable to stand another second without embarrassing himself, Shay barked, "Hey!"

He immediately realized that perfect ass was attached to Tock Lepstein, whose gorgeous curly hair briefly covered her face as she turned to look at him. With a quick twitch of her head, the hair moved and she blinked dark brown eyes at him.

"Shay?" she asked, frowning in confusion.

"Hi, Tock."

She placed her palms on his thighs and used her arms to raise her torso so she could look around.

"Where are we? What happened?"

"You don't remember anything?"

"No." She made a smacking sound with her mouth and glanced back at him. "Why do I taste cobra?"

"The snake? That kind of cobra? I do not know why you would taste that. I also don't know *why* you would know what king cobra tastes like."

She shrugged. "It's a little gamey. But with a nice sauce and fileted—"

"I can't listen to this now," he cut in before she could keep going. He didn't want to start retching while his neck was healing. "I am asking you nicely to please get off me."

"What?" She looked down and, after a brief pause, began crab-crawling away from the raging hard-on making a tent of the sheet. But that meant her ass was backing up right toward his face.

"Tock . . . Tock!" he barked, a little panicked.

She stopped, looked at him over her shoulder. All he had to do was widen his eyes and she quickly realized that he was inches away from having his nose buried in that ass. Something neither of them were comfortable with at the moment.

Gasping, she scrambled off him, which he appreciated. But then she grabbed the sheet and yanked it off. Leaving his hard dick exposed.

With a growl, he grabbed the pillow out from under his head and slammed it over his crotch.

"You're killing me, Tock," he told her, using the device draped over the headboard to lift the top half of the bed so he could sit up without moving his head or neck.

"*Why* am I naked?" she demanded.

"I don't know."

She looked him over, which made him feel even more naked. Like he didn't have a very convenient pillow covering his junk.

"Why are you in a hospital bed?" she wanted to know.

"There was an . . . incident."

"What incident?"

He took in a breath before admitting, "It's complicated."

"Oh, no. Did you get involved?"

"Uh . . ."

"I told you *not* to get involved. I told you to wait five minutes and—"

"Tock, I did all that. Then there were armed men and you were . . ."

"I was what?"

"Poisoned."

She laughed. "So?" She sucked her tongue against the roof of her mouth a few times and asked, "Is that why I taste cobra?"

"I don't mean that kind of poisoning."

"What kind, then? Cyanide? Rat poison? Ricin? Strychnine? Tetrodotoxin? VX?" When he frowned, she added, "Used during the Cold War."

"No. I don't think. I . . . uh . . . actually don't really know . . . what was used on you."

Still holding the sheet against her chest, she took a step back. "What? What do you mean you don't know what was used?"

"I don't know. Nobody knows."

"Shay . . . what the fuck is going on?"

"I don't know. Not yet. But your family—"

"My family? Which family?"

"Uh . . . I don't know how to answer that."

"Are they Black, Shay? Because that would give me a definite point to start."

"Not from what I've seen."

"Fuck," she said. "Savta. Fuck. Fuck, fuck, fuck."

She began to frantically scuttle around the room, briefly stopping to look through the glass windows before studying the floor and checking under his hospital bed.

"What are you doing? What are you looking for?" he asked.

"Where are my clothes?"

"I have no idea."

"*Why are people just taking my clothes?*"

Confused by Tock's behavior, Shay watched her attempt to twist the sheet into a makeshift dress while keeping it on her body. He'd be entertained if it wasn't so weird. He'd never seen Tock this hysterical. Not hysterical for anyone else, but definitely for her.

Tock didn't get mad. She didn't get sad. She didn't get happy. She just always seemed annoyed. But now, it was as if she wanted to jump out of her skin or out of his hospital room window. She actually opened it and stuck her head out, and he grabbed the alert button to let the nurses know that one of their patients was making a crazed run for it. But then she stepped back in.

"I gotta get out of here," he heard her saying. "I gotta get out of here."

"I think you need to calm down."

Waving him off, she jogged toward the glass front door. She had her hand on the handle when Shay, in desperation, called out, "Tock!"

She stopped long enough to look at him and demand, "What?"

He didn't know what to say. He wanted her to calm down. He wanted her to stop running. He wanted to stop her panic. But he didn't know how to make any of that happen. He knew she would bail on him at any second, so he did the first thing he could think of.

He asked, "What time is it?"

She froze, the door pushed halfway open. "What?"

"Do you know the time?"

She looked down at her left wrist, then around the room. "Where's my watch? *Who the fuck took my watch?*"

Tock released the door and faced him, and Shay quickly lifted his hands to his chest, palms out. "I didn't take it."

"I have to have my watch. I *need* my watch."

He gestured at the open window. "It looks like morning—"

"It *looks* like morning?" she repeated with obvious disgust. "What the fuck does that even mean?"

"I mean that it *looks* like morning, but it may not be. Morning. It could possibly be afternoon."

"How could you possibly think from the way the sun is positioned in the sky that it was afternoon?"

"Well—"

"How can you possibly go through life *not* knowing the time?"

He shrugged. "People tell me where to go and I go. No one ever says I'm late. If I were late, I'd hear about it from Keane."

Tock's top lip curled in disgust, but she seemed calmer. "That is an appalling way to exist in the world."

She moved toward him but stopped at the many machines that surrounded his bed. She studied each one until she pointed. "It's eight thirty-four in the morning."

Closing her eyes and letting out a breath, Tock repeated, "It's eight thirty-four in the morning." She took in another breath, let it out, and repeated one more time, "It's eight thirty-four in the morning."

When she looked at Shay, it was with calm brown eyes. He'd given her something to hold onto and it centered her.

Gazing at him, she suddenly asked, "What happened to your neck?"

Tock didn't understand. Why couldn't she remember what had happened?

As Shay told her the story of what had taken place the night before, she began to understand that the poisoning wasn't a simple ambush for a bounty or for revenge over something she or her family had done. This was much worse.

She'd been a goddamn test bunny!

"And here we are," Shay said when he was done.

Tock now sat on the edge of his bed, staring at the wall while he spoke. When he finished speaking, she turned her head to look at him and quickly noticed that his color was better and he definitely looked healthier.

"Sorry I nearly killed you," she said.

"It was an accident. Let's just be grateful neither of us are wolves."

"Why?"

"I think I'd belong to you forever. I've heard some lion males do that, too."

"I think that's done with a bite." She blinked. "Wait . . . did I bite you, too?"

"No. But don't you think that's weird?"

"It *is* weird."

The glass door opened and a She-lion walked in carrying charts.

"Oh, look!" she cheered. "You're both up. I'm Dr. Chan, the specialist who repaired your artery damage, Mr. Malone."

Slipping off the bed, Tock walked over to the doctor. She took Shay's chart from the female's hand and began to study the results of recent tests made while they were both still asleep. She was about to tell Shay his numbers were looking good when the She-lion snatched the chart back.

Hissing at the rudeness, Tock tried to get the chart back but the She-lion roared. Tock tensed, ready for a fight.

"Hey, hey, *hey!*" Shay yelled. "Do you two mind? I'm trying not to die here."

"You're not dying," Tock told him before realizing that the doctor had said the same thing along with her. They looked at each other and, after mutually sneering, backed away.

Once at a safe distance, the doctor explained, "The rat—"

"Ratel. Or just honey badger."

"—is right. Everything is looking good. I just want to examine your wound. Then you should be able to go home." She glanced over at Tock. "I'm pretty sure you're ready to go, too."

"You're sending me home? Do you even know what they shot me up with?"

"No. But I'm so sorry the original poison didn't work."

Tock hissed again, but Shay's pleas stopped her from tearing the rude bitch's face off.

"Ladies, please," Shay begged. "I just want to go home."

The She-lion nodded and walked over to a sink in the corner of the room. She sanitized her hands, put on nitrile gloves, and went to Shay's side. She carefully removed the bandage over his wound and took care to closely examine the damage.

Tock really hoped there was nothing wrong. She hated that she'd accidentally hurt him while he was trying to help.

She also felt bad he'd had to deal with her family. She didn't even ask her teammates to do that. No one should have to deal with either side of her family. They were all a little bit insane and Tock didn't think it was fair that anyone else should have to put up with the crazy. She was born into it, but her teammates had enough to deal with on their own. She never wanted to add to their stress by adding her relatives.

She'd already told Mads and the others that if something happened and she was killed during something they were doing—but shouldn't be doing—she wasn't to tell anyone but her parents until she was buried.

"Trust me," she told Mads and Max another day when they were only sixteen, "it will be better for all of us in the long run."

"How will it be better for you?" Max had asked. "You'll already be dead."

"That doesn't mean my grandmother can't still get to me. And, oy . . . the guilt that woman will pour down on my head."

"Okay, this looks great," the rude doctor announced. "A nurse will come in to help with your discharge. Your brothers are here."

"They are?"

"Been here all night. They're wonderfully unpleasant."

Shay nodded. "Yeah. They are."

"What about me?" Tock asked.

"What about you?"

"Bitch, I will cut your—"

"Discharge," Shay quickly cut in before Tock could finish her threat. "Can she be discharged, too?"

"I'll send your doctor in to move that process along as quickly as possible. We'd like to get all of you out of here."

"All of us?" Tock asked.

"All those badgers are here, too."

"Still? They're still here?"

A slow smile spread across the She-lion's face, and Tock wanted to smash her head in!

"They are here," she said, her smile getting wider. "Why don't I go get them?"

Before Tock could stop her, the bitch walked out the door.

Tock ran across the room and jumped on Shay's hospital bed.

"What are you doing?" he wanted to know.

"Getting out of here."

"Tock, you have to be discharged."

She heard him, but ignored his words and, instead, climbed on his shoulders.

"Hey!"

She ignored that too, reaching up and pushing at the tile above her head. She was having trouble pushing it out of the way, so she unleashed her claws and slammed them through the neighboring tile. Holding on with her claws, she lifted her legs and kicked in the tile next to it. She planted her feet on either side of the opening and retracted her claws. Using the strength of her legs, she stayed in position until she could bring her torso up and crouch inside the air duct.

Once she was securely inside, she leaned down and told Shay, "Meet me outside in ten minutes." After that, she scampered off and didn't look back.

Shay was still staring up at the empty hole in the ceiling when his brothers walked into the room.

"Hey!" Finn greeted him. "You're up."

"Way up," Keane muttered.

Recognizing that tone, Shay immediately looked at his lap and realized the pillow was no longer covering his junk.

"Shit," he barked, covering himself again.

"You just had artery surgery. Why do you have a hard-on?"

"Maybe he has a morning hard-on," Finn reasoned. "I love a good morning hard-on."

"Can we stop talking about my hard-on?" Shay pleaded.

Keane pointed. "Why's the tile on the floor?"

"Long story."

"Where's Tock?" Finn asked.

Shay and his brothers looked up at the hole in the ceiling, and Keane said, "That explains the hard-on."

Before Shay could tell his brother to shut up, the door opened again and Tock's family came into the room.

All of them. *All* of them came into the room.

"Where is she?" Tock's grandmother asked.

Shay grimaced. How do you tell an entire family that the person they'd been waiting for all night had run out on them?

You don't. You don't tell them anything. Instead, he simply looked up at the ceiling and all the badgers followed suit.

"Huh," one of her cousins said, still staring at the opening. "Well, that's rude."

But Tock's grandmother only chuckled. "That girl. She is just like her mother, which is probably why I want to punch her in the neck right now."

And there it was for Shay to finally see: the family resemblance between Tock and her grandmother.

Chapter 6

Shay and his two brothers got into the SUV Keane had rented at the airport. He thought the badgers would be driving with them, but they'd opted to rent their own car, which Finn seemed glad about. "Max always drives, and she drives like a suicide bomber."

Shay stretched out in the backseat. Although "stretched out" wasn't exactly correct. The SUV was of average size. Fine for most people but not for a Malone brother. He had to bend his knees, and his back rested against the left-side passenger door.

He was glad to be out of the hospital, though. Glad he was okay. Now he could just relax until he got home.

Closing his eyes, Shay easily fell asleep but snapped awake when he heard his eldest brother growl, "What the unholy fuck . . . ?"

Shay sat up and looked around. "What? What's wrong?"

Keane still drove, their vehicle now on a two-lane road. He was going pretty fast, but Keane always drove fast. Shay didn't see anything in their way. So he wasn't sure what his brother was complaining—

Another vehicle sped up behind them, trying to pass. The entire crew of honey badgers occupied the passing SUV—except for Tock. Tock wasn't inside the SUV. She was on the outside. Climbing up the front grill while they raced along whatever road this was.

Horrified, the three brothers watched Tock—now in a hospital gown, which seemed a waste because it wasn't tied so most of her naked body was exposed to the world as the material flapped wildly in the wind—make her way up to the hood. Once there, she paused to catch her breath, then started moving on all fours toward the front windscreen.

"Are we racing?" Keane suddenly asked.

Finn leaned back so he could see out Shay's window. "Max is driving. So . . . yes. You're racing. You better slow down," he ordered. "Let her go a—"

"*Shit!*" Keane abruptly slammed on the brakes; Shay was thrown against the front seats. It was a necessary move, though. A truck came from around the corner, going in the opposite direction, and all Max did was speed up while heading straight for it. Tock still occupied the hood of the SUV.

The SUV cut into their lane just before the truck could obliterate them, the driver blasting his horn and yelling.

Tock briefly paused once more—this time so she could raise her arm high and give the truck driver the finger—before she continued making her way across the hood.

She finally reached the windshield.

Shay couldn't see her for a few seconds; then he spotted her clinging to the side of the vehicle and finally crawling into the now-open passenger side window.

The window closed and Max hit the gas; the group disappeared around the next bend.

The brothers were silent for a bit as they drove on, all three staring out the front window.

Then Keane finally said, "I am so glad you risked your life *saving* that one. She so clearly needs to be saved."

Shay could only shrug. "At the time . . . it seemed like a solid idea."

"Yeah. And I'm sure it had nothing to do with that ass."

"Well . . ." Shay began, but what was the point of fighting the truth? "Yeah. It was definitely that ass."

Tock changed into fresh clothes in one of the private airport's bathrooms and stepped out of the stall. Mads had brought her overnight bag from Detroit, which was great. Tock had no desire to travel in a hospital gown all the way back to New York. She didn't want anyone assuming she was an escaped mental patient because there was nothing Max would love more than leaning into that joke until all of them were racing away from law enforcement and emergency services.

Exiting the bathroom, she stopped to look around. Saw nothing out of the ordinary and rechecked every means of escape from this airport should it become necessary. She didn't do this because she was suddenly feeling paranoid. Her grandmother had begun the drill when she took her to the mall at five years old. "Always know in and out, my little one," she'd say. "In case you need to make a run for it."

Satisfied, Tock walked over to the chairs and tossed her bag by those—where did he get sneakers that size?—big feet before dropping into the seat next to Shay. She let out a sigh and started scrolling through her phone. She was annoyed. She'd had stuff planned for the last few hours. A nice, neat schedule, but it had been shot to hell because of all this unnecessary drama.

"Do you not see me glaring at you?"

Tock looked away from the schedule app on her phone that she'd built herself because most schedule apps didn't give her what she needed, and found herself staring into the glaring face of a big cat.

"Don't you always look like that?" she asked after a moment.

"No." He pointed at another set of attached seats where two of her teammates were hanging out. "*He* always looks like that."

She hadn't even noticed Keane sitting next to Max. He was also glaring but not at Tock or Max or Streep, both of whom sat close to him. He was just glaring in general, his gaze locked on a blank wall. He was so focused on that wall, he didn't even notice or acknowledge a group of loud rich guys walking in, talking about the private jet they were about to take to Cancun. What entertained Tock, though, was watching those loud, annoying men spot Keane and, despite his having no interest in them at all, purposely stop, stare at him for a few seconds, and then walk in a big circle around their group. They ended up sitting on the opposite side of the airport, with Keane's back to them.

Once those full-human men sat down and she felt certain that Max wouldn't start a fight with them because she was bored waiting for Nelle's family jet to be fueled, Tock went back to her phone. She moved a few things around in her app, added a few things on the to-do list app she'd also made herself, and slipped her phone into the back pocket of her jeans.

As she relaxed in her chair, she realized the cat was still glaring at her.

"What?" she asked.

"I didn't think we were done talking."

"We're not?"

He threw up his hands and angrily turned away from her.

She thought that was the end of it but as soon as she relaxed again, he turned to face her once more and asked, "Are you *trying* to kill yourself?"

She had no clue what he was talking about, which was why she replied, "What?"

"Walking on the car while it was being driven by *Max* . . . ? That seemed like a good idea to you after almost dying last night?"

"Although, according to you, I didn't almost die. I did suffer, though. You know, I really don't remember much of anything from last night, but I *do* remember my cousins just wouldn't shut up, and I just wanted to *choke them until they all stopped talking.*"

When the cat didn't reply, Tock looked down and saw that her hands were mimicking strangling someone. And her teeth were so tightly clenched, she was sure she must have growled out that last part of her thought.

She lowered her hands, unclenched her jaw, and looked up at Shay.

"I hid under the SUV until we were on the road and then I crawled out. That way I didn't have to see my family. It was a weak and pathetic move, but I did it because I hate having debates that *never end*. And when you fight with my family, there's never an end. They love to argue. About *everything.*"

Shay studied her a moment. "Okay," he said. "I get that." He stopped glaring and rested his forearms on his big thighs. "But why didn't Max pull over once you guys were away from the hospital, so you could get out from under the car without risking your life?" When Tock didn't answer, he rolled his eyes. "Exactly how many times have you fallen off a moving car?"

"I have no idea."

"But should you really risk your life like that? Climbing over cars while they're moving?"

Done with the conversation, Tock didn't answer. Instead, she said, "Thanks for helping me yesterday. I appreciate that."

Shay snorted and asked, "Since when?" He shook his head. "You just want to change the subject."

"I really do. And I thought feeding your ego would help with that."

"It doesn't. But if you want to risk your life jumping around on moving cars driven by Max MacKilligan of all people . . . be my guest."

Tock studied him for a moment before announcing, "That's right. You're a dad."

"What? I mean . . . I am. But what does that have to do with anything?"

"You just really have the guilt thing down. It's impressive."

"Learned it from my mom," he admitted. "Once me, Finn, and Keane hit puberty, it was the only thing she had in her arsenal to control us besides disembowelment."

"My parents have been using guilt on me since birth. My mom is especially adept at it." Not wanting to think too much about whether her parents might hear of this latest situation—and the guilt that would ensue—she asked, "Daughter or son?"

"Daughter. Ten."

"So you were kind of young when you had her?"

"I was. Her mom's a little older. Used to play pro football but she had to get an elbow replacement after a brutal hit in a championship game. She has three other sons she's raising to be players."

"Your daughter wants to play, too?"

"No. Actually . . ."

His words faded off and he suddenly looked off. As if he was hoping she hadn't noticed. But of course she had and now she was curious to find out what he was hiding.

"Actually . . . what?"

"It's nothing."

"Tell me."

"I get enough shit from Keane. I'm not in the mood to hear any more."

"Oh, come on. Aren't we beyond this?"

"Beyond what? You being nosy?"

"You *noticing* that I'm being nosy. And after everything we've been through together."

"Really? You're using that one on me? And exactly what have we been through together?"

"You saw me pee myself yesterday. Something that was traumatic for both of us."

"That was in reaction to the poisoning and we don't need to discuss it."

"I actually do appreciate your not making that into a big deal. Most guys are not fans of girls that pee themselves."

"It's not like you got ridiculously drunk in a bar and then pissed on the DJ." When she glanced up at him, he gave one of his shrugs and added, "That happened once with a girl. It was not pretty. And we didn't have a second date."

"Understandable. Anyway, just tell me about your kid. I'm not really a kid person, so the fact that I'm interested at all is . . . impressive. I'm very impressed with myself right now."

He gave a soft chuckle before letting out a sigh and grudgingly admitting, "She likes math. And she wants to be an"—he cleared his throat—"an accountant."

"An accountant? At ten? Did she see a movie?"

"A movie about accounting?"

"It's possible. At ten I wanted to be a race car driver and a bounty hunter. Why? Because I saw two movies over a week-end, and one was about a race car driver and the other was about a bounty hunter."

"Yeah, well, she's loved math since she was three and wanted to be an accountant since she was six."

"Oh. Oh. Yeah. She might be in it for the long haul." She paused a moment, then asked, "How did she know what an accountant was at six, anyway?"

"I have no idea." He gave a little smile. "She is good at math, though. Studying at an eighth-grade level. I mean, she's not like . . ."

"Stevie?" Tock shook her head. "*No one* is like Stevie. And that's okay, because she's been in therapy since she was, like, five. It's really hard being Stevie. So be grateful."

"I am. My baby's good in her other subjects, but average good. Not terrifying good. I think that balances out the math thing."

"It does. I was always advanced with science and math, but I barely passed English. And I only find some parts of history interesting enough to remember. I mean, who *cares* about what happened in 1066?"

"The Battle of Hastings." When she only stared at him, he muttered, "That battle kind of led to the birth of the entire English language."

"Again, who cares? With some household cleaners and a match, I can take this entire building down. Isn't that more important than who started the English language a bazillion years ago when people didn't bathe?"

"Well, that's . . . disturbing."

"What is?"

"All of it. All of what you said just now. I was going to say interesting, but nope. It's just disturbing."

The fight came out of nowhere. They were just sitting on the private jet, heading back to New York. Everyone was pretty quiet. Either reading magazines or on their phones. Then it just happened.

Mads looked at Tock, who was sitting next to her and, without any warning, started yelling, *"How could you be so fucking stupid?"*

Shay was shocked. He'd never heard or seen Mads angry, much less screaming at someone. She was always the rational one of the group. The one who tried to calm everything down. But here she was, screaming at Tock.

And Tock started screaming back. The pair of them nose to nose . . . screaming. Shay didn't even know what they were saying. He could barely make their words out, they were saying them so fast.

That was bad enough, but then they were on the floor of the aisle, trying to throttle each other.

Shay got out of his seat and reached in to grab Tock. He was glad to see his brother attempting to do the same with Mads. It was necessary, too, because their fellow teammates weren't helping at all. Nelle continued to read a recent copy of Italian *Vogue*. Max kept eating honey-roasted peanuts by the handful while gleefully watching the fight. And even sweet Streep, who seemed to hate it when her friends fought, continued to text someone on her phone rather than intervene.

He was not, however, surprised that Keane didn't do anything but roll his eyes and try to go back to sleep. Worthless. His brother was worthless.

It took a bit to get the women apart. Their claws were out and caught on pieces of fabric and tangled in each other's hair. Once they did manage to separate them, Shay carried a hissing Tock to the back of the jet.

Shay put Tock in the very last seat and then pinned her there until she finished hissing in rage.

It took nearly five minutes until he could release her. And even then, he just took his hand off her face. He'd had to pin her head against the window to prevent her from biting his nose off.

Was this what it was like to work in a zoo? Did the caretakers have to worry about getting their noses bitten off? He doubted it. Those wild animals were behind several layers of fencing and metal doors. He had nothing to protect him from rabid badgers with rage issues.

Crossing her arms over her chest, Tock looked out the window that one side of her face had been pressed against and seethed.

Yeah. That was the best way to describe it. She seethed. He hadn't known she could seethe. He'd seen her annoyed. Restless. Frustrated. But he'd never seen her seething. Not even with her cousins when she'd tried to choke one of them to death.

He suddenly had a bad feeling. Was this the end of the honey badgers' friendship? Were Tock and Mads no more? That would be awful. They'd always been so close. He'd once had an argument like the one they'd just fought with a buddy on the team. It had been over his daughter's mother and it had ended their friendship then and there. Half the team held Shay back and the other half held back his fellow cat. His buddy actually transferred to another team, refusing to even be in the same room with Shay during team meetings. And life in the locker room had been way too tense. Years later, they only met on the gridiron, and it was always the most brutal game of the season.

He'd hate to see that happen between Tock and Mads.

Thankfully, the flight back was short, and the only other harm done was to the air quality because of all the carbon the jet had unleashed into the atmosphere. Not that Nelle or her family seemed to care about that at all. Finn had told him they had a fleet of jets. A fleet. How rich was Nelle's family anyway?

When they landed at a private airstrip, Shay wouldn't move until everyone else had grabbed their stuff and exited the jet. Then he stood and stepped into the aisle.

Tock hadn't said a word to him the entire time, finally focusing on her phone for the last leg of the trip. Now she moved past him without a word, and grabbed her overnight bag from where she'd placed it in an empty seat. She headed out.

Shay quickly grabbed his bag, too, and followed. He wanted to be ready if the pair got into it again.

Once they were on the tarmac, though, Tock suddenly

moved quickly and cut in front of the badgers. Shay exchanged a panicked glance with Finn and they began to move toward the group with big strides.

Tock reached behind her and Shay had a memory of all the weapons she'd carried on her—in her clothes—just the other night. He was only a foot or two away, about to grab her arm, when she pulled out her phone rather than a small nuclear device. She held it up in front of her friends.

"Did you guys see this yet?" she asked.

Mads took the phone from her and began reading while the other three looked over her shoulders. After a few seconds, she looked up and stared into Tock's eyes. She tossed the phone back to her and followed Max, who was already moving on.

"I'll call you later, Finn," Mads told his brother without even looking back at him.

Tock gave Shay a short wave before going after her friends. Then they were gone.

"What the hell just happened?" Finn wanted to know.

But none of them had an answer. Because even for badgers . . . that was just plain weird.

Chapter 7

They barely arrived in time. Max parked the car with the front passenger wheel over the curb and on the grass. They all got out of the vehicle and ran toward the house, leaping over the low picket fence and reaching the stoop from different sides.

Max slid in front of the two males, arms thrown wide, blocking them from the front door they'd been moments from knocking on. Tock took a spot in front of the door with Mads beside her. Nelle came up on the left; Streep on the right.

"Hello!" Streep called.

The two wolves looked over the five badgers, clearly uncomfortable at their sudden appearance. But Dutch Alexander, Max's best friend since junior high, had sent a group text to warn them, giving them enough time to get here and stop what was about to happen.

"Uh . . . ladies," the older wolf announced. "Nice to see you all again."

"Is it?" Max asked.

Seeing them again? Tock didn't remember the pair. Not surprising, though. She had too much in her head to recall useless information, like wolves she had no intention of dealing with on a daily basis or how the English language started. Seriously? The man knew 1066 just off the top of his head? Why would anyone who wasn't a teacher or a television historian know that?

"Is there something we can help you with?" Nelle queried, keeping her tone polite.

"We want to visit Charlie. Is that a problem?"

"Probably," Tock muttered.

"Can you smell it?" Mads whispered to her.

"Everyone smells it," Tock replied. Because there were bears lurking all around the house. The entire street of bear families had left their homes with central air-conditioning so they could sit and wait outside in the intolerable heat of the final days of summer, in the hopes that Charlie would give them what they wanted. They could rip the doors off the hinges and crash through the windows so they could get inside and simply take what they wanted, but they'd learned a long time ago that Charlie wasn't one to push around. She did not take it well. And despite her small size and inability to shift, she was meaner and more dangerous than any hungry grizzly could ever dream of being.

These wolves didn't even know what they'd walked into, but their natural arrogance preceded them, along with their model looks. Even the older one was stunning. Those cheekbones! Who naturally had cheekbones like that?

The Van Holtzes. That's who. Tock normally couldn't tell one pack from another. Wolves were wolves were wolves unless they played on her basketball team. But the Van Holtz Pack, whether from here or their original home country of Germany, stood out among the other shifter wolves because they all seemed to be stunningly beautiful and fucking arrogant.

And, normally, that made them perfect for Max to torture. Nothing she loved more than torturing arrogant beings of any gender, race, religion, breed, or species; but today she wasn't going to do that. Not today.

Because Charlie had been baking.

It was why all the bears were lurking. They adored Charlie's baking and would eat it every day if she'd open a bakery. But Charlie didn't want to make baking a job; she wanted it to be a stress reliever. In fact, baking might be the only reason she wasn't a homicidal maniac.

"You can't see her now," Max told the two canines. "That would be a very bad idea."

"It's important."

"Don't care."

"Yes, but—"

"Do you see me smiling?" Max abruptly asked.

The older wolf blinked before replying, "Uh . . . no."

"Right. And I always smile. I smile so much, I freak out my own mother. Do you know why I smile? Because I'm a fucking happy person. I love life. I love everything about life. I especially love making other people miserable. I'm good at it. And yet," she continued, "I'm warning you away from seeing my sister *despite* what I know she'll do to you. That should tell you something."

"So, you're seriously telling us—"

"If you walk into that house, you ain't walkin' out again. Instead, I'll be searching out hyena territories to bury your bones." That last part . . . she *did* say with a smile.

The wolves looked at each other, then back at Max.

"Fine," the oldest canine replied. "But can you let her know I stopped by, and I'd like to talk?"

Max nodded. "I can do that. Do you have a business card I can give her?"

The two wolves gazed at Max, looked at each other, then back at Max.

"You don't know who we are?" the eldest asked.

"Should I?"

"You and Charlie have been to my office to meet with me. You sort of work for us through Imani."

"I know Imani!" she said cheerfully. "Still don't remember you."

"How is that possible?"

"You mean nothing to me, so why would I think about you?"

"And your sister? She'd remember us."

"Doubtful."

He handed her a business card pulled from a pocket inside his expensive suit jacket.

Max looked at it and announced, "Niles Van Holtz. What kind of name is Niles? Didn't your parents love you?"

Nelle smoothly took the card from Max and pushed her out of the way. "We'll make sure to let Charlie know you came by."

"Thank you."

The younger wolf was already heading back to their sleek black limo, but the older one stopped and looked over at Tock.

"Is your grandmother in town?" he asked her, but Tock wasn't about to answer that question. She never answered that question, no matter who asked. One time Kissinger asked her that question . . . she didn't answer him either.

When she didn't respond, he walked away. Down the stoop, across the tiny front yard, and into the waiting limo.

Tock didn't even know she'd pulled her gun and aimed it at the nosy canine's head until her team grabbed her and pushed her up against the front door.

"It's always fun when visitors come to call, isn't it?" Max joked while pinning Tock to the house until the canines had driven away.

Ric Van Holtz wished he could just go home, but he had a job to do. And these days, he knew his job was more important than ever.

A shame really. That his kind couldn't play nice. Instead, they were starting wars with honey badgers. One of the worst things he could think of anyone doing. For lots of reasons.

Honey badgers weren't like the rest of them. They lived mostly in family units, coexisting with the full-humans of the world as if they belonged there. They normally had very little to do with the various shifter intelligence agencies: his organization, simply called the Group; Katzenhaus Securities, started in Germany by lions, but now worldwide and involving all cat breeds; and the BPC, aka the Bear Preservation Council, which handled all bear issues around the world.

Unless you got up close enough to catch their scent, you would never know honey badgers were anything but the full-humans most of them pretended to be. It was a mistake, however, to think they were nothing but a disorganized group of weasels that liked to steal. In reality, they were a dangerously unstable but highly organized gang of vicious predators that could shut down entire nations on a whim.

That was the thing about badgers. They were never the leaders of the countries they took down. They were smarter than that. A leader could lose his throne or be assassinated. So honey badgers were never the front-facing ones. That would only make them targets.

No, they were never the tsars of a country. They were the Rasputins. They were never the Lenins. They were the Trotskys. They were never the pope, but they were definitely one of the cardinals. Over time, depending on how powerful they became, they might become targets, but they never started off that way. And depending on what their plan was, they could topple entire ruling parties. Sometimes because they had an agenda. Sometimes because they were bored and had nothing better to do. And sometimes because they were just feeling downright mean.

One never knew with a honey badger.

So to purposely start a fight with them seemed . . . stupid. He was going to say reckless, but nope. It was just plain stupid. Reckless was when his daughter tried to juggle knives while his back was turned. Stupid was trying to kill honey badgers. A species that made hyenas appear warm and friendly.

Instead of heading back to Manhattan and the Group office, the limo turned at the corner and made its way down the street until it reached another shifter-only neighborhood. Not bears this time, but cats. They pulled up in front of a lovely house where cubs and a few moms were lounging out front. As soon as his Uncle Van stepped out of the limo, the kids were sent inside and male lions woke up from their lazy napping to unleash fangs and claws in warning.

By the time Ric got out of the limo, Imani Ako was out of her house and motioning the males away with a sweep of her hand.

"Niles," she said, coming down the walkway toward them, "how did it go?"

"How do you think? I couldn't get in to see the eldest. And the other one didn't even remember us."

"It's always better to be forgotten by badgers than to take up any of their memory. That way lies skinning."

"*Don't* remind me."

She laughed. "And Ulric—" she began before turning her head so Ric could kiss her cheek.

"Imani."

"Don't worry about Charlie and her sisters. I'll talk to them myself. Now if both of you will just follow me, I have someone else you should talk to."

"Someone I actually want to speak with?" Van asked.

Walking toward the house, Imani did nothing but laugh.

"We have to go in there."

"*We* don't have to do anything," Tock reminded Max as all five of them stared at the front door. "You, however . . ."

"My sister is very sensitive when she's upset. I don't want her to—"

"Kill us all?" Nelle asked.

"She wouldn't. I don't think."

"Why don't you go in first," Streep helpfully suggested, "and if we don't hear your dying screams, we'll follow about ten minutes later."

"We are honey badgers," Max reminded them. "I can't believe you're all being such limp dicks about this. We are afraid of nothing."

"Except your sister," Mads muttered.

"What's going on?" asked a deep voice from behind them.

The grizzly and his triplet siblings stared at them . . . and then the weapons now aimed at the bears.

"I thought we discussed your not pointing guns at us," the

female triplet said. Tock could barely tell the three of them apart. She just knew the female because of her scent, her slightly smaller size, and her voice. It was not as low as that of her two brothers. Other than that, all three Dunns might as well be clones of each other.

"Don't sneak up on us, then," Max said.

"We're bears. How could we sneak up on you?" She gestured to the big yard next to the house. "And there's nothing here but bears."

"I smell muffins," one of the male triplets announced before pushing past them and walking into the house.

"Hey!" a sun bear complained from the yard. "How come those bears just get to walk into the house?"

"Because," Max snapped back, "one of them is fucking my sister!"

"Oh."

Max faced her team. "Although, quite honestly, I can never tell which one."

"I know!"

"Right?"

"I thought it was just me."

Now that the bears had gone in—meaning they'd be the first to die if Charlie MacKilligan was "in a mood"—the badgers followed. The whole house smelled amazing. So many baked goods. Tock was betting Charlie hadn't gotten any sleep. She must have been up all night doing whatever she did in the kitchen.

Tock could only make two things: jerk chicken and latkes. Both sides of her family loved her latkes.

But the stuff Charlie made . . . she was like a magician in the kitchen.

As they walked through the living room, they saw a spread of fresh baked goods on the dining room table, the sideboard, and the top of the china cabinet. The kitchen table and counters were also covered.

The woman really should open her own bakery.

But instead of a stressed-out Charlie ready to destroy, they found a relaxed, laughing Charlie sitting at the kitchen table. Her newest sister, Nat Malone, sat on her lap, Max's wolverine friend, Dutch, in a chair to the right, and the young jackal, Kyle Jean-Louis Parker, in the seat at the other end of the table. They all seemed to be relaxed and happy. Enjoying themselves.

Tock was relieved. No running for her life. But Max seemed strangely calm. Usually, there was nothing calm about Max. A calm Max made Tock nervous.

"I see the Xanax worked," Max noted, watching the triplets pile their plates high with the available food.

"I didn't take it," Charlie said.

"You didn't?"

"Nope. I ended up teaching our baby sister here how to bake."

"But you said you didn't know how to teach people to bake," Max replied. "That you just knew how to do it, but you didn't know how to pass any recipes on."

"Maybe she just didn't want you to burn down the house," Nat Malone said.

The kid was deaf, having lost her hearing when she was much younger, but she was pretty good at reading lips. Although with the other Malones, she only used sign language. All the brothers had mastered it so they could communicate with Nat. Tock kind of loved that. Shifters weren't always the best when one of their own was a little different.

"Where's Zé?" Charlie asked before Max could respond to her youngest sister by dragging her to the floor and kicking the crap out of her.

"He's with Stevie and Shen. Stevie wanted to go to her lab to conduct tests on whatever they got from Tock, and I knew you'd want her to have more protection than a goofy panda." Then she turned to Nat. "I would *not* burn the house down," she snapped at the kid. "And why are you sitting in her lap?"

Max hadn't even known she had another sister until very recently. None of the three sisters had known about Nat. Because their father was the worst. Freddy MacKilligan: con artist, lowlife, impregnator. Just the worst. But Max and her sisters would never hold the sins of the father against the kid because people did that to them all the time. The whole MacKilligan family loathed Freddy so much, they barely acknowledged his daughters' existence, much less invited them to holiday dinners. Charlie's mom had done the best she could to raise her daughter and two of his children that were not her own, but then she was killed. Charlie's grandfather took the three girls in, but his pack didn't really want them around. When Max graduated from high school and Stevie, just fourteen, had already earned several degrees, they left the pack and started off on their own.

The fact that the three of them had survived still amazed Tock a bit.

"I heard you already did burn the house down," the kid said to Max, smirking, before wrapping her arms around Charlie's neck. "And I'm on her lap because I wanted a hug from my big sister!"

Max leaned in close so Nat could see her mouth. "That fire was not due to baking. Now get your hands off my sister!"

"Max," Charlie warned, "be nice."

"But . . . but I thought we were *all* sisters!" Nat said, sniffing, before burying her face in her hands.

Charlie was so busy ordering Max to "Apologize! Apologize right now!" that she didn't notice Nat giving Max the finger with both hands by pushing her fists into her eyes while raising the middle finger of each hand. All the while, her shoulders shook and she made sobbing sounds.

Dutch quickly stood up and walked out the back door before Max could see how hard he was laughing. Kyle simply got up, put his plate and milk glass in the sink, and headed to his rented space in the basement.

The triplet bears, having helped themselves to all the food they might need for the next ten minutes, grabbed three gallons of milk from the fridge and headed off toward the living room and TV.

"*Now!*" Charlie bellowed when Max refused to speak.

"Fine. I'm sor—"

"She can't see you," Charlie reminded her.

Max rolled her eyes before tapping the kid's shoulder. Nat slowly looked up at her older sister and patiently waited. Her eyes did look wet, if not as teary as Streep's would have been. But Streep had a real talent when it came to fake tears. She could turn them off and on like a faucet in a fancy hotel.

Still, not bad for an untrained kid. Good enough, in fact, to fool one sister, and piss the other off.

"I'm sorry if I offended you," Max said, overenunciating each word just to be a bitch.

"And we're sisters?" the kid asked. "Forever and ever?"

"Of course, we are," Charlie said, rubbing Nat's back with one hand and pointing at Max with the other. "Tell her we're sisters."

"*Seriously?*"

"*Max*," Charlie bit out between clenched teeth.

"Yessss," Max hissed. "We're sisters."

"Forever and ever?" Nat pushed, eyes wide and hopeful.

"*Oh, come the fuck on!*"

Charlie stood, placing the kid on her feet at the same time. "Max Genji Yang-MacKilligan, you be *nice* to our baby sister!"

"Fine. Forever and ever."

Nat launched herself at Max, hugging her tight. "You've made me so happy!"

"You have a Chinese middle name?" Nelle asked, ignoring everything else. "Why didn't you ever tell me?"

"Why would I tell you that? So we can bond as two Chinese chicks?"

"Yes!" She gestured to the kid still clinging to an unhappy Max. "Knowing that information could bring us closer together, Max . . . like sisters."

"I *hate* all of you."

Charlie motioned to the food. "You guys take what you want. After that, I'm giving the rest to the bears outside." She turned away from her sisters and asked, "How are you feeling, Tock?"

Tock was so surprised by the question, it took her a few seconds to reply.

"Um . . . fine?"

"You don't know?"

"No. I know. I'm fine. Thanks for asking."

"Yeah. Sure. I'm going to go take a shower."

"Van Holtz was looking for you," Max threw in while trying to pry Nat off her.

"What? Why?"

"No idea. But he wants you to call him. I have his card—"

"Later. I need the shower first." She grabbed a random muffin and walked out. Not a second later, Max and Nat began to struggle, each attempting to drag the other to the ground.

But the floor shook when Charlie slammed her foot down three times in the dining room to ensure everyone could "hear" her warning. The sisters pulled away from each other and Nat backed out of the room, both middle fingers raised at Max, a huge grin on her face and her tongue hanging out.

When she was gone, Mads announced, "If I wasn't sure about you two being sisters before, Max . . ."

Van stopped in the middle of the doorway. "What's happening here?"

He felt like he was being tricked. That this was an ambush.

"I think we should all talk," Imani said. "Calmly."

"Calmly? Really?"

"Niles!" the female greeted. "My old friend."

"We are *not* friends, Mira."

"We're not enemies."

He raised an eyebrow at that because both of them knew it was bullshit.

Van and Mira had a very long history. It wasn't that she'd ever attacked him or hired anyone to attack him. But she did tend to make his job much more difficult. Even now, just seeing her sitting there in her black business suit and low-heeled shoes, legs crossed at the ankles, understated gold jewelry on her wrists and around her neck, simple diamond studs in her ears, and her hair cut in a fashionable bob, he might take her for any other stylish grandmother with a little money in the bank. A woman who loved to play with her grandchildren and make them Sunday dinner while donating to a conservative cause.

But that was only how Mira Lepstein *looked*. In reality . . . she was a killer. There wasn't anyone or anything she wouldn't hunt down and eradicate if it got in her way. Of course, Mira came from a long line of killers. Her parents hunted down Nazis after the war, and there were some ancient relatives in parts of Russia that used to take on the Cossacks. Even her shoes were a lie. She had higher heels in her car. She wore the low heels to fool people into thinking she was nothing more than a nice, simple grandmother. But she wasn't.

That's why Van knew that when all this started, she'd come. Especially when he'd seen her granddaughter standing there with Max and her other friends. He just hadn't expected Mira to be *here*. In a lion's den, with lion males right outside the door. These were not two species that were cozy.

"I just wanted to give you a heads-up," Mira told him.

"A heads-up about what?"

She motioned him farther into the room. He took a step inside but stopped to examine the space, including the ceilings. Especially any vents or cabinets. Then he lifted his nose, sniffed the air.

"Come, little doggy," she teased. "You are safe."

"Like I was in Istanbul?"

"That was a long time ago—just a misunderstanding. You really need to get over it. We are older now. Smarter. You are a father and leader. I am a grandmother and soon, God willing, a great-grandmother for the second time. So let us put the past behind us and talk." She patted a spot next to her on the couch. He sat in a chair across the room.

"Talk," Van told her.

"Dogs," she muttered under her breath. "Always so rude." She let out a breath. "Fine. You know what situation we have."

"I know *your* situation. It's not like my situation."

"But it is. You think the de Medicis are your only problem. But they are not."

"And why is that?"

"Who do you think bankrolls this insanity?"

"Why do the de Medicis suddenly care about honey badgers?"

"I do not know. But they have become a problem for both of us."

"Don't you mean all of us?" Van asked, glancing at Imani.

"Imani no longer works for Katzenhaus," Mira told him. "She works for you. She has her own little group that includes my granddaughter."

Van began to lie but she held her hand up. "Don't bother. I already know the truth, and we don't have time to play any more games."

"I may no longer work for Katzenhaus," Imani cut in, "but I am still a retired leader. And I know that they will not challenge the de Medicis. Neither will the bears. They want nothing to do with any of this."

"That seems foolish," Mira remarked.

"I agree." Imani gave a small shrug. "But I'm not in charge anymore. Katzenhaus is not going to fuck with the de Medicis. Not over badgers."

"What about the schemes that have nothing to do with badgers?"

"I have tried, in vain, to get Katzenhaus involved in that situation as well, but they say they want more proof."

"And proof will do what?"

"Probably nothing."

"Just great." Van stood, began to pace.

"As little as Katzenhaus cares about the honey badgers, they care even less about full-humans."

"This whole thing with the badgers started when the de Medici father disappeared," Ric noted. "You wouldn't happen to know anything about that, would you, Mira?"

"Me? Why would I kill that mean bastard? Personally, I

think his sons did it. They wanted to be in charge and now they are."

"He was their leash. If he's dead . . ."

"Och!" Mira slashed her hand through the air. "I am tired of treating these bastards like they run the Holy Roman Empire."

"No one sane, Mira, wants to go up against the de Medicis," Imani insisted.

"I know. That's why I called in those who have no sanity."

Van didn't like the sound of that at all. Nope. Not at all.

"Who?"

Now Mira shrugged. "I called in Tracey Rutowski and her—"

"*Have you lost your mind?*"

"Oh, Mira. No!"

"I went to a show at Rutowski's gallery in Manhattan a couple of months ago. It was amazing." Ric blinked, looked at all of them before adding, "But I guess that's not the point of this conversation."

"Didn't she *start* Chernobyl?" Imani asked.

"No! That was propaganda from Russian cats. She was nothing but a child then."

"She did extend the Cold War," Van reminded her.

"She did *not* extend it. She simply made it a little more difficult to end. And you forget she was a teen then, dabbling in things she didn't understand."

"A teen starting shit with her honey badger friends. In foreign countries. Involving *Gorbachev*. And now you bring her into this?"

"What do you want me to do? The cats won't help," she said. "Neither will bears. And if there's anyone who can find out what's going on and maybe unearth the information that will get Katzenhaus off their collective asses, it is Tracey Rutowski and her honey badger friends."

"Is this because of your granddaughter?" Van asked. "Are you putting us all at risk to protect her?"

"My granddaughter can take care of herself. But I will not put my *species* at risk. If that means pulling the craziest of our kind out of retirement to help, then that is what will happen."

Mira stood. She put the straps of what had to be a fourteen-thousand-dollar designer purse over her forearm and paused to brush long lion hair off her black suit.

"Now, if you'll excuse me," she said, "I have other things to get to. I just thought you should know where we all stood at the moment. And I will ask both of you to let Rutowski do her work."

"And if she blows up half of Manhattan . . . so be it?"

"Oh, puhleese, little dog. Such lies you all tell. Besides," she added, pushing past Ric, "the Berlin wall had to come down sometime, and she was smart enough to make it look like *everyone* was involved!"

Chapter 8

"Tock?"

Tock froze. She'd been trying to sneak through the kitchen, hoping Charlie wouldn't notice her. Charlie was at the sink with her back to Tock, washing the last of the utensils she'd used to create her amazing baked goods. Tock had assumed she'd just be ignored now that the bears had been fed and had finally lumbered off.

She was wrong.

So she stood there, frozen.

Charlie shut off the water, shook her hands over the sink, and grabbed a paper towel to dry them. As she turned toward Tock, she asked, "Did you eat something?"

"Uh . . ."

"You need to eat. After what your body went through, food is the most important thing right now."

"I, uh, had a muffin."

"One muffin?"

"I only wanted one muffin."

"Sit," Charlie ordered and Tock immediately sat down. "You need something a little more substantial than a muffin. You don't want to suddenly pass out, do you?"

"No?"

Charlie frowned at her weak answer, then went to the freezer. "Let's see what we have . . ." She let out a sigh. "I can see Dutch has been in my freezer again. This is what happens when you have a breed that can eat frozen meat without thawing it first. He's eaten most of the bison I had in here. I have regular beef, though." She leaned out and looked at Tock. "Do you want regular beef?"

Tock didn't know what "regular beef" meant, but she was too afraid to ask. "Sure."

Charlie again looked in the freezer. "There are pork chops. Thick-cut ones. Oooh. There's a leg of lamb. Do you want lamb?"

"Uh . . ."

"You know, you probably need carbs, too. I can make you my spaghetti and meat sauce. You want that?"

"Okay."

"Great." She pulled big packages of ground meat out of the freezer. From the cabinets, she took out big cans of tomatoes, and several pounds of pasta followed.

Charlie quickly got to work, putting big pots on the stove to make her sauce in.

Not given permission to leave, Tock just sat there.

"So how do you feel?" Charlie asked.

"Fine."

"No aftereffects from that poison?"

"I don't think so."

"Good." She moved a tray of chocolate muffins from the counter closest to the stove and set it before Tock. "Eat this for now. I don't want to rush my sauce, but I don't want you passing out on me either."

"I don't think I'll—"

"You're lucky to have no aftereffects," she continued, moving back to the stove. "I got hit with strychnine once and it was *unpleasant*. Took me three hours to recover, and by then I was facedown in a dumpster. I even vomited a little, which was weird. I rarely vomit."

Why was Charlie MacKilligan talking to her? The only time the hybrid had ever spoken to Tock for any length of time was when she'd been trying to find out what Max had been up to . . . because Max was always up to something. But Charlie had never given Tock food before she ordered her into a chair and started grilling her for information. This, though . . . this was making Tock paranoid. And she liked to leave paranoia to Mads.

"Do you braid hair?" Charlie suddenly asked.

Tock stared at MacKilligan's back. "A little. Do you mean like, braid-braids? Or two ponytails?"

"Braid-braids. It's so hot these days, I've been thinking about getting micro-braids. But I don't feel like spending all day at a salon."

"Mads can do it. And she's fast. And you won't feel like she's ripped your scalp off when it's done."

Charlie looked over her shoulder. "Mads? Really?"

"Don't let her Thor's Hammer necklace fool you. Before her mother brought her to Wisconsin, she grew up in Detroit. Girlfriend knows how to braid hair. She does mine."

Charlie shrugged. "Think she'll do mine?"

"She'd be afraid not to."

Charlie stopped what she was doing and faced her. Meanwhile, Tock cringed.

"Afraid not to?" Charlie repeated. "Why is that?"

Tock cleared her throat. "Uh . . . no, no real reason. I mean . . . you know . . ."

"Are you guys still afraid of me?"

"Sh-should we not be?"

Charlie opened her mouth, glanced off, closed her mouth, opened it again, and finally said, "Fair enough. And I'll admit, I wanted you guys to be terrified of me when we were all in high school because, you know . . . *Max.* But that was a long time ago. You don't have to be afraid of me now."

"Okay . . . ?" But even Tock knew the way she'd said that sounded weak as hell.

"Let me put it to you this way: Have you guys tried to get my baby sister to make meth?"

"No."

"Did you sell Max into slavery?"

"No."

"Then you have no reason to be frightened of me."

Tock thought a moment before finally getting up the nerve

to ask, "Your father really tried to sell Max into slavery? She wasn't just blowing up that story for our entertainment?"

"Nope. He sold her into slavery. Household slavery. Not sex slavery. But yes. Twice. Max only knows about the one time, because I dealt with the second time myself."

"Was that the time your father suddenly moved out of the country?"

Charlie grinned. "It was. I blew up his car with him in it. He was really pissed about the car. It was some classic Corvette or something and was completely destroyed. He, however, survived. But I did get my point across, and he wisely moved to Ukraine for a couple of years."

She stepped away from the stove and went to the refrigerator. "I need a few things we are out of."

"Want me to run to the store?"

"No. I don't want you running anywhere until you eat." She pulled her phone from the back of her jeans. "I can just order it online and have it delivered because that's the kind of person I've become. Getting all my food delivered because I'm not a people person."

As she worked on her order, eyes focused on the phone, she asked Tock, "So, do you know what anyone is planning next?"

"For what?"

"For what happened to you. Last night."

"Oh. I don't know. I kind of . . . well . . ."

"You kind of what?"

"Ran away from my family before we could talk about anything."

Charlie's head snapped up, eyes wide. "Really? You sure that was wise? Considering."

"You just don't know my family." And Tock could hear the whine in her voice. She hated that whine. "There are just so many of them. On both sides. And they . . ." She brought her hands together. "They just bring so much energy with them. And it's a *lot*."

"No need to explain. I get it."

"I just hate whining about it because . . ." She shrugged.

"My family?" Charlie guessed.

"And Mads's. I feel guilty complaining about mine to you guys. They never dropped me at someone's house and never came back. Or actively threatened me."

"I'm glad. No one should have our lives. And I'm not going to resent someone who had better. I should let you know, though, that I did try to kill your grandmother last night."

Tock blinked. "Uh-huh."

"I know. Bad form and all. But I was angry and really annoyed about the Stevie thing. I blamed her, but Keane and Finn stopped me before I could do anything stupid." She looked away from her phone again. "Did you know shifters have their own legal system?"

"They do?"

"Yeah, apparently."

"Badgers usually just deal with full-human law enforcement. You seem less angry at my grandmother now," Tock pointed out, hoping she was right.

"I am. While I was baking, I realized *she* was not the problem. Speaking of which . . . should we invite the guys to dinner?"

"The guys?"

"Yeah. The Malone brothers."

"Why do you want to bring them over here?"

"They're involved in this, too, now. And you know how Keane is. He's a vengeful motherfucker. We're better off watching what he does than finding out after the damage is done. I know this from personal experience of being Max's sister." She chuckled and continued creating her order.

"You sure you'll have enough food? They are big cats. They eat *a lot*."

Charlie glanced off and Tock thought she was out of the woods. She couldn't explain why she didn't want to see Shay at this moment. Maybe it was because she kind of *did* want to see Shay, which was weird, and a feeling she was not enjoying. Maybe she just needed a break from the cat. She was sure she'd be back to normal in a couple of days.

Until then, if she could just focus on anything *but* Shay, that would be—

"We'll need more garlic bread if we invite the Malones." Charlie went back to her phone. "Lots of garlic bread. Ooooh. Here we go. Garlic bread already made. Just need to bake for ten minutes in an oven. Perfect."

Tock could just never get a break, could she?

They stopped at White Castle on their way home, ordering forty burgers each. Much to the annoyance of the staff. Not that anyone was about to say anything as long as they paid, but you could see the annoyance in their eyes. But was there anything about the Malones that said, "We'll only need ten burgers each, please"? As it was, this was just a treat to tide them over until they figured out what they'd do for a real meal. They sat at an outside table and ate in silence as the Malone brothers tended to do. They weren't big on conversation when food was involved. They could talk before or after, but during was not okay. Past girlfriends had learned that the hard way and never appreciated it much.

Driving down their street in their rental SUV, though, Shay realized he was already hungry again. And that meant his brothers were, too. Maybe before they had to return the vehicle, they could order something—

"Is that Dani?" Finn asked from the front seat.

Shay immediately leaned forward to look through the windshield. And sure enough, his baby girl was sitting on the front stoop with her panda backpack and a tiara on her head. Like most cats, his baby liked things that sparkled.

"What the hell?" He could tell she hadn't been inside the house. His mother was still away with her sisters, and his youngest brother was spending a few days with a few of his full-human buddies, one of whom had a pool in their backyard. So who knew how long the poor kid had been sitting outside waiting for someone to let her in?

"Why is my niece sitting outside the house?" Keane demanded, slowly turning into the driveway. "Did her mother just drop her off again? Without warning?"

"Let it go," Shay told Keane.

"But—"

"I mean it. Shut it in front of the kid!"

"All I'm saying is—"

With the car stopped in front of the garage and the brake on, Shay felt comfortable grabbing his brother by the hair and yanking his head back. "Say one bad word about my kid's mother and I'll shave your balls again. Understand?"

"Fine," Keane spat out between clenched teeth.

"Good. Now let's go."

Shay got out of the SUV, and before he could walk three feet, his daughter was leaping into his outstretched arms.

"Baby! What's wrong?"

Burying her head in his neck, he heard her say, "Your neighbor said I was abandoned and he was calling Child Services!"

"Finn!" Shay barked.

"I'm on it."

Finn headed off to deal with their next-door neighbor, who had been an ass since the day the Malones had moved into the house. He didn't like the big dogs Shay had, he didn't like Keane's glares, and he especially didn't like that their mother took no shit from the man. He was always trying to tell them how to cut their lawn or how to put out their trashcans or when they should prune their trees. He had lived in the neighborhood for decades and thought he ran it, which he sort of did . . . until the Malones moved in. Ever since, he'd been trying to bend Shay's family to his will, but they were big cats. They didn't bend for anyone.

"He said I was going into a home!"

Shay kissed his daughter's forehead and told her, "Worry lines. Worry lines. Your forehead is going to look like your Uncle Keane's if you keep it up. Is that what you want? To look like a worried kitty?"

"Yes," she defiantly replied while trying not to laugh.

"No one is taking you away from me or your mother. Now, where is your mother—"

"Did she leave you again?"

"*Keane!*"

Giving a short roar, Keane stomped off. But not before briefly stopping and kissing his niece on the top of her head.

"Uncle Keane is mad," she whispered when he had gone inside the house.

"Uncle Keane is always mad. Don't worry about it. Where's your mom?"

She leaned back a bit in his arms but didn't look him in the eyes. "She had to do something with the boys. Something with football, of course. She texted you yesterday and I asked her if she heard back, but—"

"Don't worry about it. I, uh, lost my phone last night somewhere and I just didn't get her message. It's okay."

Small fingers brushed his neck. "What happened, Daddy? Were you hurt?"

"Just a little. But I'm okay now. And I see worry lines again."

"Sorry. Sorry."

"Keep it up, you're going to become a growling, snarling, man-beast!"

And to show their niece what that would like, Finn walked up to them and yelled toward the house, "The neighbor is not being reasonable!"

Keane was out the front door like a shot, heading over to the next house. Snarling and growling the whole way.

"No one messes with his niece," Finn said, taking Dani from Shay's arms and lifting her up so she could sit on his neck.

"Is he going to hurt the man?"

"Of course not, baby. Because your uncle fears prison. The idea of being locked up behind bars terrifies him."

"It terrifies me, too!"

Shay stared at his daughter. "Why are you worrying about going to prison?"

"Or being put in a zoo. That's like prison, right? Our class went to the zoo last year and I was thinking, 'What if I get put in here?'"

"You're not going to be put in a zoo, Dani."

"I *could* be put in a zoo. If full-humans find out what we are, they could put us *all* in zoos."

"Do you think about that a lot, baby?"

"Don't you?"

"No," Shay and Finn said together.

"Must be nice. Flittin' through life without any worries."

Shay crossed his eyes but didn't bother arguing with his child. She could be as stubborn as her mother on good days. And today probably hadn't been a good day.

Once they were inside the house, Finn's phone rang. He handed Dani off to Shay, who held her in his arms until she pointed out, "I haven't touched the ground in about ten minutes. I can walk, Daddy."

"Right. Sorry."

As soon as her feet hit the floor, she took off toward the backyard.

"Stay away from those filthy dogs!" Finn yelled after her before turning toward Shay and asking, "You want some spaghetti?"

"You made spaghetti?"

"Charlie made spaghetti. That was Mads. We've been invited. For spaghetti."

"Will there be sauce?"

"I don't know. I didn't ask."

"We could buy some sauce. If they don't have sauce."

"I'm sure they'll have sauce."

"Who will have sauce?" Keane asked, walking into the kitchen.

"Charlie invited us to her house for spaghetti. Did you threaten that old man?"

"He's not that old. He's just lived in that house since he was a kid. And yes. I threatened him. But don't worry. Nothing that could be used in a court of law. I did it with my eyes. And why do we need to see the honey badgers again?"

"We'll also see Nat."

"I do like Nat."

"We all like Nat."

"But we don't know if Charlie will have sauce?"

"Why wouldn't they have sauce?"

"They only mentioned spaghetti."

"You should ask. In case we have to bring our own."

Finn texted Mads. A few seconds later, he said, "There'll be sauce."

"I like sauce."

"I do, too."

"We all do."

"Are you really all talking about sauce?" Dani asked, gazing up at them and petting something in her hands.

"What's that, honey?" Finn asked.

"A puppy."

"Where did you find a puppy?"

"Outside with the dogs. Looks like one of them had puppies."

"How many puppies?" Shay asked.

"Six."

"Jesus, those things are huge. Now we'll have to get *more* food," Finn complained.

"Princess had six puppies?"

"You call that drooling animal 'Princess'?" Keane demanded.

"I love Daddy's dogs," Dani informed her uncles in a tone that would tolerate no dissent. "Do not roll your eyes at me, Uncle Mean."

Keane leaned down until he was nose to nose with Shay's daughter. He rolled his eyes again and again until she laughed.

"Are we going to get spaghetti or not?" Finn wanted to know.

Keane stood tall and asked, "What about the kid?"

"She can come."

"To the honey badger house?"

"Nat will be there."

"I love Auntie Nat!"

Keane put his hand over Dani's face, and as hard as she tried to get him to remove it, he wouldn't budge.

"Are you really okay with your offspring hanging out with those badgers?" he asked Shay.

"My *offspring*, as you call her, has named you Uncle Mean, and you're worried about Mads and her friends?"

"I'm not mean to her. I'm mean to everyone else."

"I don't know how that's better. But it doesn't matter. I need to talk to Charlie."

Keane glanced at his niece, who was still trying to wiggle away from his big hand.

"Talk to Charlie? About last night?"

"No. About the puppies. I'll bring the puppies. And the mom. In case the puppies get hungry."

Shay slapped Keane's hand off his daughter's face. "Want to get all the puppies together? We'll bring them with us."

"Yay! Puppies!" Dani cheered before rushing out again to the backyard.

"Why are we bringing the puppies?"

"I need Charlie's advice about them."

"About what?"

"How to take care of them."

"By leaving them alone in the backyard with their mother?"

Disgusted, Shay shook his head, and went to get the crate for the back of the SUV.

"Are you doing this for Tock?" Keane asked and Shay immediately stopped.

"What?"

"Are you bringing puppies with you to impress a woman we were, at one time, pretty sure was going to blow up a kitten?"

"Mads said later Tock wasn't going to blow up the kitten."

"You're friends with someone who blows up kittens?" he heard his daughter's sweet voice ask, and both he and Keane looked down to find her staring at them with wide eyes and three tiny puppies in her hands.

"Of course, I'm not. I'd never be friends with someone like that. Your Uncle Keane was just joking."

"He's not laughing."

"Your Uncle Keane never laughs, baby."

Dani thought on that a moment, those worry lines forming on her forehead. Finally, after a full minute, her forehead cleared and she said, "That's true."

She walked off, and Keane glared at him.

"What?" Shay was not going to fight about bringing his kid to Charlie's house. But that was not the issue bothering his eldest brother.

"I laugh," Keane insisted with an angry snarl. "I have quite a healthy sense of humor."

"Oh, my God!" Shay gasped loudly before lowering his voice and adding, "I never knew you were delusional."

Chapter 9

When Nelle realized that what was supposed to be a short stopover at Max's Queens home had turned into a dinner party with pool access, she slipped out and went across the street to change. They all kept extra clothes in Mads's house because they knew they'd be crashing there at some point. It was a great place to heal from wounds or lie low after some socialite had discovered their half-a-million-dollar painting was missing.

When she opened the front door—using the set of keys she'd made for herself while setting the place up—Nelle walked inside to find Tock sitting on the big couch, watching TV.

Moving across the room, she studied Tock's expression.

"Why are you pouting like a child?" she asked when she stood next to the couch.

"I'm not pouting. Just watching TV."

"Watching TV while pouting." She glanced at the television. *"Animaniacs?"*

"What? I like cartoons."

Nelle sat down in one of the accent chairs she and her designer had chosen for this front room. When first seeing it, she'd thought of the space as a foyer with access to stairs leading to the second floor, a half bath, an extra bedroom, and the kitchen and great room with glass doors looking out over the backyard. A room that Nelle, personally, would have called the living room. She knew her teammates better than she knew her own family, however, and Mads wouldn't look past the first room she walked into. That was where she would dump her bags when she first moved in and that's how she would think of it. As the living room. Because it would be days, if not weeks, before the woman even noticed the room next to the kitchen.

She knew Mads was still pissed that Nelle had taken it upon herself to have the entire house decorated and stocked with food, clothes, and supplies. But what did Mads expect Nelle to do? Sit around in lawn chairs and pretend to be okay with that? They were no longer eighteen, and nothing was worse than twentysomethings still acting as if they were living dorm life.

"What's going on?" Nelle asked when Tock refused to do anything but stare blindly at a show for children.

"I didn't want a party," Tock complained.

"It's not a party. It's a casual dinner involving pasta and Charlie's amazing meat sauce."

"She invited the Malones."

"Of course she did. They're family now."

"I just wanted to relax."

"And you can't do that in a house filled with badgers, cats, and bears who will be doing nothing more than swimming, eating, and sunning themselves like lizards on a rock?"

Tock's eyes locked on Nelle and she asked, "Why can't you just let me be miserable?"

"You're too good at it. When you get in one of your moods, it takes days for you to come out of it. And I'm guessing we don't have time for you to lock yourself away in a tiny room with all your tools and equipment so you can build baby bombs until you feel better."

"I guess."

"So, instead, why don't you find a way to entertain your-self?"

"And how do I do that?"

"Well . . . Mads is walking around with a basketball and dressed like she's about to be teleported back to the nineties so she can actually witness one of the Chicago Bulls' champion-ships." Nelle grinned. "Now are you just going to let that go unchallenged?"

★   ★   ★

After stopping first to pick up a new phone for Shay, the Malones arrived at the MacKilligan house with Dani, Princess, and a crate filled with puppies. Unwilling to deal with any of it, Keane simply walked away from the SUV. Finn offered to carry Dani, but she wanted to "help Daddy with the crate," which really meant putting her hand on its side and walking beside Shay on his left, while Princess stayed on his right.

While they walked together, Shay and Dani discussed her math camp. It was a day-camp thing that her mother had wisely gotten her into. Why a kid wanted to spend their summer break learning about math, Shay didn't know. He hated math when he was Dani's age and he hated it now. He used the calculator on his phone for everything and had a very smart brown bear accountant handle his taxes. Anything was better than attempting to do it himself. His baby, though, loved math, and if she wanted to work on equations over the summer, Shay wouldn't let anything get in her way.

"I go Monday through Friday. Mom takes me there before she takes the boys to practice. Or Aunt Lei takes me."

"I can always take you, if you want."

"Really?"

"Of course."

"Can you hang around and meet some of my friends and the teachers? Or will Uncle Keane be mad? I know you have practice."

"Uncle Keane will probably want to come, too, to make sure everything is up to his standards."

"I've been in math camp all summer. He wants to come *now*?"

"Baby, don't try to use logic when dealing with Keane. You know better than that."

Laughing, she pulled open the screen door to the MacKilligan house and walked inside. Shay began to follow but had to stop immediately.

Shay wasn't sure what he'd expected when he walked into that house, but what he *didn't* expect was the wave of nostalgia that swept over him like a minor tsunami.

Maybe it was the delicious scent of tomato sauce. Or the grizzly triplets in the living room, sitting around the huge coffee table playing Scrabble and arguing about which were real words and which were made up. "Josaltude" was definitely made up. Or maybe it was the laughter and conversation he could hear coming from the kitchen and outside from the yard. He really didn't know what it was, but when Nat came out and saw Dani, the pair squealing and running at each other for a big hug, Shay had to turn around and leave the house, taking a seat on the porch bench.

His heart raced. His hands shook. And he was positive he was on the verge of tears. He just didn't know why.

Princess sat in front of him, resting her big head on his knee while he carefully placed the crate filled with her puppies on the chair cattycorner from him. She patiently waited while he tried to sort through his feelings. Not an easy task. He wasn't big on, you know . . . feelings. Shay usually just went through life doing what he needed to do. Being dependable. Being a good dad. Trying not to twist people on the F train into pretzels when they got on his nerves. What every shifter did to survive life in New York.

"You okay?"

Shay slowly raised his gaze. Taking in Tock's red Nike hightops, bright blue knee-high sweat socks, long blue shorts, and cutoff blue-and-red Detroit Pistons jersey.

"Pistons?" he asked. "You're from Detroit, too?"

"No. Only Mads. This is just to irritate her. She still worships at the throne of Michael Jordan and the Bulls. And this is a signed Isiah Thomas jersey." Tock tossed the blue-and-red basketball she had in her hands up in the air rather than dribbling it. He appreciated that.

"You cut a signed Isiah Thomas jersey in half?"

She shrugged. "I don't care about Isiah Thomas. Mads does." She jutted her chin toward him. "So what's going on with you?" she asked. "You look positively . . . Irish."

He shook his head. "I walked in that house and . . . it just reminded me of my dad. Everyone hanging out. Having fun.

Waiting for dinner to be ready. It hasn't felt like that with my family since he died. It just . . . the feeling . . . it took me by surprise."

"Yeah. I call that the Gift of Charlie."

"The Gift of Charlie?"

She sat down beside him on the outdoor love seat, but turned to the side so she could look directly at him. "No matter what's going on, no matter where we are, Charlie has this amazing ability to make it all feel like home. Even when she's yelling at Max and ordering the rest of us around, it still feels like a family thing. All this," she said, jabbing her thumb toward the house, "is because she wanted to make sure I ate some carbs before I passed out."

"You feel like you're going to pass out?"

"No. Not even a little. I feel great, thankfully, which is good because it's taken her all day to make this sauce. But Charlie likes to feed people and I'm not about to turn down her spaghetti."

"It does smell good."

"*Right?*"

They went silent after that, and Shay tried to think of something to say to keep the conversation going. He didn't want Tock to think he was silent because he didn't want to talk to her. He just didn't have anything interesting to impart. He was really bad at small talk. He left that to Finn, who was really good at it. Keane didn't like small talk either, but he did love to complain. He could complain for hours, and some people didn't mind listening. But Shay . . . he only spoke when he had something to say. One of the things he loved about his daughter was that they could sit for hours, drawing or reading or watching TV, and never had to say a word to each other. They just enjoyed each other's company. Dani's mother, though, tended to call it "plotting cats ready to pounce." But they weren't plotting anything.

He glanced at Tock. She was staring off, not really appearing to focus on anything specific. He tried to come up with something that could start a conversation. The weather? No. Shifters didn't care about weather. The rivalry between Michael Jordan and Isiah Thomas? Nah. It seemed her current ensemble had more to do with pissing off Mads rather than honoring Thomas. The state of the country?

God, he was pathetic.

Tock suddenly pointed at the carrier.

"What's that?" she asked.

The dogs! Of course!

"Puppies. My dog had puppies. Thought Charlie could give me some advice."

She frowned a little. "Advice about what?"

"The puppies. I don't know how to take care of them."

"Then why did you let her have them?" she questioned, pointing at Princess.

"Let her?" Shay asked.

"If you didn't want her to have puppies, why didn't you have her spayed?"

"Seemed wrong to spay *her*, but not the males."

Tock's head twitched to the side. "Wait . . . why wouldn't you neuter the males?"

"Take their balls? That seems cruel."

Now she leaned forward, pointing her finger at him. "Are you telling me you didn't get your dogs fixed because you didn't want to cut off the males' balls?"

"I love *my* balls. Why would I do to them what I wouldn't do to myself?"

"Are you fucking kidding—"

Tock's words abruptly ended when Charlie walked out of the house and onto the porch.

Shay started to ask Charlie to weigh in on the question of dog balls—because that seemed like something people would do to keep a conversation going—but Tock was suddenly in his lap. He just didn't know why. If he'd been a few inches shorter, she'd have completely blocked him from Charlie's view.

The thing was, Charlie didn't even stop. With keys in hand,

she rushed away from the house and down the street to an SUV.

"What are you doing?" he asked the top of Tock's head.

"Shhhh."

A few seconds later, Charlie was back. Now she had a big box of kitchen trash bags in her hand. Before she made it into the house, though, she stopped and pointed at him and Tock.

"What's going on here?" Charlie asked, almost smiling.

"Nothing," Tock replied.

"I have no idea," Shay admitted.

Charlie laughed. "Well, whatever is going on, you two make a cute couple."

"Oh, please."

"Thank you!"

Once Charlie was back in the house, Tock glanced over her shoulder at him.

"'Thank you'? Really?"

"What? I was just—"

Charlie came back out on the porch.

"Did I just hear a puppy?" she asked.

Tock threw her arm up so that it covered his face before she replied, "Shay wanted you to meet the newest members of his family."

He pushed her arm down and asked, "Family . . . ? Ow!"

This time, he pushed her elbow out of his chest, but Tock kept talking.

"Because who doesn't love puppies?" Tock asked.

"I do love puppies," Charlie whispered, but whispering didn't matter at this house.

"*You are not getting any more dogs, Charlie MacKilligan!*" one of the bears yelled from inside the house.

"I'll be right back," Charlie said with a forced smile before walking back into the house.

"What's going on?" Shay asked Tock while Charlie and one of the bears yelled at each other about dogs, the "sanctity" of their bed, and how "we're not having this argument again!"

"If you tell Charlie you didn't get your pets spayed because bros back up bros when it comes to balls, she's going to take *your* balls and rip them off your body."

"That seems a little extreme."

"Not for Charlie when it comes to dogs."

"What about cats?"

"She could give a shit about cats." Still on his lap, Tock reached over and released the locks on the top part of the crate and pulled it off. "Just don't talk about balls or spaying or what your plans are for these puppies."

"Plans? What kind of plans do you need for puppies?"

Tock's head dropped. "Oh, my God. She's going to kill you."

"Daddy!" Dani called out, running around from the other side of the house. "They said I can go swim—"

Shay cringed when his daughter managed to get her feet tangled with the air, apparently, and face-planted into the yard.

"You okay, baby?" he asked his daughter.

"I'm fine," she replied directly into the dirt. Placing her palms flat, she pushed herself up until she again stood. "Can I go swimming?" she asked.

He reached over the banister behind him and waved her over. She ran, this time keeping her footing until she reached him and Tock.

Shay used his left hand to wipe off the dirt still clinging to his daughter's face. "Yes. You can go swimming. Your bathing suit and towel are in the gray duffel in the back of the SUV. But make sure Nat or one of your uncles is with you."

"I'm not a baby, Daddy. I know how to swim."

"I know that. I taught you. But you're not going swimming alone. No arguments."

"Fine."

"Fine."

Her eyes glanced at Tock, then back at Shay. After that, she came around the porch, up the stairs, and stood in front of them. Then she just waited. Slowly blinking.

And, knowing his daughter, Dani would wait forever until she got what she wanted.

"This is Tock," he finally told her. "Tock, this is my daughter, Dani."

Tock held her hand out and Dani shook it. Like two proper business strangers meeting for the first time.

"I like your watch," Dani told Tock, pointing at the giant monstrosity on the woman's wrist.

"Thanks. I like your headband."

Dani smiled, touching the crystal-encrusted headband with the tips of her fingers. "Me, too. It sparkles!"

When the kid touched that headband, which was decorated with a crystal-covered butterfly, Tock didn't know what to think. She really wasn't a "kid" person. Even when she was a kid, she didn't really like kids. They talked too much, had no idea how to manage their time, and . . . well . . . talked too much. Her mother used to tell her, "No man is an island." A statement Tock didn't really get until her father explained, "Everybody needs somebody, baby. Even you." Tock hadn't really believed them because she'd been doing fine without friends, but then she'd met Mads, Max, Nelle, and Streep. Having those badgers hanging around her house now and then seemed to make her parents feel better, so it made sense to keep them. Besides, they weren't as annoying as most kids her age . . . except Streep. Streep was always annoying. Tock didn't think it had anything to do with age. But she was a beautiful distractor when they needed one.

The main thing, though, was that the kid was Shay's daughter, which meant any protection Tock might provide for the big cat because he'd protected her, also applied to the cub. Besides, how could she not protect the kid? She was actually quite cute. A mini-version of her father with shoulder-length black hair, a strong jaw, and full cheeks.

The pride she saw in Shay's eyes when he looked at his daughter reminded Tock of her own father. It was a goofy expression that her father sometimes wore, but it meant a lot. Especially knowing he still felt that way despite everything she'd put him through over the years.

"What are all those dials on your watch?" the kid asked, leaning in to study it.

"Date. Local time. Stopwatch slash timer and time in Israel."

"Israel?"

"I have family there."

"You also have family in Wisconsin, right?" Shay asked.

"Is it really that hard to subtract an hour from current time?" Tock asked.

"My dad is not a math guy," Dani said.

"I know the basics. I just can't do that fancy math you do," Shay said.

"Fancy math?" Tock asked.

"He means fractions. Daddy struggles with fractions. I'm sure it's because he's been hit in the head so many times."

"That doesn't really affect our kind the way it does full-humans," Tock explained. "But like all animals, some of us are just not as smart as the rest of us. That's okay, though. He's your father and you love him despite that."

"Wow," Shay said from behind her. "Just . . . wow."

"Math is important," she told him. "Just like science and time."

"Time is a human construct," Dani put in.

Tock glared down at the kid. "Excuse me?"

"It's a human construct. It only exists because we brought it into being. Science and math exist because they just do. One is only as important as the power we give it. While the other two are important because they simply are. Without science or math, we wouldn't exist."

"Time management is extremely important. We couldn't function as a society without time and the brutal, heartless control of it."

Eyes wide, the kid gawked up at her, but Tock didn't know why. That was a completely rational argument, and she didn't need some ten-year-old telling her that time was not important! Time was *always* important! How could it not be? People running around, showing up whenever? No specific time or day to be where they needed to be? That was insanity! That was chaos! And chaos due to lack of time management was a world Tock refused to live in!

Charlie walked out onto the porch, yelling a "Fine!" over her shoulder.

With a little growl and shake of her head, she returned to stand in front of them.

"The puppies," she said. "You were saying . . . ?"

Tock opened her mouth to speak but the cat jumped in first.

"Tock and I were debating dog balls."

Closing her eyes, Tock shook her head. Dumbass!

"Dog balls?" Charlie repeated, glancing at Shay's cub. "Um . . . what about them?"

"Is it really necessary to cut them off? Because my boys—"

"You haven't had the dogs fixed?" Dani suddenly demanded, startling all the adults standing on the porch.

"Well—"

"Oh . . . Daddy." And she said it with such infinite sadness and disappointment, neither Tock nor Charlie could say a word. "How could you?"

"I didn't."

"I mean, how could you *not* get the dogs fixed? My favorite math teacher rescues dogs and cats, and she says all dogs should be neutered and spayed so there are no unwanted animals." She pointed at the crate. "Those are unwanted animals that *you* have put at risk. And why? Why, Daddy?"

"Um . . . if I wouldn't want the same thing, why would I do it to my—"

"Oh . . . Daddy." Lowering her head, the kid shook it slowly and very sadly. "Daddy. I'm so disappointed."

"I see that."

Putting her arm around Dani's shoulders, Charlie wisely intervened. "It could be that your father just didn't know."

"How could he not? It's not just my math teacher! I see stuff about fixing dogs all over the place! People are trying to help these poor animals roaming the streets!"

With one arm still around the kid's shoulders and her other

hand patting her right arm, Charlie briefly glanced off. And Tock knew it was to stop herself from laughing. The kid was just so damn earnest, concerned as only kids could be when it came to something they truly cared about. Of course, most ten-year-olds cared about comic books or butterflies. Or whatever kids were into these days. But worrying about whether dogs were fixed or not? Didn't seem like a normal thing for a kid to concern herself over.

Clearing her throat, Charlie said, "How about this . . . ? Wait here."

Charlie went back into the house while Shay's daughter made "tsk-tsk-tsk" sounds and shook her head, all the while staring at her father with dark brown eyes.

When Charlie returned, she had a thick book. "Here." She handed the book to Dani. "Read this. It's a helpful book on how to care for your dog from birth to the end. You read it and you tell your father what you learned."

"Shouldn't *he* read it?" Dani asked; Tock was barely able to choke back her laugh at the haughtiness she heard in the kid's tone.

"But we both know he won't. So *you* read it and tell him what he needs to know. Okay? But first, take these puppies to the vet and get them checked out. You have a vet, right, Shay?"

"Uhhh . . ."

"Oh . . . Daddy."

There was that unequivocal sound of disappointment again. Tock loved it. Especially when Shay tossed his arms out wide and said, "*What?*"

Dani looked the book over. "Thank you so much, Miss—"

"Just Charlie, sweetie. Now why don't you get a bathing suit and go swimming? You might fit in one of Stevie's bathing suits."

"Because Stevie has the body of a ten-year-old?" Tock asked.

Tock ducked the back of the hand coming for her face by leaning into Shay, and Dani told Charlie, "I have a suit in my dad's car. I'll go get it." She held the book to her chest. "And

I'll make sure my dad gets up to speed on taking care of Princess's puppies."

"Thank you, sweetie."

After another look of disappointment directed at her father—"*What?*" Shay demanded again—Dani held her hand out so her father could give her the car keys and ran off toward the car parked down the street.

"Really?" Charlie said with a chuckle once the kid was gone. "You didn't want to take your dogs' balls?"

Shay shrugged. "I wouldn't want anyone to do that to me."

"Oh, my God," she said, laughing and picking up the crate filled with puppies. "You're an idiot."

She disappeared back into the house, Princess following right behind her, while one of the bears growled, "Why are you bringing those puppies in here?" as soon as the screen door slammed shut.

"That wasn't so bad," Shay noted.

"You can thank your daughter for that," Tock told him. "She was so upset, she completely diffused the Charlie Rage." Turning her upper body to look directly at Shay, she pointed a finger and said, "And just so you know, you and your brothers *never* want to trigger the Charlie Rage."

Shay gazed at her. "Why?"

"Because"—she stood, vacating his lap and leaving it cold and lonely—"I don't feel like digging the size graves you three cats would need. I've done enough of that in my life."

"Wait . . . what?"

Tock didn't bother answering him, because Mads had walked out onto the porch and the pair stood there, staring at each other. Well, Tock was staring. Mads was glaring as she looked her teammate up and down.

"Really?" Mads asked.

"What? I thought you'd want to get a little practice in, so I changed my clothes."

"To *that?*" Mads's eyes narrowed and she took a step forward, bumping her shoulder against Tock's. And Tock bumped her back.

"Uh . . . ladies?" Shay weakly called out. But it was too late.

"Let's do this, *Isiah*," Mads sneered.

"Okay, *Michael*."

Mads spun around and marched back into the house. Tock picked up the red-and-blue basketball, but just as quickly as Mads was gone, she came back, snatching the ball from Tock's hands. She imbedded her unleashed claws in the ball, deflating it while staring Tock right in the eyes. When she'd made her ridiculous point, she tossed the useless piece of leather aside and walked back into the house.

Once the screen door shut behind her, Tock started laughing. That's why she liked Mads. Her teammate entertained her in ways no one else ever had. She was ridiculous! Who loved basketball this much? Except maybe Michael Jordan himself! And even he liked golf and baseball, too. Mads could not say the same.

"I don't have to worry about you two, do I?" she heard Shay ask from behind her. He was standing up now. Thankfully, the house the MacKilligan sisters were renting had been built for bear shifters, so Shay's head didn't scrape against the ceiling of the open porch.

"Worry about what?" she asked, truly confused.

"You two fighting it out like at the hospital."

"Mads and I don't fight."

He pointed at the leather on the floor. "She punctured your basketball with her claws."

"And?"

Shay threw up his hands. "Okay. Maybe I just don't understand how your relationship with Mads works, but—"

Shay landed face-first at Tock's feet with Finn on his back after his brother had leaped over the banister to attack him from behind.

Grabbing Shay by the back of the neck with his hand, Finn announced, "We're going swimming before dinner. Let's go." With that, he lifted his brother high enough to toss him over the banister and into the yard.

"Ow!" Shay complained.

"Stop whining!" Finn grinned at Tock. "Nice outfit. It's like you're trying to start a fight with Mads."

"We don't fight."

Finn shook his head and muttered, "Whatever," before heading out the way he came in. Over the banister and onto his brother's back. By the time they both were on their feet, they'd shifted to cats and were in the midst of a battle involving claws and fangs.

"The Malones sure do fight a lot," she said to herself just as her head jerked forward. Forced by the power of the basketball that hit her in the back of the head.

Snarling, she glared at Mads over her shoulder.

"Ready, bitch?" the psychotic Viking demanded.

Shay thought the whole dog discussion with Charlie was over, which was good. He wanted to focus on the absolutely *brutal* one-on-one game taking place on the half-court across from the pool he was lounging in with his daughter and three siblings. But he knew he couldn't relax just yet when Charlie, sitting on the ground near him, asked, "So you're not going to breed her again, right?" She pointed to Princess. The dog seemed to have attached herself to Charlie, even when Charlie didn't have the puppies with her—although at the moment, there was a large pup splayed across the top of Charlie's head, fast asleep. Maybe Princess was making sure the little fella didn't fall off its perch.

"I didn't breed her in the first place," Shay explained. "She breeded herself."

"The word is 'bred,' and you *allowed* her to breed."

"Not on purpose."

"Oh . . . Daddy."

"Stop saying that," he told his daughter as she swam around behind him. From the corner of his eye, he watched Dani lift her hands out of the water and sign to Natalie, "He is pitiful."

"I know," Nat signed back. "We all know."

It had been a mistake, teaching his daughter to sign before she could walk and then enrolling her in ASL classes from the time she was three. He knew that now. Because Nat was a bad influence.

"It was an accident," Shay insisted. "And now I plan to read that book you gave Dani and learn all I need to know about dogs."

"You'll need to read more than one book to do that," Charlie told him.

Shay couldn't help but roll his eyes. "Why are dogs so much more complicated than cats?"

"Because people let their house cats stay wild. They don't know where they are half the time. I see them roaming around neighborhoods. No leash. No person attached to them. Shitting wherever they want. But they belong to somebody because they usually have a collar on, sometimes with a little camera attached. If I did that with any of my dogs, I'd get tickets from the city."

"Because dogs are disgusting," Keane cut in, swimming up to Shay's side and resting his arms on the rim of the pool. "They shed. They drool. They stare at you with their dumb dog faces. I don't know how any of you put up with it."

"While you cats have such a wonderful temperament."

"I don't have to have a wonderful temperament," Keane replied. "I'm an Amur tiger. My kind roamed the Mongolian flats before Ghenghis Khan was even born. In my cat form I'm more than eight hundred pounds and nearly ten feet long. You're all just lucky I have deigned not to eat you."

"What?" Keane pushed when everyone simply stared at him. "Speaking of which . . . where are *your* dogs?"

"Over at Berg's house. Hiding from you. The mean cat that wants to eat us all."

"I don't *want* to eat any of you. Quite honestly, you look a little gamey. I'm just saying I could. Luckily for you . . . I'm benevolent."

"Yes, yes. So very benevolent. Like a loving king." That voice came from a long set of legs strutting by the Malone brothers. While the other honey badgers had on shorts and T-shirts or tank tops, Nelle Zhao had on an extremely tiny bikini with straps that crisscrossed around her muscular mid-section, and heels that seemed to make her legs go on forever.

Shay watched those legs strut by until he saw Tock and Mads get into a tug of war with the ball they'd been using during their game. Neither would give the stupid thing up. They eventually landed on the ground, kicking and growling while trying to pry the ball from each other.

"Can you believe this shit?" he asked, glancing over at Keane. His brother didn't answer, though. He was still gawking at Nelle.

"Forget it," Shay bluntly told Keane. "You haven't got a shot in hell."

Blinking, Keane looked at him. "What?"

"You heard me."

"I'm just sitting here. Minding my own business."

"And her ass."

"She does have an amazing ass," Charlie interjected. She now hugged the puppy that had been on her head against her chest, both hands wrapped around its small body. A look of pure bliss on her face. "And she'll crush you without even working up a sweat."

"Exactly." Shay focused again on Tock and Mads. By now, Streep had pushed the two crazed females apart and was holding the ball.

"This is ridiculous!" she yelled at them. "Both of you acting like this."

The pair got to their feet and stared at their teammate in confusion.

"What are you talking about?" Mads asked.

"Why don't you two just admit how much you love each other?" Streep demanded.

"What?" Tock asked, laughing a little.

"You guys are best friends but you never say it. You never admit it. If you did, you'd understand that all of this"—she swung her arms wide—"is just an attempt to hide the fact that the two of you are simply worried about each other. That you just want to protect each other. Like all good friends do."

It was quick. The look that passed between Tock and Mads, but Shay caught it. He just wasn't sure Streep did.

"That's stupid," Mads bluntly told the little actress, taking the basketball from her. "You're stupid."

"I'm just saying—"

"We're teammates," Tock told her. "That's all. I could not care less if Mads gets hit by a bus."

"Or a train," Mads added with a knowing nod.

"Exactly."

Streep started to rant but immediately stopped, clasping her hands together and lacing her fingers as if she was praying. She held her clasped hands close to her face, closed her eyes, and took in a deep breath. When she released it, she said, "We all know you two are very close friends. Just admit it. Just say the words."

Tock and Mads exchanged a more obvious glance before replying in unison, "No."

Streep slapped the ball from Mads's hands—nearly hitting a ducking Charlie in the process—grabbed each woman by the throat and dragged them close, choking them while screeching, "*Just say it! Say it!*"

"Okay." Max, who had been standing by a nearby tree, bickering with a neighbor bear about some recently raided bee hives—she had *nothing* to do with the raid so why did everyone keep accusing her?—quickly rushed over to rescue her two teammates. Preferably before a hysterical Streep choked them to death. "Let's all just calm down." She pulled hands from throats and pushed a gasping, coughing Tock and Mads away before wrapping her arms around Streep and pulling her close.

"It's okay," she told a now-sobbing Streep. "It's okay." Max pulled the badger as close as possible and rubbed her back.

"Why are they so fucking awful, Max? *Whyyyyyy?*"

"Because they're horrible, horrible people. But you already knew that."

"I did. I *did* know they were horrible people."

"Exactly." Max held Streep by the shoulders and took a step back so she could look the overemotional female in the eyes.

"Now, let's go help set up the tables. We'll be dining *al fresco* today. Won't that be lovely?"

"It will. It *will* be lovely!" She glared at Tock and Mads. "And you two are horrible. Horrible! *Stop laughing at me!*"

It was a little bit of Italy in the middle of Queens, New York. Charlie's sauce was amazing, the pasta perfectly prepared, the garlic bread and salad perfect accompaniments. She even had the perfect wine for the few who wanted it.

What started as a quick early lunch in the middle of the day to make sure Tock wouldn't pass out had turned into an early evening feast while the sun slowly lowered. Charlie's dogs finally came out to play in the yard, Mads's illegally harbored coyote came over to steal a loaf of the garlic bread, Stevie's kitten hung from a tree limb, and all those predators feeding nearby managed not to scare any of the domesticated pets.

It was heaven. And Tock didn't believe in heaven.

Halfway through the meal, Stevie returned from her lab with Shen and Zé. The look on her face made it clear that Max's kid sister hadn't made a breakthrough on whatever toxin had been used on Tock. But Stevie wouldn't stop until she'd figured out what was going on. In fact, she could be obsessive over that sort of thing. As it was, she only sat down to eat because Charlie and Max forced her. Well, Charlie got her a plate and filled it with pasta and sauce and some salad, while Max physically forced Stevie into a chair as they fought like two cats in a bag. But the scuffle led to Stevie actually eating, which was all any of them wanted. Whether she was honey badger or tiger, she was still way too thin to be either. Picking her up was like picking up a bag of chips.

If it weren't for her shifted form, Tock would have been much more worried about Stevie's daily safety. They didn't discuss her shifted form, though. It was better for Charlie to believe that "Max's friends" didn't know what Stevie actually turned into when she became animal. They did know, of course, and it was horrifying; but not in a scary movie way, just in the size of what she became. Like a mini-Godzilla. While Charlie couldn't shift at all.

Maybe Charlie was right. Her father *did* have fucked-up genes that had affected his offspring.

Once Stevie was eating her spaghetti while still managing to continue arguing with Max, everything seemed to calm down. Tock and Mads relaxed, too, and took a few minutes to just eat the remainder of their meal in silence. Mistake, because when Charlie suddenly put her arms around their shoulders and leaned in, she startled them. Both females let out loud snarls.

"Whoa." Charlie leaned back a bit. "You guys okay?"

"Uh-huh," Tock and Mads replied, trying not to sound as panicked as she always made them feel. It wasn't her fault, really. Other than that she was naturally terrifying, and over the years they'd seen her do some really horrifying things.

Charlie leaned back in, her arms around their shoulders again. Tock had to fight hard not to spin away and back up, hissing in warning. A reaction appropriate for a pride of hungry lions, but not for a friendly Charlie MacKilligan.

"Do me a favor," Charlie said. "Before you guys head out for the night, grab the others and meet me at Mads's house for a quick chat. Okay?"

"It was Max," Mads abruptly announced. "She did it."

Charlie shook her head at the sudden statement. "What are you talking about?"

Mads scratched her forehead, eyes downcast. "Nothing. I'm not talking about anything."

"Okay." Charlie frowned a little, confused. "Anyway, give me a heads-up when you guys decide to go and we'll meet at Mads's."

When Charlie had gone back inside the house, Tock turned to Mads and hissed, "You *rat*."

"I know!" Mads whispered back, briefly covering her face with her hands. "But I just panicked! She's my same height, size. But she terrifies me."

"Some Viking you are."

"Oh, shut up! You panicked, too."

"Yeah," Tock said with a wink and a smile, "but my people hide it better."

Shay packed up the duffel bag with Dani's wet swimsuit and towel, which he would toss in the washer when he got home. His daughter handled the puppies, looking them over before she'd put them back into the SUV along with their mother.

"Daddy . . . we're missing a pup."

"We are?"

"I counted and we're—"

"Here you go." Charlie's bear, Berg, placed the puppy into the crate with the others. He nodded at Dani. "Sorry about that. The woman I love has a hoarding problem."

"I am *not* a hoarder!" Charlie yelled from the kitchen.

The bear looked at Shay. "Do me a favor, cat. Don't bring any more dogs here. I have enough trouble keeping her away from Mads's damn coyote."

"That coyote comes to *me!*" came the kitchen retort. "*I* was the one who sent him back to Mads's house!"

The bear rolled his eyes. "I'm going home. Do not take another puppy!" he barked toward the house before lumbering off the porch. A few seconds later, the house shook a bit as the other two triplets followed their brother. Even the female lumbered, but she was way cuter than the males, smiling and waving goodbye to Dani before going down the steps and heading to their house across the street.

Keane passed the bears without saying a word, despite having spent nearly a whole day with them. He came onto the porch and said to Shay, "The SUV is packed up. You two ready to go?"

"Will be in thirty seconds."

"Okay. Wait with Finn. I need to go talk to Charlie before we leave."

Shay immediately stood up straight and gazed at his brother. "Talk to her about what?"

When Keane didn't answer, Dani charged across the porch and slid to a stop in front of her uncle.

"Don't be mean," she ordered him.

"Excuse me?"

"I was clear."

Shay briefly glanced away so that he didn't laugh out right. It would only piss off both of them.

"I am not mean," Keane told Dani.

"I *call* you Uncle Mean for a reason."

"I thought it was just a play on words."

"It's not."

"This, little miss, is none of your business." He reached down and picked Dani up by her arms, carefully placing her by Shay and out of the way. "Now if you'll excuse me—"

Dani ran back over and grabbed her uncle's leg, holding on tight.

Keane sighed. "What are you doing?"

"I like her. I like Charlie. And if you're mean to her, we can't come back here. It'll be Popeye's Chicken all over again."

"We're only barred from the Popeye's Chicken in Amityville. Now release me, tiny child."

Frowning deeply, Dani let her uncle go and watched as he walked into the house.

"I'll never be able to swim here again, will I, Daddy?"

"Knowing your Uncle Keane . . . ? Probably not."

"So, how's it going with my sister?" Keane asked Charlie MacKilligan as she moved across her kitchen with several bottles of spices in her hand.

"Except for her meth addiction and whoring herself for extra cash, she's doing great. Why?"

Keane was about to tear the house apart with his rage when he was distracted by Charlie's opening one of the cabinet doors.

"Why is Stevie hiding in there?" he asked.

"She's not hiding. She's taking a nap. She was up all night working."

"Fascinating, but that doesn't really answer my main question. Why is she in the cabinet?"

"Shen and Zé went to get ice cream."

Keane expected more to the reply but he didn't get it. He wasn't sure if he should follow up . . . but he had to know!

"Why is she *in* the cabinet?"

"She's napping."

"In a cabinet!"

"She feels safe in there. There are man-eating tigers around."

"*She's* a man-eating tiger!"

"Only half of her. And that's only because our father has fucked-up genes. If he didn't, she'd be all honey badger and she'd still be in the cabinet. Would you rather she medicate her anxiety so she's nothing but a useless zombie until you and your brothers leave?"

"Why is that the only option?"

"It's not the only option." She gestured toward the cabinet. "See? It all works out."

Deciding this was too stupid a conversation to continue, Keane went back to the subject of his baby sister. "Nat. How is she doing?"

"You saw her, she's fine."

"I can't believe my mother agreed to let her stay with all of you."

"Why not? She's family."

"You don't know her like we do."

"We're learning."

He decided to be honest. "Look, Nat is a seventeen-year-old She-cat—"

"Honey badger."

Keane took a moment to get his annoyance under control. He let out a long breath and said, "*Half* honey badger. And there are things about her that you simply may not be able to handle."

"I understand your concerns. I really do." Charlie walked back across the kitchen and opened one of the drawers. "I have been dealing with Max, Stevie, and their issues since I was a kid. I know what's involved in managing a MacKilligan girl."

"She's a Malone."

"Uh-huh." Charlie moved over to the counter that stood directly under the open window looking out over the backyard. The window had been slightly raised so a thin arm could snake in and dig through a big purse that had been sitting on the counter; a wallet was half hanging out of it.

"I understand your concerns, Keane," Charlie continued. "I really do. But your sister is at that age when she can be quite a handful, and I'm not sure three brothers who adore her are going to be able to manage her the way a honey badger needs to be managed."

"What does that—*Oh, my God!*" he barked out, watching as Charlie grabbed the hand digging through her purse, slapped it flat onto the counter, and stabbed it with a fork she'd taken from the drawer.

"*Owwwwww! Motherfuckerbitchwhoreburninhell*—"

"Stop whining," Charlie calmly ordered, releasing Nat's hand, but only so she could drag her halfway through the window so Keane's younger sister could see exactly what Charlie had to say. "If you're going to steal, Nat, don't steal from family. And be good at it. If you're not good at it, you'll get worse than a fork to the hand. *Capiche?*" She shoved Nat out the window and turned to Keane, letting out a charming little giggle. "I guess I'm still feeling a bit Italian today."

Keane pointed at the now empty window. "You stabbed my sister in the hand."

"Yeah. If she's going to steal, she needs to be better. Or she needs to not give a fuck about being stabbed in the hand. She can't have it both ways."

"What?"

Tossing the fork into the sink, she explained, "With honey badgers, there are two types of thieves: the brazen, and the smart. The smart ones steal from you, and you never know until you open your safe to get the bonds your grandmother gave you twenty years ago and just find a little card where the bonds used to be. And on the card is a smiley face. Or a middle finger. It really depends on the mood of the badger."

"And brazen?"

"They just take what they want. I have several uncles and cousins like that. They just walk in and take what they want and dare you to call the cops on them. Brazen is what you do when you like going to jail sometimes or getting slapped around by people much bigger and stronger than you. There is, sadly, a little too much brazen in the MacKilligan bloodline. But since I don't want my sisters to go to prison, I train them in the smart ways. And the smart way is no stealing from family, and everyone else never knows you were there."

"And that means *stabbing* your sisters with forks?"

"No, no. I never stabbed Stevie. She doesn't steal. She thinks it's morally wrong."

"She's right."

"Although she does love stealing magazines from doctor's offices. Just to see if she can get away with it. And I'm okay with that—it keeps her natural skills sharp."

"But you stabbed Max with a fork?"

"No." She shook her head. "I stabbed her with a knife. More than once. But she was stealing from everybody, including the Pack, which would have ended much worse than getting us thrown out. Plus, she's a little bit of a sociopath, so she doesn't have a memory of pain the way normal people do. She doesn't fear its reoccurrence."

"Oh, my God."

"I know. That one has taken a lot of work, but she's come a long way. And Nat," she added, gesturing to the empty window, "is a fast learner. I know that she'll never try to steal my wallet from my bag again while I'm standing right there because she's *not* a sociopath. She absolutely remembers pain. It's a deterrent."

"You know, Charlie, I'd prefer you *not* stab my baby sister."

"You want me to punch her?"

"No!" He stopped, forced himself to calm down. He knew he couldn't be his usual self with Charlie. She was . . . different. Not like anyone—full-human or shifter—he'd ever known. And unlike everyone else, she wasn't scared of him. Not even a little. "We try to avoid abuse in our family. That's kind of what Nat's used to. What's so funny?" he asked when she laughed.

"I've seen how you treat your baby brother."

Keane let a snarl slip before he could stop it, but he quickly recovered. "The idiot—" He stopped, gave himself another second. He began again. "*Dale* is a bit of a momma's boy."

"So are the rest of you!" she retorted, still laughing. "All four of you are momma's boys. You just give him shit because he enjoys his momma-boy status. Don't hate the player, Keane, hate the game. And as much as you don't want to believe it, Nat is not a cat. She's a honey badger. Loud and proud about it, too. And if we're not careful, she will go from trouble-making Rasputin right into Lucrezia Borgia territory, and then where will we be? I'll tell you where: talking to your sweet little Nat through plexiglass at Rikers while she does twenty-five to life for—as her defense team will argue—accidentally poisoning someone to death. Is that what you want?"

"Uh . . . no."

"Exactly. So let me handle it. Because, honestly, after Max . . . everyone else is a fucking cake walk."

Keane didn't know what else to say. What *could* he say? He didn't think Charlie was wrong. He knew his sister. Better than he probably wanted to, and she was, in a word, trouble. Max MacKilligan was nearly thirty and hadn't gone to prison yet, so maybe . . . ?

He started to walk toward the front door, but stopped to look back at Charlie.

"Lucrezia Borgia?"

"Dude . . . her father became *pope* despite his litter of children and many mistresses. Of *course* the Borgias were honey badgers. But," she added with a smile, "they were the smart ones."

With a nod, Keane walked out of the kitchen. He was near the front door when Charlie called out, "I gave Finn extra sauce for you guys. But don't leave it in your car too long. The bears will start tearing that thing apart to get to it. Especially since it's after dark."

Keane took off running, pushing past both his brothers on the porch. He ran down the stairs and stopped on the sidewalk. That's when Keane roared toward his SUV. Lions and wolves on other streets responded in annoyance and panic with their own roars and barks until Keane bellowed out, "*Get your grizzly asses away from my SUV! That sauce belongs to the Malones!*"

Chapter 10

"Why does Charlie want to see us?" Streep asked. She looked at Max. "What did you do?"

"Why do you guys always ask me that? It hurts my feelings."

"You don't have feelings."

"And after I let you cry on my shoulder when these two were mean to you," Max admonished Streep.

The front door opened and Charlie walked into Mads's recently purchased house. Along with cash, Mads had given up one of her paintings to the former owners in order to secure the house. She didn't mind. It had been worth it. She'd never had her own place before. She'd really only lived in the apartment above her great-grandmother's store in Detroit. When she'd been forced to move back with her mother's hyena clan, Mads hadn't really lived with them. She was honey badger more than she'd ever been hyena, so she did what badgers do: She found small spaces to hide in. Sometimes in someone's kitchen cabinet or under their bathroom sink or even under a couch. She avoided sleeping under strangers' beds because she was too young to hear all that might be going on there. Then she'd met her teammates, and they invited her over to stay in their cabinets or under their sinks or under their couches. They were all honey badgers, too, which meant two things: their parents were unfazed to find a child badger sleeping in their cabinets; and all the honey badger parents hated hyenas anyway and didn't blame the kid for not staying at her "official" home.

When Mads was finally old enough to move away from her

mother, she rented an apartment for a while but didn't really live there. Not after that time she'd come home to find a couple of the clan's males standing outside, watching it. That's when she went back to crashing in people's cabinets. It was safer. Even if she had to break into a stranger's house and risk arrest, it was safer than dealing with her mother and the rest of the Galendotter Hyena Clan.

When Charlie closed the front door behind her, Mads heard the coyote that had taken up residence in her house suddenly charge across the bedroom he had been sleeping in and race down to the first floor. He had already confronted her team-mates, and that had worked out fine. Max had simply smiled at the wild animal, sending it fleeing deep into the house. It was disturbing but nothing they hadn't seen before when it came to Max.

But Mads didn't think Charlie had dealt with the coyote yet and she didn't want anyone hurt. The coyote could be mean. Charlie could be meaner. As it was, Finn kind of hated the little guy. Then again, he wasn't really a dog fan. "They just look dumb to me," he'd say when he saw one of Charlie's dogs running around her backyard.

Mads walked over to Charlie, planning to step in front of her to block the coyote from getting close. But the little bastard used Mads as a ladder, jumping at her and climbing up and over Mads's shoulder before launching himself into Charlie's arms.

"Hello, you!" Charlie greeted the coyote. Mads watched Charlie rub her nose against the canine's muzzle before she allowed it to lick her face like she'd just come back from war. That was something even Mads didn't let the animal do. It was gross. She knew where that tongue had been. Mads only allowed the animal to roam around her property because he kept the place clean of vermin and it was funny to watch Finn argue with a wild beast as if he expected it to reply in full sentences.

After a lot of kissing and cuddling, Charlie finally placed the coyote on the ground and walked over to the rest of the team, flopping down in one of the stuffed chairs near the big couch.

Charlie briefly studied the chair before letting her gaze roam around the room. "Nice job with the furniture, Mads."

Before Mads could say anything, Nelle replied, "Thank you."

"I never asked you to decorate my house," Mads reminded her teammate.

"You weren't going to do it," Nelle shot back. "And none of us wanted to have these kinds of discussions while sitting on a hard, unclean floor."

"How do you know my floor is unclean?"

"Have you cleaned it?"

"I haven't had time—"

"That's why I also got you a cleaning service."

Mads walked back over to where her teammates were sitting and gawked at Nelle. "You got me a cleaning service?"

"Yes. They'll come by once a week. Clean the place and keep your refrigerator stocked after throwing out anything that's expired. It's a very good service."

"How will they get in my house?"

Nelle frowned. "They have keys."

"There are strangers with keys to my house?"

"If we don't want to be sitting in coyote filth . . . *yes*."

Mads started toward Nelle—you know, to beat some sense into her—but Tock grabbed her arm and pulled her onto the couch beside her.

"Leave it," Tock told her.

"But—"

"Leave it. You know Nelle fights dirty."

"All while looking amazing in these shoes," Nelle added, holding one long leg out so they could all witness her ridiculously high "whore shoes" as Mads liked to call them. Whore shoes that cost at least five figures per pair.

The coyote jumped into Charlie's lap, climbed onto her shoulders, and curled himself around the back of her neck. He looked like a large fox stole except he was glaring at all the other badgers in warning.

With the coyote now situated, Charlie leaned forward and rested her elbows on her knees, clasping her hands in front of her.

"So," she began, "how are we all doing? After what happened with Tock."

There was an extremely long moment of silence before Max finally asked, "Huh?"

A sentiment that made Mads feel better. It proved she wasn't the only one confused by the question.

"How are you guys doing?"

"In what sense?" Nelle wanted to know.

"What happened to Tock was traumatic."

"It was?" Tock asked.

"Yeah. Sure." Charlie shrugged. "I guess."

Eyes narrowed, Max asked, "What are you doing?"

"I'm managing my team. You guys are my team," she said with a sweeping arm. "And I'm managing . . . you."

"Why?" Mads finally asked. "Why are you doing this?"

Charlie threw up her hands before pulling her phone out of the back pocket of her jeans. "I think I have to."

"Why would you have to?"

"It's in the book." She pointed at her phone and Max quickly went over to her sister's side.

"What is this?" she asked, taking the phone out of Charlie's hand. "*Managing Your Team*," she read out loud. "Dear God, what is this?"

"When they hired us, they sent me that book. I didn't really think about it, but then Imani called and she was all, 'Have you talked to your team? And are they doing okay?' And when I responded, 'I guess they're okay. They ate,' she made this sound of disgust. Like I was fucking up somehow."

"She knows we're honey badgers, right?" Max asked. "We don't really get . . . you know . . . traumatized."

"Yeah," Streep agreed. "That sounds like a cat issue . . . definitely a dog's."

"Canines are sensitive," Charlie agreed, petting the coyote's muzzle. "But I just want to make sure you guys are okay."

"We weren't even there," Max noted.

"I was pissed she would put the upcoming championship at risk." Mads felt the need to point out, ignoring Tock's enormous eye roll. "But other than that . . . I'm fine."

"*I*," Streep announced, hand pressed to her chest, "was very concerned about Tock. I kept thinking, Is she safe? Is she alive?" Tears began to fall. "What if we'd lost her forever?" She wiped her face with the back of her other hand. "We are *all* friends and Tock means the world to us. We can't lose her! Not like this!"

Charlie gazed at a sobbing Streep for several seconds before telling her, "You know you gave me almost the exact same speech that time we couldn't find Max, right?"

Looking up, Streep said, "Sorry?"

"Remember? You guys were in tenth grade, and I was worried that she'd either been kidnapped by that drug dealer trying to kill Dad *or* she'd decided to track down the drug dealer and kill him herself. Turned out she was just with her boyfriend, but you guys were covering for her. And that's when you gave that speech. That speech you just gave. Tears came in at the same time, too."

"Oh." She sat up straight, tears now gone, and sniffed. "Well . . . in answer to your question," she replied calmly, "yes. I'm fine."

They all looked at Nelle, but she was texting on her phone. "Yeah, yeah, yeah," she said, waving with one hand before going back to her texting, "Devastation. Tragedy. Blah blah blah. Glad she's alive."

Max handed Charlie her phone back. "Maybe badgers and wolverines should have their own team-managing handbook." She sat down in her chair and pointed at Charlie's phone. "Because if they suggest forced frivolity and team-building exercises that involve trust falls"—she shook her head—"that information is *not* for us."

Shay followed Keane into the house; Finn came behind him with Dani "helping" her Uncle Finn to carry in the crate with all the puppies.

"Where do you want it?" Finn asked.

He shrugged. "Out back, I guess."

"Oh . . . Daddy."

Shay faced his daughter. "What did I do now?"

"Outside? In the harsh elements?"

"Harsh elements? It's summer."

"And their dog houses are air conditioned," Finn added. "Much to my disgust."

"Princess and the puppies will go in my room," Dani informed them with a superiority only found in tiger and lion cubs. "She'll need blankets and space so Princess can care for the puppies."

"Or," Keane said, "we can just put her back outside where she was doing a great job of being a dog mom."

Dani's silent glare was so intense, Keane turned around and walked away. Dani was a naturally sweet girl, but like any cat, she had a temper.

"Is putting them in your room necessary?" Shay asked. He wasn't put off by his daughter's glares. That was why she rarely bothered to level them at him.

"It's the cleanest room in the house because I make sure it's the cleanest."

"The house isn't dirty."

"But you could eat off my floor if you were so inclined."

"If I was so inclined?" Shay said with a laugh.

"And," his daughter went on, lifting her arm high, her hand holding the tome that Charlie had given her so Shay couldn't avoid seeing it, "according to the book, at this age, the puppies need to be fed every three to four hours. And they need warmth. And their mother needs to lick them to help with their"—she stopped short and looked around at her two uncles and Shay before whispering—"bodily functions."

"Ew," Keane said, lip curling in disgust.

"Cats do the same thing," Finn argued.

"Ewwwww."

"Not shifter cats, you idiot. Cat cats. We, shifters, are born human . . . and like most humans, we start pooping and peeing on our own, I guess. Wait . . . do we?"

"So they're going to be in your room, peeing and pooping all over the place?" Keane asked. "And you want that?"

"I want them to be safe and healthy and confident in their surroundings. Not outside with two big male dogs and all sorts of other animals running around, scaring them. And you're not going to get in my way, Uncle *Mean*."

"Uncle Mean, huh?" Keane demanded, picking up a squealing and laughing Dani. "Let me show you how mean I am!" he said, tossing Shay's daughter in the air.

He loved watching his older brother with Dani. It was one of the only times the man ever smiled or laughed. Not since their dad had died . . . well. Yeah. That horrible day, when they'd gotten the news, they'd all changed. Everything had changed. Only when he was with Dani or Nat did Keane remind Shay of the brother he used to be.

Shay's new phone vibrated in his pocket, and he pulled it out. As soon as he saw his daughter's mother was calling, he said to Keane, "Put her down. And you"—he pointed at Dani—"get your room set up so Princess and the pups can relax. They had a big day."

"According to the book, Daddy, you shouldn't have taken the puppies or Princess out of the house. They're not vaccinated yet and—"

"Can you chastise me about all the things I did wrong later, baby?"

"Okay."

Shay waited until Dani led Finn and Princess up the stairs to her room.

Once his daughter was gone, he walked outside and called her mother back.

"Hi, Chu," he said as he leaned his ass against the front of the SUV, facing away from the house so he could have some privacy.

"Hey, Shay. How's it going? How's life?"

Shay immediately rolled his eyes. He always knew Chu was up to something when she started out asking him how he was doing, because she really didn't care how anyone was doing. A true tigress, Chu didn't bother with memories of good times or arguments over . . . well . . . anything. She didn't even worry about child support. Instead, they'd equitably worked it out so Shay paid for Dani's private school education and future college tuition and let the kid stay with him and his family anytime Chu wanted her to, which was way more than one would think.

Honestly, he'd be fine with Dani living with him full time, but she loved her mother, and he didn't want her to ever feel she had to choose. Because she didn't. Not when he understood Dani's mother the same way he understood Keane. At the end of the day, the pair of them only cared about two things: grudges and football.

"What's going on, Chu? What do you need?"

"Would it be okay if Dani stays with you for a little bit?"

"Why? What are you doing?"

"I . . . uh . . . I have a boyfriend and we're going to go to a hotel and bone for a few days."

Shay sighed. "Chu, don't lie to me."

"Fine! I was with the boys at their two-week football training camp, and I was showing the coach some moves he hadn't seen before—"

"Because they're full-human and haven't seen anything that shifter football has to offer."

"Whatever. I promised I'd stay and help out as a team mom. But not if Dani can't stay with you—"

"Of course she can stay with me."

"Are you sure? Because if it's going to be a big deal—"

"My daughter staying with me is never a big deal."

"I bet Keane has a problem with it."

"Keane doesn't have a problem with Dani staying here. He has a problem with you. Mostly because he still hasn't forgiven you for that playoff game six years ago."

"He got in my way."

"We were on the same team!" Shay stopped, let out a breath. "Look, Chu, it is what it is. I just want my baby to know she's loved."

"She's loved. I let her know she's loved. I love my daughter."

"Then stop dropping her off at the house without telling me. No one was home when she came today, and I'm worried we're going to give her a complex."

"It was a last-minute thing."

"I don't care. She can be here whenever she needs to be. That's never a problem. But I don't want her to feel like she's being tossed around all over the place. She needs to feel confident and safe. Oh, shit."

"What?"

"That's kind of what she said about the fucking puppies."

"What puppies?"

"Forget it. Do you want me to put her on the phone so you can talk to her?"

"She has a phone. I already texted her."

"You . . . you *texted* her you were leaving her here?"

"Yeah. Why?"

Shay closed his eyes and shook his head. "Nothing. Just . . . nothing."

"Don't be such a drama cat, Shay. I swear, all you Malone boys. Thankfully, *my* daughter is not nearly as sensitive as you."

"Uh-huh."

"And just so you know, she could have come with me today. She didn't want to."

"I can't believe I have to say this to you again, but *our daughter hates football!*"

"No need to yell it. I know. But I just want *you* to know she did have options, and when she said she wanted to stay with you instead of coming with us . . ."

Not wanting to have this discussion yet again, Shay said, "I'll take care of it. Talk to you later, Chu."

She disconnected the call. Didn't even say goodbye. An action which in no way signified she was angry. It was just Chu's way.

Still shaking his head, Shay turned back toward the house. Only to find Keane standing in front of the door.

"She's leaving her here again?"

"It's for football."

"I don't care. This is *my* niece we're talking about." He came down the two steps and whispered loudly through clenched teeth, "*I won't let her hurt Dani.*"

"Let me handle this."

"But you handle it *poorly.*"

Unwilling to have this discussion with his brother, Shay walked back into the house after pushing Keane out of his way with his shoulder.

"That was weak!" Keane yelled after him. "I expect better hits at practice tomorrow!"

"How are we doing on the Malone case?"

The teammates traded glances; it was Nelle who spoke up first. "We didn't know it was one of our cases."

"I put it in the system," Charlie said.

Max leaned forward. "We have a 'system'?" she asked with air quotes.

"We have a system. They keep giving me stuff, like the office, the computer stuff, the weaponry, the system, and I just take it. Looking at the equipment and guesstimating prices . . . we're better equipped than most SEAL teams."

"That's awesome." Max let out a happy sigh before she abruptly stood. "Come on! Let's go kill somethin'!"

"Down, Max," Charlie ordered. "You can't use this stuff unless you're on one of our cases."

"You think they'll check?" Tock asked.

"They do the cleanup . . . they'll check."

Tock had toyed with the idea of maybe using the new equipment to build the devices she used to get in and out of anything—especially safes—but now she wouldn't. Although it would save her money and effort, she didn't like the idea of these people being in her business.

"All we've found out so far," Mads admitted, "is that the

BORN TO BE BADGER   161

Malones' father was CIA, and he was investigating something on his own when he was killed."

"CIA? He was a spy?"

"Human division."

"Did the brothers know?"

"No. Not at all."

Charlie leaned back in her chair and the coyote licked the side of her face before nuzzling her neck.

"I don't know anything about the CIA," she admitted. "The shifter division did try to recruit Max, but I put a stop to that."

"I could have had a fabulous career," Max said.

"Or started World War Three," Tock muttered.

"What's going on with them now?" Charlie asked about the brothers.

"Finn convinced them to take a break from trying to find out what happened," Mads explained. "But that won't last long. Not with the Malones."

Charlie focused on Tock. "Can your grandmother help?"

Tock's entire body tightened, and she grew hot, then cold. "What? Why . . . why would you even ask me that?"

"If anyone has CIA contacts, it's got to be your grandmother."

"No."

"No . . . she doesn't have CIA contacts? Or no—"

"No. As in no, you're not involving my grandmother. That is not a good idea."

"Why not? She could get the information quicker than we ever could. And she kind of owes Keane and Finn."

"Owes them?" Mads asked. "For what?"

"They stopped me from killing her when Tock was in the hospital. Because I was about to. But they stopped me, so she owes them."

"And why were you trying to kill her?" Nelle asked.

"Because we had talked about her staying away from Stevie and, apparently, she didn't believe how serious I was about that."

"Wait." Tock sat up straight, shocked by this new information. "When did you talk to my grandmother?"

Charlie shrugged. "I don't know. I was fourteen, maybe fifteen. And she showed up at the Pack house wanting to talk about taking Stevie to Israel. It was a very nice conversation. We had tea and cookies. But I thought I made myself clear."

"Didn't Stevie say she just started working with her?" Max asked.

"I didn't put an age limit on it. I didn't say, 'My baby sister is untouchable until she turns twenty-one.' I was extremely clear. Stay away from Stevie." She thought a moment before adding, "And Max."

Charlie wasn't the only one who'd made things clear. So had Tock. She'd sat down with her grandmother and told her to stay away from her teammates and their families. All of them. She'd gone out of her way to ensure they'd never directly meet. To find out her grandmother had gone behind her back . . .

"I cannot have you guys involving my grandmother," Tock said.

"But she's already involved."

"Not with us. With the ones using that toxin against us. Let her focus on that." When everyone simply stared at her, Tock said, "Look, my grandmother can be very . . . manipulative. She's basically Rasputin in a designer suit with a Glock tucked into the back of her skirt. And what starts off with, 'Can you do this one thing for me, *metuka*?' turns into, 'You did so great with that, can you also help me with this?' Until you wake up one day and you're living in an Israeli kibbutz, waiting for her next command."

"Us?" Charlie asked, incredulous. "You think she can do that to *us*?"

Tock shrugged. "She did it to Margaret Thatcher. Gerald Ford. Leonid Brezhnev." She winced a little. "The family rabbi."

Charlie shrugged. "So?"

"Well, if she can do that to a man of God, what will she do to you idiots?"

★   ★   ★

Shay forced himself into a very uncomfortable position on the floor beside his daughter, pulling his long legs in and crossing them so that he didn't kick Princess in the face. Dani had seated herself on the floor, right by the puppies and their mother.

His daughter had taken a big wooden box from the backyard and filled it with thick, warm blankets. She sat outside the box but stretched her arm in to gently pet one of the sleeping pups while some of the others nursed from their mother. It was a serene moment, but he didn't like the look of sadness on his daughter's face. He never wanted her to be sad, but he knew from his own experience that parents could only do so much. Being sad was just part of life. What he didn't want—and what always worried him deep inside—was for her to wallow. Keane wallowed. Shay didn't want his daughter to become like Keane.

"You're not staying up all night watching them," he told her.

"I wasn't planning to."

"Good. Their mother knows how to take care of them."

"That doesn't mean we can't help her. These little guys have needs, and we should help as much as we can."

That was the moment when Shay noticed that she'd adjusted the AC so that it felt as if the house was being heated rather than cooled. In the summer.

"What's going on with the temperature?"

"According to the book, puppies need to be kept warm."

"Your uncles aren't going to like that."

"My uncles are not defenseless, innocent pups. They can grab a fan."

Shay dropped his head quickly. He didn't want her to see him smile. He wasn't laughing at her, but she might think he was. His Dani was very sensitive to what she considered insults.

"Uh . . . did you get the"—he hated saying the next word—"text . . . from your mom?"

"Yes. And before you ask, I'm fine. She said I could go with them, but I'd rather drive nails in my hand than watch a bunch of gross boys run around like idiots."

"Okay."

He saw her look at him from the corner of her eye before she asked, "Are you okay with me staying here until Mom is done doing summer football stuff for the boys?"

"Why are you asking me stupid questions?"

Now she looked directly at him. "It wasn't a stupid question. It was polite. You should never assume people have time for a houseguest."

"Dani, you're my daughter. You're not a houseguest. You're my daughter and you live here just like you live with your mom. This is your house as much as it's mine."

"Uncle Finn says he paid for the house."

"Uncle Finn is delusional!" he snapped before getting control. "I put in the down payment."

"But Uncle Keane says—"

"I don't want to talk about that. I'm not having this argument again."

The sides of her mouth turned up a little as she fought not to smile at his annoyance. "Okay. But you may want to check in with Gran, because she seems to think this house belongs to—"

"Oh, my God! This family!" He smiled at his daughter's giggling and said, "Tomorrow. What's the plan? Math camp, right?"

"No. Puppies. They need to go to the vet. According to the book—"

"Please don't mention that book again tonight. Okay? We'll just figure it all out in the morning. But whatever we do, I can't miss team practice. Keane is not going to be okay with me missing that."

"Uncle Mean will have to suck it up. The puppies come first."

"You're free to argue that point with him—"

"And I will."

"—but let's not go into this situation looking for a fight with the man you call Uncle Mean."

"He's not mean to me," she replied. "He's just mean to everyone else."

Dani suddenly rested against his arm. "And thanks, Daddy."

"For what?"

"I don't know. Just felt like saying it."

"Yeah. I totally get that." He kissed the top of her head. "I love you, Deacon."

Dani sat up and glared at her father. "Why did you give me a football nickname?"

"You can pretend it's religious."

"But it's not. You named me after Deacon Jones!"

"The man came up with 'sacking the quarterback.' He was part of the Fearsome Foursome. He was the secretary of defense! Just like you are . . . by protecting these puppies."

Shay spread his arms wide and grinned, proud of how he'd made that whole thing work.

His daughter's face, however, scrunched into an expression of obvious disgust, and she again hit him with "Oh . . . Daddy."

"Why don't *I* handle your grandmother?" Charlie asked. "And leave the rest of you out of it? Because I know you weren't calling *me* an idiot."

"I was not," Tock replied. "I was definitely not calling *you* that."

"Look"—Charlie stood, the coyote still on her shoulders— "I've already dealt with your grandmother before. We've had tea. You guys don't even have to be involved."

"That works for me."

The voice came from the other side of the living room, and Tock's teammates reacted as she would expect them to. Mads, Streep, and Nelle pulled out the handguns they had tucked into the back of their jeans or shorts. Max unleashed two of the six blades she had strapped to her back, one in each hand. And Charlie had a blade in one hand and a gun in the other. While the other four waited to see who had managed to sneak up on them, Charlie immediately let her blade fly; she probably didn't want to disturb the neighbors by firing her gun.

Tock didn't do anything, though. Because she instantly recognized the voice.

Her grandmother's head moved to the side just enough to avoid the blade while she continued to eat from a plate of reheated spaghetti ladled with the sauce they'd brought back from Charlie's house and stowed in the refrigerator nearly an hour ago.

Meaning her grandmother had been somewhere in the house all this time. Just . . . hanging out.

Standing by the hallway on the other side of the living room, which led to the kitchen, she slurped spaghetti into her mouth while calmly gazing at the others. Not even acknowledging Tock.

She gestured at the food with her fork. "This . . . is amazing. You made this, yes, Charlie?"

Charlie nodded but didn't verbally reply.

"So good. I have been around the world many times, and this might be the best meat sauce I have ever had." She took in another mouthful before motioning at the team with her fork. "Keep going," she mumbled through her food. "Don't mind me. I'm just eating."

"I have to say"—Charlie looked at the others—"you getting in here without us knowing . . . that's impressive."

She began to politely applaud and the others joined in. But not Tock. She felt no need to applaud anything.

"Thank you, dear." Mira Malka-Lepstein walked toward them in designer shoes that gave her an extra five inches. Shoes Tock would never dare wear because she was sure she'd fall on her ass. "Look at all of you. So lovely. And how you have grown. So beautiful. So honey badger. Your families must be proud." Stopping in front of Tock's team, her grandmother said, "For years, I have wanted to meet you, but my sweet Emily wanted to keep us apart. I have no idea why. The two of us have always been so close."

Disgusted, Tock simply walked out of Mads's house.

She just couldn't stand there and listen to her grandmother another second.

As she slammed the door shut, she saw two of her cousins relaxing against a brand-new black Mercedes-Benz. She gave them a short wave—her mother would kill her if she was rude to her cousins—and started off down the street. As she walked, she saw something flash in another car and realized that other cousins were in a car parked at the end of the street. The ones planning to follow her, maybe. For her "protection," she knew, but it still bothered her.

She couldn't go to the place she'd been staying. She knew her family would be there waiting for her. She was starting to see they were all over this street. Watching Mads's place and Charlie's. Even the triplet bears' house. Because her grandmother had to insert herself and her five-inch designer heels into everything.

And Tock was just not in the mood to deal with it.

Chapter 11

"*What is that noise?*" Keane roared from his room, waking Shay up.

"It's the damn puppies!" Finn yelled back.

"They're just whining a little! Stop complaining!" Dani ordered.

"Do you have to wake me up like this every morning?" Dale yelled from his room.

Shay had thought his youngest brother was going to be gone for a few more days, but he should have known better. All Dale's "buddies" were full-humans, which meant they were instinctually terrified of Dale's "big" brothers. But when they annoyed Dale enough, they would also become terrified of him. They simply didn't know why.

Chances were that once Dale hit his "growth spurt," they would be terrified of him all the time. But that hadn't happened yet. Instead, he just looked like your typical tall, skinny teenager who was about to go to college.

Shay didn't know what was taking his brother so long. Shay hit his growth spurt when he was fifteen. Finn when he was sixteen. And Keane when he was thirteen! Making him one of the most complained about kids in junior high football in American history. Every parent on the opposing teams was sure that he was a thirty-five-year-old man trying to relive his glory years. Eventually, their mother had to find a shifter-only league on Long Island for cubs and pups. But both Keane and Shay still had to go into the older group because of their sheer size.

Swinging his legs over the side of the bed, Shay sat up and ran his hands through his hair. Some people used an alarm clock or their phones to wake them up every morning. Shay just used the screaming of his family. For natural-born predators known for their silent hunting, the Malones certainly were a noisy gang of tigers.

Needing some orange juice and whatever meat he could find in one of the family refrigerators, Shay made his way downstairs. His mother still wasn't back, and he had no idea when she would be. Once she and her sisters started gambling, they could be gone for a while. Shay didn't get it, though. Gambling. Then again, he never found losing fun. With football, he had a modicum of control over things, but there was no control over poker or dice unless you cheated, and Shay didn't cheat. He, like his brothers, found it distasteful.

Yawning and making cat sounds most past girlfriends found "weird and unholy," Shay pulled the orange juice out of the refrigerator and put it on the kitchen table. He then opened a cabinet door and grabbed a glass. As he poured himself some orange juice, he stopped . . . and blinked. Putting the half-full glass down on the table, he opened the cabinet door again.

"Uhhhh . . . hi."

With her body contorted so that she didn't damage any of the glassware, Tock still managed to make it appear that being stuffed in a cabinet was normal. "Hey," she grumbled.

"Need anything?"

"No."

"Okay." Shay closed the door again and finished pouring his juice. He was draining his second glass when Keane arrived in the kitchen.

"I cannot deal with those dogs being in our house."

"Talk to your niece. I'm not getting involved."

"You *are* involved. You brought those disgusting animals into our house and now we're dealing with their offspring."

"For eight weeks. Then we'll give them away."

"Who in the world would want puppies? I mean, besides Charlie?"

"Lots of people. Lots of people want puppies."

Keane growled and went to the cabinet to grab his own glass. Shay didn't turn around because he didn't need to. He simply heard the cabinet door close and his brother snarl, "Why do badgers keep ending up in our cabinets? Did this one even bring Danish?"

"Tock, did you bring Danish?" Shay said loudly so she could hear him through the wooden door.

"No."

Shay faced his brother. "No. She did not bring Danish."

"Then get her out of our cabinet."

"It could be worse," he reminded Keane. "It could be like that time we had a racoon living inside our walls. It took us forever to get that thing out of there, and then we had to sanitize and repair everything. We won't have that worry with Tock."

"Are we sure?" Keane sneered before stomping off with his glass of juice.

Finn walked into the kitchen seconds after Keane walked out. "What's going on?"

"Tock is in the cabinet."

"Oh! Did she bring Danish?"

"Should I tell Mads that you're here?" Finn asked through the cabinet door.

"I don't care."

"You okay?"

"I'm fine."

A few seconds later, the cabinet door opened again and, to Tock's surprise, she was faced not with one of the Malone brothers but with Shay's daughter. Her father held her up so she could look directly at Tock.

"You don't look fine," the ten-year-old told her. "Would you like some coffee?"

"Coffee?" That actually sounded good.

"Yes. I make coffee for my mom all the time. She usually needs to spend a lot of time managing my brothers in the morning. I'm very self-sufficient."

"That would be nice. Thank you."

"Sure. I hope it's okay, but I usually make it strong and black. Just the way my mom likes her—"

"Okay!" Shay barked, quickly closing the cabinet door before his daughter could finish that well-known phrase. And, for the first time in several hours, Tock laughed. Hard.

By the time the kid was pouring the coffee into a big mug with ROCKY MOUNTAINS written across the outside, Tock had slipped out of the cabinet and was now standing in the middle of the Malones' kitchen.

"Here you go," Dani said, handing her the mug.

"Thank you." She took a sip, and the coffee was very good. "Where's your father?"

"Daddy jumped in the shower before Uncle Keane because he takes too long in there. They argue about it all the time."

Dani gestured to a chair at the kitchen table with a grand sweep of her arm. "Please, have a seat. And relax."

Kind of charmed by Shay's kid being quite the little awkward hostess, Tock sat down.

"Would you like some toast?"

"No, thank you. I'm fine."

"Okay." Grabbing her bright pink backpack from across the room, Dani sat down at the table, catty-corner from Tock.

Tock cringed. She was not in the mood to have a conversation with a kid. She was just not good at that sort of thing. For her, such conversations were always frustrating and uncomfortable; right now, she didn't want to do anything but drink this delicious coffee and be annoyed thinking about her grandmother.

She loved her savta. She really did. But the way Mira wormed her way into people's lives had always pissed Tock off. If she wanted to do that with heads of countries, that was fine. But treating everyone else the same way, especially family . . . Tock didn't need that from her or anyone.

Still, after using the Malone kitchen cabinets as a hotel room, Tock knew it would be rude to tell the kid to stop talking to her. Especially since she was kind of sweet.

After ten minutes or so, Tock finally realized something . . . The kid wasn't talking to her. She just opened her pink backpack, pulled out a pink notebook, a pink, rhinestone-covered box of pencils, and a textbook. She opened the book and notebook, took out a pencil, sharpened it, and got to work. Quietly.

Allowing Tock to just enjoy her coffee and the silence until the third time the kid erased something with her separate big white eraser. She didn't use the pencil eraser for some reason.

"What are you working on?" Tock finally asked after the fourth time Dani erased something on the same page.

"Equations. I can't figure this one out."

She moved the notebook over so Tock could see it. And Tock instantly knew the answer. She was even about to say it, but then remembered that she used to hate it when her mother just gave her the answers to problems. She wanted to figure them out herself. She was guessing Dani probably felt the same way.

"Okay," Tock said, putting down her coffee. "What's the first thing you do when you look at fractions?"

Shay finished tying his sneakers and quickly combed his hair back with his fingers. When he walked out of his room, Keane was just coming out of the bathroom. He gripped a towel around his waist and was brushing his teeth with an electric toothbrush while striding down the hallway to his room.

"Wha'?" Keane asked around his toothbrush because he knew what Shay's glare meant: *Why do you take so long in the goddamn bathroom?*

Dani took less time!

"I'm leaving in ten minutes," Shay informed Keane.

"Wh'?"

"Because we're taking the puppies to a vet before practice."

"Gonna be 'ait."

"I will not be late," Shay replied, wiping the toothpaste that had hit his chin. "There's a vet in the arena building. We'll just need someone to watch Dani and the pups afterward, until practice is done."

" 'ale."

"Good idea. Dale!" Shay called out.

"What?"

"You're going to need to come with us to practice so you can watch Dani and the puppies while we're training."

"I have a life, ya know!"

"You only have as much life as we allow you!" Finn yelled, dressed and already heading down the stairs. "Just get ready!"

"I really can't! I'm going to a college thing. You know I start in a few weeks."

"Okay, okay!"

"Don't worry," Shay told Keane when he came back out of the bathroom after spitting out his toothpaste and rinsing. "I'll just bring Dani with me to practice. We've done that before."

"But now she'll have those dogs."

"You'll just have to deal with the dogs, dude."

"Whatever. I'll be downstairs in ten," Keane added as Shay followed Finn to the first floor.

Together, the brothers headed to the kitchen. Tock and Dani were leaning over one of Dani's notebooks. He really didn't think about what they were doing, but they were clearly deeply involved. Both with pencils out, staring at something intently.

He also didn't bother *asking* them what they were doing. He simply went to one of the kitchen drawers and pulled out what he needed for Dani while Finn put together food for the family to eat while at practice.

As Shay worked, his daughter continued to focus on her notebook, but after a few minutes, he realized that Tock was gawking at him.

"What?"

"I . . . uh . . ." She gave a little shake of her head. "Huh."

Tock knew that Shay and Finn were moving around the kitchen, but she'd focused on the math instead. Much more interesting. Until she realized that Shay stood behind his daughter's chair. When she glanced up, she saw him parting the girl's hair with the end of a rattail comb. He held two black hair ties in his mouth. Once he parted the hair, he spritzed a little water on it, put in a little gel, and began French braiding first the left side, and then the right.

Initially, when she saw what Shay was doing, she was going to offer her assistance, but Shay didn't need it. At all. The man knew how to braid his daughter's hair. He didn't fumble around or look overwhelmed. Not the way her father used to when he had to manage her curls. Poor guy. Her father, like most of the men in their family, kept his hair short, so he didn't really know what to do with Tock's long, unruly locks. She used to joke that her father's hair was "Almost half an inch long! How did you let it get so out of control?" It was her mother who had curls similar to Tock's, and she had even put in a few dreads in her younger days that she never took out. She loved the hippy, living-by-the-beach look she maintained in the middle of Wisconsin. But her mother also made it her business to know how to do her Black daughter's hair. She didn't want anyone in her husband's family looking disgusted. Because they would.

And though Dani's hair was thick and bone straight—easy enough for most people to braid—Tock was still surprised to see any dad doing his daughter's hair. Not just brushing it and slapping a hairband on to keep it out of the kid's eyes, but actually doing a style. And doing it well!

"Are you ready to go?" Shay asked his daughter while he twisted the hair tie on the end of the second braid.

"Just need to get the pups and Princess."

"Can't believe all we're doing for that dog," Keane complained as he entered the kitchen and kissed his niece on the forehead.

"They're your responsibility, Uncle Mean. They live in your house."

"I didn't bring those things here. That was your father."

"Mads wants to know if you need a ride," Finn said to Tock, "or if you'll be coming in with us."

"You told her I was here?"

"Of course I told her you were here. Why wouldn't I? So she could yell at me for *not* telling her?"

"Your weakness disgusts me."

"Why are you hiding from your team?" Keane asked between downing several more glasses of orange juice.

"I'm not hiding from them. I'm hiding from my family."

"How is that *less* weird?"

"So you go out of your way to say 'good day' to all the Malones you meet on city streets?" Shay asked his brother.

"Fair point." Keane put the juice glass in the sink and asked, "Are we taking separate cars?"

Shay checked his daughter's hair carefully before appearing satisfied with the braids. "Do you want to drive with a bunch of whining puppies?"

"See you guys there. Shay, do not be late."

Keane and Finn left, grabbing big duffel bags with their team's colors and logo on them as well as a cooler filled with food and drink.

Shay ran up to the second floor, and Tock helped Dani put her school stuff back into her backpack.

"So you're in summer school?" Tock asked.

"No. This is for math camp."

"You're in math camp?"

"Yes."

"Trying to get your grades up for college?"

Dani laughed. "No. Just wanted to get a head start for fifth grade. That's when the pressure's really on."

"Pressure for what?"

"Okay, fine." She zipped up her bag and looking directly at Tock. "I just like math. I could have gone to a regular camp with fun outdoor adventures and s'mores and all that stuff every day. But I just wanted to work on math and occasionally do the s'mores thing and outside adventures every couple of weeks. I find math fun. Okay?"

Tock stood up. "I went to science camp every summer until ninth grade. While the other kids were working on their baking soda volcanos or were prodigies preparing for their fresh-men years at MIT, I was figuring out the physics of bringing down the cabins we slept in."

"Really? Why?"

She shrugged. "I like science."

"Not why were you in science camp. I understand going to science camp. Why were you trying to bring down the cabins?"

"They were there."

"Okay!" Shay suddenly announced before shoving a crate of puppies into Tock's arms. "Enough of that. Baby, why don't you leash up Princess—I think she's in the living room—and take her out to the car. I'll get your backpack."

"Do I really have to hold the crate?" Tock asked as the kid went in search of the adult dog. "These puppies smell weird."

"Could you *not* tell my daughter how you like to bomb things?"

"It's science."

"It's terrorism."

"It is not. I am very anti-terrorist."

"Good for you. If you want to talk the basics of math and science to my kid, feel free. But she doesn't need to hear about the felonies you and your friends were or are up to."

"Not friends. Teammates."

"Spare me," he sighed, slinging the bright pink backpack over his shoulder. He looked ridiculous, but also adorable. "Just no felony talk."

"Understood."

"Thank you. Ready, Dani?"

"Coming!" she yelped, attempting to hold onto the leash as Princess dragged the kid from the living room to the side door.

"Shit. Dani, give me the leash."

"I've got it."

"Dani—"

"I've got it!"

Shay threw his hands up. "Fine. But I want no tears when she drags you across the gravel."

"Thanks for your confidence, Dad."

Shay glanced at Tock, his eyes crossing. Tock chuckled at his fatherly exasperation while she grabbed her own black backpack with one hand and held onto the big crate containing the puppies with the other.

Shay was right. Telling a ten-year-old about her childhood felonies was probably not a good idea. Even if she did get away with all of them.

Mark didn't know what had happened. One second he was walking home from the gym, the next thing he knew, he was in a cage, chained to the floor. He wasn't alone. There were others in separate cages. About fifteen of them. Women and men, ranging in race and size and age.

He didn't get it, though. He was a strong guy. Six-two and could bench press two hundred and fifty pounds. Women asked him to walk them out of the office at night when they worked late. He was seen as a protector. Not some victim. But the ones who seemed to be controlling this situation were some international scumbags, speaking in a range of languages and willing to slap a girl around if she got too mouthy or cried too much. And there were others working with them. Giants. Massive males who gave one-word commands and growled.

Mark had never been scared before. Not since he was a kid. But he was scared now. Terrified. Because none of this was normal. Guys like him might get mugged. They might get shot. They definitely got challenged in drunken bar fights. But they did not get kidnapped for sex trafficking. It just didn't happen. Not to guys like him.

It got even worse when he realized they were on some kind of cargo ship, trapped in a massive container, and would be setting sail soon. On the ocean, anything could happen to them. He just didn't know what he could do. He'd tried to pull the chains from the floor. Tried to communicate with the other victims. Tried to kick their giant captors with his feet when they came into his cage, snarling at him to be quiet. But these massive men had dealt with Mark the way he and his brothers dealt with his five-year-old cousins, one of them holding him down while another chained his feet to the floor. They didn't even work up a sweat.

He also knew it was a bad thing that none of these scumbags hid their faces. They didn't wear masks and they didn't blindfold the captives. He watched a lot of streaming true-crime shows . . . he knew what that meant.

When the cargo ship's engines revved up, he began to pray. It was a last resort, but he was out of options.

The smaller guys were outside the container doors and the massive guys were coming through the container with clipboards. As if they were making sure they had enough cases of Rice-A-Roni for delivery rather than human beings locked in cages.

One of them stood outside Mark's cage, looking at each captive before jotting something down with the tiny pencil he had clutched in his massive hand. He glanced at the blond, older woman in the cage across from Mark's, looked at the clipboard and began to walk away . . . but then abruptly stopped. The giant studied the clipboard again, then—weirdly—lifted his head and sniffed the air. He did it several times, each sniff getting bigger and more dramatic.

He stomped back over to stare at the older woman in the cage. She was standing right by the bars, looking up at him with big blue eyes. Mark had heard her speak before. She had an accent. Russian, he guessed. She seemed to have been talking to herself ever since one of the smaller guys had unceremoniously dumped her in the cage a few hours ago.

The giant leaned in and took another sniff. Mark couldn't see the man's face, but he saw his entire body tense before he started to back up. He didn't get far, though. He was suddenly jerked forward toward the cage bars, a growl turning into a roar before he stumbled away.

He turned toward Mark's cage, hand over his throat, blood pouring from between his fingers, eyes wide in panic.

Shocked, Mark gawked at the woman. Her expression hadn't changed. It was still weirdly bored and unafraid, but now her mouth and jaw were covered in blood. Staring Mark in the eyes, she spit out what he could only guess was a thick piece of flesh.

Another one of the giants dropped his clipboard and ran over. He took one look at the bleeding male on the ground and suddenly charged at the woman's cage, his arm reaching between the bars to grab her.

She took hold of the man's arm and dug her teeth into his wrist, ignoring the screams of her victim as she tugged and pulled.

Mark couldn't look away from what he was seeing until he heard feet running over the top of his cage. He lifted his gaze in time to see a small woman launch herself at the back of the man getting his wrist ripped apart. She wrapped something around his neck and began to pull.

The giant tried to yank his arm away from the blonde, but she just went with him, allowing him to slam her, face-first, into the thick metal bars again and again. The other woman continued to pull whatever she held tight. Mark thought maybe it was rope, but when he saw all that blood dripping on the floor . . . piano wire, maybe? Did people still use that as a weapon?

Apparently. And it was doing the trick. The giant was getting weaker and weaker. The other giant was already dead on the floor from blood loss.

He could hear people calling to one another from outside the container. He could also hear gunshots. A lot of them.

The giant stumbled back now that the blonde had released his arm. But Mark soon realized she'd released his arm because she'd chewed off his hand. She tossed it over her shoulder and moved forward as the giant took several steps back. She put her hands on the bars of her cage and pushed, the door swinging open easily. Mark had no idea how she'd got that open. Or how long it had been unlocked.

The giant dropped to his knees, but somehow, despite the blood loss from his neck and wrist, he was still alive.

The blonde motioned to the other woman. "Move. You take too long."

"Give it a second."

"We have no seconds. Move!"

The woman did as told, pulling the piano wire from around the giant's throat and stepping off his back.

"Give me," the blonde ordered, holding out her hand; a semiauto handgun was slapped into her palm.

She pointed the weapon at the giant's head and without a wince or even a blink, she pulled the trigger. The man's brains splattered across the space between cages, hitting Mark in the face and chest.

Horrified, he quickly wiped the mess off as best he could, just in time to see two more older women walk into the container. They dragged a man with them. One of the smaller scumbags that had kept them all trapped. He was bloody and beaten, a bad wound on his shoulder telling Mark he might have been shot. But he was still able to walk. Or, more accurately, be dragged along.

"Tell them," one of the women ordered the man.

He spit at the floor and the second woman, an Asian with one side of her head shaved, grabbed his uninjured shoulder. He began to scream, although Mark didn't know why. But then he saw blood flowing from his shoulder and he wondered how long the woman's fingernails were. They must be long and thick to cause such damage. She must be strong, too, because Mark could hear the crunching of bone as she squeezed.

"Tell them," the man was ordered again.

The man barked out a reply in Italian, and the woman who liked piano wire argued back in Italian. She didn't look Italian, though. More like a dark-skinned Latina with long, black-and-white curly hair that reached down her back. She wore a sleeveless shirt, showing off a colorful skull tattoo on her shoulder that reminded him of an ex-girlfriend's love of Mexico's Day of the Dead.

After a few minutes of arguing, she shook her head and said, "He won't tell us anything."

"Doesn't his speaking Italian kind of answer the question, though?"

"It doesn't answer this." The one holding the scumbag's arm pulled something out of her back pocket and held it up. It was a tube filled with liquid. Mark didn't know what kind of liquid. "There are cases upon cases of this shit in another container. Headed to Italy."

"Motherfuckers," the Russian growled. "I say we go over there now and kill them all."

"No. They're not our problem. Not yet, anyway."

"We can't let that shit go."

"We won't. But first we're going to burn this thing to the ground."

"Good plan, my friend," the Russian said before raising her semiauto again and pulling the trigger at the last man.

"Dude!"

"Come on, Ox!"

"What is *wrong* with you?"

"We were going to keep him alive?" the Russian asked the other women. "For what?"

"I'm not in the mood to argue. Let's just go get the captain."

"I say we kill entire crew," the Russian announced.

"We are *not* killing the entire crew."

"Okay, sensitive Sally."

The four women strode toward the exit until Mark yelled out, "Hey! Heyyyy! What about us?"

The Russian faced him. "What about you? All so pathetic and weak. We should just leave you here to die."

"Oh, my God!" one of the other women snapped. "What is wrong with you today?"

"She is in a *mood*."

"I know. Right?"

The Latina quickly searched one of the huge males until she found keys. She briefly studied each one before choosing a key and using it to open Mark's cage.

Pressing the keys into his hand, she said, "Make sure everyone gets out in the next ten minutes. Understand?"

"Yeah."

She started to move away, but abruptly turned back, adding,

"So sorry about your trauma. Don't be afraid to go to therapy after all this. It does help."

"Therapy?" the Russian repeated. "Only Americans need therapy."

"You know who needs therapy right now?" one of the women told the Russian. "You. For whatever is going on with you. Deep, every day, *hours-long* therapy. That's what you need."

As the women walked out, one of them, the Asian, spun around at the last moment to point at Mark and add, "And you never saw us, kid." Then she made finger-guns, clicked her tongue against her teeth, and winked at him. It was weird.

Once the women were gone, Mark quickly helped the others get out. Those who were strong enough to walk on their own helped those who were nearly catatonic with fear, and together they escaped their cages, the container, and the cargo ship.

They were on the dock when the ground beneath them shook. They turned in time to see the cargo ship begin to go down as crewmen jumped into the water or scrambled onto the dock to get away.

When the cops, the Feds, the Coast Guard, and every other government agency assigned to the case asked Mark and all the other captives what had happened on that cargo ship, they all had the same answer:

"No idea."

Chapter 12

"Was that you?"

Tock looked away from the waiting room TV screen with BREAKING NEWS splashed across it and glared at Shay.

"No. That wasn't me. I am much more eloquent . . . and subtle," she answered.

"Subtle?"

"There is a skill involved in what I do."

"What do you do?"

Tock and Shay looked down at the child who'd just asked that question and both replied, "Basketball."

"I play basketball," Tock reiterated.

"What does that have to do with that ship going down at the docks?" Dani asked, gesturing to the TV news they'd all been watching.

"You need a stupider child," Tock informed her father.

"I really do."

"Okay. Dr. Maurice is ready for you now." The trio was led into another room with Princess and her crate of puppies.

Sadly, the shifter vet who handled dogs and cats as well as broken fangs, cracked claws, or torn groins after nasty fights couldn't look at Shay's puppies due to a packed schedule. So that meant they had to go to the vet's office on the upper-level floors that were filled with full-humans. Not a problem, though. Tock was used to working with full-humans.

But while Tock felt completely comfortable, Shay clearly did not. She understood. All those full-humans in the waiting room who were completely unaware of the building's lower levels that housed shifter-only sporting events, shifter-only food outlets and stores, and shifter-run offices didn't know what to make of such a large man. To them, he looked terrifying.

Good thing Keane hadn't come with them. These people might be taking their sick animals out of here just to get away from the terrifying Asian guys who had to turn slightly in order to get their massive shoulders through the average-sized doors.

It really didn't help things either when Shay suddenly yawned and the noises that came out of him were not what anyone would call human. It wasn't a growl or a roar, but it definitely wasn't human. His daughter had giggled at the noise, but everyone else just seemed . . . well, yeah . . . terrified. Tock had never heard a noise like that come out of anyone. It was loud and low and his tongue rolled out of his mouth like a red carpet rolled out at a movie premiere.

Thankfully, Dr. Maurice didn't seem put off by Shay's size, even though the cat took up a lot of space in the small exam room.

"I am really blown away," the vet said, gawking at Princess in obvious wonder. "I have never seen a Tosa Inu before. They're very rare in the States. She must have cost you a fortune."

"Uh . . ."

"And very well trained if your daughter can hold her leash." She smiled. "Which breeder did you get her from?"

"Uh . . ."

Fighting hard not to smile, Tock turned in her chair so she could look directly at Shay. She couldn't *wait* for the cat's answer.

"Actually . . . I got Princess and her brothers from the back of a truck at a King Kullen parking lot."

Eyes wide, the vet began pointing at Princess. "This . . . *this* dog, you got from a grocery store parking lot?"

"Yeah. A man was giving them away and wanted to get out of there before the cops came. So I took three of them."

"And . . . and you have those two brothers living together with their sister? At your house? With your very tiny daughter?"

"Well, before you worry, it wasn't one of her brothers that . . . you know . . ."

"Knocked her up?" Tock asked.

Shay nodded. "Yeah. Exactly."

"You're sure?" the vet pushed.

"Yes. It was this stray pit bull that had been hanging around the neighborhood for a while. I caught them, uh . . . you know."

Now the vet looked even more concerned. "So you're telling me these puppies are a mix of Tosa Inu *and* pit bull?" the vet asked.

"Yeah. He was a big pit, too. Like, at least a hundred pounds."

"Let me see if I understand . . . You bought dogs—"

"No. The guy just gave them to me. They were the last ones there and he had a scanner that told him the police were coming. He just wanted out of there."

"Okay. So you got these dogs, tossed them into your—"

"Backyard."

"Right. Backyard. Let a pit bull mate with one of them, and you now have a whole gang of random puppies."

"Yes."

Tock nodded her head and furrowed her brow as if she was simply listening intently to the conversation, but she had her hand across her mouth so Shay couldn't see her grin. She hadn't been so entertained in . . . years? Yeah. Maybe years.

Poor Dani, baby drama queen that she was, simply lowered her head and placed her hand over her face. She radiated embarrassment.

"Okay, first," the vet said, "I'm going to suggest you take the leash from your daughter while I get out one of our emergency muzzles."

"Why?" Shay glanced at his daughter and a calm Princess. "They're fine."

And sure, maybe Tock was wrong and there actually was a God, because it was at that moment the exam room door opened, and a vet tech walked in with a folder and—

Fangs bared, her vicious snarl filling the room, Princess hit the end of her leash, nearly taking poor Dani with her. But Tock grabbed the leash with one hand and smiled at the vet while Shay grabbed his child around the waist and pulled her onto his lap.

The vet tech immediately ran from the room, slamming the door behind her, and the vet tossed Shay the muzzle before announcing, "Well, we now know Princess is very protective of your daughter . . . so that's nice!"

"Princess is a Tosa Inu," the vet explained. "A very strong, very powerful dog from Japan. They look a lot like a mastiff but they're not. They're a Tosa Inu and they were originally bred for fighting."

"What's wrong with men?" Tock felt the need to ask Shay. "Why do you always have to make animals fight?"

"Why are you asking me?"

"I don't know." She shrugged. "You're here?"

"And," the vet continued, "because of their strength and power, they can be a very hard breed to handle."

"Meaning . . . ?"

"That the only reason that dog hasn't ripped your face off and used your daughter like a chew toy is because of what you are."

Confused, Shay frowned and asked, "Mongolian?"

Tock covered her mouth but the laugh slipped out.

"What?"

"Daddy, I think Dr. Maurice means what you *are*. What *we* are."

"What are you exactly?" The vet looked him over. "Bear?"

Now Tock just laughed out loud. The comment would only be a bigger insult if she'd called him a wolf.

"My daddy's a tiger, Dr. Maurice."

"Oh. Sorry."

Now Shay was panicked. This vet was definitely a full-human. "How do you know about . . . Would you *please* stop laughing!"

"Sorry, sorry." Tock waved her hand in front of her face.

The vet lifted a puppy out of the crate and began her examination by weighing each one on a small scale.

"My husband is African wild dog," she informed Shay in response to his partially asked question. "We met when I was in vet school. Sorry about calling you a bear. I don't spend much time around big cats."

After weighing each pup, she checked their heartbeats, claws, paws, and teeth.

"The puppies look great. Very healthy. Now, time to take a look at the momma."

Shay put his arms around Princess and lifted her as he stood. Before he could put her on the exam table, though, Tock took the muzzle from Dani and stepped over to the pair so she could put it on the dog. That's when Princess bared her fangs in warning at Tock for the first time.

"I *know* you didn't just growl at me," Tock told the dog.

Princess's mouth relaxed, her hackles went down, and she yawned. Tock stepped close and put the bucket muzzle around the dog's closed mouth.

Once secure, Shay put her on the exam table.

The vet examined the dog and took some blood. She asked about vaccines, and when Shay only gazed at her, she began writing furiously on her chart.

When Shay put Princess back on the floor, the vet said, "Mr. Malone, my strongest suggestion to you at this point is that you don't place these puppies with anyone other than the big shifters. That includes the smaller cats and dogs. No bobcats. No foxes. No jackals. Apex predators only, please."

"She's fine with me," Tock said. And when the vet only gazed at her, she added, "I'm honey badger."

"Ah. The psychotic, rage-filled assholes of the wild? Yeah,

I'm sure she's fine with you, but my suggestion still stands. Bears. Lions. Tigers. Wolf Pack. And start socializing those puppies *now*."

"You mean . . . socialize them outside their uncles and mother?"

The vet clenched her fists and, for a brief second, Shay was sure that the woman was going to punch him. But his daughter stepped forward and said, "Don't worry, Dr. Maurice. I'll be handling the puppies from now on."

"Well, thank God for that. Unbelievable." She shook her head at Shay. "You got them at a parking lot. Unbelievable."

"She wanted to beat you to death."

"I am aware."

"Who knew you could make a vet so mad? She deals with animals all day and yet you pushed her to the edge. It was hilarious."

They had left the vet's office and were making their way down to the world beneath. Of course, that sounded way more dramatic than it actually was. All you had to do was walk down some stairs and pass a couple of shifter security guards who gave a good sniff to make sure you were one of them.

"You want something to eat, baby?" Shay asked Dani, placing the crate with the puppies on a table near the Starbucks.

Tock dropped into a seat and Dani took one of the others.

"No, thank you, Daddy. Just some water."

Shay had walked into the coffee shop but walked right back out. "You're not hungry?" he asked, gazing down at his daughter. "What's wrong? You don't feel well? Do I need to take you home?"

"Um . . . no. Just wanted some water."

"When was the last time you ate? Did you eat before we left? What about some fruit? Do you want some fruit? Or cereal? I can get you some cereal."

"You are freaking her out," Tock told him. "You know what I'd love? A small coffee. Black. No sugar." She pushed a ten-dollar bill across the table, but Shay waved it away before looking his daughter over one more time and finally walking into the Starbucks.

"Thanks for coming with us today," Dani said once her father was gone.

"No problem. Your father is always so cute in his inherent confusion."

"I think I'm going to stay with him and my uncles until we find homes for the puppies."

"Probably a good idea. Will your mom be okay with that?" Tock's mom had become weepy when she spent the night at Streep's house or Nelle's mansion. Even now she received regular texts from her mother that basically said the same thing: "I haven't heard from you in days. Are you dead?" Tock had never wanted a sibling, but she always wondered if her mother would be less clingy if there were another child to distract her.

"My mom has my brothers in football camp, then they will start practice for football at their school, so I won't be missed. She'll be busy until after the Super Bowl."

"Does that bother you?"

"No. My test scores are always higher during football season."

Tock laughed at that.

Shay returned to their table. After watching the cat stare at the crate of puppies, Tock picked it up and placed it on the ground next to her legs and Princess.

With a grunt that she guessed was a thank-you, Shay put down a large coffee in front of Tock—she'd asked for the small—and a plate with several honey buns, which she hadn't ordered at all. He put a giant bottle of water in front of his daughter, as well as a bottle of orange juice, and a plate filled with cinnamon buns.

"Here. Eat," he ordered.

He went back into the coffee shop to bring out his own food.

"I don't want this," the kid said.

"How about the honey buns?" Tock loved honey but she wasn't a honey bun fan. There wasn't enough honey for her and the bun just felt gummy against her tongue. She'd rather just squeeze the contents of one of those bear-shaped honey containers directly into her mouth.

"No."

"Well, I'll take the cinnamon buns." She loved those. "Orange juice?"

"I really just wanted the water."

Tock took the juice, opened it, and drank it all in several gulps. She closed the bottle and put it back in front of Dani.

"You drank that," she said, pointing at the empty bottle.

Shay returned with his own three plates full of pastries, a large coffee, and a large bottle of water.

He sat down, carefully arranged everything around him, and then began to eat. But not before noting, "At least you drank the juice, baby."

Nodding, eyes wide, Dani replied, "Uh-huh."

"Here." Tock pushed her honey buns toward the big cat.

"You don't like?"

"They're okay. But I like cinnamon better. I like my honey plain and unfettered by stuff."

"Whatever that means."

They ate in silence while the kid pulled out her notebook and began working on her fractions again.

When Shay had finished shoveling food into his mouth with a speed Tock found fascinating, he reached across the table and took Tock's arm. As he turned it so he could see her watch, she no longer felt the desire to punch him for touching her without permission.

"Okay. I've got to get to practice. You ready, baby?"

"Do I have to go?" Dani whined.

"Baby, I can't leave you here." Shay gestured at the others sitting at nearby tables. "These are all killers and you're just a little cub. I can't leave you alone with any of them."

Tock dropped her head to hide her smile when she saw all the insulted glares leveled at the back of Shay's head.

"Um . . ." Tock cleared her throat. "I don't have practice for a couple of hours. She can hang with me."

"Oh, *please,* Daddy! Please, please, please, please, pleeeeeeeeeeasssssseeeee! Can I stay with Tock?"

"Well—"

"*Please!*"

"Okay! If you're really okay with it, Tock."

"Why wouldn't I be?" she said with a shrug. "She's doing math."

Dani nodded. "I am."

"I'll drop her off just before I go to practice."

"Okay." He stood and pointed at Dani. "Be good." He raised a brow at Tock. "You, too."

Chapter 13

"**Y**ou left our baby with a honey badger?"

Shay took a step back from his eldest brother's sudden burst of rage. "First off, she's not *our* baby. She's *my* baby. And second, it's Tock."

"Yeah," Finn agreed. "I'd be more worried if it were Max."

"Exactly."

"As we speak," Keane snarled, "she probably has her involved in a heist!"

"They're doing math."

"About diamonds?"

"Possibly, but not to steal them. Besides, I trust Tock." Shay blinked. "Huh. I trust Tock. Didn't see that coming."

"Not after she cut your throat," Keane muttered.

"That was an accident. And she just nicked the artery. Who among us hasn't lost control of their claws?"

"That's it. I'm going to find my niece."

Shay and Finn grabbed Keane and yanked him back.

"Dani is fine," Shay insisted.

"And Mads will be here in a few hours for basketball practice," Finn said. "She'll make sure everything's fine."

"What makes you think I trust Mads with my niece any more than I trust Tock?" Keane wanted to know.

"Because Mads is family."

"Since when?"

Shay grinned. "Since Finn fell in love with her."

Finn nodded and grinned back at Shay. "Yeah."

Keane looked from one brother to the other before announcing, "Both of you are idiots."

Dani didn't know how long she'd been working on her math problems before Tock said, "Let me see your work."

Annoyed, she snapped, "Oh, come on. It's been five minutes."

"It's been four hours, and if I hadn't put a smoothie in your hand and the straw to your lips, you would be a dehydrated husk right now."

"Four hours?" Dani hadn't noticed. That happened sometimes when she worked on math. While time ticked by so slowly she could scream when doing history or English—nothing was more boring! She already knew English anyway! She spoke it every day!—math time sailed by. Her mother might complain about her lack of interest in football, but she loved that she didn't have to worry her youngest child was getting into any trouble when she was quiet. Not like Dani's brothers. When they were quiet . . . something very bad was about to happen and Mom was about to send a whole lot of money to a whole lot of angry parents.

"Four hours," Tock confirmed. "I have to be honest, though. I didn't really notice. I was reading this book on . . . never mind. Let me see."

Dani pushed her notebook across the table. While Tock looked over Dani's work, Dani checked on Princess—she was fine. Asleep on the floor next to her feet—and the pups' crate. The crate sat on a chair, and Dani could see they were sleeping, too. But she'd need to find a place to let them nurse from their mother. Dr. Maurice had already sent a long-term feeding schedule, and Dani would need to look that over to learn when to transition the pups to more solid food.

She knew she wasn't supposed to be so involved in the care of these animals. As far back as she could remember, her mother had been telling her that dogs were nothing but "behind-sniffing losers that do nothing but beg and whine and eat. You're better off getting a goldfish as a pet." Dani didn't know if she believed her mother. She only half listened to her on most days. But her wonderful math teacher rescued animals. She had four dogs, five cats, a three-legged squirrel, a one-eyed racoon, and a very aggressive duck. Her dogs were all pit bulls, and she'd brought one in as an example of the good that could come from rescue work.

Dani had avoided the creature at first. He was big and slobbery and his breath smelled really bad. But he kept coming to her. At first, she didn't know why. She hadn't been welcoming and she knew the dog understood her true nature. But then she realized that two of the students—a boy and a girl—were making it uncomfortable. Kind of hurting it. The pair's love of bullying was the reason Dani avoided them herself. They were jerks. It was the same day her teacher had also brought the aggressive duck—where she'd found a muzzle for that thing, Dani didn't know—and she wasn't paying as much attention as usual to her dog. When the dog came over once again, Dani understood it wanted her protection. Without even thinking about it, she gave the animal just that. The same way her daddy and her uncles would. They never talked about it or made a big deal of it, but when some parents got crazy angry at her school soccer games or someone needed to be walked to their car after a late school function, her daddy was always there. So that's what she did. She turned into a protector. Of course, the situation did turn into a fight with those two kids, and they all got detention afterward, but that was fine. It was worth it.

"I marked the ones that you need to work on," Tock said, pointing at Dani's notebook. "There are only two of those, so you can get that horrified look off your face. You clearly grasp the concept of fractions now, so accept that you will still make mistakes and fix the ones that are wrong. Then, we'll move on so you don't become an obsessive psychopath that no one can stand to be around. Now . . . are you hungry?"

Dani was going to roll her eyes and tell Tock not to be like her dad, always worrying about Dani eating. She'd already had breakfast! But then she remembered it was actually almost one o'clock and she was, in fact, hungry.

They didn't have to go anywhere to get food, though. They'd decided to move from the coffee shop hours ago when they realized how busy it was. People coming and going, needing a caffeine fix. Eventually, they'd located a corner table in the back of the food court. It was the perfect spot. There was an outlet right under the table, so Tock could use her phone without worrying about a dead battery and the table was big enough so that Dani could spread out her textbooks and notebooks. Plus there was space for the dog and puppies so they didn't get in anyone's way.

After they were all comfortable, Dani lost all track of time until Tock asked about what she might want for lunch.

"Burger and fries?" Dani suggested.

"Sure. What do you want? Bison? Gazelle? Zebra's always good. Oh . . . and with cheese or without?" When Dani simply stared, Tock nodded as she walked off. "Right. For the baby cat, beef it is."

Dani carefully closed her notebook and textbooks and slipped them into her backpack. She put her pencils and eraser into the pink case her father had given her, taking a moment to organize them by size, and zipped it into the backpack's front pocket. When she was sure everything was secure inside the bag, she put it on the floor against her chair, bending at the waist to make certain she placed it exactly, perfectly on the—

The sound of the crate being opened had Dani sitting up straight in the plastic chair. Some kid she didn't know was holding one of the puppies. He stared at her with dark gold eyes; wild blond hair that appeared to have never been touched by a comb hung in his face. He kept jerking his head to get the strands out of his eyes. Two other boys with matching eyes and hair stood behind him, watching.

Princess snarled a little and Dani pressed her hand against the back of the dog's neck to calm her.

"Cute," he said, lifting the pup. "How much?"

"How much for what?"

"To buy. I want to buy a puppy."

"They're not for sale."

"Then let us play with them. Just for a little while. We'll be right over there. You can even watch us."

"No."

"Why not?"

"Because I said so."

Dani was getting angry. She hated when boys got pushy. It happened all the time at school, and more than once her mother or father had to go in to talk to her teacher about "Dani's aggression problem." It seemed her aggression problem was the fact that she didn't let boys her age push her around.

"I don't know why you're being this way," the boy argued.

"He said he'd pay for it," one of the other boys told her. "Just give it to him."

"No." She tried logic. "They're too young to be away from their mother."

Practically snarling at her, the boy holding the puppy asked, "Why you gotta be so difficult?"

Okay. She was done with logic. It was really making her mad that the kid kept pushing, expecting her to give in. Except . . . Dani didn't give in. Ever. She was a Malone.

"Put the puppy back in the crate," Dani ordered.

He snorted. "Or what?"

"Or"—Dani slammed her hands against the table and stood—"I'm going to climb over this table and *rip your face off!*"

The three boys reared back at her bellow, but before they could bolt off with the puppy, Tock was there. She didn't run over either. It was as if she just . . . appeared.

Standing between Dani and the boys, arms straight out to hold them away from each other if that became necessary, Tock asked Dani, "What's going on?"

"He—" was all Dani got out before Tock cut her off by asking, without turning around, "Where do you think you're going with that puppy?"

The three boys froze in the midst of walking away, and the one holding Princess's pup then proceeded to outright lie! "She said I could have him."

"You lying little—"

One upheld finger silenced Dani immediately. She didn't know why she responded like that to her father's friend. Because, by now, Dani's mother would have torn someone's arm off and ripped apart most of the building. Tock, however, remained calm and soft spoken. It was kind of underwhelming.

"We both know," Tock said to the boys, "that she didn't give you that puppy. So put it back in the crate and walk away."

"It's mine," the boy insisted. "She *gave* it to me."

With her finger still raised to keep Dani quiet and her head turned so she could keep the boys within sight, Tock said in the same calm tone, "Put the puppy back in the crate and walk. Away."

Then Tock smiled. It was just teeth and gums. No fangs. If Dani saw someone walking down the street with a smile like that, she wouldn't think anything of it. But coming from Tock the smile seemed . . . weird. Really, really weird.

Dani wasn't the only one who thought so. With his gaze locked on Tock's face, the boy slowly walked forward and put the puppy back into the crate. He started to move away, not bothering to close and secure the crate door. Still smiling, Tock tilted her head just a bit and he stopped, waited a beat, then secured the crate. After taking a few steps back, he and the two other boys turned around and took off running.

When Tock faced her, she asked Dani, "Are you okay?"

"I'm sorry, Tock. I didn't mean to get you into that."

"What are you apologizing for?"

Dani frowned. "For . . . for starting that fight."

"You didn't start anything. I heard the entire conversation while I was ordering the food. You were clear, concise, and very direct. And he ignored what you said. That was unacceptable, and you have absolutely no reason to apologize for a damn thing. Understand?"

"Yeah . . . ? I guess." She shrugged, not really wanting to discuss it anymore. "At least it's over."

"Oh, sweetie," Tock sighed, actually looking sad. "It's far from over."

Tock turned away from her just as five women stomped

around a nearby wall. They were all tall, had dark blond hair, a lot of makeup, and a lot of big gold jewelry. They also had dark gold eyes like the boys who stood just behind them. But they were adults and very angry.

"Was it you?" the one wearing the New York Rangers jersey and three thick gold chains demanded, pointing at Tock with her forefinger angled from a fist. "Was it you that put your hands on my son?"

Oh, my God! That kid was *such* a liar!

Still calm, Tock said, "I didn't do anything to your son. But you should have a talk with him about respecting boundaries. When a girl tells him 'no,' he should learn to respect that. Or you'll be talking to his big lion head through plexiglass."

The woman took in a breath. "You got something to say about my son?" she wanted to know.

"Yeah." Tock walked over to the woman until she stood right next to her, tilting her head up so she could look directly into her face. That's when Dani realized that Tock had her hand behind her back and with the same finger that had silenced her earlier, she now motioned Dani away. It was just a twitch, but she knew what Tock was telling her.

Tock was sending her away because she thought things might get bad with that woman, and she wanted Dani to be safe. And it would be all Dani's fault because she didn't know how to be nice to idiot boys.

Tock knew the second the kid took off because the She-lion's eyes flickered away from Tock's face. But she wanted to hold her attention until the kid was gone. She didn't want Shay's kid to see what she might be forced to do to this woman. Dani still had that adorable cub-innocence and Tock didn't want to be the one who stripped it away. Cats and dogs and especially bears were all such cute, sweet pups and cubs.

But honey badgers . . . well, they were born ready for a fight. It was how they survived in the wild. The only other cubs Tock could think of with that kind of edge were the hyenas. Of course, they weren't born with an edge like badgers;

they were just born mean. It was said that twins had to be separated at birth because they'd fight in their crib even though they still hadn't learned to crawl. Tock once watched a hyena baby knock out another with a left hook when they were both strapped into separate baby strollers.

It was funny, of course, but still . . .

Tock quickly moved her head to keep it right in front of the She-lion so she wouldn't notice Dani's escape. It worked, too. The She-lion glared down at her with the irrational rage of a mother with a horrible child.

"What the fuck you staring at?" the cat asked with one of those thick Staten Island accents that Tock found so offensive. Who could listen to that all day?

Of course, Tock's response to that very New York question would have to keep the She-lion's and her friends'—most likely sisters'—attention. The problem was that Tock wasn't like her teammates. She didn't have Streep's ability to burst into dramatic tears in less than three seconds. She didn't have Nelle's perpetual cool. She didn't have Mads's brutal rage. And she especially didn't have Max's off-putting good cheer, which could somehow stir a life-ending brawl at a royal wedding.

No. Tock had to go with what she was good at: being kind of weird.

"Oh, I'm not staring at anything," she said to the She-lion, letting her voice ease out of her like smoke from a chimney. "Just waiting for you to die."

Yep. That was weird. And the She-lion responded by shoving Tock back thirty feet.

"*What the fuck is wrong with you?*" the female wanted to know.

Sadly, that was a question Tock had heard many times before.

Shay was listening to one of Keane's rants about commitment and loyalty and "being on time"—that last one had been directed at him—when he heard "*Daddy!*" yelled across the training field.

Although he immediately knew his daughter's voice, every

other father in the arena looked around. It was instinct. A few of them might not be with the mothers of their children, but most of them insisted on being involved in the lives of their offspring. The idea of their exes hooking up with some full-human male who might try to raise their shifter child was too much for any of them to take.

"Dani?" He started to run over to where she stood, asking, "What's wrong?"

"Tock's about to get into a fight with a She-lion because her kid wanted a puppy!"

Shay slowly came to a halt and nodded. "Oh. Okay." He turned back to his brother to hear the end of the rant.

"Daddy?"

"She'll be fine, D," Keane called out. "Badgers and She-lions fight all the time. Don't worry about it. We'll finish the team meeting and then we'll go with you. Okay?"

Shay had nearly returned to his team when *"Daddy!"* was viciously screeched across the field. And it was not a plea. It was an order. One that must be followed. So Shay turned back around and started running toward the exit.

"Burt!" he called out to a black bear sitting on the sidelines, eating spoonfuls of honey from a jar. "Watch my kid."

"We can watch her," Keane argued, indicating himself and Finn. "We're not going any—"

"Go with him!" Dani ordered her uncles.

"Listen to me, little miss—"

"Nowwwwwwww!"

Shay was not surprised when his brothers caught up to him a few seconds later as he ran down the hall, following his daughter's scent back to the food court.

Keane stopped his brothers as soon as they got to the food court. He didn't want to be involved in this mess. He didn't want his family involved either.

The Malone name had a bad enough reputation; he wasn't about to make it worse by entangling himself and his brothers in what his father would have called "a Malone family reunion."

Tock wasn't even part of the fight! She'd been pushed aside by her teammates, who had probably just arrived at the sports complex for their own team's practice but decided it was a good idea to get into a screaming match with She-lions instead.

"I am not getting in a fight with Anya Morozov. We're leaving," Keane told his brothers.

"Going back without Tock?" Shay asked. "Dani will have your ass."

"Then go get her," Keane snarled between clenched teeth. Because this was embarrassing!

"Okay, okay. Calm down." Shay lumbered off like he had bear genes or something.

"You know she won't leave the others, right?" Finn asked with that smugness in his voice Keane was ready to beat out of him. He'd only gotten that tone since he'd been hooking up with Mads, and Keane didn't like it one bit!

"What?"

"Tock isn't going to leave her girls in the middle of a She-lion fight. So if you want us to move them out of here, you better step in yourself."

"Why me?"

"You know why."

"I'm not dating a She-lion. I'm definitely not dating a She-lion from Staten Island."

"I can't express to you how much *no one* wants you to date anyone, but you can still end the fight just by being yourself." Finn chuckled. "And one bad date with Donna Datolia, and the entire female shifter population of Staten Island is doomed?"

"Yes."

"Hey, Tock."

Tock looked away from what she liked to call "the crazy yelling" of her friends to find Shay standing next to her.

She'd forgotten the time—and that team practice was only

an hour away—when she got into it with the She-lion, so it surprised her when her teammates came running in, yelling at the She-lions and pushing Tock out of the way. While Max, Nelle, and Streep kept up the yelling, Mads had turned to her and asked what happened.

"Nothing, really. Just something with the kid and the dogs."

"Dani?"

"Don't worry. I sent her back to her dad. Didn't think she should see this."

"I've spent time over at the Malone house. Trust me. The kid has seen cats fight before."

"Not when we're involved."

"Good point." Mads had looked back at the She-lions. "Want me to shut this down?"

"The kid's safe, so I don't care."

"Well, it might be a good idea to do this before practice. Get it out of our system and all."

"Pre-practice fights do cut down on the rage explosions during layups and in the showers."

"Exactly. But keep an eye out," she had added before stepping back into the fray. "Charlie drove us here and is looking for a parking spot. Let us know when she gets up here so we can pull Max out. Because Charlie will just assume—

"—Max started it," they had said together.

So that's what Tock had been doing. Keeping an eye out for Charlie while her friends got all that natural aggression out of their collective system. So it took her by another surprise to see Shay standing beside her.

"What are you doing here?" she asked.

"Dani wanted me to rescue you." When she frowned, he added, "No. Really. She thought you were in true danger."

"Oh, my God, Shay," she said softly. "That is so cute."

"Not so cute when she snarled at me," but he said it with a smile.

Tock covered her mouth with three fingers to keep from smiling. "She snarled at you?"

"Apparently I wasn't moving fast enough for my little princess. You know, because clearly you needed to be saved from the big bad cats."

Together, they looked over at the still-screaming badgers and lions. It was a tactic Tock and her teammates had used for years. Sometimes it was a distraction during a job. Sometimes it was because someone was being rude but not rude enough to warrant getting their head blown off. But usually it was just Tock and her teammates trading crazy for crazy. This allowed them to work off their aggression without actually having to think too much about what they were doing or saying. Sure, there was still angry pointing and raging hysterics, but if anyone listened carefully, they'd realize that Mads and the others were simply screaming nonsense.

"*I'm a ho! You're a ho! We're all hos!*"

"*Four score and seven years ago, I wasn't even born!*"

"*If you live like an animal! You will die like an animal! And you're nothing but animals!*"

"*And then I told that director, you don't know what love is! That was in the eighth grade and he* still *doesn't know!*"

See? Nonsense.

"I have to admit," Tock said, turning her attention back to Shay, "I was impressed that Dani left when I signaled her to go."

"She's been trained to do that since birth. By both me and her mother. I seem to attract fights without even trying. Just walking by. And Dani's mom is . . . well, she's rude. And we needed to ensure that Dani knew how to run and hide when shit started."

"Smart. I like that."

"Thanks for protecting her."

"I was pretty certain you didn't want your baby to see me pummel a She-lion within an inch of her life before shooting her in the back of the head. If that became necessary, I mean."

"Yeah. I agree. I wouldn't want her to see . . . that."

"She's too young," Tock reasoned.

"She's too young," Shay echoed.

Gazing at each other, they both laughed.

"Look," Tock told the cat, "they've just been playing with these cats. If you want us to shut this down—"

"No need. It looks like Keane is going to handle it. And that should entertain you and your friends for another five minutes."

Keane pushed his way into the middle of the screaming, finger-pointing females and bellowed, "*That is enough!*"

He spread his arms wide, forcing the two groups of females to separate.

"There is no reason for any of this," he told them. "So let it go."

The She-lion leader raised her arm high, forefinger pointing at Tock. "That *bitch*"—Tock pressed her hand to her chest, mouth dropping in faux shock at the insult—"came at *my* son?"

"Really?" Keane briefly glowered at Tock and she thought for sure he was about to yell at her. But he turned back to the She-lion and said, "Tock is the most calm and rational of this unholy group of insane badgers—"

"Thank you, brother to my half-sister!"

"—so I have to wonder what your son did." Crossing his arms over his chest, Keane took a step forward so he towered over the She-lion despite her six-inch, tacky, knockoff designer heels. "By that, I mean what your son did to my *niece*. Or did it involve my brother's dog and her puppies? You see, my niece is very attached to those puppies. And I'd be very cranky if someone upset her. Whether it was about the puppies. Or the dog. Or standing near her. Or even just looking at her weird. Whatever upset her, I would take it very personally. You understand what I'm saying to you, Anya?"

The pair glared at each other for several extremely long seconds until male lions came out of the nearby sports gear store and walked toward them.

"What's going on here?" one of them asked.

Keane replied by locking his eyes on the three males and roaring. Just once.

Looking up. Then down. Then remembering they had left

something in the sports store, the males retreated. The free food and housing provided by their mates apparently weren't worth the trouble of engaging three male Amur tigers.

The She-lion rolled her eyes, clearly disgusted with the males she'd chosen to help father her pride's offspring, and took a step away from Keane.

With one more glare for Tock, the lioness spun around and walked off. Her tacky sisters and cousins followed.

The She-lion did keep talking, though, but now she spoke Russian.

Unfortunately for them, Tock knew Russian. Just as she knew Polish, German, French, Czech, Slovak, or any other language that her people might have spoken before immigrating to Israel.

It didn't matter that she understood, though. Because she was going to be the bigger person and just let it go. She was just going to ignore those females. Yeah. She had been *going* to.

Until she heard the She-lion say in Russian, "Forget those ugly cunts and that alley cat's fat, lying niece."

Tock had a lot of issues with what was said, yet she could still have ignored it all . . . except what was said about Dani. It was bad enough that the misogynistic full-human society they were forced to live in would do their best to give the kid a self-image problem. It was bad enough that she called a ten-year-old fat. What Tock couldn't ignore was the disloyalty of female to female. It was bad enough they had to put up with males' bullshit all day, every day. Did they actually have to attack each other, too? It was fine if instinctive enemies went after each other. Tock did that all the time. But she never went after another female just because she was female. And she would never do that to a female *child*!

That was something she couldn't and wouldn't ignore.

So Tock walked past her silent teammates, stopping a few feet in front of them and yelling out in Russian, "Your son doesn't know how to take 'no' for an answer. And if you don't teach him now about how to interact with women, one day, when he's older, someone like me is going to cut his throat.

And no one will miss him. And no one will miss *you* if you get in my way."

The She-lion spun around so fast, the females with her took several steps back, staring back and forth between Tock and their leader with wide gold eyes. A few had their fangs out; others, their claws. Because they were expecting a reaction. So was Tock.

She braced herself, her right hand pressed against the small of her back. Max pressed the handle of a tactical knife into Tock's palm and Tock waited. It didn't take long. In fact, it happened in seconds.

The She-lion dropped her purse, started running and, in mid-stride, shifted to lion. Her clothes and shoes flew off as her arms and legs, now covered in animal muscle and fur, stretched out. Like a ballistic missile, she headed right for Tock.

Tock took in a breath and tightened her grip on the blade, but she never had a chance to use it.

The She-lion was so focused on Tock, she never saw Charlie MacKilligan coming until the hybrid's shoulder slammed into the five-hundred-pound cat. Since Charlie couldn't shift, it was her human body that hit the She-lion and, in theory, she should have bounced off like a ball against a wall.

This was Charlie, though. Charlie couldn't shift, but her strength had become legendary. Not only did she send the cat flying in the opposite direction, the She-lion didn't stop until she crashed into the far wall hundreds of feet away.

Charlie, however, immediately stopped right in front of Tock and her teammates.

"Everything okay here?" she asked with forced good cheer, her gaze locked on Max.

"It wasn't her," Tock explained, handing the tactical knife back to Max. "This one is kind of on me." She pointed. "And him."

Charlie narrowed her eyes on the She-lion's lying son, and the kid gave a baby hiss before running into the sports store with the two other young males.

Princess barked and Charlie smiled at the sight of her. "God, she is such a cool dog."

"If you bring home another dog . . ." Max warned.

"I know. I know. But," she suddenly added with actual good cheer this time, "what I can do is take Dani home with me for the rest of the day." She focused on Shay. "She can bring the dog and the puppies."

Keane stepped in front of Shay before his brother could respond.

"What are you going to do with her?" Dani's uncle asked with clear suspicion.

"Well, I'll get her home. Get the dogs settled. Put Dani to work in a sweatshop making cell phones until I start sending her out to deliver sweets to strange men in vans."

"Why do you *try* to make me angry?"

"Because it's easy?" She shrugged. "What do you think we're going to do? She'll hang out with Nat. She'll swim"— she held up her hand before Shay could say anything—"under strict supervision. I'll make sure she's fed and that the adult bears don't mess with her. Stevie's working from home today, so they can talk math or whatever. It'll be fine." She reached her arm out and up, gently placing her hand on his bicep, and said with disgusting sweetness, "We're all family now."

"Ech."

Charlie laughed and turned toward Princess and the puppies.

"Did you forget you also have practice?" Keane asked her. "Which you've already missed most of."

Charlie turned back to Keane and asked with all sincerity, "Really? You think *I* need more practice tackling people?"

They all looked at the She-lion, now human again, trying to pick her naked, battered body off the floor, but unable to do it without help from the other She-lions.

Keane returned his gaze to Charlie. "Try to come at least twice a week."

"Yeah," she said with a nod, "I can do that."

Chapter 14

Practice could have gone better. Coach was in a mood, so she pushed more than usual. And seemed to have no patience for Max being Max or Streep being Streep. And, of course, Mads didn't understand why they weren't playing at the highest level . . . at a practice. She was going to be a real pain until the championship was over.

Eventually, though, Tock remembered she still hadn't discussed her teammates' talk with Tock's grandmother—adding to her general stress. After the fight with the lion pride, they'd gone straight to practice and Coach didn't allow any talk during training because, again, she was in a mood.

Tock was okay with that, though. She didn't want to talk about her grandmother. She didn't want to hear about how great her grandmother was or why hadn't Tock introduced them before or how she had a small job for them, and why was it a big deal to handle it as a tiny favor?

In an effort to delay hearing any of that for a few extra minutes, once practice was over, Tock helped one of the assistants gather up all the basketballs and put them on the rolling stand. Then she went into the hallway and headed toward the locker room for a nice hot shower and maybe some time with one of the PTs. The team had been given temporary accommodations since they'd been in the playoffs. And now, with the finals coming up, they'd keep their lockers until it was—

Tock was used to getting grabbed and dragged into rooms. It had happened enough that she didn't even bother counting how often anymore. So she wasn't shocked that it happened again, but that it was her coach who grabbed her was a bit off-putting.

Since she didn't wear a gun or blade during practice—unlike Max and Nelle—Tock unleashed her claws, slashing them through the air. But Coach grabbed her wrists and pushed Tock into a chair before sitting at the desk across from her, seemingly unfazed by the fact her face had almost been torn off by one of her players.

"Hey," Coach said once she'd sat down and taken a few seconds to get comfortable.

"Hey."

"How's it going?"

Tock was confused. The only time Coach Diane Fitzgerald asked that question was when Tock and the others came to practice or a game with bruises or open wounds. Once they'd all come in to practice with gunshot wounds and all Coach said was, "That shit better not fuck up your layups, ladies." It hadn't, so it was never mentioned again.

Frowning, Tock asked, "Am I in trouble?"

"No, of course not."

"Did Max do something?"

"No."

"Because if she did something, I know nothing about it. But if I did know about it, I probably wouldn't tell you anyway."

"Uh—"

"And if I were you, I wouldn't ask. It's best not to ask when it comes to Max. The last thing you want is her oldest sister involved—"

"Tock," she cut in, "I just need your opinion on something."

"*My* opinion? You sure you don't want Mads for this? I mean, she lives for this shit."

"No, no. I want to talk to *you*. Get your opinion."

"Okay."

"Now . . . how loyal are you to our team?"

Tock felt a little bolt of anger. "Are you trading me?"

"What?"

"I mean, if that's what you want, if you think I'm the weak link rather than Janice, Fine."

"Tock, I'm not trading you."

"Then why are you asking me about my loyalty?"

Coach took off her baseball cap and removed the tie from her hair, letting the brown-and-gray mass fall to her massive She-wolf shoulders. The female could have easily played football with other wolf shifters, but she said she really loved basketball. Felt it was more graceful and took more skill. She would also say, "I like my brain not binging around my skull after some grizzly hits me from behind."

Tock had to agree. As much as she loved basketball, she'd never understood the allure of football. Why would anyone sign up for that level of injury? She was even more worried about full-humans playing football than she was about shifters. Their kind was just so . . . brittle. Like empty corn husks easily crushed by rampaging pigs. They intentionally slammed into each other and then were surprised when they turned forty and their bones turned to dust.

Nope. Tock agreed with her coach. Basketball was a much better, safer sport.

"I've been made an offer," Coach suddenly announced.

"To trade me?" she asked.

"I am *not* trading you," she snapped. "I'm not trading any of you. Stop asking me that."

"Well, you brought up my loyalty. Implying I'm not loyal."

"I'm not implying you're not loyal, Tock. I'm simply wondering if you think you and the rest of the badgers would follow me to another team. Or if they're specifically loyal to the Butchers."

"Why would we be loyal to the Butchers? Wait . . . let me rephrase. Why would we be loyal to the Butchers without *you?*"

Coach blinked. "I don't—?"

"You do realize that Max only lasted this long with *any* team because of you and your innate ability to tolerate her bullshit. With anyone else, Streep would have headed to Broadway or Hollywood by now. Nelle would go wherever Mads went.

And if Mads was going to leave while you were still coach, she would have done it when we had that two-year run that we didn't even get into the playoffs."

"And you?"

"I do what I want. And I don't like being ordered around. You're one of the few people who know how to manage me without pissing me off. That's a skill very few have. You are literally the only person I take orders from when not trapped in a firefight. Especially if whoever is in charge does not truly understand the concept of time management. It's not just about *being* on time, you know?"

"Yes, I know."

"There is a lot more to it and it really irritates me when people don't understand that."

"Yes, Tock. I know." She moved some papers around on her desk, but Tock got the feeling it was just so she'd have something to do with her hands.

"So," Coach eventually continued, "if I said there was an opportunity to go to another team—"

"It's not Alaska, is it? Mads would go, but I'm from a desert people and an island people and Wisconsin is cold enough, thanks. Mads is Viking. She can handle that cold shit. But the rest of us?"

"No, no. Not Alaska. It'd be here. In New York."

"The New York team wants you?" Tock asked on a laugh. "Doesn't the owner call you Fido?"

"Not to my face." She cleared her throat. "And we've worked through that."

"Is she insisting Mads and the rest of us come, too?"

"No, no. Actually," she admitted after another throat clearing, "I'll probably have to fight to bring all five of you. The owner does have issues with—"

"The MacKilligans?"

"No. The Gonzalezes. She's very Catholic and she thought she was purchasing actual artifacts from the Vatican, but they were, in fact, excellent fakes."

"Ahh. Yeah. Streep's family does do that sometimes. I mean,

they probably"—she paused a moment to think of a safe word to use—"*acquired* the originals from the Vatican, but those are in the main family home in the Philippines or at one of their local churches. They're big fans of the pope. Anything he's touched means a lot to them."

"Well, whatever. It doesn't matter to me. I want you guys with me. You guys are my secret weapon. Nothing is concrete yet, but I wanted to see if the five of you would even be interested."

"Interested? Well . . . let me think a moment." And Tock did, though she did her thinking out loud. "Mads just bought a house here. And she's fucking one of the Malone boys. So that will definitely go in your favor. Max just met her very young half-sister, and I know she's not ready to leave her yet, at least until they know whether she's more MacKilligan sociopath or MacKilligan sociopath adjacent. Nelle has access to a bunch of private jets, so she can travel wherever, whenever and doesn't really stress about which team she's on as long as Mads and the rest of us are there. Nelle doesn't say it much, but she really likes to win. As for Streep, she'll be near Broadway. She'll happily move here."

"And you?"

"I don't care."

"What do you mean, you don't care? You don't care about what? Basketball? The team? Life? Oh, my God, are you depressed? Should I get you mental health assistance? There's no shame in asking for help, Tock."

"No, I'm fine," she said simply. Because she was. "But I can live anywhere as long as my team's with me. Well . . . anywhere except Alaska. I refuse to move to Alaska."

"I didn't know you were so anti-Alaska."

"I'm not anti-Alaska. I just know my limits. And not being able to walk from the local grocery store to my house without being mauled by a wandering polar bear does not sound like a good time to me."

"Don't Max and Mads currently live on a street—"

"Full of bears. Yes. But that's different. Those are suburban bears. Not crazed, full-blooded polars that have lost most of their ice shelf. Besides, Charlie keeps them under control by making this upside-down honey-pineapple cake that is to die for."

"Is it really that good?"

"It's amazing."

"So if I made you guys an offer . . ."

"Very high probability."

"Okay. This is good." She nodded. "This is very good. Just don't mention it to anyone yet."

"So you want me to *pretend* I won't tell Mads and the others . . . ?"

She sighed. "Fine. Tell them but keep it among you five, please. I am still working out offers and whatnot."

"Are you sure you want to tie yourself to us?" Tock asked her. "I mean, I know we're great in a game and all. But . . . it's *us*. I could say we start shit, but really, shit tends to follow us."

"Are you worried about prison time?"

"Why do you mention prison? Have the cops been sniffing around?" Tock leaned forward. "Do we need to use our extra passports?"

"No, no," Coach quickly replied. "And I don't want to hear about your 'extra' passports," she said with air quotes. "Plus, I already know you guys are not welcome in many Florida cities." She thought a moment. "And all of Idaho."

Relieved she didn't have to tell the others to "make a run for it!," Tock relaxed back in her chair. "Oh, yeah. Yeah. That's true. But no. We're not worried about anything."

"Good. Okay. That helps." She again played with some papers on her desk before finally asking, "What happened in Idaho anyway?"

Tock shook her head. "Coach, unless you want to risk being pulled into a federal grand jury, I'd probably let it go. I mean, we were underage and everything, but there are some things that have *no* statute of limitations."

Coach let out a long sigh. "Thank God you guys are good at basketball."

"That's funny."

"What is?"

"My mom has always said the same thing. And she hates basketball."

"What are they wearing?" Jerry asked his coworker Gregg. Jerry didn't mind Gregg. True. The others found him freakish and cold and a little terrifying. But the dude was just tall. And wide. Like a Mac truck or a building.

It wasn't just his massive size, though. It was the silence. Gregg didn't say much unless he had something to say. He would just stand there, staring. It was easy to be freaked out by that. But since Jerry was one of the few who didn't mind being around Gregg, they were always assigned to work together.

Jerry was okay with that. He made lots of extra money at times like this due to Gregg's connections. But this was the first time Jerry had ever felt the need to involve himself beyond letting people in and out and pretending nothing had happened. This time, however, how could he ignore what he was looking at?

Both women looked like they'd been in a bad 1970s baseball-related soft porn. Both wore cutoff denim shorts, sweat socks, sneakers, and blue baseball jerseys. The sleeves had been torn off the slightly taller one's jersey, revealing giant shoulders; and the dark-haired hottie—who was actually chewing gum like a true seventies' soft porn star—had a cutoff jersey that barely covered her ample chest. Both also had on blue baseball caps, but the hottie had hers turned backward, so you could easily see her pretty face. The other one, though, had her cap pulled so low you could barely see her eyes. Her cold, weird, off-putting eyes.

The plan had been like all the others: to allow two people inside to pick up their "cargo," and get them out before anyone asked any questions. The problem now, though, was how could that happen when the two people who had been sent were these women. And they were looking like *that*?

"He's kind of right," Gregg grumbled to the women.

"Sorry, but we just came from a game," the hottie said.

"Softball league?"

"The Malone Pub against Dolly's Dinner Den."

"Did you win?"

"Got our asses handed to us." She shook her head. "We're kind of the worst at softball."

"It'll be fine, y'all. Let's just go," the tall one muttered with an accent that made his skin crawl. Made him think of the movie *Deliverance*. He had seen that movie when he was twelve and he had never recovered.

"Yeah," the hottie said. "We're supposed to be meeting people for beers."

"But," Jerry argued, "they're going to have to walk past—"

"It'll be fine," Gregg insisted with a sigh.

Look, if that's what they wanted, Jerry wouldn't argue the point. But if he was female . . . he'd never do it. To walk past prison bars and have the scum of the earth say things to him that absolutely *no one* wanted to hear . . . Well, it was up to these women and Gregg. Jerry just wanted to make his money.

Gregg unlocked the gate and Jerry walked through, leading the women toward the closed-off room at the end of the long hall.

As soon as the two women walked in, the men they had temporarily locked up in these cells until they could be moved into more permanent housing, slammed into the bars, arms reaching out, trying to grab them; jeering and yelling. It went from generally loud to unbearable in less than a second.

Jerry was sure it wouldn't stop until they got the women out of here and even then, it would continue for days. Already Jerry was wondering if the money was truly worth it.

He started to walk faster so he could rush the visitors down the hall. He expected them to keep their heads down and their bodies as close to the far wall as possible so no one could put hands on them.

But the women abruptly stopped moving and, to Jerry's horror, turned and faced the bars. The uproar should have gotten worse at that very moment. The yelling. The screaming. It should sound like the beginning of a riot. Except . . . it was as if a switch had been hit or a weird lever pulled. Because the noise stopped. Instantly. It didn't peter out. All that yelling and screaming and attempted grabbing simply stopped in that very moment.

Staring at the women, the men lowered their arms and shut their mouths.

Jerry had only seen this sort of thing happen when Gregg suddenly entered without warning. But Jerry had always assumed that was simply because the men were intimidated by the man's size and silence, just like everyone else.

But these were . . . women. Guys who ended up in these particular cells weren't intimidated by any woman, whether they were guards or cops or nurses trying to help a wounded inmate. Women meant little to them except as something to grab and harass. At least that's how it had always been . . . until now.

Fascinated and more than a little terrified, Jerry watched the women silently walk toward the bars. As they did, the men on the other side stepped back and back . . . until they were by the far wall. As far away from these two as they could get, but Jerry had the feeling that still wasn't far enough.

Though the men moved away from them, the women continued to stand there, staring boldly at each inmate, locking eyes until each and every man looked away. They looked down, looked up, turned away . . . anything to avoid the direct eye contact that seemed to be terrifying them.

That's when Gregg stepped in and led the way down the hall, toward the last door. Jerry followed, glancing over at the inmates to see at least two of the men quietly crying.

Maybe the women were the girlfriends of high-level gang members or something. Although when he thought about that even a little bit, it didn't make sense. Not if Gregg was involved. He was the cleanest guy Jerry knew. Even moving these inmates didn't seem like a backroom deal of some kind, but a government-run thing that helped keep the identities of those being moved a secret.

He'd helped Gregg with these kinds of transfers before and they'd always been relatively easy: Guys in suits would come in, quietly remove someone from a cell, and Jerry received an envelope filled with a healthy amount of cash. Funky, yes. But he knew fellow government employees when he saw them.

But these two women and the energy they brought to what should be another run-of-the-mill, underground event was just plain weird.

Finally, they all reached the end of the hall. Jerry was surprised that the inmates remained quiet. Not a sound from any of them. They were never quiet. The place was filled with noise day and night. Until right now.

"You ready?" Gregg asked the women.

The taller one rotated her finger while muttering, "Let's just get this over with."

"All right." Gregg unlocked the metal door and pushed it open.

The inmate sat at a large table bolted to the floor. His legs were also shackled to the floor, and his arms were shackled to the chair.

"You've got five minutes," Gregg told them.

The women nodded and entered the room. As Gregg closed the door, Jerry heard the taller one say, "All right, hoss. Ready to get this done?"

With the door closed, Gregg relaxed against the wall and waited. Jerry took a step back, wanting to take a quick look to make sure all that quiet was simply the men waiting—like him—for this to be over. And not that they were up to something.

But before he could reach a spot that would allow him to see what was going on, something heavy hit the metal door.

Jerry stopped and stared. That door was thick and only opened and closed so easily because of well-oiled hinges. But whatever had hit the door was thrown with such force that the metal door shook. That was weird.

He waited for Gregg to do something since he was closest to the door, but he didn't do anything other than gaze down at his huge feet. Did he have to get his work boots specially made like Shaq did his NBA sneakers?

The door was hit again, the heavy metal actually bending this time. Like it might be knocked off its hinges. Jerry began to slowly walk backward. But when the door moved again and he heard snarls and growls from the other side, he immediately stopped.

After about a minute of door-rattling banging, the door opened just enough for the taller woman to stick her head out. She was no longer wearing her baseball cap and she was bleeding from bruises to her face and neck. Her weird-colored eyes—they seemed to glow in the harsh prison light—locked on Gregg.

"Uh . . . we could use some help in here."

Gregg rolled his eyes and walked over to the door as the woman stepped back into the room. He grabbed the handle but stopped to look over his shoulder at Jerry.

"Don't come in here," Gregg warned. "No matter what you hear, okay?"

Jerry could only nod his head in reply. Because behind Gregg, Jerry could swear he saw a . . . a . . . well . . . a *tiger* leaping across the room, briefly passing by the partially open door.

But that was crazy, right? *Right?*

Gregg went inside and closed the door behind him. That's when the roaring started. It didn't stop. The door was hit so hard, several times, that Jerry was sure it would be torn out of its moorings.

Taking more steps back, he briefly glanced into the cells. There was no plotting going on. No grand schemes to start a riot or find a way out. There was just abject fear as every man huddled against the wall, waiting for all this to be over.

Finally, after what felt like a lifetime, the door was wrenched open and Gregg came out, dragging the prisoner with him. Hog-tied with chains, the man was pulled across the floor until he was outside the room.

Bloody and battered, his clothes an absolute mess—as if he'd taken them off and put them on hastily—Gregg didn't seem fazed at all, gripping the humongous white-haired man under his left arm. Still in the room, the two women were quickly putting their clothes back on, which was beyond weird. Why had they taken their clothes off in the first place? There hadn't been time to have sex . . . right?

The women were as beaten up as Gregg, but they were moving with ease and didn't seem bothered by all the blood they kept wiping from their faces. The hottie was still chewing her gum.

Once they were back in their bloody clothes, they strode up to stand on either side of the prisoner. They each grabbed him under the arm and proceeded to drag him down the long hallway back to the exit.

"Thanks, Gregg," the hottie called out, as cheery as she'd been when the women had first arrived.

"Hate polars," the taller woman mumbled, which made absolutely no sense to Jerry.

"I told you we should bring someone else," the hottie shot back.

"Shut up."

"You shut up."

The taller one released the man so suddenly his face bounced off the floor; he grunted in pain as the taller one stepped on the back of his head, so she could square off against the hottie.

"I ain't in no mood for your shit, Malone."

The hottie didn't back down. Instead, she stepped closer, putting her face so close to the other one that their noses practically touched.

"Back off, Smith, or I'll finish the job that dumb bear started and rip your face off."

"Just try me."

The two women silently eyed each other for a long moment, and then the taller one's lip curled and she snarled. The hottie hissed and, for just a second, Jerry was sure he saw fangs . . .

But then Gregg got up right beside both women and he . . . well . . . he . . .

It sounded like a roar. An actual . . . *animal* roar.

So loud and powerful that the floor underneath Jerry's feet trembled and one of the inmates pressed against the wall peed his pants.

"You two trifling house pets," Gregg said when he had the women's attention, "take this seal-eating idiot and leave my prison. *Now.*"

Both women snarled at Gregg but didn't challenge him any further. Just grabbed hold of their prisoner again and walked a few more feet. Then the hottie stopped and said over her shoulder with renewed good humor, "Oh, before I forget, Gregg, if you still want your daughter to try out for the team, bring her by tomorrow."

"We don't have time for your hockey shit," the taller one complained.

"There's always time for hockey." Then the hottie grinned and the taller one let out a short laugh.

After that, the women walked out. And once they were gone, the men remained silent. And stayed silent. In fact, the entire wing, for the first time that Jerry could ever remember, was silent for the next two days until new inmates came in and older ones were moved out.

When his coworkers asked him, "What's going on over there?" he gave the same answer every time:

"No idea."

Tock stepped out of the SUV, still answering questions that had begun during the after-practice shower.

"I don't know," she said again.

"You didn't get any other information from her?" Mads demanded, sounding almost hysterical.

"What kind of information?"

"Like, what does all this mean for the championship? For the next few practices? How good is the New York team? How much playing time will we get or will we just be riding the bench? Is Coach planning on bringing anyone else from our team? What plans does she have for the new team and how will her choices affect *this* upcoming championship?"

Tock shrugged. "I'm pretty sure she's planning on losing the championship so she can go on to the next team as a failure. Owners love to pay for coaches that fail."

Mads stood in front of her, gripping the car keys, and glaring. A lot of Viking-like glaring.

"That's sarcasm, isn't it?" she asked.

"What do you think?"

Another, bigger SUV pulled past them and parked a few cars ahead. The three Malone brothers got out at the MacKilligan house to pick up Shay's daughter.

On his way toward the brick home, Shay stopped and waved. Tock waved back, not thinking much about it. But when she turned around, her teammates were staring at her.

"What now?"

"What's going on with you two?" Mads demanded. "Is *he* why you suddenly want to switch teams?"

"Oh, my God!" Streep gasped, hands clasped together. "Are you two in love?"

"Are you planning on stealing one of those puppies?" Max asked, smiling. "Now that we all know how much they're actually worth, I say we take them all. Those idiots will never know."

Nelle asked nothing. She was too busy taking a selfie.

"He waved at all of us," Tock pointed out.

"But he meant it for *you*!" Streep cheered.

"I'm sorry," Tock told Streep. "But clearly I'm going to have to kill you before this gets out of hand."

"What was that?"

Shay stopped on the porch and faced his brother. "Huh?"

"You're waving to her now?"

"I was waving to all of them."

"Bullshit."

"I was just being nice."

"We're not nice."

"*You're* not nice. That's why my daughter calls *you* Uncle Mean."

"Look, it's bad enough this idiot—"

"Hey!" Finn barked when his brother pointed at him.

"—has involved himself with a badger. I'm just glad it's Mads, who is less annoying than the others."

"I'm not involving myself with anyone," Shay explained. "I've got too much going on."

His brothers stared at him.

"What exactly do you have going on?" Finn asked.

"Lots of things."

"Like what?" Keane pushed. "And you better not say those fucking dogs."

"They're puppies. They'll need a lot of care."

"Oh, my God." Disgusted, Keane pushed past him and opened the screen door so he could bang his fist on the hard wood of the front door.

He knew his brother was annoyed, which was why he banged on Charlie MacKilligan's front door and didn't think about the consequences. Shay cringed, though, when that door was snatched open and the muzzle of a semiauto was pressed against his brother's chest because he was too tall for Charlie to reach his head.

"Oh," she said. "It's you."

She lowered the weapon.

"You have guns around my niece?" Keane demanded before Shay could.

"I have guns around everyone. That's how we survive. That's how I protect your niece and our sister. Because I'd rather stop those who want to hurt us instead of getting revenge later."

"I don't like it," Keane growled.

"You don't like anything. But I have brownies, if you're interested."

Shay raised a finger. "I'm interested in brownies."

Keane snarled at Shay.

"What?" Shay wanted to know. "I'm hungry."

Chapter 15

Tock looked down at the big brownie on a paper plate Charlie had just put in front of her.

"Thanks."

"I need you guys to come with me tomorrow," Charlie said, sitting at the kitchen table with her own brownie on a paper plate.

"We have practice," Mads said, unable to help herself.

"Dude, when have we ever gone to practice every day?" Max asked their teammate.

"You're captain of the team. You should want us all to go to practice, every day, until we win the championships or die trying."

Tock let out a sigh. Mads was going to continue being this unreasonable until the championships were won or lost. So it was best simply to ignore her.

"What's up?" she asked Charlie.

"The ship that went down earlier today . . . ? We need to look into that."

"Why? It wasn't me."

"I know."

"You do? Because everyone else keeps asking if that was me."

"No. You're subtler."

"Thank you," Tock said earnestly. It was nice to be appreciated.

"We'll meet in the morning and go over together."

"You guys can crash at my place tonight," Mads said, clearly resigning herself to no practice time the next day.

"Are you sure?" Streep asked, batting her eyelashes in a really annoying manner.

"Why would I not be sure? And stop doing that with your eyes. You look like you're having a seizure."

"I'm just assuming that you'll want to invite Finn over tonight. Since he didn't stay at your place last night."

"First off, stop tracking when guys I'm fucking come over to my house. And second . . . I don't care if you crash at the house when Finn is there."

Max hopped onto the counter behind her so she could sit without sharing a kitchen chair. "You don't mind us hearing your nasty sex noises, Mads?"

"Who says we make nasty sex noises?"

"He's a cat, isn't he?"

Chuckling, Nelle eased into a chair, phone clutched in her hand. "Is that why you spend all of your time over at Berg's house?" she asked Charlie. "So you don't have to hear Max's nasty sex noises with Zé?"

"I've had to wear headphones to bed since Max hit puberty. She was always having dirty, nasty sex dreams and she kept waking up the entire Pack with her incessant screeching."

"I'm a horny badger," Max happily admitted. "What can I say?"

"Nothing," Tock told Max. "You can say nothing. I know it's unusual for you, but try."

"Come on." Mads stood. "Let's go over to my place. Order some dinner. Watch some TV. We'll bring the brownies with us. We'll meet you around eight tomorrow morning. Okay, Charlie?"

"Sure. And don't let the bears see you with those brownies," Charlie warned. "They will just rip them right out of your hands."

"No, Dani. You can't."

"*Pleeeeaaaasssssseeee!*"

He stopped in Charlie's kitchen and turned around to face his daughter. She was starting to get red in the face, which meant a real healthy tantrum was about to happen.

"I said, no."

"I want to stay with Aunt Nat," she repeated, yet again. "Just for tonight."

"She can stay here if she wants," Charlie said, putting away recently cleaned dishes and pans. "I don't mind."

"No offense, but your house is a nightmare of gun ownership."

Charlie shrugged. "She can stay at Berg's place with me and the triplets. There's a room she can share with Nat."

"Aren't the triplets a professional security team? Which means more guns."

"Yeah. But they put their guns away in a safe. A real safe. It's like a big closet with a massive, metal door that even they can't tear open. If it's bear safe, it's cub safe. And Princess and the pups are already over there."

"What are they doing over there?"

"Let's just say that Princess was not comfortable having my dogs around her puppies. She nearly took Shotzy's ear off."

"Oh, my God. I'm so sor—"

Charlie waved away his apology with a quick swipe of her hand. "Shotzy was asking for it. He's like Max. A little shit-starter."

"Was the damage bad?"

"I had the jackal and the wolverine take him to the emergency vet for me."

"I like Kyle," Dani said on a near-whisper as she stepped forward. "He's dreamy."

Shay, now standing behind his daughter, pointed at her and mouthed to Charlie, *What the fuck?*

Charlie cleared her throat to keep from laughing and said, "He is a handsome young man, Dani. But very busy."

"He's an artist, Daddy," his baby told him, tilting her head back so she could look at him directly. "An *artist*."

Shay knew a little about Kyle Jean-Louis Parker. He was an

eighteen-year-old jackal with shoulder-length hair and the title of "art prodigy." A title that Shay had no respect for. It was bad enough the kid was hanging around his baby sister, who might or might not think he was "dreamy." But to think his innocent daughter was getting all googly-eyed over a boy—*any* boy—was beyond upsetting.

She was just a baby! His little girl! She was too young to be mooning over some artistic pretty boy who acted like he knew better than everyone else because some of his artwork had already sold for six figures.

"Please, Daddy!" Dani begged, her arms now wrapped around his right leg. "Can I stay with Auntie Nat and the bears? *Pleaaaaaaassssseeeeeee!*"

He looked at Charlie. "You'll look out for her?"

"Of course. And if you pick her up by eight a.m. tomorrow, I'll make sure you guys get breakfast."

He trusted Charlie. Didn't know why. She was half canine, and he barely trusted his own wolf teammates to cover his back on the field. But he was entrusting his only daughter to a woman who'd greeted them at her front door with a semiauto and an offer of brownies.

Shay looked down at Dani, her head tilted all the way back so she could focus on him with those eyes just like his own.

"Okay. Fine."

The squeal his cub let out nearly shattered his eardrums, and even Charlie covered her own.

Using her strong cat legs, his daughter catapulted herself into Shay's arms, making him laugh.

"Thank you, Daddy!"

"You're welcome. But," he quickly added, "I don't want to hear tomorrow that you caused any trouble. Understand?"

"When do I ever cause trouble?"

"What I'm saying to you, Dani Malone, is that there will be *no* treating the Dunn Triplets like they're giant teddy bears."

"Even though they *look* like giant teddy bears?"

"*Especially* because of that, baby. That's how they lull their victims into a false sense of security."

★ ★ ★

Finn found his older brother sitting on the stoop and staring across the street at the bear triplets' house. He tried to sit next to him, but their shoulders made that impossible, so Finn went down a step and looked up at Shay.

"What's wrong?"

"Dani's spending the night at the bear house."

"Why?"

"She wants to spend the night with Nat, and I refused to let her spend the night in a house filled with guns."

That was probably a good idea. Not long ago, Finn had found a sawed-off shotgun taped under the kitchen table. He hadn't told his brothers because he trusted Charlie MacKilligan when it came to weapons. But it was one thing to have their seventeen-year-old sister living here with angry, armed women. And quite another to have their ten-year-old niece stay the night.

At the same time, Finn also understood why Dani wanted to stay. Nat was the girlfriend-slash-sister that every ten-year-old girl needed in her life. Her mother was not that woman and neither was their mother. But with Nat, Dani could play with makeup and clothes and learn how to take down a deer without getting her face battered by a hoof. Important things all female cubs needed to know.

"I wouldn't worry," he told his brother. "You know Nat will watch her."

"I do. I do know that. I just don't want her to think she's getting tossed off somewhere. Again."

"Didn't she ask *you* if she could stay?"

"Yeah."

"And wouldn't she have just thrown a fit if you'd said no?"

"Yeah."

"Then stop worrying. It's not like you're leaving her here for weeks."

The screen door behind them opened and Shay could hear the heavy human footsteps of his brother seconds before Keane stepped over them to get down the stoop stairs.

"Are you two coming with me?" he barked at them. Keane wasn't in a bad mood. He just spoke to everyone *as if* he was in a bad mood.

"No," Finn said before Shay could figure out what he wanted to do. "Shay's going to hang at Mads's house with me for a little while."

Keane gazed down at him for a second before asking, "You gonna try and fuck Tock?"

"What? No!"

"What is wrong with you?" Finn demanded on a surprised laugh.

"She's just a friend," Shay insisted.

"So, you're saying you're *not* gonna hit that? Is that because she's too short for you? You know, there's a benefit to banging a short woman. If they're tough enough, you can just toss them around like a Tonka toy," Keane said.

Without another word, Shay got up and stormed across the street, heading to Mads's house.

Finn shook his head and, grinning, asked his eldest brother, "Why do you insist on starting shit with him?"

"He lets me," Keane admitted.

"What do you want to eat?"

He stopped short when a phone was shoved into his face.

"What?"

"What do you want to eat? We're ordering dinner. And we need to order dinner now because in another twenty minutes all the good restaurants will stop delivering."

Shay carefully placed his hand on the top of the phone and slowly lowered it so he could see Tock's face.

"I don't care what I eat," he told her. "Just make sure there's meat."

"So then you do care what you eat, but you don't want to make a decision."

"I'm not a bear. I need protein. Not vegetables and honey."

"I'll just ask Finn," she said with an annoyed sigh, looking back at her phone. "You'll eat what he eats, right?"

"Yes. We're interchangeable."

"I noticed that," Max said, pirouetting around him in the big kitchen of Mads's newly purchased house. "But Stevie said I was being racist. How can I be racist, though?" She stopped, arms up like a very big-shouldered ballerina. "I'm Asian, too."

"We'll take care of dinner," Finn said, pushing Shay out of the kitchen and toward the living room.

Shay sat down on the couch and examined the room around him.

"Nice, right?" Nelle asked, sitting in a club chair near him.

"It is."

She winked at him. "Thanks."

Apparently, Nelle had designed Mads's house without Mads's knowledge or consent and it was definitely a sore spot between them. He didn't know why, though. Nelle had done a really nice job. Not that Shay would ever say that with Mads around. Finn had and she'd bitten his head clean off.

"Okay," Tock said, walking into the room. "We ordered Chinese food, but Max keeps saying just calling it Chinese food is racist. We've chosen to ignore her."

Shay and Nelle exchanged mutual eyerolls. Max was . . . a lot. How that black jaguar put up with her, Shay didn't know. Maybe his breed had more patience with irritating weasels than tigers did. Of course, Zé Vargas was currently in his cat form, asleep on the top of a cabinet across the room, his long black tail twitching and turning on its own. They played football together, and Vargas was a pretty good running back.

Tock sat down next to Shay, tapping furiously on her phone.

"Everything okay?" he asked, trying to seem like a normal houseguest and not a weird, silent, giant cat that slept on cabinets.

"Huh?" She paused to glance at him before returning to her phone. "Oh, yeah. Everything is fine. Just reworking my schedule. All my time with Dani and those dogs made me miss a ton of appointments today."

Shay cringed a little. "Sorry about that." Not about his daughter—she was worth anyone's time as far as he was concerned—but the dogs. He had no excuse for the dogs.

"She's not talking about doctor appointments or anything like that," Max announced, dropping into another nearby chair.

"Tock is talking about her thirty-minute blocks of time," Nelle explained.

Streep sat down on the floor, resting her arms on the big coffee table. "She books all those little blocks of time with stuff to do. Sometimes weeks in advance. And then moves them around as she deems necessary."

"But only *she* can move them," Max said, whose neck-length purple hair was suddenly in two ponytails. Shay hadn't seen her do that. When she first sat down, her hair was just hanging down, free. "Tock gets really pissed when anyone else fucks with her schedule."

"Because all of you keep fucking with it," Tock replied. "If you guys just used the app I created and my time management method . . . your lives would be so much more—"

"Sad and desperate?"

"Uptight?"

"Riddled with despair?"

"I was actually going to say 'functional,' but whatever."

"Do *you* enjoy time management, Shay?" Streep asked him with a sweet smile.

"Uh . . . what? Are your eyes okay? They're blinking a lot."

Tock snorted a laugh and dropped her head.

"My eyes are fine," Streep replied, her smile now a little strained. "I just mean, how do you manage your time? With apps? Or an old-fashioned datebook? A big wall calendar? Post-it notes? Writing notes on your hand?"

Not knowing what to say, Shay said nothing.

"So, are we not going to talk about your grandmother?" Max asked while staring at her phone. Now her hair was in one high ponytail. Again, Shay hadn't seen her change it.

Tock briefly closed her eyes and took in a deep breath before answering. "Sure, we can talk about her." She lowered her phone and looked at Max. "What would you like to say?"

"She was great!"

Tock's face tightened. Shay saw it. Like she was gritting her teeth or something. He just didn't know why. "Uh-huh."

"Friendly," Streep added. "Charming."

"Nothing like you," Nelle joked.

Tock nodded. "All very true."

"Still, we were surprised you never told us," Mads said as she entered the room with Finn and dropped onto his lap once he'd sat in the love seat across from the others.

Tock lifted her hands and immediately dropped them. "Never told you what?"

Mads leaned forward, hands clasped in front of her, and replied, "How much that woman fucking *hates* us."

Tock studied her teammates.

"What? No," she argued. "My . . . my grandmother doesn't hate you."

"You don't think I know when someone hates me?" Mads asked. "I lived with someone who hated me. Actually," she self-corrected, "two someones. My mother and my grandmother. Every day, I looked into their cold, dead eyes and saw hatred. And I saw the same thing from your grandmother."

Tock refused to believe any of this. "Why would my grandmother hate you? You're all honey badgers. You're all good at what you do. You've always had my back. And she's a big believer in loyalty. I've only been keeping her away from you guys because I didn't want her recruiting you."

"She would have recruited us," Max noted, "just so she could be sure we were dead by the time we were eighteen."

"No way!"

"As you know, Tock, I feed on the hatred others have of me. It gives me life. It gives me motivation. It's like Popeye's spinach. And I left that conversation quite satiated. Almost *over-full*."

Tock took another look around the room, studying each of her fellow badgers. They were being serious with her. They all felt this way. "Did she say something to you guys? Was she rude?"

"No," Mads said. "She was wonderful. Couldn't say enough nice things about us."

"Just so we're clear," Nelle said, "she has no problem with you."

"She adores you," Streep said.

"I think you're her favorite." Max glanced at her phone. "Which is impressive since you seem to have so many cousins, and she seems to be the grandmother of them all."

"Yes, but as for us . . . ?" Nelle spread her hands out, glancing around the room. "Pure hatred."

"And you know what that means," Mads said before looking at Max.

Grinning, Max promised, "That means I'm going to have so much fun fucking with her."

"What are you doing?"

Shay, now sitting on the stoop at the back of Mads's house, overlooking a surprisingly large yard, pointed. "Watching."

Tock sat down beside him. "Watching what?"

"Wait. You'll see."

They did, sitting there in silence, staring at an empty backyard. It didn't feel awkward or strange, though. Just quiet.

Finally, the silent waiting paid off.

"Is that your dog?" Tock asked.

Shay turned his head to look at her. "That's a coyote."

"Oh." She leaned against him and whispered, "Don't tell anyone, but all dogs look alike to me."

"I see that. But this is actually interesting."

"It is?"

"Yeah. Mads's coyote has moved his girlfriend in. And their kids!"

For the last thirty minutes, before Tock had come out here, Shay had been watching a female coyote carrying pup after pup to the den the male had created under Mads's house.

"How many puppies does he have?" Tock asked.

"So far . . . ? Five, I think."

"Wow. What a whore he is."

"Huh?"

"After everything Mads has done for him, he knocks up another woman and then moves her and their kids into the home Mads has paid for. It's like a Maury Povich episode."

Shay laughed. Hard.

"Finn's going to be pissed when he finds out there are more coyotes," Shay said when he could finally speak.

"He does not seem like a fan."

"He's not." Shay glanced at Tock. "Um . . . hey. Listen . . . thanks. For today. Dani really enjoyed her time with you. And helping with the dogs and her math. All that was really . . . cool."

"Sure. We need more women in STEM." When he just gazed at her, she explained, "Science, Technology, Engineering, and Math. When we find girls who really love math and science, we need to support them because insecure boys will try to push them out. And I can't have that. So, if she needs any more help with her work or whatever . . . just let me know."

"Thank you. I appreciate that. Stevie said something similar . . . but she said it from a kitchen cabinet. Because the"— he made air quotes with his forefingers—" 'maneaters' were around. And she felt safer in the cabinet until the panda came back with her ice cream. So, long story short, I'd prefer you tutor my child rather than someone else."

"That's probably for the best. Not because Stevie is terrified of her own kind—which she is—but because Stevie just *knows* this stuff. Like, it's in her blood or something. The rest of us have to read books and study and work on equations and work with teachers and think about next steps and make mistakes along the way and take our SATs more than once . . . at seventeen or eighteen. Not at eight. The problem is, it's hard for her to understand how to get from point A to point B when she's already at point Z and heading toward the infinity of time and space."

After glancing around, Tock leaned in again and whispered,

"I've heard a rumor that once, while working on her physics homework, she accidentally opened a worm hole into another dimension."

"Do you believe that?"

Tock shrugged. "I don't disbelieve it. And if anyone could do it, it's definitely Stevie."

They were both silent for a moment, contemplating Tock's words, when, at the same time, they both began to speak.

"Yeah."

"Yeah. It's best she works with you."

"Absolutely. And I'm happy to do it."

"Great."

"Great."

Tock stood. "Mads set up the couch for you to sleep on."

"I should probably head home."

"No one believes you're going home with your cub spending the night at a bear house. So don't even try to lie. Instead of standing outside the Dunn house all night, just sleep on the couch. With your hearing, you'll know if she sneezes in her sleep."

A little embarrassed that Tock had so easily sized him up, he simply replied, "Thanks."

He felt her turn toward the back door, but she didn't walk away. Instead, she crouched down and placed her hand on his shoulder. "She'll be just fine tonight. I promise."

"Thank you. I appreciate that."

She kissed him on the cheek, taking him by complete surprise and charming him all at the same time.

"See you in the morning," she said.

"Yeah." He waited until she opened the back door before he looked at her over his shoulder. "Night, Tock." But his voice was so low, he wasn't sure she even heard him.

He opened the door to his brother's room in their New Jersey home. He didn't like being the one to wake him up, especially this early in the morning. It was risky. The big cat took his sleep very seriously. They all did, but his older brother was the only one who wasn't afraid to make his displeasure painfully known.

This couldn't wait, though.

Splayed across his bed in his lion form, his brother slept hard. But he knew what would get his brother's attention.

"It's happening today."

One gold eye immediately opened; the left side of his face was smooshed into his pillow so he couldn't open the other eye. Still, even with that one eye, he knew his brother's question without having to hear it.

"It's going to be very nasty."

Slowly, his brother pushed himself up on all fours, standing on the double king mattress. He threw his head back and began to roar. Powerful, short roars with a few seconds between each. Then a series of staccato ones that went on for nearly twenty seconds, until he went back to the short powerful ones.

Finally, they heard their next-door neighbor's loud girlfriend scream, "*Oh, my God! What the fuck is that shit?*"

Chapter 16

Shay expected the morning to be bad, but it wasn't. And that was because Tock was in charge. She woke people up based on how long they normally took in the shower—he did not ask how or why she had that information, but she had it. By the time she tapped him on the shoulder to wake him up, everyone else was either dressed or nearly dressed. Ready to start the day.

"You've got twenty minutes," she informed him. "Clean clothes from your brother in the main bedroom. You can also shower in the bathroom. Breakfast at Charlie's. Waffles and bacon."

"Wolves love waffles," he mumbled, sitting up and scratching his head. "Am I the last to get ready?"

"Finn says you take short showers while Streep insists on wasting water for forty-five minutes."

"I've been up since five!" Streep announced as she walked through the room in shorts and a T-shirt, her feet bare.

"Why are you not dressed yet?"

"I'm not naked."

"Shoes! Boots, preferably. No idea what's going to happen this afternoon."

Shay frowned. "Everything okay?"

"Yeah. Just looking into something."

"Need backup?"

"Max, do we need back—"

"Nope!" the MacKilligan announced on her way through the hallway toward the kitchen.

"Why is no one wearing shoes?" Tock demanded. "Put your shoes on!" She focused on Shay's face again. "We'll be fine."

After that he'd taken his shower, put on his brother's clothes, and headed over to Charlie's. As promised, she had made bacon and waffles and baked goods for the bears lurking around her windows. Dani was already at the kitchen table, enjoying her waffles and bacon, when he walked in and kissed her on the top of the head. She looked so happy that morning, he was glad he'd let her stay with Nat, who ate and then went back to bed as any teenager would in the summertime.

Keane showed up in time to have some breakfast before getting them into his SUV—including the "damn puppies" and Princess—and headed off to Dani's summer camp out on the Island. Sitting in the front with Finn, Keane complained about the cost of gas and all his traveling "back and forth between Long Island and Queens. I hope you appreciate the money I'm spending."

While his brother continued bitching, Shay pulled his daughter close and watched as she worked on math problems in one of her notebooks.

"Daddy?"

"Uh-huh?"

"Do you like Tock?"

Uh-oh. Shay had to be careful here. Kids could get attached easily, and he hated disappointing his daughter. He needed to set up strong boundaries now before she started thinking Tock would be a permanent part of their life just because she might occasionally tutor Dani in math.

"Of course I like Tock. She really helped us when we needed it."

"But do you *like* like her?"

"No, baby, I don't. She's just a friend."

"Really? Because Auntie Nat thinks you *like* like her."

Dammit, Nat! What was wrong with his baby sister? Not everything had to be a stupid rom-com.

"I've barely spoken six words to Nat in the last four days. How could she possibly know what I like or don't like right now?"

"Well, Auntie Charlie thinks Tock likes *you*."

Shay rubbed his forehead with his free hand. "You do know that Charlie, Stevie, and Max are *not* your aunts, right?"

"Don't change the subject," Finn said from the front passenger seat. "Do you *like* like Tock or not?"

Shay glowered at the back of his brother's super-slapable head. "Shut. Up."

They parked the SUV more than five miles away and walked to the docks. They couldn't get close to where that boat went down, though. Federal agencies of every stripe were there, blocking the area and conducting investigations.

After a few minutes of just standing around, watching the Feds along with the crowd of curious onlookers and press, they spread out and followed their noses around the rest of the massive New Jersey dock until they could sneak past the full-humans guarding the place.

And as soon as they got closer to where the action had happened, all Tock could smell was bear. Big, male bears.

That wasn't unusual at any dock. Shipping required big burly people to help move all those products and the crates they were in. But along with the scent of bear, she could smell gun oil and . . . lion.

Tock rolled her eyes. She had no patience for lion males. Lion females were bad enough, but she only fucked with them when they started shit. But lion males . . . True, they'd helped her and her teammates take down the hyena clan led by Mads's mother, but that didn't matter. Good will one day did not guarantee good will later when it came to wild animals. It especially didn't guarantee that with shifters.

"I don't know why he's mad at me," Mads complained beside Tock while Tock just kept sniffing. "It's not like I invited that coyote and his family into my home. He was already there. He had imminent domain."

"It's *eminent* and I don't think you're using that term correctly. At all."

"I just don't think it's fair to consider running off a coyote that's not bothering us when he's just trying to take care of his family."

Tock stopped by a large container and sniffed the door. She kept smelling bears. Bears everywhere! She continued moving.

"Don't you think it's dangerous to have an animal on your property that could be riddled with disease and fleas?"

"He's very clean. He doesn't have fleas."

Again, Tock stopped, but this time she faced Mads.

"What?" Mads asked.

"Have you bathed that animal?"

"Of course I do. When we're not home, he gets into the house and sleeps on our sheets."

"That's disgusting."

"You're just uptight."

"When it comes to vermin . . . yes, I am."

"Coyotes are *not* vermin."

"Just because it's cuter than a rat, that does not make it any less vermin-y."

"I thought we were working."

"*I'm* working," Tock reminded her teammate. "You're obsessing over your boyfriend not liking the wild animal you're trying to make into a house pet."

"Finn is not my boyfriend."

Tock stopped a third time and faced Mads. They stared each other down the way they would a player on an opposing team.

"Fine," Mads said when the insane staring went on for way too long. "He's my boyfriend. But, quite honestly, I don't know if I'm his girlfriend."

"He puts up with the rabid animal you allow to sleep on your clean sheets. Trust me. He's your boyfriend."

"He's not rabid. He's had his shots."

"The vermin-y dog or the oversized cat?"

Mads shrugged. "Both."

Disgusted her normally sensible teammate would do any of that for a dog that wasn't even domesticated, Tock started walking again, her nose high, each sniff bringing her closer to . . . something. She just hadn't figured out what yet.

They came around the corner of a container but found their way blocked. Not by another container or even a wall but by big cats. She glanced over her shoulder and found even more behind her and Mads.

The tigers—their massive size that told her they were Amurs—appeared to be dockworkers; a few were even wearing badges identifying them as such.

"Badgers," one of them said, "lurking around these containers make us very nervous."

That actually made complete sense to Tock. When honey badgers "lurked," it was usually because they were about to steal something.

Having decided not to bring her guns when the docks were filled with federal agents and cops, Tock only had a tactical knife on her. But that would do the job. She started to reach for it, but before her hand could wrap around the handle of the weapon strapped to her back, Mads was holding up her smartphone toward the cat that had spoken.

The tiger looked down, leaned in a bit, and squinted. "Finn?" he finally asked the screen image. "Is that you?"

"Back off, Donovan," Finn warned over the phone.

"Or what?" the cat scoffed.

"Or I tell your mother what you did in the fifth grade."

The cat's expression went from mocking to fear to anger. "My own cousin . . . the disloyalty."

"*Disloyalty?*" Keane exploded from the other end of the phone.

Tock couldn't see Keane's face but she could easily imagine him snatching the phone from his younger brother and yelling into it. And watching the restless reactions of the cats standing right in front of them, they'd heard all this before. "You've got the *nerve* to spout off about disloyalty to *us*, motherfucker? *Fuck you!*"

"Okay," the cat said over Keane's ranting. "*Okay!* But they better not be here to steal. That'll be a problem."

"They're not," she heard Finn reply. He must have taken the phone back from his brother. "Just back off."

The cat nodded and Mads lowered the phone, disconnecting the call. The tigers moved off without saying another word, leaving Tock and Mads alone among an endless sea of shipping containers.

"Did you tell Finn what we are doing here today?" Tock asked Mads when they started searching again.

"No. Why?"

"But he blindly backed you with his borderline-criminal Malone cousins anyway?" Tock waited until Mads looked in her direction and then she mouthed, *Boyfriend*.

"I can't believe they actually said that to us."

Shay cringed. His male cousins weren't always the brightest. For the Malones, the true intelligence went to the females of the family. The males ranged from their dad—smart enough to be recruited by the CIA—to their Uncle Seán, who thought it was a good idea to tell his wife that she did look nice in that dress . . . but she was prettier when she was twenty-two.

So, yeah. He didn't expect his cousins to think too deeply about whether it was a good idea to say some dumb shit to Finn, Shay, and Keane about "loyalty." A loyalty the family never showed their own blood kin when Shay's old man died.

Of course, now that Shay knew his father had been a federal agent, it made more sense that the Malones had had so little to do with their brother and his half-Asian family. Federal agents, in their minds, were no better than NYPD. Cops were cops were cops. And the Malones didn't deal with cops.

Keane didn't care about the Malone credo, though. The Malones had done nothing to avenge his father's death and even less to care for his kids and wife. As far as Keane was concerned, they weren't family at all. Just more enemies for the eventual funeral pyre he was working to build.

Shay got angry about it at times. So did Finn. But nothing topped the rage that tore Keane Malone's soul apart.

Keane parked the SUV and they all got out.

"Do you need anything from me?" Shay asked his daughter as he helped her to put on her overfilled backpack. He saw the other kids rolling their backpacks around, but not his daughter. She didn't want rollers on her bag. She just wanted sparkle and the Hello Kitty brand.

"Just ask Uncle Dale to look in on the dogs if you go out today."

"Dani—"

"Please, Daddy."

"I'll take care of it."

She threw her arms around his waist and hugged him. "Love you, Daddy."

"Love you, too, baby."

She pulled away and ran toward math camp. What his ten-year-old self would have thought of as the most boring camp ever, his daughter *ran* toward. Happily! He'd never seen her more excited. Well, at least she had the smart female genes from his Malone side.

"Call Dale," Keane suddenly ordered, staring at his phone. "Tell him to stay home and take care of those dogs."

"Why?" Finn asked.

"Because we're going to the docks."

"Why? What happened?"

He gripped his phone so tight, the glass started to crack. "Those motherfuckers have been texting me."

"Our cousins? What did they say?"

"Just get in the car."

"Keane, we're not getting into a fight with our Jersey cousins."

Keane glowered at Finn and, for a brief, horrifying moment, Shay was afraid he'd have to kill his eldest brother to save his younger one.

But then Keane blinked and said, "No. We're not. We're going there to protect Shay's new girlfriend."

"From what?" Shay asked.

"We can't trust our cousins to leave her and her badger friends alone. So we'll go there and calm the situation down ourselves."

"Calm the situation down? By what? Starting a fight with the Malones?"

Keane shoved his damaged phone into his back pocket. "That's on them."

Shay watched his brother walk back toward the SUV, but he couldn't let this go . . .

"And Tock is *not* my girlfriend!"

Tock and Mads continued searching around the containers until they got a text from Charlie telling them to meet her by the car. They had turned around, about to head back, when Mads's head suddenly lifted and she started walking toward a big container.

She checked the door and reared back, nearly crashing into Tock.

"What?" Tock asked, steadying Mads before she could fall on her ass.

"Decomp." She pointed at the container. "From in there."

"Could be mob guys just working out their own shit."

"With bears? Because that's what I'm smelling. Dead bears."

Pulling out her set of lockpicks from the back pocket of her jeans, Tock crouched down and got to work on the thick padlock. It was currently protected by a lockbox of some kind so she couldn't just cut through the padlock. She had to work on it from underneath. A deterrent for run-of-the-mill thieves but not for badgers. Or wolves. Tock knew for a fact wolves could break into and out of anything.

She twisted the pick but briefly froze when she heard a new sound. Then she realized it was just Max and Streep coming around the storage container, followed a minute later by Nelle.

"You smelled it, too?" Max asked.

"Mads did," Tock said, continuing her work.

With her teammates watching the area around them for trouble, Tock asked, "Where's Charlie?"

"She's already at the car. Waiting for us."

"Should we let her know—"

"Not until we're sure," Max replied. "I don't want to waste my sister's time. She hates that."

Tock felt the *click* of the padlock and relaxed when the lock finally opened. She tossed the lock aside and opened the handles near the bottom of the doors. With Mads's help, they grabbed one of the long handles and dragged the right door open, leaving the left one closed.

The smell of decay hit hard once the door was open, but they didn't cough or choke the way most full-humans did when hit with such a strong scent. Decomposition was just another stage of life; many predators were able to feed off decaying corpses.

Tock stepped inside, Mads behind her, and the rest of their teammates followed along.

They found the bodies at the end of the container. About eight of them. All bears. Grizzlies, one black, and a couple of polars. They smelled of death and the ocean. Not Tock's favorite scent, but what could a girl do? Flies and maggots already swarmed the bodies, but that didn't stop Max from digging around the pockets of the grizzlies until she found a wallet.

"Giuseppe Romanov."

"That is *not* a common name," Streep noted.

"Text Charlie and see what she wants us to—"

Max's next words abruptly stopped when the sunlight coming in from the opening began to disappear. They all looked up in time to see a woman Tock didn't recognize closing the door. Seconds before she closed it completely, the woman smiled and gave them a little wave.

The next second they were in complete darkness. That wasn't a big deal, though. Badgers were nocturnal.

But still, Streep probably summed it up best when she muttered, "I don't know about the rest of you guys . . . but I find all this disconcerting."

Shay knew his brother wasn't really concerned about "backing up" Mads and Tock at the New Jersey dock. They didn't even know where the badgers were, and the docks were huge. He did, however, think Keane would at least pretend to be doing so. But that did not happen. Not once he spotted Seán and a healthy chunk of Malone cousins eating tacos near a food truck. They weren't even by the docks, but several blocks away.

Why argue, though? Why bother reminding Keane that they were supposed to be in Jersey to help the badgers? Especially once Keane pulled to a stop, got out of the SUV, and charged over to their cousins like a rampaging rhino.

"You got something to say to me?" Keane challenged, stomping up to Seán, who was mid-bite of his taco. And interrupting an eating tiger . . . such a bad idea.

Instead of replying, though, Seán took another bite from his taco.

That's when Keane slapped the rest of the taco out of his cousin's hand.

Charlie leaned back against the SUV, stared at her phone, and waited for Max and her friends. Max had texted that they were "looking at one more thing," so Charlie wasn't too concerned that her sister and teammates were taking their time.

Besides, online shopping always kept Charlie busy when she had to wait for one of her sisters.

She was checking out a matching leash and harness that Dani could use to walk Princess and the male dogs—Charlie would normally not be okay with a ten-year-old walking a potentially aggressive dog, but she knew the father and uncles wouldn't allow it unless they were going along to protect the kid—when she got that feeling in the pit of her stomach. It was her personal warning signal. It let her know when something bad was about to happen. It made her hyperaware of everything within a five-mile radius. Sounds. Smells. Everything.

Charlie lowered her phone and turned toward the SUV, her stomach pressing into the hood while her head moved. She could hear arguing a few blocks away. Angry arguing. The scent of pissed-off cats. She heard Keane Malone snarl in the distance, but before she could pin down his location, the air around her changed.

Jerking her shoulders, Charlie moved her head to the side as a blade slashed the air where her head used to be.

Charlie dropped her phone and spun around, slamming the back of her fist into the head of her attacker, sending him face-first into the passenger-side window of the vehicle. But there were more attackers.

And they all came at her at once.

Tock only had a moment to exchange a look with Mads before they hit the ground and bullets tore through the side of the storage container.

The weapons being used were definitely semiauto handguns, but the bullets . . . they had to be 50-millimeter, armorpiercing rounds. Tock would guess the Desert Eagle .50 AE. The one weapon that could actually take down a honey badger.

They all shifted to their badger forms, making them a little smaller, a little harder to hit. Zigzagging while sprinting, they headed toward the doors.

The first bullet hit Tock in her left front leg. Then her left side. Max got hit in the ass, her pained yelp almost making Tock laugh. Mads took a hit to the shoulder, causing her to flip head over tail before she got back to her feet and continued running. Somehow the rain of bullets seemed to miss Nelle completely until a shot nailed her through the neck. Nelle kept moving.

They were nearing the door when a bullet ricocheted off the ground and went into Streep's chest. The tremendous force sent Streep sliding across the floor and into the wall; Nelle was forced to jump over her teammate's limp, bleeding badger body so she didn't crash into her.

Shay pushed his cousins away from his eldest brother's back while Finn worked to get Keane's hands from around their Uncle Seán's neck.

It wasn't that Shay didn't think his brother was being an asshole. He was an asshole most days. But he also wasn't going to let his cousins beat up his brother.

Sadly, this wasn't the first time this sort of thing had happened. Their grandmother's birthday. Their great uncle's funeral. The Malone family reunion. That christening at the church. Of course, their priest uncle started that shit, and their

cousin who had taken a vow of silence for her order broke
Finn's nose. So this fight was fairly typical.

Annoyingly . . . painfully typical.

"What is wrong with your brother? Why is he acting like
this?" Georgie Malone demanded of Shay while reaching for
Keane from behind.

"*Him?*" Shay yelled back. "You guys started this! Texting
him about our dad!"

"No, we didn't!"

"What?"

Georgie started to answer but stopped, staring off into the
street, becoming so distracted he stopped trying to tear Keane's
jaw off with his bare hands. Shay turned to see exactly what his
cousin was looking at.

It was a white van. And Shay had always believed that if it
wasn't a plumber's or painter's van, a white van was never good.

Shay stepped away from the scrum and watched as the van
followed the curving path of the street. As it neared their bat-
tling group, the van's side door slid open and the muzzles of
automatic rifles slid out.

"Holy—"

"—shit!" Georgie finished before he and Shay tackled the
fighting cousins and their uncle as bullets sprayed the area from
at least four separate weapons.

Hands dug into her hair and threw Charlie through the plate
glass window of a recently shutdown deli. Her body slammed
against a table, bounced, and hit the floor. By the time she got
up, the attackers had stepped through the destroyed window.

They were shifters, but to Charlie's shock, they raised Desert
Eagles. Charlie was shocked because they weren't badgers. They
were lions. Lions, tigers, and bears rarely used guns against
other shifters. As apex predators, they felt it was beneath them.
Guns were weapons only weak full-humans and tiny shifters
needed to survive. That belief apparently hurt foxes' feelings
and they also rarely used weapons against fellow shifters. But
badgers didn't have feelings to hurt. So they did whatever they

had to do to stop an enemy. But to see a bunch of lions pointing guns at her . . .

The cats didn't even wait; they just pulled their triggers. The Desert Eagle was a gun with ammo powerful enough to go through metal or rock or honey badger.

Charlie grabbed the table she'd fallen on, lifted it, and flung it across the room. Then she charged forward, dodging to the right, then left, then straight at the last two lions still standing and shooting because the table had missed them completely.

The shooting stopped as the van careened off. The cousins focused on Georgie. He'd been shot through the leg and the lower back. But Shay hadn't been hurt. Neither had his brothers. But they'd been shot at. And they were not happy.

Keane may have been the one known as the "mean" Malone Brother. But all three of them had an issue with rage. And vengeance.

Snarling, not caring they were shifting in the middle of the street, in the middle of the day, the Malone brothers took off after the van, streaking past stunned full-humans who had managed to drop to the ground when the shooting started.

Shay didn't care who saw him. He didn't care what was caught on camera. He didn't care what repercussions there might be from him showing the world what he was. He didn't care and neither did his brothers. They cut across the street and leaped onto the roof of a small union building. They sped across the rooftop, well aware their speed would only last so long. Tigers were sprinters, not marathoners. That was wolves.

They jumped from the roof. Shay and Finn landed on the back of the speeding van, Finn gripping the back door with his claws, Shay holding onto the roof rack. Keane landed on the hood. Shay made it across the top toward the front just as Keane rammed his paw into the windshield. The force shattered the glass and Keane shoved his body inside. Not even a second later, the van took a hard turn, hit the curb and flipped, sending Shay and Finn spiraling along with it.

★   ★   ★

Charlie held one She-lion around the neck and shot the male through the head with the Desert Eagle she'd taken from one of the other females.

Brain and bone blew back on her before she put the gun to the She-lion's head.

The She-lion clawed at her arm and yelped, "*Aspetta*—"

But she wouldn't wait. Charlie pulled the trigger, blinking as more blood and bone hit her face. She released the body in her arms and was about to walk out of the store when a bullet slammed into her from behind, breaking her collar bone on its way out of her body.

Still standing, Charlie looked down at the wound. Her fangs slid from her gums and she slowly faced the lions who had come in the back door of the deli. The one who had pulled the trigger gazed at her with wide eyes.

"*Cazzo,*" he cursed, backing up and pulling the trigger of the weapon he held. But the kick from a Desert Eagle was brutal. He had to keep re-aiming the weapon before he could take his shot and Charlie just kept moving out of the way of each bullet. She was moving so fast, she knew the lions could barely see her.

Charlie jumped up on the deli counter, charged across it and over the lions. By the time they realized she was no longer in front of them, she'd buried her claws into the spine of a She-lion. While staring into the eyes of the male lion standing to the female's right, Charlie yanked her claws up until she'd split the female's spine into several pieces.

Holding up her blood-and-gore-covered hand, she moved to stand in front of the male lion.

"*Ti prego.*"

"Yeah," she said, hearing the lion behind her running out the way he'd come. "It's a little too late for begging."

Tock reached the doors; there had to be a way to open them from the inside.

Shifting to human, she pushed at the right door, but it was securely locked. Even with her claws, she'd never get through that metal. She quickly moved to the left door, ducking as a bullet came dangerously close to her head. That one moved and she realized the person who'd shut them hadn't thought it necessary to lock the other door. The one they'd unlocked but hadn't bothered to open.

"Mads!"

Mads rushed to her side and shifted. While the others helped Streep, Tock and Mads pushed on the heavy door. They had gotten it halfway open when Tock heard squealing tires and a gunned engine. She grabbed Mads's arm and yanked her back, expecting the truck to hit the doors.

The container moved a foot or two when the truck hit it, but that truck didn't slam into the doors. It scraped against the side of the container as—based on the roars, snarling, screaming, and disturbing thuds—the truck mowed down whoever had been shooting at them.

Tock motioned for Mads to stay put and then slipped past the partially open door and went to the edge of the container. She peered around the corner. The truck's brake lights were bright red and the attackers on the ground, at least two of them now shifted to lion, were starting to get up. But then the engine revved again, and the brake lights went off. The big blue van sped back and, again, slammed into the ones who had been shooting at Tock and her teammates.

The van kept going until it passed the container and stopped. An Asian woman with part of her thick hair shaved on one side leaned out the driver's-side window and asked, "Tock?"

Stunned, because Tock didn't recognize this woman at all, she nodded.

"Get your friends and get your asses in the van, kid. We've gotta move."

Looking down at the carnage and using the butt of the gun she still had in her hand to rub her bloody brow, Charlie briefly wondered what prison would be like. That's when she felt eyes on her. She turned, raising the weapon.

A blond woman watched her from outside the busted window, but she didn't move. Didn't run away. Didn't even flinch.

Another badger.

Still, Charlie thought about killing her, too.

"The Desert Eagle," the blonde said with a thick Eastern European accent, "it jams. You are better with CZ or Makarov."

"The Makarov? Do they even still make those?"

The blonde motioned to Charlie with a twitch of her forefinger. "Come, little freak. We must go."

God, Charlie was just so tired. All she really wanted to do was crawl into one of the empty cabinets in the back kitchen and get some sleep before the cops showed up and handcuffed her.

"Lady," she finally sighed out, "I don't know you. As it is, I am thinking of killing you, too. Might as well, right?" Charlie added. "If I'm going to prison, I might as well go out with a bang."

"Prison? You think they would ever allow *you* to go to prison? They would kill you first. Or have me do it. But for now . . . we just need to move you to some place safe."

"My sister—"

"My friends have her." The blonde wagged the finger she'd just been gesturing with when Charlie's fangs made a sudden reappearance. "Now, now, little freak. No need for that. She is alive. We're here to help. Not to kill. Unless you make us. So come. Move that pretty ass and let's go."

Charlie looked at the jammed gun in her hand, dropped it, and followed the woman as she walked to a waiting Mercedes.

As they all got back into the clothes they'd quickly grabbed before making a break for it, the van they were in turned hard at a corner, and Tock nearly landed on poor Streep.

"Sorry. Sorry," she said, pushing herself away from her teammate's prone body.

"They drive like Max," Mads complained.

"They really do," Max agreed. "And do we have any idea who these people are? Friends or enemies?" When all she got back were shrugs, Max nodded and said, "Great, great. Always good to know we might die any minute."

"We have to do something," Nelle pointed out. "We've already lost poor Streep."

Streep's eyes opened. "I'm not dead."

"Yet, sweetie." Nelle patted her head. "Yet."

"Tock said I'd be fine!"

"Tock is not a doctor. But don't worry . . . we'll miss you when you're gone."

"How are we going to get out of here?" Mads wanted to know.

Before any of them could think of a way, the van suddenly stopped.

Tock knew they hadn't gone far. They were still near the docks and all the shipping containers and the people trying to murder them.

She went to the back doors, expecting them to be jury-rigged so she couldn't open them from the inside. But they swung open easily and Tock jumped out.

"Wait here," she told her teammates before going around the vehicle.

The Asian—whom Tock had realized was a fellow badger before even driving away from the containers—stood in front of a severely damaged white van, the back doors flung open and facing them.

"Come on!" the She-badger yelled into it. When she spotted Tock easing up behind her, she motioned her over. "Can you please help me here?"

Tock didn't understand what the woman was talking about, so she stepped closer and took a look inside.

"Maybe they'll listen to you? Because we have to go. Now."

Tock walked closer to the van and said, "All right, guys. Let's go."

The three Malone brothers—still in their tiger form—just stared at her. Tock had to admit . . . it was off-putting. They were so fucking big, they completely filled the inside of the van. It also didn't help they were covered in blood and didn't seem to recognize her at all. Those cold, cat glares just . . . staring at her.

"Guys," she tried again, "let's go. We have to go."

The three males exchanged glances before a massive Keane jumped out of the van and loped over to the other vehicle.

Tock knew he'd reached it when she heard Max exclaim, "*Holy shit! More cats!* Oh. It's just the Malones."

Finn quickly followed Keane, but when Shay tried to do the same, Tock stopped him with one raised finger.

"Drop the head," she told him.

Shay took a step back; a giant male lion's head was securely locked between his jaws. You'd think, with all that golden mane getting in his eyes, Shay would be happy to get rid of the thing. But he clearly didn't want to release his prize. Instead, he growled a little and shook it.

"Shay Malone," Tock barked, using her mother's authoritarian tone, "drop that head and get the fuck out here!"

Shay's prize hit the floor and rolled out of the lopsided van, landing on the ground with a wet thud. A second later, Shay followed, running over to the van and jumping inside.

"Let's go," the She-badger ordered, already moving back to the driver's side.

Tock began to follow but a full-human woman was standing on the sidewalk, gawking at her. She was so stunned, she hadn't even bothered to use her phone to record what she had witnessed. It simply hung limply from her hand.

With a shrug, Tock told her, "Wild animal trafficking gone horribly, horribly wrong. Never put different apex predators in the same van."

When the woman only frowned in confusion, Tock walked away. She didn't have time for further explanation.

Tock forced herself inside between three really big Siberian tigers and her teammates, all of whom were trying to give Streep some space, and leaned back out to grab the doors and slam them closed.

The van began moving again and Tock sat down on the floor, a now-human and naked Shay sitting beside her.

Both covered in a good amount of blood, the pair glanced at each other, then away.

"How was your morning?" Tock asked the cat.

"Pretty bad. And yours?"

"Shitty. Quite shitty."

"Yeah," Shay said on a long sigh. "Yeah."

Chapter 17

Captain Desiree "Dez" MacDermot watched in fascination as nearly the entire Eastern Seaboard was shut down in record time. Not by the United States government. They'd only managed to shut down the Jersey docks.

But the United States shifters? They didn't play. As soon as they heard about what was going on at the docks, they moved with a speed she'd never actually witnessed before. The area was blocked off in all directions for up to ten miles. Communications were completely shut off. Suddenly, cell phones didn't work. There was also an immediate media blackout—local and national news were unable to get anywhere near the epicenter of "animal trafficking gone very wrong."

At least that was the story the media was getting and would continue to get. About how some very bad men had been moving apex predators through the docks to sell to rich billionaires when the animals got loose and went on a rampage.

What about the bullet casings? And reports of drive-by shootings? No, no. That was just the bad guys trying to get their animals back under control. Yes, there were guns, but no one was actually hurt.

If one did not count honey badgers, apparently.

Dez wasn't surprised to find that honey badgers were somehow a part of the disaster. Of all the problems she had to deal with as head of the NYPD's Shifter Only Unit, the badgers were always the worst to deal with. A few years ago, she would have said it was grizzly bears hopped up on cocaine-infused honey that were her biggest problem. But she'd quickly learned that particular issue was easily rectified with a tranq gun normally used on elephants and a media report about meth-head body builders.

Honey badgers, though . . . they were a nightmare. Because they didn't act like other shifters. They were nothing like Mace, Dez's husband, or their son—both very moody lion males who took lots of naps and ate a *lot* of food. She loved them both, but she fought hard to manage them. Especially with each other. But she was from the Bronx. Managing two males with machismo issues was something she was used to after years as a cop and former Marine MP.

The badgers, however, didn't have machismo issues. They didn't think because they had a lot of hair and a big attitude, the world should automatically back away and let them roam free. Instead, badgers insinuated themselves into the full-human world and then started shit. Whether it was the young badgers who nearly burned down a school so they could get out early and go to a concert at Madison Square Garden, or adult badgers who somehow managed to start a fistfight between diplomats at the UN. Diplomats! Their whole business was *not* to fight. But, as Dez had been saying since she found out that actual honey badger shifters existed, "Leave it to a badger."

Leave it to a badger to steal Romanian royal jewels on loan to MOMA.

Leave it to a badger to get moms to literally spit at each other during a parent-teacher conference when all Dez wanted to know was how to help her son pass his English course because he found it "soooo boring!"

And leave it to a badger to shut down the Eastern Seaboard because someone wanted to kill a whole bunch of them.

She examined the shipping container that her former partner told her some of the badgers had been stuffed in. There were bullet holes and blood everywhere. Plus, dead lions on the outside and dead bears on the inside.

That was concerning. Especially the lions. The New York Lion prides could be an issue, sure. But always easily managed. They, like everyone else, just wanted to live their lives. Some were really rich. Some less so. But their goal was always to protect the pride. Nothing else mattered.

But the lions she saw scattered around the shipping container and in the white van that had done the drive-by . . .

First off, they weren't American. The few IDs that had been found on them said they were from Italy. Again, Dez was always a little surprised when she discovered something new. Like Italian lions. It made sense, of course. But still . . . she was just a full-human cop from the Bronx who happened to fall in love with a lion. Stuff that her husband had grown up knowing, she was still discovering almost each and every day.

It was fun and interesting, but definitely terrifying. How could it not be? A human being able to shift into an apex predator! One just had to hope and pray those unusual beings didn't get bitchy about how full-humans were fucking up the planet and each other. Dez knew if those shifters ever decided to turn on the rest of them . . . they would all be screwed.

But for eons, shifters had made one thing their focus: protecting their kind. Not just from one another—bears hated wolves; lions hated hyenas; tigers hated everybody—but from the dirty shit full-humans so often got up to with anything they considered "other." Shifters kept their kind secret because they didn't want to end up strapped to a lab table, about to be dissected. That was one of the reasons Dez had taken the job she currently had, because she wanted to help protect the most important things in her life: her husband and her son. Big-headed lazy bastards that she adored like the moon and stars.

And if protecting them meant closing down the entire Eastern Seaboard until the shifter-run federal agencies fixed the problem, she was okay with that.

"Are they all dead?" she asked her old partner, Lou "Crush" Crushek. A polar bear who looked like a giant old biker but who was really just an undercover cop who managed to terrify everyone around him simply by standing up. The man was nearly seven feet tall, with long white hair and muscles on top of muscles on top of muscles. He was one of Dez's best friends.

"The lions? Yeah," he said. "They're all dead."

"No." She motioned around the shipping container with a wave of her hand. "The badgers."

Crush sort of snorted. "No."

"What do you mean 'no'? I've seen the casings. They used .50-caliber ammo. Hollow points. And I've seen what the Desert Eagle can do. Are you telling me those badgers aren't dead somewhere?"

"We don't know where they are, but they definitely walked out of this shipping container."

"And that's not weird to you?"

"MacDermot, my wife is a tiger. I walk in sometimes and find her on our couch, in her cat form, with her legs up in all directions while she licks her own ass and watches a Rangers game on the TV. So what I consider weird may be vastly different from what you do."

"Yeah." Dez nodded. "I can see how it would be."

The van didn't go far before it stopped again and the doors opened. They'd reached a private airport; four running helicopters waited for them.

"Let's go," an older Latina badger ordered, her sleeveless T-shirt showing off powerful, tattooed shoulders and arms. "Head to the copters."

Only Nelle moved forward, stepping down from the van in those ridiculous shoes she insisted on wearing. Who walked around a dock in six-inch designer heels except Nelle?

Towering over the Latina, Nelle said, "We're not going anywhere until you tell us who you are and what you want."

The She-badger stepped back, looking past the van.

"They're being assholes!" she called out to someone.

"Maybe they're just being cautious!"

"Okay. They're being cautious assholes."

Tock glanced at Shay and he muttered, "I'm not going anywhere without my kid."

"What was that?" the Latina demanded, badger gaze locking on Shay.

"I'm not going anywhere without my daughter," Shay announced, louder.

"Doesn't she have a mother who can deal with her?"

Nelle quickly put her hand on Keane's chest before he could launch himself at the badger.

"Her mother's at football camp," Shay said.

The Latina frowned. "On purpose?"

"I have to get my kid," Shay insisted.

"You're all covered in blood, the badgers have bullet holes *all over*, and you three cats are naked," she added, pointing at Shay and his brothers.

"They didn't have time to go back and get their clothes," Nelle explained.

"So . . . what? You want us to run them home first to get their clothes and then get them out? We don't have time for this."

"Make time."

"You don't seem to understand the situation all of you are currently in." An S-class Mercedes pulled in near the van and the Latina glanced at it before finishing with, "A situation that could get all of you put down like dogs with rabies."

Nelle crossed her arms over her chest. "*We* were attacked. *We* were ambushed. For once, in fact, we did nothing wrong."

The doors to the Mercedes opened and Charlie got out of the passenger side. Max jumped out of the van then, running into her sister's open arms.

"Are you okay?" Charlie demanded. "Are you?"

"I'm fine."

That's when Charlie pulled away and slapped the back of her sister's head.

"What did you do?" Charlie barked.

"Nothing! I swear!"

"Then it was Dad." Charlie became somber. "We've gotta kill Dad."

Max shrugged. "Okay."

"It wasn't Fred MacKilligan," a dark-haired She-badger said as she closed the driver's-side door and moved around the front of the Mercedes. "Although none of us are shocked you'd jump to that conclusion. I've never met a greater fuckup."

"Oh, my God," Tock heard from behind her. She glanced back at Mads. Her teammate had been sitting next to Finn with her head on his shoulder for almost the entire ride. But now, eyes wide as she reacted to the female speaking, Mads slowly got to her feet.

"What's wrong?" Finn asked.

Mads didn't answer, but instead asked, "Aunt Tracey?"

The She-badger grinned. "Hi, sweet girl."

Mads bolted forward, pushing her way through everyone in the van until she could jump off the vehicle and right into the female's arms.

Tock knew of Mads's Aunt Tracey. The pair had stayed in communication through discreet emails over the years. That was all they could do because Mads's bitch of a mother had made it very clear that if Tracey—or anyone in the Rutowski family—tried to have anything to do with Mads, she'd be killed. It was a threat they'd taken very seriously because they all knew that Mads's mother was mean enough to do it, and her hyena clan would happily join in. It was too great a risk to hope someone in that clan would have a moral issue with killing a kid. So, the Rutowskis had stayed away. Until now. Until Mads was old enough and powerful enough to take not only her mother and grandmother down, but the entire clan. All with the help of football-playing lions who loved nothing more than destroying hyenas for shits and giggles.

Putting her arm around Mads's shoulders, Tracey Rutowski turned her niece around to face their small group.

"Now, I know we need to go, but I just want to take a few seconds—"

"It's always a few seconds with you, and then we're running from the KGB," one of the older She-badgers complained.

"*Anyway* . . . I want to introduce you, Mads, to my very best friends." She pointed at the Latina. "This is Cecilia Álvarez. We all call her CeCe. You might know her as C. E. Álvarez."

"The painter and sculptor?" Charlie asked.

"Yes."

"Hey!" Max said, "I stole one of your paintings. Sold it to my fence for, like, a mil-five."

Rutowski blinked. "Huh." After a quick head shake, she motioned to the Asian She-badger with the partially shaved hair. She had lots of earrings on that side and several big scars on her neck. But the prettiest smile Tock had ever seen on a woman not selling toothpaste.

"This is Stephanie Yoon."

"Just call me Steph."

"Steph Yoon?" Tock asked. "The founder of Yoonotics? The company that created the killer robots and drones that turned on their human handlers?"

"*That* is an incorrect summation of what transpired and something I can't talk about until the lawsuits are resolved. But yes . . . that's me."

"I bought a drone from your company and the first time I used it, it definitely attacked me."

"Yeah . . . it probably did. But we have a patch for that now you can get off our website."

"And," Rutowski quickly cut in, moving everyone's attention on to the last of her friends with a sweep of her arm, "this is Oksana Lenkov."

"Doesn't she have an adorable nickname, too?" Max asked, her voice so cutesy, it could only be mocking.

"Yes. We all call her Ox."

Tock looked at "Ox." She was blond. Stunning. With big blue eyes and sharp cheekbones. Dressed in thousands of dollars' worth of designer clothes and shoes. She also had what could only be called a permanent sneer. She looked like she was ready to kick someone in the face with those designer shoes for doing nothing more than passing her on the street and saying, "Excuse me."

"That is my nickname," Ox sneered at a silent Max in a European accent of some kind. Tock would guess Russian. "I like it. Do not annoy me, tiny Asian badger."

Eyes wide, Max looked at Tock; and as soon as that grin spread across her teammate's face, Tock knew Max was going to make it her mission in life to torture Ox.

It wasn't surprising, though. Max hated being called "tiny."

Listening to the badgers banter back and forth was irritating Shay to no end. He wanted to get to his daughter. He wanted to make sure she was okay. He wanted to wash the blood out of his hair. He wasn't worried about his mother. He just had to give her a heads-up and she would go underground with her sisters. She'd done the same thing with her sons when his dad was murdered. They'd almost missed the funeral the Malones had the nerve to arrange.

Yeah. He needed a phone and to get moving.

Oh. And he should check on his baby brother, too. He kept forgetting about Dale.

"I need to get my daughter," he repeated when there was a brief lull in the conversation.

"How?" Álvarez barked; clearly fed up with him. "Again. You are covered in blood and naked. There's no way to get from Jersey to the Island without people noticing."

"How the fuck do you know we live on the Island?" Keane demanded.

"Maybe it's your annoying accent."

"Okay," Tock interjected as Nelle again placed her hand on Keane's chest to prevent him from attacking. "Before this gets out of hand, Shay and I will go get his kid and then we'll meet you wherever you say. Sound good?"

"Absolutely," Rutowski replied. She handed over the keys to her Mercedes. "Take the car and meet our choppers here in"—she looked at her watch—"four hours?"

Tock looked at her big watch. Nodded. "Got it."

"Like a last flight out of Saigon, huh, Tock?" Max joked before glancing at Stephanie Yoon. "No offense."

"That was Vietnam," Yoon sighed out. "I'm Korean. Dumbass."

"Does anyone care that I'm in here dying?" Streep called out from deep inside the van.

"No," all her teammates replied.

Tock texted one of her cousins—grudgingly—and found out there was a safe house not far from where Mads's aunt would have choppers waiting for them. She drove Shay there while he stayed low in the backseat. While he took a shower in the upstairs safehouse bathroom, another one of Tock's cousins showed up with appropriately sized clothes for the extremely large cat and Tock.

"How are you doing?" her cousin asked.

"Fine."

"Really? Because your bullet holes are still bleeding," her cousin pointed out. Which was true, but that didn't mean she wasn't fine. The wounds were still bleeding because they were healing. Bad blood pouring out so the wounds could heal up without infection. Ahhh. The wonders of being a honey badger shifter.

Not that the healing didn't hurt. It always hurt to be a honey badger, but Tock would take temporary pain over permanent death any day.

Her cousin helped her clean the wounds and wrap them before finally leaving, briefly pausing at the front door to warn, "You know *Savta* is involved now, right? I mean . . . more than she was before. And old gal is *pissed*."

But Tock wasn't exactly surprised to hear that. Her grandmother protected their family with an Angel of Retribution approach that she took very seriously. Whatever Mira Malka-Lepstein might feel about Tock's teammates didn't matter, because whoever had attempted to kill them had also gone after

Mira's granddaughter. A mistake one simply did not make if one hoped *not* to have the older honey badger involved.

Once her cousin had gone, Tock packed up her stuff quickly and tossed anything with her blood on it into the trash that would be taken to an incinerator later that afternoon. By the time she was ready, Shay was bounding down the stairs, hair wet from the shower, black T-shirt, sweatpants, and sneakers covering up almost all the scrapes and bumps from the earlier attack.

"Let's go!" he ordered, heading toward the front door.

Tock grabbed his arm and pulled him toward the couch in the living room.

"Sit."

"We don't have time—"

"Sit," she said again, pushing him down until he was on the couch. "You're bleeding a little."

"Dani—"

"Don't worry," Tock told him as she dug into the leftover first aid supplies so she could deal with the bleeding scrape on his forehead. "I have eyes on her. She'll be safe until we get there."

"Eyes?" Shay lifted his frowning face, gazing right at her. "You called in your family?"

"Something like this . . . They're going to be involved anyway. Might as well get them involved in a way I can manage. So, I've got eyes on your daughter, your mom, and your little brother. And my one cousin who likes dogs is picking up the puppies and the three adults from your house."

"Seriously?"

"Dani is *not* going to forgive you if you don't grab those dogs and bring them along. I don't want her feeling any panic over this. She's too young for that."

He suddenly gripped her wrist, gazed at her with those big green-gold eyes. "Thank you."

Shay said it so earnestly that Tock had to frown to keep from feeling things. She hated feeling things. Feeling things was just an annoying weakness. She was not weak.

"That's fine. No big deal." She cleared her throat. "We STEM daddy's girls have to look out for each other."

Tock pulled her wrist away and focused on the wound across his forehead.

"There," she said, once she'd cleaned and bandaged it. The cut wasn't that deep, so she hadn't had to sew it closed. And she couldn't help but chuckle when she'd first seen all the different shades of bandages in the bag her cousin brought. Her politically correct cousins wanting to make sure there was something that would match Tock's skin tone. But there were ones light enough to match Shay's skin tone as well and that was actually kind of cool. "All done. Now you won't freak your daughter out when she first sees you."

She looked at her watch. "Let's get going. We have thirty minutes to—"

Tock stopped talking when Shay took her hand and held it.

"What? What's wrong?" she asked, worried he might be hiding more serious damage. Then again, he'd been naked until the last five minutes, so she would have seen any additional wounds.

Shay got to his feet, towering over her. She thought he was about to say "Thank you" again and she really didn't want to hear it. But he just stood there, looking down at her with this intense expression on his face. She had no idea what to make of it until he leaned in.

Leaned in to kiss her.

He didn't just grab her, though, and pull her close. He leaned in until he was kind of close and then he stopped . . . and waited.

Shay waited for her.

He didn't know why he was doing this. Why he was risking what was turning into a very nice friendship with this move. But he really wanted to do it. He wanted to kiss her. He just needed to know she wanted the kiss as much as he did. He wouldn't force himself on her. That was not something a woman like Tock would appreciate one bit. She didn't play games. She didn't tease. She was just Tock. A dangerous honey badger who had been shot at least seven times and was still standing strong, making sure his daughter was safe.

How could he *not* want to kiss this woman?

He had to wait, though. He had to wait for her.

"We have to go," she said, staring back at him.

"I know."

"We don't have time for foolishness."

"I know."

"We're on a schedule. That helicopter is not going to wait for us."

"I know."

"People clearly want us dead."

"I know."

Still . . . he waited.

"So, we should really go."

"Okay."

As she stared at him, her entire face abruptly scrunched into what appeared to be a huge frown. Shay had no idea how to read her expression, but he figured it was his cue to walk out the front door.

She pulled her hand away from his, and he started to straighten up until she pressed that same hand against his cheek.

Startled, Shay looked down at Tock again and watched in awe as she went up on her toes. When that wasn't enough, she slid her hand around the back of his neck and pulled him closer until their lips met.

The first touch shook him hard. Harder than he expected. He could feel that first touch down to his toes. Then she turned her head a little and he opened his mouth. Her tongue slid inside and brushed against his.

That's when he slid his hands into her curly hair and held her in place as he kissed her back. When he did, she gripped the back of his neck with one hand and his waist with the other.

It was the kind of kiss that seemed to go on forever and not last long enough.

When she finally pulled away, Shay let out a little growl. He didn't want it to end, but he knew it had to. Because life was unfair.

Brushing her hand against her throat and blinking, Tock said, "We really . . ." She pointed at her watch. "Time," she said.

Her momentary incoherence gave him tremendous hope.

"Right," he replied. "Time."

She pushed away from him and strode toward the door. Shay happily followed.

Chapter 18

Charlie gazed up at the mile-high ceilings and down at the marble floors. This wasn't some small, overpriced Hamptons summer home for those trying to *pretend* to be wealthy.

Nope. This was a mansion. A true *Dynasty*-type TV show mansion for the extremely wealthy. There were at least three floors that she could see from the front of the house, she didn't know how many rooms, a sweeping marble staircase, and acres of land surrounding the whole thing.

Charlie had always known of Tracey Rutowski. Not only as Mads's aunt, but also as a very important art dealer. Her company had galleries all over the world, and she'd helped bring up some of the most important artists of the last thirty years. Many of them people of color. Rutowski was also feared. Stealing from her gallery was not a wise move. Every honey badger avoided it. Full-human thieves eventually learned to avoid any gallery or show the female was involved in.

Still, this mansion didn't just imply a successful business. It implied old money. And Tracey Rutowski was definitely *new* money.

Even stranger, the entire mansion reeked of badger and . . . wolf?

"Did you know your nose was a little . . ." Steph Yoon lifted her hands and moved them around her face without touching it, indicating that the pain Charlie had been feeling was from a busted nose. Again.

"I did not."

"Want me to try and—"

"Max," Charlie called out.

Her sister appeared at her side, turned Charlie to face her, put her hands on her face, and roughly twisted her nose around with strong fingers until it was back in place enough to heal on its own.

Charlie took in a deep breath. She never breathed better than after she got her nose broken and repaired. But it wouldn't last. In a few hours, her allergies would be irritating her once again. For now, though, that wolf smell came through even stronger.

"Thanks," she said to her sister.

"The Malone girl—"

"Nat."

"—is on her way with those bears," Yoon told her. "Will be here in a little while."

"Great."

"And we're working on getting Stevie out of her lab." She glanced at her phone. "She's not making it easy, though."

"Let her bring some of her lab stuff with her. She's working on a problem, and she hates being interrupted."

"Right. Okay." She texted someone before asking, "Are you hungry? Thirsty?"

"I would love some water. And something for a headache."

"Oh, sure. This way."

Yoon walked away and Charlie started to follow, but she immediately stopped and spun around. Max and her friends all froze. They hadn't actually been doing anything, but Charlie wanted to make sure they didn't start doing anything. Not until she knew *exactly* what was going on.

Charlie pointed her finger. Mostly at Max, but she made sure to make eye contact with the other two. Tock was off with the Malone brother and Streep had been put into a bed with a doctor and nurse to care for her.

"While we're here," she announced to the women, "there will be no stealing, no lying, no setting anything on fire. No parties, no ambushes, no casual get-togethers that turn into riots." She started to turn away, but stopped again and quickly added, "You will also not gnaw on the furniture, claw your way into any crawl spaces, or chew through any wiring."

"Are they racoons?" Yoon asked.

"Sometimes."

With one more glare at her sister and her friends, Charlie followed Yoon from the room.

"If we can't gnaw on furniture, what are we supposed to do?" Nelle asked. Only half joking, Max guessed. The woman did like to gnaw.

"A place like this must have a basketball court somewhere on it."

"We are *not* going to practice, Mads." Max looked up at the walls. So much expensive artwork and she couldn't touch any of it without her sister kicking her ass.

"You're practically drooling," Nelle told her.

"Dude," Max sighed, staring up at the large wall beside the stairs, "that's a real Chagall."

"They'll definitely notice if that one goes missing."

Mads joined them. "If we're *not* going to practice—"

"Oh, my God, seriously?"

"—we should check on Streep."

Nelle nodded. "Good idea . . . Max? What's wrong?"

"I feel like we've forgotten something."

"Like what?"

"I don't know. But something."

"Think we should be worried?" Kyle Jean-Louis Parker asked the male sitting across from him at the kitchen table.

"Worried?" Dutch Alexander was a wolverine who called himself Max MacKilligan's "best friend." It seemed, though, to Kyle, that he was more of "just a friend" to the honey badger as she spent more time with the She-badgers on her basketball team than she ever did with Dutch. "Worried about what?"

"No one is here. And those three bears from across the street hustled Nat out of the house about an hour ago. Without saying a word to us." Kyle looked down at the sleeping dog in his lap that Charlie had recently rescued. As a jackal, he had a soft spot for some canines. And after spending most of the night in the vet ER with this guy while he got his ear repaired, Kyle had grown a little attached. Not that it would last. He was an artist with no time for true connections beyond the connection to his work. But since he was just sitting here and the dog had crawled right into his lap, looking for affection, he didn't have the heart to toss him off. Seemed unnecessarily cruel. Even for him. "It just seems like something is going on and we've been . . . I don't know . . . forgotten."

"No way. If something was up, Max would definitely let me know."

Max racked her brain for a good minute or so, but nope! She couldn't think of anything she might be forgetting.

With a shrug, she started walking up the big staircase to the second floor, her teammates right behind her. "Let's go check on Streep."

Charlie looked around and sighed, "This kitchen is . . . amazing."

Rutowski smirked. "My husband likes to cook."

"I could get so much baking done in this kitchen." The big room had giant glass doors that let in bright sunshine and looking out over a perfect lawn. It spoke to her on so many levels. How could it not? With four stainless steel double ovens, six gas stoves, four refrigerators, and two freezers that could easily hold several zebra carcasses in each, marble floors and counters, Italian tile, and all the equipment she could ever need or use, she'd never been so envious in her life. "I'd have bears lined up around the block. That could be bad, though. They start going through your trash. Looking for the honey buns you burned."

"Bears," Rutowski chuckled. "They'll eat anything." She gestured to a plate covered in a glass dome. "Arizona bark scorpion?"

Charlie couldn't help but curl her lip a little, unable to hide her disgust. "No, thanks. Max and her friends will like that, though. Although you may want to keep anything that squirms or scuttles or slithers out of sight once Stevie gets here. Or the screaming will start, and it will never stop."

"Good to know." She gave a vague gesture. "Your head feeling any better?"

"Yes."

"Do you need anything else? You seem a little anxious."

"Me? No. I'm fine. I'm fine!"

Rutowski placed her hands over Charlie's, and Charlie realized that all ten of her fingers were tapping incessantly against the marble counter.

"Sorry. Sorry." She pulled her hands away and began rubbing them against her bloodstained jeans. She just needed to think. To figure out what to do next. To manage the situation.

Sitting here, though, in these high chairs at a marble counter that might cost more than the SUV she'd left behind in Jersey, with these old She-badgers watching her . . . that was just not working for her right now. Nope. Not at all.

Tracey watched, fascinated, as the eldest MacKilligan sister jumped off the chair and began moving around the family kitchen. She thought the kid just needed to pace. Badgers could be pacers when they were thinking, planning, plotting. But things only got weirder from there when, while talking nonstop, the kid began going through the kitchen cabinets.

"Does anyone know what's going on?" MacKilligan asked. "Who targeted us? The ones who came after me were Italian. I know that. But what does that mean? Does it mean anything? Or was it just a cheap hire? And did they lure us all to the docks? How? And why? Should I get my sisters out? And are you sure my father has nothing to do with this? He usually does." She briefly paused, a five-pound bag of flour clutched in her hands. "You have geese," she noted, gazing out the big windows. Slowly, Tracey and her friends turned in their chairs and stared at the geese walking by the big double doors.

"I don't understand," the kid said, suddenly speaking again.

"For once we didn't do anything. We weren't there to start shit. We were just . . . investigating. And they tried to kill all of us. Do you have more flour than this?"

Tracey blinked. Surprised by the second sudden change of topic. "Um . . ." She pointed at a door that led to the pantry.

The kid disappeared inside, gasping at the sight of everything that Trace knew was in that room. Just wait until the kid got a look at their walk-in freezer.

Tracey could hear that the kid was still talking. She couldn't make out the words but she had a feeling the girl was still analyzing what had happened that day. She was beginning to feel sorry for the poor thing. She was half wolf. Maybe that's where all that self-analyzing came from. Honey badgers didn't really do that. They might analyze why a heist went wrong or why they'd ended up in jail, but only so that sort of thing wouldn't happen again. What they didn't do was tear themselves apart over emotional bullshit.

The kid walked out of the pantry with two unopened sacks of flour, each fifty pounds. She carried them with ease but that wasn't Tracey's concern. Instead, it was knowing how crazy her husband would get when he saw his pantry had been invaded.

"Oh, honey," Tracey said, slipping off the stool and moving toward the kid, "maybe you should *not*—"

"Uh . . . Aunt Tracey?"

Tracey stopped and looked at the doorway that led into the hallway. Her niece stood there. So strong and fierce. She'd survived a really shitty childhood as only a true honey badger could. She doubted her niece spent any time overanalyzing emotional bullshit like MacKilligan.

"Could I speak to *all* of you?" Mads motioned with her hand. "Please?"

Gesturing to her friends, Tracey headed out of the kitchen and into the hallway. Mads kept walking, so Trace kept following until they reached the foyer.

"Is Charlie . . . baking?" Mads asked when they'd stopped.

"I think so. She started going through the cabinets and then the pantry—"

"She turned the oven on," CeCe noted.

"Okay . . . yeah." Mads nodded her head while her face cringed. "You need to stay away from her right now."

"Uh . . . my husband isn't going to be okay with her baking in the family kitchen."

"I say this with love, but he's going to have to suck it up."

"Pardon?"

"When Charlie gets like this," Mads explained, "when Charlie starts *baking* . . . just back off and hope we're all alive when it's over."

"What the hell does *that* mean?"

"You were right," Mads said when she walked back into the bedroom where they'd put Streep. Their wounded teammate was stretched out on a queen-sized bed, appearing feverish and pale. Her chest was covered with blood-soaked bandages that had been traded out many times in the last couple of hours by a nurse and doctor. Both were cats and had no patience for the honey badgers in the room, but Mads and her teammates were not about to trust some cats with Streep's life. So they refused to leave . . . no matter how many times they asked. Or demanded. "Charlie was baking."

"I knew it," Max said. "You got your aunt out of there, right?"

"Yeah. But she wasn't happy. Apparently, her husband is real protective of his kitchen or something." She shrugged. "I have no idea who her husband is so I don't know how deep his panic might go over a single room in his giant house."

"You don't know her husband?"

"I didn't know she was married until she just said, 'my husband.' I'd heard she had kids, though. Grown ones. But I've never met them either."

"Awwww. You have cousins."

"I've always had cousins, Max. Aunt Tracey's kids just haven't threatened to eat me yet . . . so that's been nice."

The doctor motioned to Mads, and she swiftly went to her side.

"We're very concerned," the female said.

"Streep is that bad?" Mads asked, her gaze turning toward her teammate.

"No. She's not. The fact is that she had a hole right through her chest. The bullet went through the rib cage, through the heart, and out the back, cutting through the spine. All of that should have killed her instantly . . . it didn't."

"But she looks feverish and unwell . . ."

"Yes. It's called 'milking it.' "

Mads tightened her lips together to keep from smiling because she had the feeling the doctor was ready to kill them all simply out of principle. "Uh . . . is there anything we can do to help her heal?"

"I don't know," the doctor replied, tossing her hands in the air. "Usually when anyone—shifter or human—is shot through the heart with a .50-caliber hollow-point bullet, I just cover them with a sheet, have them put in a body bag, and taken to the morgue. But this"—she moved her hand around, gesturing toward Streep and the others—"unholy scenario is something I don't know how to handle and refuse to involve myself in any further. You people are on your own."

With that, the doctor grabbed her designer purse, her computer bag, her black doctor's bag, and her car keys. She walked out without another word, slamming the door behind her.

Mads glanced down at the nurse. She was sitting silently in a straight-back chair, busy filing her claws, and didn't seem to be in any rush to leave.

When Mads simply kept staring at the cat, she finally volunteered, "I'm getting paid by the hour and I like money. So you badgers can be as unholy as you like."

They pulled up to the math camp and, to Tock's surprise, Dani was already standing outside the doors with a teacher. Or was it counselor? Anyway, the fact that she was already outside was weird since they hadn't actually called anyone or told them to have the kid ready. Shay was just going to go in and get her.

"Why is she already outside?" Shay asked.

"I'll go check."

He looked at her. "Why you?"

"Because you can be terrifying, and we don't have time for that right now." She pointed to her watch. "Do you see the time?"

Tock didn't wait for Shay to answer. She got out of the car and quickly walked the distance from the vehicle to the kid.

"Hey, Dani. Everything okay?"

Dani didn't answer; just rolled her eyes.

"I was hoping to speak to Mister or Mrs. Malone," the teacher announced.

"My mother is not a Malone," Dani practically snarled, "and she already told you to call my dad because she couldn't come."

"I tried to contact your father, and your mother has refused to pick you up again."

"Thank you for making me feel bad about my family, Mrs. Latimer."

"That's not what I meant—"

"Mr. Malone's phone was damaged earlier today," Tock quickly cut in. "But we're on a schedule, so can this important discussion wait until another—"

"Dani punched another student."

Tock gazed at the teacher, waiting to hear more. It took her several seconds to realize that the teacher had thought that was more than enough. She wanted Tock to say something.

"Was it a boy?" Tock asked Dani.

"Yes."

"Did he deserve it?"

"Absolutely."

Tock shrugged at the teacher. "Sounds like he deserved it."

"It's not that easy, Miss—"

"I'm sure it's not, but it can wait until later."

"It really can't."

One of the glass front doors was pushed open and a full-human man stomped through; his kid was just behind him.

And yeah, Dani had definitely punched the kid. In his left cheek. It had a golf ball–sized swelling under the skin, which might mean the kid had a broken cheekbone. Dani was young but she had some true cat strength. No wonder her mother was constantly trying to get her into football.

"Is this the mother?" the man demanded, finally reaching them. Tock and Dani glanced at each other and both giggled a little. They looked nothing alike, but . . . okay! "Look what your daughter did to my son," he said, pushing the boy forward.

"She says he deserved it, and as someone who has dealt with boys in math departments for many years . . . I totally believe her."

"If you think I'm letting this little brat get away with assaulting *my* kid, you've got another think coming, lady!"

"If we could all calm down," the teacher offered, "I'm sure we can come up with a way to . . ."

Her words faded off as something very big blocked the sun behind Tock. She watched the father's gaze lift up and up as Shay—who had already had a very bad day—came up to their small group and then kept coming. Until he stood directly in front of the man, who quickly shoved his son behind him.

"What . . . what is this?" the man finally stuttered out.

"This is the *brat's* father," Tock said with her arm around Dani's shoulders. "And if you have a problem with her, you should really address it with"—she reached her arm up and patted one of his giant shoulders—"him."

Shay stared down at the man but said nothing. Instead, he just stared. Really . . . it was more of a glower. It reminded Tock of Keane actually, in its complete animosity. But Shay wasn't completely silent. Tock could feel the low grumble emanating from the big cat's chest.

"I . . . uh . . . um . . . uh . . ." the man stammered. Was this how full-humans acted when they stumbled upon black bears in the woods? All stammers and shaking? Putting themselves between the apex predator and their kid. Like that would prevent or help anything.

"Well, if you think of something," Tock continued, "I'm sure Mr. Malone would be happy to discuss the issue with you.

Here. And now." She waited a beat. "Or we could go. Because we do have a schedule to adhere to." When the man did nothing but shake his head, unable to speak, Tock turned Dani around and shoved her in the direction of the car. Then she reached back and grabbed Shay's arm, dragging him along behind her. It wasn't easy. He weighed a lot, even while human, and didn't seem to be in the mood to leave his prey undigested. But they'd have nothing but more problems if he bit the guy's face off. It was best to keep moving.

Thankfully, when she intertwined her fingers with his, Shay followed, letting Tock pull him to the car. She got back in the driver's seat, and when everyone was buckled in, she took off.

"I guess I can't go back to math camp now, huh, Daddy?"

"Probably not, baby."

"That's okay," Tock interjected, stopping at a light. "Stevie and I will set up a math camp for you. It'll be great."

"We were going hiking tomorrow."

"In the woods?" Tock asked, looking in the backseat at Dani. "On purpose?"

"And there was supposed to be kayaking next Friday."

"I thought it was math camp. Doesn't that mean *math*?"

"We do math, but we also do some outside activities. Like regular camp. I like that part, too."

"You do?"

Shay finally looked at Tock. His anger seemed to have faded away and was now replaced with curiosity.

"Not a big outdoors person?" he guessed.

"Not when I'm doing math."

"If you didn't get Mommy's messages, Daddy, why did you guys pick me up so early?"

"For your safe—"

"We're going on a little trip," Shay cut in. Apparently, he didn't want to tell the kid the truth and Tock got that. She kept forgetting that most shifter cubs were much more delicate than badger cubs.

"To where?"

Tock and Shay exchanged a glance. Neither of them really knew.

"It's a surprise!" Tock said, using an old gambit Max pulled out anytime they had to get preteen Stevie out of dangerous situations without alarming her.

"I hate surprises."

Tock sighed. "Yeah. Of course, you do." So had Stevie.

Mads had just parked herself back in the chair next to Streep's bed when the bedroom door opened and Streep's girl-friend, Ashley Baker, rushed in. She took one look at Streep and charged over to the bed, kneeling beside it and taking Streep's hand.

"Baby? Baby, can you hear me?"

"Ash?" Streep squeaked out. "Ash . . . is that you?" She reached out one limp arm, fingers barely able to move. "Ash. Take my hand. Let me know you are there before I go."

"Oh, Cass!" Ash said, using Streep's real name and grabbing the weak hand the idiot held out. She placed that hand against her cheek, then glanced over at Mads. When Mads crossed her eyes, Ash quickly hid a smile and said, "My poor, poor baby! What did those bastards do to you?"

"Don't cry, my love. You will find happiness again . . . once I've left this harsh, horrible world."

"No, Cass! No! You know I can't live without you!"

Max, standing slightly behind Ash, pointed at the back of Ash's head and mouthed to Mads, *Who is this?*

Shocked, Mads looked at Nelle, who could only shrug and shake her head in surprise and confusion.

"What do you mean, 'Who is this?'" Mads said out loud.

"Dude!" Max cringed before forcing a smile at Ashley. "I'm sorry, hon. I'm just terrible with names and faces."

Ashley frowned, also confused. "Max, it's me. Ashley."

"Ashley . . . Ashley . . ." Mad scrunched up her nose. "Yeah. Sorry. I'm drawing a blank."

"Seriously?"

"I'm assuming we've met before."

Now even Streep was staring at Max, eyes wide open and clear.

"Max," Ashley pushed, "we've all known each other for, like, a decade."

"Oh! Right!" Max nodded. "Ashley from high school!"

Ash briefly closed her eyes. "Yes. Also from high school. But I'm *also* with Streep."

"Yes!" Max cheered. "We're all with you, Streep. Go, Streep! You'll be fine in no time."

Streep pushed herself up on her elbows. She couldn't even be bothered to continue milking the situation anymore. Instead she gazed at Max with her mouth open.

"What?" Max asked, completely clueless. "What's wrong?"

Stevie jumped out of the helicopter and practically army-crawled away from it toward the Hamptons mansion. She was afraid to walk upright. That's how you got your head cut off by those blades slashing through the air. And she'd kept her eyes closed the entire trip here because she knew exactly how many copters crash-landed around the world. She was terrified she'd be the next victim!

Honestly, she wouldn't have boarded the fucking thing if it hadn't been for Shen. He'd gotten really good at putting her in vehicles she didn't want to be in. He had a lot of patience and always kept things fun. Or as fun as they could be when Stevie was worried about dying painfully.

Right now, she would have army-crawled all the way to the house if Shen hadn't picked her up by the waist and lifted her into the air. Stevie squealed until he put her on the ground and kissed the top of her head.

"Feeling better?" Shen asked.

"Now that I'm out of that flying death-mobile and have my feet on solid ground . . . yes."

Walking beside them, Zé asked, "Who are they?"

"By those supermodel looks and the funk of wolf coming off them, I'm guessing those are elder Van Holtzes."

Stevie silently agreed with Shen. There was something about the males of that family. No matter the age, they stood out in an average crowd of men, and they all shared a resemblance. Once you saw even one of the Van Holtzes, you could recognize all the others no matter where in the world you might spot one.

And the three older males she saw exiting a black SUV and heading toward the mansion were definitely Van Holtzes, although scruffier than she was used to seeing. They looked like they'd just come back from some kind of rough-and-ready backpacking trip in a foreign country.

As the three males neared the mansion, one of them spotted Stevie, Shen, and Zé not too far behind them. He stopped and faced them.

Stevie recognized him. There were two tiers of this generation of Van Holtz brothers. There was the eldest, Edgar, who oversaw the entire pack in the U.S., working closely with the German Van Holtz Pack and the U.S. government when necessary. The second oldest, Alder, who had once run the restaurant business in the U.S. but had been forced out a few years back. The rumor was embezzlement, but Stevie didn't know how accurate that was. The family never discussed it one way or the other. And then there was the third oldest, Niles, who was also known as Van. He ran the Group, a government organization protecting shifters all over the world, especially hybrids; he was also family negotiator when anyone had to deal with Alder.

But there were three more Van Holtz brothers connected to the first trio. These were the three who had been walking toward the house. In no particular order, since she didn't know their ages, there was Heller, also called "Hel"; Lothaire, also called "Lot"; and Gerulf, *only* called "Wolf." Stevie didn't blame him for insisting on a ridiculously redundant nickname for a wolf shifter. Because who wanted to be called "Gerulf"? These three wolf brothers had very Old German names and very little was known about them. While the three oldest were outward facing, seamlessly gliding between the shifter and full-human worlds without problem, Stevie rarely heard about the three younger brothers. She knew they were rich. She knew they were trained chefs . . . and that was about it.

"Gentlemen," Stevie greeted them as she approached.

"Stevie MacKilligan," Wolf said, greeting her with a head nod. The fact that he knew her name was a little unnerving. Stevie had never met the three youngest brothers before. She knew of them, of course, because Charlie had showed her pictures once of the family so Stevie could recognize them on sight. Edgar and Niles Van Holtz's involvement with the government had made that necessary. Still, she hadn't met these three before now. And yet, Wolf had greeted her as if he'd known her for years. "Not to be impolite, Stevie, but why are you here?"

She shrugged at the question. "We were brought here."

There was a momentary look of confusion on Wolf's face but it quickly changed to outright annoyance and anger.

"Dammit!" he barked, spinning around, stomping to the front of the house and throwing open the door to the mansion.

"*Tracey!*" he bellowed as he stormed into the entryway. "*Get your ass down here!*"

As Lot stepped inside behind his brother, he sniffed the air. "I think . . ." He sniffed again. "I think someone is baking in our kitchen."

Realizing it had to be Charlie, Stevie looked at Shen and mouthed, *Uh-oh.*

Charlie looked up when three very handsome wolves entered the kitchen.

"What the hell are you doing?" one of them asked.

"Here." Charlie went around the big counter and pushed a brownie into the male's hand. "Try this."

"I don't want to try your brownie."

"Eat it. I tried this fancy unsweetened cocoa you had in your pantry. I usually just use Hershey's, so I'm curious how this one will work in my recipe."

"Dear God," one of them gasped. "You used our cocoa?"

"Wench!"

Mads's aunt burst into the room with her three honey badger friends.

"Wolf! You're home!"

"She's baking in our kitchen!"

"Let's talk outside."

"You brought them here and let this one bake in our kitchen!"

"Outside." She forced a smile at Charlie. "Excuse us."

She grabbed an arm and began dragging. Two of her friends followed suit with the other wolves.

Charlie thought about following, finding out what the problem was. But she knew herself. What would start out as a calm and rational conversation would quickly turn into a nasty fight and, eventually, a mass burial that she simply didn't want to be involved in.

"Better to bake," she told herself. "Always better to bake. Mass murder bad," she reminded herself. "Baking good."

With that bit of wisdom, she went back to what she loved.

"You need to calm down."

"You brought them here?"

"What did you want me to do? She's my niece."

"Bring your niece. I don't give a shit. But you brought *all* of them here." Wolf pointed an accusing finger at his wife. "I smell cat, too."

"Yes. There are tigers in your home. Malones, specifically."

"Why don't you just poison the entire pack?" Lot asked. His tone suggested reasoned thinking, but his words revealed what a nut he was. "Quick and easy. That way we don't have to worry about watching our children being eaten by tigers."

Trace gestured at the canine and asked CeCe, "Seriously?"

"When did *I* become responsible for Lot's insanity?"

"When you married him!"

"A drunken night of irresponsibility that I immediately regretted."

"That you have not dealt with in more than thirty years."

CeCe sighed. "All that paperwork for a divorce. I'm an artist! Who has time for all that paperwork?"

Lot, who'd been sitting between his wife's legs on the couch, looked back at her and said, "I love you, too, honey."

"I don't see what the big deal is," Steph tossed in. "They stay for a couple of days and then we get them out."

"Unless Edgar comes." Hel looked around the room. "Do we know if Edgar's coming?"

"You males sound like panicked puppies," Ox interjected. "If Edgar comes, *I* will deal with him."

"No!" the entire group shouted at her.

"You're not killing our brother," Lot told Ox.

"What is this connection you boys have with each other?" Ox wanted to know. "When I was two, my sister tried to strangle me in the crib. I survived, and I'm stronger for it."

"We do love these little *amuse-bouche* that you provide, Comrade," Wolf snarled, "but they're not particularly helpful."

"Look, don't worry," Trace promised Wolf. "I've got this all under control."

He almost believed her. She could tell. They'd known each other for over three decades, and she knew her husband. He was right there with the believing . . .

"Charlie?" a young honey badger called out from the foyer. Must be the younger MacKilligan sister. She had a bear and a cat with her as her protection detail. "Where are you?"

"In the kitchen. I'm baking!" The two males began to head that way, but Stevie MacKilligan quickly stopped them, stretching both arms out to block them.

"*Okay!*" she continued to bellow from her spot in the foyer. "*Well . . . when you have a chance, I need access to a freezer! I have samples to test and I don't want anyone to be accidentally poisoned by this stuff!*"

"Told you," Lot snapped.

"*No problem!*" Charlie screamed back. "*They have a bunch of freezers in this kitchen! Just give me a few minutes to see which one will work for you!*"

"*That's great! Thanks, Charlie!*"

"*No problem!*"

"*Hey! Where's Max?*"

"*With Streep! Upstairs!*"

"*Okay! Thanks!*" Stevie looked at the bear and cat. "Go, go, go!" she quietly ordered, pointing. Then all three scrambled up the stairs and disappeared to the second floor.

The wolves again focused on Tracey, and she smiled and started to reassure them, but the nearly two-hundred-pound female dog that had been brought to the house for some reason—along with her very young puppies—appeared in the archway and began to bark at her. And bark. And bark. Demanding food, most likely.

Two male dogs came down the stairs and joined the female. Together, like a little team, they all barked and barked and barked.

"Princess!" Charlie MacKilligan called out from the kitchen. "Come here, girl! I have treats!"

That's when the three dogs ran off . . . into her husband and his brothers' pristine kitchen, where no one with fur was allowed for health-safety reasons.

While all three wolves now glowered at her, Tracey said, "See? Complete control . . . just like always."

"Which is *exactly* what you said to Gorbachev," Wolf reminded her. "*And you were wrong then, too!*"

Chapter 19

Stevie burst into the bedroom with Shen and Zé behind her to warn everyone, "Charlie's baking . . . in a strange kitchen! We're all going to die."

"Not necessarily," Max debated.

"I smelled brownies."

"Dear God." Max pressed her hand to her mouth. "We *are* all going to die."

"I like Charlie's brownies," Mads admitted. Who didn't love a good brownie?

"Brownies are her stress-bake," Stevie explained. "If it were pies, cakes, even a torte, she could be just baking. But brownies? She'll burn this house to the ground."

Stevie stopped and smiled. "Ashley? Oh, my God, Ashley!" she cheered, nearly knocking her sister out of her chair to get to Streep's girlfriend. The pair hugged and laughed.

"Stevie, girl! Cass told me you were back in the States. How was that spa in Switzerland?"

"It was more a mental health facility. And it was good for me."

Ash leaned back to smile into Stevie's face. "Did you take over the group sessions?"

"I had to. They didn't know how to run those things. I always get to deeper shit when I jump in."

"I have always said you should go back to school and get your psychiatry degree. Get your own shingle, girl! Then maybe you can explain to me why your sister never remembers who I am."

"Charlie? She loves you!"

"Wait . . . even *Charlie* knows her?"

"Oh . . . Max," Stevie sighed out.

Tock entered the massive house right behind Dani.

"Wow. This is really nice," she said to Shay. He nodded, closing the door behind him. "I couldn't live here, though."

"Why not?"

"All these rooms?" she noted. "There could be attackers in every one, and I'd never know until they were coming at me with an axe."

Dani turned to face her, eyes wide.

"Not here, though," Tock quickly corrected. "It's totally safe here. I promise."

Shay sniffed the air. "My brothers are here . . . and wolves. Why are wolves here? Why would those badgers take us to a place with wolves?" He shook his head. "Keane is not going to stop complaining about that."

"I need to check on Princess," Dani said.

"You do not need to check on Princess. I'm sure she's fine."

"In nature, wolves and dogs don't always get along, Daddy. She might be frightened."

"Princess isn't scared of anything. She's not even afraid of your Uncle Keane."

Dani lifted her head and took several sniffs. It was so cute! The kid trying to track down her dog by using her senses. When she hit puberty, those senses would overwhelm her a bit before she got full control of what she was seeing, smelling, hearing. But as a ten-year-old, she was probably just confused by all the scents bombarding her nose at the moment.

Unless, of course, one scent stood out.

"Brownies," the kid sighed. "I smell brownies."

Now Dani's father lifted his head, but instead of just sniffing, he opened his mouth, pulled his lips back over his teeth and stuck his tongue out. It looked ridiculous, but it was something that tigers did to catch different scents in the wild.

"Dani's right. Brownies. I think Charlie's baking."

With that announcement, father and daughter started toward the kitchen, but Tock grabbed them both by their T-shirts and yanked them back.

"What the hell—"

"Run," Tock ordered. "Run for your lives."

Shay and his daughter exchanged confused glances before Shay offered, "Or we could just . . . you know . . . go get a couple of brownies."

Walking through the halls of his New Jersey home, he triple-checked all the windows and the doors. Made sure all his nieces and nephews were safe inside the house. Made sure nothing was on his territory that wasn't supposed to be there. He wanted to be sure everything was secure.

He had known from the start that today was going to be a bad day, but he hadn't known it would be like this. Idiots. What had they been thinking? They could destroy everything by trying to kill all their problems at one time on the same day.

He pushed open the door to his den with his lion head and stepped inside.

What had gone down was absolutely insane and put them all in danger. But he'd have to deal with that later. For now, he just had to protect the ones who lived under his roof.

So he'd had the house locked down with everyone safe inside. His siblings were watching every possible entrance. Any entry point where someone could—

He spotted the red dot on the floor and stopped, wanting to pounce on it. Wanting to chase it around the house. But it moved from the floor to his chest. He sat back on his haunches as more red dots hit his chest and, he was sure, his head.

Although there were many intruders in his den right now, he couldn't see any of them. He couldn't even smell them, which was strange. He also knew, if they were planning to kill him, he'd be dead by now. But that wasn't what they wanted. At least not yet.

He looked toward his favorite chair. The one by the window, where he sat and read from actual books made of paper and thread and ink. She sat in that chair now, looking so tiny.

In one hand she had a glass of his favorite scotch. In the other she had a Desert Eagle that, with the right ammo, could easily blow a huge section of his lion head into juicy chunks.

"Giovanni Medici," Mira Malka-Lepstein greeted him. "It seems you have a little bit of a problem, my friend."

Shay watched as Tock slowly pushed open the swinging door that led into the kitchen. He looked at Dani, but she could only shrug. Because Tock was acting so weird. He'd known her for a little bit now, and she never seemed scared of anything. Especially not baked goods. Who'd be afraid of baked goods?

She leaned into the kitchen and almost immediately pulled back.

"Dear God," she whispered, hand pressed against her chest.

"Can I just get a brownie?" Shay asked.

"You don't want to go in there," Tock whispered. "Stay away!"

"I'm going in," Dani announced.

Shay wasn't sure that was a good idea and was about to tell his daughter so, but Tock actually tried to stop Dani, grabbing at her with both hands. But Dani was fast and slippery, and she made it into the kitchen.

"Wow!" he heard his daughter say after a moment.

Panicked, Shay shoved past the door and into the kitchen. He stopped short right next to Dani, taking a moment to look around the giant room.

Every possible clear space had been filled with baked goods. Shay didn't know how Charlie had had time to make so much stuff. Cookies, cakes, pies, pastries. She was still going, too.

"Hey, Dani," Charlie said. "Hungry?"

"I was hoping for one of your brownies."

"Sure." Charlie came over holding a platter filled with brownies. Different types of brownies. Even blondies.

"Do you have any nut allergies?" Charlie asked.

"No."

"Good." Charlie held the platter out and Dani reached for a brownie. "That's dark chocolate. With walnuts. Do you like dark chocolate?"

"Uh . . . I don't know."

"Then try the lighter brownie next to it first. That has pecans."

Dani took the lighter brownie and took a bite. His daughter closed her eyes and made a low growling sound from the back of her throat.

"Daddy, you have to try one!"

With a closed-mouth smile, Charlie held the plate out to Shay. He didn't like that smile. It was ridiculously off-putting. But the smell of those brownies . . .

"The dark chocolate one," she pushed when he started to grab the same kind his daughter had.

"I don't really like dark—"

God, the way she was staring at him.

"Okay." He grabbed the dark chocolate brownie instead and took a bite. "Oh, my God," he gasped, no longer caring about how off-putting Charlie was at the moment. "This is the best thing I've ever had in my mouth."

"Thank you." Charlie looked around. "Where's everyone else?"

"I think they're hiding from you," Dani said. She was still at that age where she just said the truth when asked. Especially when she was in the thrall of delicious brownies, her face and hands already covered in chocolate.

"They're avoiding me?" Charlie repeated. "Why?"

Shay let his gaze move over all that food out on display before looking back at Charlie and replying, "Who can say?"

Tock burst into the bedroom and announced, "I left them both to die!"

"Who?" Mads asked.

"Shay and the kid."

"Tock!"

"*She wanted a brownie!*"

"Charlie does make good brownies."

"What is it with you and those brownies?" Max wanted to know.

"I like a good brownie," Mads said. "Most people use a mix. But your sister makes them from scratch."

Tock moved across the room and hugged Ashley. "That's not all she's made, though."

"How bad?" Max asked.

"Dude, she's filled that kitchen with baked goods. And it's a really big kitchen. It looks like a bakery."

Nelle leaned forward. "Should we make a run for it?"

"No!" Stevie pointed at the floor. "We should tunnel our way out."

"Why are you all acting insane?" Ash asked. "It's true that Charlie bakes when she's stressed, but she's just working through stuff. She's just trying to figure out what happened to you guys and why and what her next steps will be. The time you have to worry about Charlie is when the first thing she does is grab a knife. We all know that's when rational thought is not part of the equation. She's literally just reacting. Reacting Charlie is bad. Baking Charlie is good!"

While the rest of them grudgingly nodded in agreement, Max just stared at Ash. Tock didn't know why until Ash, staring back at Max, suddenly exploded, "Oh, my God, Max! Cass and I have been together since tenth grade! You've come on vacation with us! I spent a week in Switzerland with Charlie and Stevie while you five were doing that heist in Marrakesh! You RSVP'd to our wedding next year! In fact," she added, "you checked off the steak for your entrée, but then you crossed it out and wrote in lobster, then wrote, 'Why are you doing paper invites anyway? You should just do this shit online!'"

Max gave a small shrug. "It's just not ringing any bells."

"That's it!" Ash moved onto the bed, stretching out beside a much-better-looking Streep. "I'm done with this. I don't know you. You don't know me."

A tiny knock at the bedroom door paused the ridiculous conversation and Tock gave a relieved smile. "You're alive."

Dani, frowning and gazing at Tock, bit into the brownie she had in her hand. When she finished chewing, she said, "Charlie wanted me to tell you that if you want anything she's made, you'd better come down and get it now."

"Why?"

"The wolves are coming."

Mira followed the massive cat up the stairs for five whole floors until they reached a doorway that led out onto the roof. He snarled at one of his brothers or an older nephew—she didn't really feel like figuring out who was who among all these big cats—to leave and walked over to the edge. That's when he finally shifted to human. Naked human, but at least he had a very good body.

Giovanni Medici didn't live the life of most lion males—fighting his way into a pride and letting the females feed him and breed with him until he was forced out by younger, stronger males. Some moving on to have their own families with full-human women; those who were particularly lazy might end their lives living with their sisters if they got along at all. Most older, full-blood lion males, however, just ended up dead in the Sudan.

But the Medicis—like the de Medicis in Italy—were not a pride. They were a coalition. A coalition of brother lions that ran their own family. It was rare but was known to happen in the wild. Over the centuries, there had been other coalitions, but none as powerful or long-lasting as the de Medicis. None as brutal, either.

Mira walked over to stand next to Giovanni. She no longer had her weapon trained on him. Wasn't sure she needed it.

"You certainly have brought a lot of problems on yourself today, kitty."

"It wasn't us."

"Don't lie to me, Medici."

"It wasn't us. If it was, I'd have eaten your head by now and left your gnawed-on bones in front of the Israeli Embassy."

"Just like your father would have?"

"Exactly." He took in a deep breath, then let it out. She wondered if he did that any time he had to talk about old Giuseppe. "Only my father could authorize an attack like this on protected soil, but I seriously doubt he would. He's not a nice man, but he's never stupid or crazy."

"Whoever authorized that attack has put a target on the back of the entire—"

The harsh laugh that cut her off was bitter and angry.

"There will be no one coming for my father or any other de Medici. Katzenhaus won't do a damn thing. The BPC will only sanction bears that work for the family, but the pay is so good, there will *always* be bears working for the family. And the Group's excellent snipers will never get close enough to put a bullet through any de Medici's head. So if your hopes are resting on any of them, forget it."

Mira turned to look at Giovanni. He looked just like all the other de Medicis. That blond mane, mixed with thick layers of brown. Over six and a half feet tall with those massive lion shoulders. The de Medici lions were swamp cats, used to fighting their way against the current. When Giuseppe's early ancestor and his brothers were forced out of the Pride by their mother, with no money and no prospects, they started their own coalition. And his first move as the head of that coalition was to eat an entire Mafia family during some Roman Catholic holiday. He and his brothers tore through that family's compound, killing everyone and eating most of the bodies. When a clan of hyenas showed up to scavenge the next day, they were shocked to find that no one had survived the massacre. Not even the children or the pets.

Centuries later, nothing had really changed. Except for one thing . . .

"We're not with him, you know," Giovanni said. "The Medicis are *our* own coalition. The *de* Medicis, and my father, run Europe—"

"And you run the States?"

"We leave that to Katzenhaus. We just manage our little domain here. In New Jersey."

"Then your father has invaded your 'little domain' and has left a trail of bodies for you to follow."

"If you think I'm going up against my father . . . I'm not. I have too much to protect right here. And trust me when I say he wouldn't hesitate to kill one of his own sons if any of us even thought about getting in his way."

"You weren't kidding," Mads said to Tock when she saw all the food Charlie had laid out. And she was still going. Even letting some dough rise so she could make her amazing cinnamon buns at a later time.

Sitting down at a table by the floor-to-ceiling glass windows in the kitchen, Tock and her teammates began to eat the baked goods that were right in front of them. Shay and his brothers were tearing through the pastries placed on the marble counter. The brothers weren't even speaking to each other; too busy just . . . devouring.

Dani had been right. The wolves did come, but they stayed outside. Most of them were in their canine forms, running back and forth at the glass windows and the glass double doors that led into the kitchen, but not daring to enter.

After about thirty minutes, Mads's aunt entered the room with her three badger friends. She went to the double doors and pulled them open. "You can come in and eat," she loudly announced, "if you'd like. Charlie has clearly made enough for everyone."

The wolves stopped pacing long enough to stare at Tracey Rutowski, but none of them entered.

Leaving the doors open, Tracey came over to their table and sat down.

"They never listen to me. More than thirty years and they still don't trust me."

"Are you the . . . *Alpha* here?" Max had to ask.

Rutowski and her friends laughed.

"God, no!" she said. "They loathe me. Wolf's sister is Alpha Female. That one," she said, pointing at a black wolf staring into the house, "Carrie Van Holtz. Head chef of the Van Holtz Steakhouse in the Village, Alpha Female of the New York Pack, and eternal pain in my ass."

"So you're just here, making friends and choosing love?" Tock joked.

"I fell in love with the man. Not his family. Definitely not his pack. But they've never given me a chance. And I have to say, I am fucking delightful."

"They're probably worried you'll steal something."

"Anything of importance the Van Holtzes have is in Germany . . . and we already got that shit."

When Tock and her teammates stared at her, Rutowski just smiled. It was off-putting.

Rutowski's phone vibrated and she looked down at it, made a face, and dismissed the call.

"Any news?" Mads asked between bites of a puff pastry filled with blueberries.

"I have every organization trying to contact me, but I don't want to talk to them yet. Not until I have the information I need."

"This wasn't our fault," Nelle said.

"No. It wasn't. But tigers running loose in the city . . . that can be a problem."

"What did you want them to do?" Mads asked.

"Not shift into tiger. Even their idiot cousins didn't do that."

Mouths full of food, the three tiger males turned on their high stools and glowered at Rutowski.

"*What?*" she demanded. "Each of you is nearly a thousand pounds and more than seven feet tall. Even in fucking Manhattan that's not going to be ignored."

With an angry snarl, Keane got off the stool, shifted to tiger, shook off his clothes, and charged out the open double doors.

The wolves outside barked and growled at the sudden invasion of big cat, but—wisely—scattered so that the cat could make his way around the compound on his own.

Sighing, Finn followed his older brother. "I'll keep an eye on him," he said to Shay before shifting and running out.

Grabbing several more Danish and a paper towel, Shay also walked out. As human and in the opposite direction from his brothers. Tock guessed he wanted to check on Dani.

"That went well," Nelle sneered.

"I am not here to baby a bunch of cats," Rutowski snapped back.

"They haven't done anything wrong," Streep argued, rubbing her sore chest through the fabric of her T-shirt.

"*They* wouldn't let it go."

"They wouldn't let what go?" Mads asked, but she only got a raised brow from her aunt. "You mean the death of their father?"

"The *murder* of their father," Max amended.

Tock folded her arms over her chest. "What's that got to do with anything?"

"That's what I'm waiting to find out."

"From the Group?" When she only got another raised brow . . . "My grandmother? You're working with my grandmother? You have to be kidding."

"Don't get your titties in a vise."

"Ew. What?"

"We've been working with your grandmother for decades. She already knows us."

"'Working *with*,'" Álvarez said with finger quotes, "is a generous way to describe our relationship with Mira, Trace."

"That's true. But only because that woman does know how to hold a grudge."

"So you work for Mossad?"

Rutowski and her friends burst out laughing.

"Fuck no!" Álvarez finally said when she could manage to speak.

"We don't really have an affiliation with anyone," Yoon added. "We're what you would call . . . independents."

"We had a lot of impact, though," Rutowski added. "I mean, do you really think the Berlin Wall just came down due to the desire of the German people and the end of the Cold War?"

Tock looked at her teammates and, together, they replied, "Yes."

"No," she immediately replied. "It was us. It's amazing how much damage four honey badgers can do to a concrete foundation when they keep burrowing under it to escape into and out of East Germany."

"Why were you *escaping* into East Germany?" Tock asked.

The four older honey badgers studied her with narrowed eyes before Rutowski said, "You ask a lot of questions."

"I really don't."

"Did you know that, according to my sources, your father came into the States about five days ago?"

The lion male finally faced her, his gold eyes wide. "What are you talking about?"

"You didn't know?"

"That can't be right. Did he arrange all this as a distraction or something?"

"No. He just took his private jet to Teterboro Airport with a small security team, drove off in an SUV . . . and that was the last anyone has heard from him."

"Why would he do that? My father hates coming here. I haven't seen him since I was thirteen, when I stopped going to Italy. Why did he come here?"

"I thought maybe you could tell me."

"What? You think my father came here to see me and I killed him?" Medici snorted a laugh. "I may not have seen my father since I was thirteen, but I also haven't *talked* to him since I was thirteen. Me or my brothers. We're all dead to him.

The only sons he has are my half-brothers in Italy. Paolo and the others. And before you ask, we're not friendly with them either. Medicis and de Medicis . . . like Hatfields and McCoys. So my father coming to the States to see any of his American offspring just wouldn't happen. Ever."

He turned away from her again. "But I'm sure my father is somewhere. Plotting. You just have to find him."

"Anyone you know who might be willing to tell me why he came?"

"My Uncle Silvio might know. He lives in Little Italy. He's the only one who deals with both sides of the family, kind of a diplomat. But I should warn you that doesn't mean he'll tell you anything. Silvio's a little nuts."

"Aren't we all?"

"No, no. I mean, he's *nuts*. Like if you go there, watch out for the towering piles of old newspapers and the big bottles of urine he keeps around his shitty apartment."

"Great," Mira said on a sigh. "Thanks."

"And the cats."

"Pardon?"

Medici looked at her over his shoulder and, for the first time, smiled. It was not friendly, though. "He has a lot of cats. And they're not big fans of strangers."

Chapter 20

The wolves finally invaded the kitchen once Charlie made plain vanilla cupcakes with an icing made of vanilla yogurt. It was the yogurt. Wolves, for some unknown reason, loved yogurt—and tequila, but everyone knew why they loved tequila—and they couldn't get enough of those cupcakes or, after that, anything else Charlie MacKilligan made.

Tock smirked when she saw those upright, uptight Van Holtz chef siblings acting like they were having orgasms every time they bit into one of the delicacies. And their overwhelming devastation when Charlie suddenly announced, "I'm going for a walk." Meaning she wasn't baking anymore. They watched her leave the kitchen as if they were watching the love of their lives abandoning them for a younger, smarter partner. It was hilarious.

Although no one knew why the attack had happened—still—things had settled down inside the Van Holtz compound. Mostly because Niles Van Holtz and his younger cousin Ulrich had shown up. The disaster at the docks had been contained and the story out to the world was "wild animal smuggling gone wrong!" Tock hadn't been sure that would work, but it had. On social media, everyone was having a blast, making jokes about the new "Tiger Mayor running City Hall" and the "Tiger Cops taking down criminals." Jokes, sure. But closer to the truth than most of those people would ever realize.

Tock was still worried about what her grandmother might be doing at the moment, though. That badger would tolerate a lot, but not a direct attack on her granddaughter. It didn't help that Tock's mother had texted an hour or so ago asking, *What's going on? Family coming in from Israel? Are you okay? Should I be worried?*

After that, Tock got rows of question marks, which was something her mother would do with absolutely no clue how annoying it was. Tock lied and told her mother everything was fine and she'd talk to her soon. Then she begged her to "stop abusing the question mark!"

As day finally turned into night and they enjoyed a dinner cooked by wolves—beyond delicious, by the way!—Tock wished she could say the "trauma" that she'd been through was catching up with her. But it wasn't. She was wide awake. And the only reason she used the word *trauma* was because Streep kept saying it. "All the trauma I've been through today," and "so much trauma! It's a miracle I survived." She even threatened to become "a better Christian. A better Catholic." But none of them believed her because Streep always said that after getting hurt. Sure, she might head to Rome to see if she could get time with His Holiness the Pope, but she never came home from those trips empty-handed. Her family really loved their Vatican "finds."

Once the wolves had eaten, they'd disappeared as wolves liked to do. Maybe they went out for a late-evening hunt. Or maybe they simply didn't want to spend any time around strange honey badgers. It was obvious that Rutowski and her friends weren't the wolves' favorites, so it made sense they wouldn't welcome more badgers. Especially mouthy young ones who couldn't bake like Charlie. They had even less interest in the big cats who had invaded their compound. True, there were only three of them and a cub, but Amur tigers were big, mean, and known to be quite vengeful. The wolves had the numbers but the tigers had the rage. Especially these tigers. Keane stayed outside in his tiger form, sitting on a small hill and staring off into the distance. Finn shifted back to human but kept an eye on his older brother. Not that Tock blamed him. Keane was pissed, and the energy coming off him was deadly. He was just looking for someone to tear apart.

The four older honey badgers took off for places unknown, and the rest of them settled in to watch the ginormous TV in the "family room" and relax.

With everyone else more or less settled, Tock went looking for Shay. To make sure he was okay. She found him in the room that had been given to his daughter. Actually, it had started off as his room, but he'd put his daughter in it along with Princess, her puppies, and the male dogs. The wolves had even provided a proper whelping box for the puppies.

As soon as Tock walked into the room, she could see that having the dogs nearby was making the kid feel better. Of course, there were wolf pups at the compound but they never made it into the house; their parents brought plates of food to their residences on the property instead. They didn't want their canine pups playing with the feline cub. But that was okay. Tock already had something to keep the kid busy.

"Here," she said, handing Dani the notebook she'd been working on for the last two hours. "Problems for you to work on."

"Oooh!"

"Tomorrow," Shay said, trying to pull the notebook from his daughter's hand.

"Daddy!" Dani yanked the book back. "I just want to look through it."

"Do not start working on problems tonight," he ordered while she flipped the pages. "I want you to get some rest. It's been a long day."

"For you. Even though you won't tell me what happened."

"Did you talk to your mother tonight?"

"I did. She wants you to call her when you have a chance."

"Of course."

"Don't fight."

"We never fight."

"Really?" Tock asked.

"I don't like arguing with people," Shay explained.

"But what if they're wrong?"

Shay just gawked at her, so Tock let it go.

Gently taking the notebook from his daughter's hand, Shay put it on the dresser across the room and motioned to the two male dogs. They immediately jumped on the bed with Dani. One faced the doorway; the other rested his big head on Dani's chest, staring at the big window. Protecting her and keeping her pinned to the bed all at the same time. Ingenious.

Shay leaned over his daughter and kissed her forehead. "I love you, baby."

"I love you, too, Daddy."

Tock was walking out of the room when she heard, "Tock?"

She turned back, and Dani motioned to her. She leaned over so the kid could whisper in her ear. The dog resting on Dani snarled a warning at Tock when she came close, but she snarled back and the dog settled down.

"What is it?"

Leaning up as much as the heavy dog head would allow, Dani whispered, "I don't have any clean underwear for tomorrow."

"Didn't your dad bring you clean clothes?" Tock whispered back.

"He grabbed the bag I used when I stayed the night with Aunt Nat, but I refuse to re-wear underwear—"

"No, no. I'd never expect you to do that. I'll take care of it."

"Don't tell Daddy."

"Why?"

"It's embarrassing!"

Honey badgers didn't really experience embarrassment, but Tock still understood that a ten-year-old girl didn't want to talk about her dirty underwear with her dad.

"I'll take care of it," she whispered. "Don't worry."

"Thank you!"

That's when the kid hugged her and Tock froze. She'd never been much of a hugger. If they won a game or whatever, she would hug her teammates in the heat of the moment, but even with her parents . . . her mother did most of the hugging. And it kind of annoyed Tock.

This, however, wasn't annoying. It was sweet. The kid had been kicked out of math camp—a late-evening voice mail from the head counselor confirmed that—she hadn't seen her mother in a few days because the She-cat was bonding over football with Dani's big brothers, and now she was in a strange house with wolves who wouldn't let their pups play with her. If Tock could make her feel more at ease after all that, she'd do whatever had to be done.

So . . . she hugged Dani back.

"Sleep well, okay?"

"I will."

Once Dani lay back again, Tock tried to pull the sheet over her a little more, but the dog lying on her was making that impossible. Tock ended up using one hand to lift that concrete block of a head up and the other to tug the sheet. Once she did that, she gently laid that big head back into place. She didn't want to just drop it. It might crush the kid's organs!

Grabbing the pink duffel bag that had Dani's clothes, Tock followed Shay out. She closed the door behind her and headed to the stairs.

As they walked to the first floor, Shay asked, "Dirty underwear?"

"She hasn't figured out you can hear her even when she whispers?"

"No. And I haven't had the heart to tell her."

"Plus, you always know what she's up to."

He grinned. "And I always know what she's up to."

Shay reached over, trying to take the duffel from Tock, but she pulled back.

"I promised."

"You don't have to wash my daughter's clothes, Tock."

"I promised her, and she doesn't want you doing it."

"I'm her father."

"It's embarrassing!"

⋆   ⋆   ⋆

It took a while to locate the stairs that led to the finished basement. There they found a bowling alley, a movie room with a massive screen, and, off the hallway, a large laundry room that looked like a damn new age laundromat.

"This is amazing," Tock said, clearly marveling at the rows of brand-new or nearly new machines in a variety of bright colors.

"I know. How much laundry could they possibly do here?"

"It's a big pack. With a lot of pups."

"None of which will play with my kid."

Tock picked a washing machine and put Dani's clothes in it, along with detergent and some softener.

"Your daughter doesn't want to play with those kids anyway."

"How do you know?"

She closed the door and punched a few buttons, setting the machine to wash.

When she faced him, she replied simply, "She's an introvert."

"No, she isn't."

"She punched that kid today because he wouldn't stop bothering her while she was working. He definitely needs to learn the rules of consent, but most extroverts would have just gotten up and gone to play with other kids. Your daughter punched him because she just wanted to be left alone to work. That's an introvert who is completely fine being alone with herself. She's just like you."

"What? I'm not an introvert. I like being around people."

"Yeah, but you're just as happy being on your own. And I get it. I'm an introvert. Mads is an introvert. Max and Streep are *not* introverts. And we don't know what the hell Nelle is. She keeps her own counsel." She tapped her watch. "You have to call Dani's mother."

"Oh. Right."

Tock left as he dialed up Dani's mom. While his ex warned him that she'd take his skin off "if anything happens to my baby," Shay was shocked to see Tock come back with a note-book and a pencil case. She hopped onto a dryer, took out a pencil, sharpened it, and got to work.

Baffled, Shay muted his phone and said, "I thought you were going to bed."

"I'm not tired. And I promised I'd get her clothes done to-night."

"I can finish."

"I promised."

He didn't know how to respond to that, and Dani's mom was asking, "Are you even listening to me?" So he refocused his attention and took the phone off mute.

"I'm listening. She'll be fine. But you and the boys should be careful, too. Until this . . . is over."

His ex paused before asking. "Shay, are you okay?"

"Yeah. It's just . . ."

"Dani's going to be fine. There's no one I trust more with my little girl than you and your brothers."

"But I don't want her in therapy for the next twenty years because Daddy was in a firefight."

"Give the kid some credit. Our baby is kickass. As long as you and your brothers are protecting her, she'll be just fine." She laughed a little. "She does seem a little disappointed about math camp, though."

"She is. But don't worry. I've got friends keeping her busy with math problems. We'll make sure she's entertained."

"Friends, huh? Would that be the impressive *Tock*?"

"Uh . . . what?" He glanced over and Tock was still writing in the notebook, so he moved a little farther away.

"You don't know? Our kid is really impressed with her. She teaches Dani math, doesn't like football either, and is appar-ently very cool."

"It's not what you think."

"I am surprised to hear she's a honey badger. You'd think they'd be too small for you."

"It's *not* what you think," he repeated.

"Is it serious?"

"There's nothing to be serious about."

"It better be serious if you're involving my kid. I don't want her getting attached to your whores."

"I don't have *that* in my life."

"You better not," she said, almost singing the words. "Or I'm going to be pi-i-ssed."

"You're not going to be pissed because there's nothing going on."

"Dani says you *like* like her."

"I'm hanging up now."

"But, seriously, do you *like* like—"

Shay disconnected the call before the mother of his child could finish such a stupid statement.

"You okay?" Tock asked.

"I'm surrounded by crazy cats."

"Also called family, but yeah." She nodded. "You totally are."

"So what do you think?"

Tock looked up from the math work she was creating for Dani. "What do I think about what?"

"About all of this."

"Are you asking if I think we will now live in a world of misery and despair, forced never to see the sun again as we live by our wits and eat human flesh for sustenance? If that's what you're asking, then yes . . . that's what I think will happen."

"You're mocking me."

"Of course I'm mocking you," she said with a laugh. "We're going to be fine. The *kid* is going to be fine."

"How do you know?"

She shrugged. "I won't allow for anything else."

"I'm afraid to ask what that even means."

She closed the notebook. "How did it go with Dani's mom?"

"Chu handled the situation better than I would have. But she's fine with Dani staying safe with us." Shay leaned over the machine Tock sat on, resting his arms on the cold metal and interlocking his fingers. "She loves our girl."

"Was that ever a question?"

"Keane thinks I should fight for full custody."

"Do *you* think you should do that?"

"No."

"Then you follow your instincts. She's your kid, not Keane's."

"Yeah, but—"

"If Keane had his way, he'd buy this entire compound, put an electrified fence around the whole thing, and put your entire family inside. Never to leave again. Not really surprising considering what happened to your dad. But you know that's not healthy for your daughter. And, honestly, he should cut Dani's mom some slack. She's trying to manage three adolescent tiger males and she wants to prevent them from growing up to run Manhattan streets, chasing down vans filled with lions that shot at them."

Shay smirked. "Very funny."

Clutching the notebook in her hand, Tock slid off the dryer. "Let's go up and watch some TV with everyone."

She started to walk away but he lightly grabbed her wrist and stopped her. "You know, Dani told her mom about you."

"What? Why?"

"She seems to think you *like* like me."

"*Like* like you? I didn't realize we were back in fifth grade."

"You *don't like* like me?'

"I am not having this conversation with a grown man."

"You kissed me like you *like* like me."

"Stop saying that," she laughingly ordered. "It's so . . . weird."

"But is it true? Do you *like*—"

Tock put her hand over his mouth. "Please stop." She felt him smile against her palm. "And in answer to your question, I find you very . . . interesting."

Shay pulled her hand away. "Is interesting good? Or is that, like, what you say when someone shows you a weird mole on their neck?"

"If someone showed me a weird mole, I would tell them to have it removed and biopsied. If I say something is interesting, it's because I find it interesting. And I don't find many things interesting. But you . . . I do."

Shay finally straightened up and stepped in front of her. He slid his hands from her elbows to her hands, ignoring the notebook she was still holding. "Well, then, I think you're interesting, too."

They gazed at each other for several long seconds before Tock finally asked, "Should we be doing something specific?"

"I'm not exactly sure what you mean, but we could go up to my room. Or yours. Together. To do something specific."

Tock shook her head. "No, no. We're in someone else's house. Not even a friend's. We don't even know these people. We probably shouldn't do anything here, huh?"

"You're probably right."

"Besides, if we head upstairs together, everyone will know what we're up to."

"Good point. Not sure either of us is in the mood for *that.*"

"Right." She let out a sigh. "We'll just wait, then. Until we're back home or can get a hotel room."

"Okay."

"Okay."

Tock felt nothing but regret. And a little resentment that the world was getting in their way. She wasn't an excessively horny badger, like Max and Streep. She did, however, find sex a healthy release when she needed it. She didn't think about it all the time or need to think about it all the time. Still . . . Shay was beautiful. And she wanted to know what it was like wrapping her body around his.

It would wait, though. No need to get Max and Streep focused on her love life. Or tipping off Shay's brothers. Because the pair of them could be major ball breakers.

No, no. They'd wait until, you know, it could be perfect.

The look of disappointment on Shay's face made her feel a little better. Knowing she wasn't the only one bummed out.

Unable to help herself, Tock reached up and pressed the palm of her hand against Shay's face. He immediately closed his eyes and leaned into that hand. They stayed like that for a bit. Tock expected him to pull away so they could go up to the first floor and watch TV with everyone else.

But Shay didn't pull away. Instead, he began to push his head into her hand, moving it around a bit. She'd seen the feral cat that lurked around Charlie's yard do something similar with Stevie when it allowed her to get close.

She moved her hand in response, circling her fingers in the opposite direction. As an amateur scientist, she simply wanted to see what that move would do.

And holy shit! Did it do a lot!

Shay growled and pressed his head closer to her hand. When she dug her fingers into his hair, his hands slapped against the dryer she'd been leaning against, his arms caging her in place. She didn't mind. The heat from his body made her tense and a little sweaty in the air-conditioned room.

Suddenly, Tock didn't care where they were. Whose house it was. What her friends were doing. She was only touching him with one hand but that alone was making her squirm. Tock did not squirm a lot. Squirming when working with explosives was never a good idea. She was well known for her stillness.

Shay's eyes opened and they were pure gold. Cat gold.

She didn't bother waiting anymore. She leaned in and kissed him, pressing her mouth against his. His lips parted and their tongues met, and it was like one of her homemade pipe bombs going off while she was too close. Every part of her seemed to be vibrating and stunned.

And that was just from a kiss.

His arms were around her now, pulling her close. She decided then they could worry about foreplay later. She had other needs that had to be dealt with right now.

But when she had his sweatpants pushed halfway past his ass, Shay abruptly pulled away.

She watched him, wondering if she'd done something wrong, when he suddenly announced, "I'll be right back."

"What?" she snapped. She didn't intend to sound mean, but she was a honey badger and he was taking her meal away!

"Don't move," he ordered. "I'll be right back. I promise."

Then he was gone. Leaving Tock to think of all the ways she could strangle him when he came back.

Finn was sitting on a couch with his arm around Mads. For the last five minutes, he'd been hearing heavy footsteps running back and forth past the "family room." The footsteps seemed to stop near or in the many bathrooms in the house, but he wasn't sure. He only had a general idea of the layout of this place. And since he didn't know who was running or why, and no one was calling out a warning, he chose to ignore the sound altogether.

He didn't want to interrupt the horror movie they were all watching. He wouldn't say he was a fan of the genre, but it was the one thing the MacKilligan sisters could agree on. Since Finn didn't want to hear hours of arguing from the three sisters, he'd agreed on their movie choice. And Keane, the Dunn triplets, Nelle, Streep, and Streep's fiancée, Ash, didn't seem to care one way or the other. So far, they'd already gone through "The Conjuring" series. And had just started "The Exorcist" series when Finn heard more heavy footsteps and then felt a hand on his shoulder. Before he could react, he was snatched out of the family room.

He unleashed his fangs, assuming a crazed wolf wanted to fight, but instead he found himself in the kitchen staring at his brother Shay.

"What are you doing?"

"Do you have a condom?"

"A condom? Why would you need a . . . oh. Oh!" He grinned. "Ohhhhh."

"Stop it. Just give me a condom."

"I don't have one. Unlike you, I didn't get a chance to go home to get my shit. At this moment, I'm wearing *wolf* clothing. It smells like them, too." He pulled the T-shirt up, sniffed it. "And Downey. Anyway, my current lack of condoms is why I'm watching horror movies with bears rather than fucking my girlfriend in the room they gave me."

"I *need* a condom."

Assuming this was all about Tock, he asked, "Can't you two wait until we get home?"

When his brother grabbed his sweatshirt and lifted him up against the wall, Finn said, "So that's a no? You can't wait?"

"What's going on?" Mads asked. Not surprisingly, she'd been the only one to notice Finn was gone. Kind of hurtful after the day they'd had. He'd think his other brother would notice that Finn had been snatched from the room. What if Finn was in danger? Again!

"Shay needs condoms."

"Condoms? Oh. Oh!" She frowned. "Oh, yeah. We don't have any. I just figured later we could suck each other off."

"Could you not?" Shay snarled while Finn smiled. He loved his girlfriend.

"Calm down," Mads soothed. She'd gotten really good at managing his brothers. His past girlfriends had just avoided them completely. "Put Finn on the floor and let's go see what we can do for you."

The bedroom door opened and Mads's aunt stood there in nothing but a sheet wrapped around her body and held there by her free hand. Her tousled gray-and-black hair practically covered her eyes. It did not appear that she had been sleeping.

"What?" the older She-badger abruptly asked Shay, Finn, and Mads. She didn't sound mad or annoyed. Shay got the feeling that was just how she talked to people.

"Do you have any condoms?" Mads asked without even a little bit of subtlety, making Shay cringe in embarrassment.

"Are they going to fuck in our house?" a male voice snarled from inside the bedroom.

"Ignore him," Tracey Rutowski said with a dismissive hand wave. "And in answer to your question, after more than thirty years of marriage, four dangerously unstable children—"

"And don't forget menopause," that male voice added.

The She-badger's mouth twisted and her eyes briefly closed. That Van Holtz wolf she'd married did like to play with danger, didn't he?

"Anyway," she finally went on, "we do not have condoms, but let's see if someone else does."

Part of Shay was dying. He didn't need the world to know he was planning to have his way with Tock. But they were dealing with honey badgers, weren't they? They weren't known for being a subtle species. Or cognizant of other people's feelings.

Mads's aunt pushed past their small group and over to the bedroom door across the hall, the gray sheet fluttering behind her. She knocked and, after a minute or two, another Van Holtz wolf answered. He hadn't bothered with a sheet, so the door was only partially opened; he seemed to be naked, too.

"What?" he asked. What was with the people in this fancy house? None of them knew how to answer a door?

"Do you have condoms?" Mads's aunt asked.

"No. We don't—"

"I do!"

With an angry snarl, this Van Holtz wolf demanded, "Why the fuck do you have condoms? We don't use condoms!"

"Oh, calm down. I got a bunch of them in a gift box from Dalia's performance-art show, *Sex Is My Despair.*"

The wolf was pushed aside and CeCe Álvarez opened the door all the way. Unlike her wolf, she had no problem with everyone seeing her naked. And Shay had to admit, he was impressed. She looked amazing.

She handed a bright pink box to Mads. "Here you go, hon."

"Thanks."

She winked at them. "You guys have fun now."

"I really don't want them fucking in our—"

The door slammed shut before they could hear the rest of the wolf's complaint.

"Need anything else?" Mads's aunt asked.

"No. This was it."

"Great. 'Night." She walked back to her room and, as the door shut behind her, they heard her growl, "I can't believe you brought up menopause. Bastard!"

Mads handed the box over to Shay. "Here you go."

"Thanks."

He started to run back downstairs but Finn caught his arm and pulled him back. He removed the securing tape from the box and opened the top. He took a condom. Then took one more.

"Now you can go."

Bastard!

Keane heard heavy footsteps run past the archway again, but by the time he turned to look, there was no one there.

"That was Shay," Nelle told him. How she could tell since she never seemed to look up from her cell phone, he had no idea.

"Why's he running?"

"No idea." Suddenly she was pressed up next to him, their faces touching.

"What are you doing?"

"Taking our picture."

"I don't want my picture taken."

"Don't worry. I'll put a black bar over your eyes. It's those cheekbones I'm really trying to get."

"Why? What's wrong with my cheekbones?"

"Nothing. That's the point."

She relaxed back into the couch and returned to ignoring him completely.

Maybe he should just go to bed, like Finn and Mads probably had. The day had been weird enough, and he wasn't in the mood for anything else to fuck up his life.

The laundry room door opened and Tock tossed her hands up. "Where the hell have you—"

She didn't even get a chance to finish what she was going to say. Originally when Shay didn't come right back, she'd had a whole speech ready: *"If you want to wait, that's okay. No pressure. It's fine."* Or something like that. At the ten-minute mark, though, she began to feel hurt. He'd just left her here. Still squirming!

Before she could unleash her full annoyance, though, he had her in his arms, and his mouth was on hers.

His kiss was so desperate, so hungry, her anger and insecurity faded away.

Tock wrapped her arms around his shoulders and he lifted her up and plopped her on top of the dryer. Big hands tossed off her running shoes and went right for her black leggings and panties. He tugged them down, continuing to kiss her. On the mouth. The throat. The chest. He pushed her T-shirt and sports bra up and out of the way, and his warm mouth latched onto her nipple.

Tock held his head against her as he moved from one breast to the other, sucking with his lips and teasing with his tongue.

She dug her fingers into his hair, massaged his scalp, because she knew he liked that. His growled response radiated through her breast and down her spine.

Shay reached around her and she felt him grab for something behind her. She was too distracted, though, to look. To investigate.

Grabbing her hips, he pulled her to the edge of the dryer and stepped fully between her legs. He was tall, so the extra height of the dryer was perfect. He just bent her hips a little and then he pushed inside her.

Tock gasped against Shay's chest and gripped his shoulders. When he started to rock his cock in and out of her, she threw her head back, mouth open. Shay kissed her then, the pair clinging to each other as they fucked and kissed and groaned.

As they kept going, she could sense that Shay was about to come. Wanting to join him, she loosened the hand she had gripping his hair, about to use those fingers to circle her clit until she also came. But then, without any additional help, she did come, her entire body clamping onto Shay's, both of them screaming into each other's mouths.

When they'd wrung themselves out, they collapsed onto the floor, on top of their discarded clothes. They sat there, still clinging to each other and panting. Not saying a word.

Because words weren't necessary.

Chapter 21

If there was one thing Tock really loved, it was getting head. Nothing more gratifying than having a guy's tongue between her legs as he did nothing but try to make her happy.

They were on the long table that people probably used to fold their clothes. It was thankfully empty and Shay had placed her there with a lot of care after their first round. Then he'd spread her thighs and gone to work. He didn't seem to be in any hurry either, languidly licking her with that rough tongue of his. All Tock had to do was lie back and play with her nipples. It was awesome.

But then there was that moment, when it went from enjoyable and relaxing—because she'd already come once not long ago—to intense. Because she wanted more. The licking was great, but she needed more. She put her hands behind his head and he took the hint, grasping her clit between his lips and rolling it around. That had her squirming again. Honestly, she'd never squirmed so much. But the cat had a way.

He stopped rolling and began sucking. That's when Tock's thighs tensed and the rest of her began to shake. She made weird little grunting sounds that she would normally stop because they sounded kind of stupid, but she couldn't think past what was happening to her body.

She rocked her hips against Shay's mouth and let the rest of her body do whatever it wanted as the cat took her to and over the edge.

Tock let out short, harsh screams as the orgasm rolled

through her. And it kept going. Shay kept it going. She didn't know if it was simply one long orgasm or several in a row, but it just went on and on until, finally, he let her go and she came down hard. Her body splayed on that table, legs hanging off the side, unable to move.

The heat from his body moved away but quickly returned. He rolled her over and lifted her ass. Tock didn't care. She was too out of it to care about anything.

He entered her from behind, slowly pressing his latex-covered cock deep inside her. He was big, filling her almost more than she could stand. He stayed there a moment while her muscles continued to throb around him in the aftermath of her orgasm.

When he finally began to fuck her, Tock was sure she might simply go to sleep while he got what he needed. She was exhausted.

The way her muscles rippled around his cock made his knees weak. He wasn't sure he could keep standing. But he didn't want to just dump her on the floor. She deserved better than that. Actually, she deserved the best suite at the Ritz-Carlton on a king-size bed with the softest sheets. But what she was getting was fucked on a table in a wolf pack's laundry room. Not exactly fair, but the world couldn't ask him for any more right now. She smelled too good. Felt too good. Tasted amazing. Licking her was like licking his favorite ice cream off a spoon. Except that didn't make his dick hard and his mind numb.

She was just lying there when he pulled her ass closer. Maybe he should wait . . .

Except then her pussy tightened around his cock and any hope of waiting was lost. Instead, he just angled her a little better and began to fuck her. He was so hard, he could make it quick. Get them what they both needed. No big deal, right?

Tock wasn't that out of it, though. Her hands gripped the other side of the table, and she began to push back against him.

And each time she pushed back, she tightened her muscles. It felt like being dragged, the way her body pulled him in.

When Tock began to pant and groan, Shay wasn't sure he could keep going. But he did. Holding her tighter, fucking her harder. Their groans mingling with each thrust. He wanted to let go right now, but he held on for her. Tried anyway. Until she gripped his cock so hard, he couldn't keep himself from coming even if he wanted to. Luckily, that grip was because Tock was coming right along with him.

They both cried out; Tock still pushing back and Shay still slamming forward. They kept going until they simply couldn't anymore. Arm around her waist, Shay laid them both on the table, still tight together. He didn't want to pull out yet. Not when it felt so good to be buried inside her.

It was the last thing he thought until his stomach growled and woke both of them up.

Shira Lepstein waited outside the Little Italy apartment with her cousin Uri. It was late. She was tense. She really wanted to go home. Back to Israel, where she'd lived since her parents had moved there twenty years ago. But this was important. Family was always important. The Malka-Lepsteins protected each other. Without question. Without complaint.

Still . . . Shira was ready to go home! All this because her boneheaded cousin insisted on hanging with MacKilligans. She'd always thought Tock had better sense. Because those three girls attracted trouble the way shit attracted flies. Only the shit didn't start anything. The MacKilligans always started something. More than any other badger Shira had ever known or learned about through history. While all honey badgers were accused of being shit-starters, their shit-starting usually had a point.

Rodrigo Borgia, who eventually became Pope Alexander VI, wanted the power of the Church. Livia Drusilla poisoned her way to the role of wife and empress, and eventually mother of the emperor when her husband, Augustus, died so she could have the power of Rome's all-powerful throne. But the MacKilligan sisters? What did they want? What were they hoping to gain when they started their nonsense?

Shira had no idea.

Her grandmother bolted out the front door to the building, desperately swatting at her clothes, face, and hair.

"Check me! Check me!"

"Check you for what?"

"Everything! Lice! Roaches! Anything disgusting!"

"It was that bad?" Uri asked while Shira was forced to look over her grandmother to make sure nothing had crawled out of that old lion's apartment.

"I don't even know what to say about what I saw. No one should live like that. No one."

"You're fine, Savta," Shira told her grandmother.

"Are you sure?"

"I'm sure. Nothing has attached itself to you."

"Good. Then let's go. We have to talk to the MacKilligans."

Because of *course* they did.

Shira rolled her eyes and pulled out her phone. She texted her husband that she was still working and she didn't know when she'd be back. Then she wondered again why her cousin insisted on hanging around *those* badgers!

"Where did you find more brownies?" Tock asked, pulling one out as soon as Shay took the top off the plastic container. "I thought the wolves ate them all."

"Charlie put some aside for Dani. But she'd had so many already, I was worried she would just throw them up. So I put these in my room."

"Did you piss around the bedroom door to mark your territory and protect the brownies?"

"This compound is filled with predators that would love more brownies, so I did think about doing just that. But in the end, I just let it go, hoping my general cat funk would do the trick. We can't afford to be tossed out of here yet."

"True," Tock said around a mouthful of dark chocolate brownie with walnuts. She pointed at the brownie she was devouring. "This was for Dani?"

"I think Charlie is trying to turn her into a dark chocolate lover, but she's still too young for that. Thankfully, she also has regular brownies in here. For the kid . . . and me."

Shay had also brought cold milk and she poured them both glasses. They ate in silence, finishing off the brownies. Tock would have felt bad for Dani, but she had no doubt that Charlie would happily make the kid more of her favorite sweets. She seemed to like having a kid around who wasn't Max or Stevie. Taking care of her two sisters from such a young age had been a lot for her.

When Shay put his empty glass down on the table, he said, "You know they're going to make our lives hell tomorrow."

"Today," she amended, showing him her watch so he could see the time.

"Yeah. You okay with that?"

A little confused, Tock asked, "Okay with what?"

"You know . . . the teasing about . . . us."

"I don't let other people dictate my life. Even my grand-mother, which is one of the things she hates about me. Will it be a problem for you?"

"Not at all," he said quickly, his eyes locked on her face. "But my brothers . . . they can be a lot."

Tock couldn't help but snort. "We spent several hours today reminding Max that Streep is gay."

"Reminding her? She forgot? Or never knew?"

"Of *course* she knew. We all knew. We have always known. Streep's parents have always known. The cheerleaders in our school always knew, which was why they were mean to her, and why we stuck wolf spiders in their lockers and milk snakes in their beds. Yet still . . . Max remembers none of it. So, I have no worries about your brothers because no one can be as an-noying and insane as Max."

"That is a good point."

"I know."

Shay suddenly looked off and, for several seconds, didn't speak.

"What?" she pushed when his silence went on and on.

"I feel like I should tell you . . . I think I *definitely like* like you now."

"Oh, my God! Are we still doing this?"

"I thought I should warn you."

"Why?"

"I'm a cat. We don't like anyone. So when we *do* like someone, it's not something we just get over."

"Meaning you're a level-five clinger?"

"I'm not a clinger," he quickly replied. "Unless I'm hanging from a tree. Then it's kind of fun," he explained, a big grin on his face. "You just dig your front claws into the wood and let your legs dangle. Total blast."

When she only gazed at him silently, he cleared his throat and continued. "Anyway, I just want to give you a heads-up—"

"For when you start stalking me?"

"I won't ever stalk you! If you want to break up, just say you want to break up!"

"Break up? When did we start dating?"

"Fine! Fine!" He tossed up his hands. "Just leave me, then."

"Leave you?"

"Alone. Despondent. Broken." He looked off, let out a sigh. "A bitter, unhappy cat that will never recover from the hurt."

"Will your foster family have to lure you out from under a couch before they can put you up for adoption, too?"

"Maybe."

Shay loved to hear Tock laugh. Too bad she didn't realize he was being kind of serious. Cats didn't get attached easily. Whether it was the big ones that were nearly extinct because full-human men with small penises couldn't stop hunting them into oblivion or the small ones that pissed all over someone's yard to annoy the family dog—cats got attached. That's why people sometimes woke up in the morning and found a cat they didn't have the day before living in their house and expecting to be fed. That person had been chosen and the cat wouldn't change its mind just because the person felt they weren't "pet people." The cat didn't care.

Not that Shay would ever force his attachment on Tock. That's what full-humans did to each other. A few of them would become obsessed with their partners and take it way too personally when they were dumped. But Shay wanted to make it perfectly clear to the naked woman sitting across from him on the long table in the laundry room that he was here for more than a "we nearly died so let's fuck" night.

"Let me see your watch again," Shay asked.

Tock held out her arm, turning it so he could easily view her watch. "I think Dani wants me to get her a watch like yours."

"This one was two hundred and fifty thousand dollars."

"Excuse me?"

"It was handmade in Switzerland by an award-winning watchmaker. We've been working together for years, so I actually got a discount."

"I am *not* spending two hundred and fifty grand on a fucking watch!"

"Now you sound like *my* dad."

"Okay. I'm just going to get Dani's clothes out of the dryer. She's going to be up soon and I completely forgo—"

"Already done."

"Huh?"

She poured herself another glass of milk. "I put her clothes in the dryer earlier. Then I took them out and folded them, put them back in her duffel bag."

"When did you do all that?"

Tock gulped down her milk before replying, "While you napped." She wiped the milk off her lip with the back of her hand.

"You didn't have to do that."

"She didn't want her father touching her underwear."

"I do her laundry all the time! So do her uncles."

"Stop using your boring male logic with a ten-year-old girl. Besides, I didn't mind. And I get it."

"You get it?"

"In our house, my dad did laundry. My mom did the dishes. Nothing is weirder than walking into your bedroom and finding your dad folding your panties before putting them away. By the time I started wearing bras, those horrifying days were over."

"Well," he said, leaning in close, "since we have a little time before she's awake—"

"*Tock!* Are you down there?"

"Fuck," she sighed.

"We were about to," Shay muttered.

"Even worse, that's not Mads or the others."

"Who is it—"

"Tock?" The laundry room door opened and a female badger walked in. Shay remembered her. She was one of Tock's cousins that he'd met that awful night Tock got poisoned. "There you are . . . Oh." Her nose scrunched up. "Ohhhh . . . ewwwwwww. Really? I mean, *really*?"

"What do you want, Shira?"

"Savta needs to talk. In the kitchen. Maybe take a few minutes first to wash the cat funk off you, though."

"Nice to see you, too," Shay tossed out as the female spun around and walked out, slamming the door behind her. "I love your family," he told Tock.

"Don't start lying to me now, Shay."

"Yeah. Because I really won't be able to keep that lie going."

Ric Van Holtz was exhausted. He hadn't been sleeping the last few days. Sometimes because he didn't get to bed. Other times because he got to bed but didn't sleep.

It felt like the New York streets were a war zone. Not due to full-humans, whose antics he was used to and mostly ignored. But due to his own kind, who'd been rampaging around as if they were on the Serengeti instead of East 59th Street.

They couldn't keep doing that. One bad situation every century or so could be explained away. But several in a short time frame would be very bad for them.

Unfortunately, the one witness who could answer a lot of his questions was not answering anything. Polar bears were notoriously tough and taciturn, using general grunts more than words. Sometimes not even using grunts. And the Italian bear locked in one of his interrogation rooms wouldn't say anything. Which left him with a very unfortunate decision:

Bringing in someone who could get what they needed out of this bear in a way that few of them wanted to even attempt. His cousin was *not* happy about it. Van grew up during the Cold War and he didn't like to return to those days, when both sides did really shitty things to get the information they wanted and needed.

But they were running out of time and options.

Cella Malone sipped her coffee and stared at her phone. Mary-Ellen Kozłowski, head of the New York branch of Katzenhaus, restlessly paced the room like the annoying cat she was. And Bayla Ben-Zeev, who ran the Bear Preservation Council, wrote notes out longhand in Hebrew, going right to left across the page. Van, however, appeared rage-filled, standing with his back against the wall, a to-go cup of coffee in his hand.

He became even less happy when Dee-Ann Smith walked in with her father, Eggie Ray Smith.

"Smith," Van sneered.

His father-in-law grunted back, which was more than Ric got on a good day. The wolf wasn't "much for talking," as his daughter put it. In fact, Eggie Smith spoke to exactly three people on a regular basis: his wife, his daughter, and, now, Dee and Ric's daughter. Otherwise . . . grunts were usually the best you were going to get out of him.

"You know what to do?" Van asked.

This time Eggie Smith didn't even deign to answer. Simply nodded at his daughter and walked into the room where they had the bear chained to a chair.

He walked back out a few seconds later, though, with a big tactical knife in his hand and, to Ric's eternal surprise, suddenly announced in a voice that sounded like ten miles of bad gravel, "He's dead."

"*You killed him already?*" Van exploded. "You just walked in there!"

"Wasn't me, rich wolf. He was already dead."

Dee-Ann and Cella rushed into the room but quickly returned.

"Yep," Dee-Ann announced. "My daddy's right. Old boy is dead."

That's when Bayla and Mary-Ellen went into the room.

"How?" Ric asked.

"Bullet to the back of the head," Cella explained. "Very clean and quick. Very professional. Dee-Ann couldn't have done it better."

"Not sure I could get in and out of there, though. The air vent ain't nothin' but a little bitty thing."

"She's right," Cella agreed. "Her giant shoulders could never get through there."

"Neither could your fat ass," Dee shot back.

Ric thought a moment. There was only one door into the room that they'd put the bear in. And Dee was right, the air filter was not some large, roomy space an assassin could easily traverse. It was, in her words, "a little bitty thing."

So then how did someone get into the room?

When Bayla returned, Ric asked, "Where's Mira Lepstein?"

"Why are you asking me?"

"Because, Bayla, you used to run the shifter division of Mossad."

"And Mira didn't work for me. She worked for the full-humans. I have no idea where she is or what she's doing."

"But . . . ?"

"But I will say that trying to kill the granddaughter of Mira Lepstein was a foolish move, and New York City is about to be *invaded* by a lot of honey badgers."

★ ★ ★

There was a full bathroom next to the laundry room. It wasn't fancy, but it was functional, allowing Tock and Shay to take quick showers and put on clean clothes before heading upstairs to face Tock's grandmother.

And she was waiting for them. In the kitchen. Along with Keane, Finn, Tock's teammates, Mads's aunt and her friends, the Van Holtz brothers, and a couple of Tock's cousins.

Shay wasn't sure he was going to sit in on the conversation. He needed to go check on his kid. But he saw his daughter outside already playing with Princess, the two male dogs, and Nat. She was laughing and running in the sun. Even a few pups from the Van Holtz Pack had joined in when they saw her rolling around with the three big dogs. Since no one from the Pack was complaining, he'd let her keep going and, by staying in the kitchen, he got to keep an eye on Dani through those big glass windows and double doors.

Even better, Charlie had clearly been up for a few hours and had done more baking. Danish! He grabbed a platterful and slid onto one of the counters beside Tock.

"Are we all settled now?"

It took him a second to realize that Tock's grandmother was talking to him.

"Uh . . . yeah," he replied, half a Danish already in his mouth.

The She-badger took a cup of tea handed to her by Charlie. "Thank you, dear."

Taking a sip, she glanced off, then announced, "The de Medicis."

"That pride out of Italy?" Streep asked.

"No," she corrected. "They're not a pride. They're a coalition."

"What's that?"

"The de Medici brothers run the family. Not the females."

"Didn't we just do some work involving the de Medicis?" Mads asked.

"Yeah," Max said. "We were supposed to be taking down their businesses."

"What businesses?" Keane asked.

"They sell humans to high bidders. For food."

Shay looked at Tock, and she let him know that accusation was true with a tilt of her head.

"Wait," Finn said, "you guys are serious?"

"Don't the hyenas kind of do the same thing?" Keane said.

"No," Nelle explained. "There are hyena clans that you can call in to clean up an . . . event so no evidence is left behind. Some just dispose of the bodies. Some feast. But it's still scavenging just like any hyena on the African plains would do. What they don't do is have breathing humans shipped to their location like they're ordering a pizza."

"But that's what the de Medicis do?"

"I think Mrs. Lepstein is saying," Nelle continued, "that the de Medicis handle the pizza delivery."

"I've heard about shifters hunting humans for sport, but—"

"This is different," Charlie told them, placing new platters of honey buns on the table. Even if Shay's brothers had wanted to try them, the Dunn triplets got there first. Snarling at the badgers when they tried to get a few. "The operation we saw was human trafficking on a pretty big scale. They're doing high volume."

"For someone's food supply?" Streep tried to clarify, her lip curling in disgust.

Charlie shrugged and went back to her baking.

"Human trafficking of any kind is indefensible," Mira said. "Why they take these people does not matter. What matters is that they take them at all."

"Which is why we were attacking their businesses," Nelle pointed out. "Although we've only dealt with one of their operations."

"Have you done anything else?" Mira asked, looking over her teacup.

"Anything else?" Nelle glanced at their team. "I don't think so. Just the one operation so far. And the only shifters we took down that day were bears. American bears. No Italians." Nelle's eyes narrowed on the She-badger. "Why do you ask? What's happened?"

Tock's grandmother placed the teacup back on the saucer, balancing both on the top knee of her crossed legs. Shay would expect it to slide over and fall to the floor, but it just sat there. Perfectly poised. He found it kind of frightening.

"That day," Mira Lepstein said, "you may have only killed bears but then, soon after, you killed someone much more important. And now the entire de Medici Coalition wants all of you dead."

Tock, and everyone else in the room, immediately looked over at Max.

"Why are you all looking at me?" she asked.

"What did you do?" Mads demanded.

"I didn't do anything."

"Max, come on," Nelle pushed.

"I didn't!"

"Wait," Tock cut in. Her grandmother had a knack for setting people at odds. She wasn't going to let Mira do that to her teammates. "Savta, who are you talking about?"

Glaring across the room directly at Max, her grandmother snarled out, "She killed Giuseppe de Medici."

"Ohhh, fuck," one of the Dunn triplets gasped. Tock didn't know which one. She was too tired to tell the difference between them. But maybe the girl . . . ?

"Who's Giuseppe de Medici?"

"He was the father and head of the Coalition," the Dunn triplet explained. "But if he's dead . . . that means his oldest boy is in charge." She shook her head. "That's not good."

"Jesus, Max," Streep complained. "What is with you?"

"I didn't kill anybody!" She stopped. Thought a minute. "I mean, I don't think I've recently killed anyone important. And definitely not some old man from Italy."

"Just admit it."

"It wasn't me! I don't even know what this Giuseppe person looks like! How would I know to kill him?"

Nelle quickly typed into her phone, then showed it to Max. "This is him."

Max, Mads, Streep, and Tock all moved closer to take a look. Max immediately shook her head. "I did not kill him."

For once, Tock had the feeling Max wasn't lying. "Are you sure?"

"Positive. Look at the big white-and-brown mane on that old dude. I would remember killing him."

"Max is right," Charlie said after looking at the picture herself before putting down a plate of cinnamon buns. "She didn't kill him."

"Why do you insist on protecting such an unstable badger?" Tock's grandmother sneered, as if she didn't protect her own blood just as insistently.

"I'm not protecting her."

"Then how do you know she didn't kill him?"

"Because *that* dude?" Charlie pointed at Nelle's phone. "*I* killed him."

There was a moment of stunned silence before Savta slammed her teacup and saucer on a nearby counter and stood. "What do you mean *you* killed him?"

"I mean, I killed him."

"Why?"

She shrugged. "He and some big-muscled cats were in my house. Uninvited. So, yeah!" she said, without any remorse or concern. "I killed them. I killed them all."

Max crossed her arms over her chest. "I told y'all it wasn't me."

Chapter 22

A few days ago . . .

Charlie loved baking and cooking, but she hated doing the dishes. It was literally her least favorite thing to do in the world. She tried to keep the workload manageable by washing things along the way, but usually when she finished mixing up her last batch of anything, there was still a mess to clean up.

That was what she was doing when she sensed someone sitting at her kitchen table.

She was busy scrubbing a baking pan with her back to the kitchen. Deep in her thoughts about whether she should take a couple of classes at the closest community college. She'd always wanted to go to school, but lacking money and needing to protect Stevie, there hadn't been the time and/or the finances. And although her time was still short, she did have money now and Stevie had Shen.

But then these people suddenly appeared in her house and she realized that maybe an academic career was just not in the cards for her.

"*Signorina* MacKilligan," she heard a voice say from behind her. "We should talk."

With her hands still stuck in hot soapy water, she looked over her shoulder. Even with her allergies acting up, preventing her from smelling much of anything at the moment, she'd still know these lion males. All that hair. Italian lions, in fact. The old man's accent was thick.

"Before you try to run, *signorina* . . . think of your family. Think of your sisters. Think of what I can—"

He stared at her with wide eyes, his words cut off as he tried to take in a breath. The ten-inch chef's knife she'd used to cut up almonds an hour ago was buried so deep in the side of his upper chest, it had impaled a lung and stopped him from talking.

She'd moved so fast, the old cat's protection detail didn't even realize what she'd done until she'd slammed a smaller paring blade into another cat's jugular. That's when they went for their guns. But they didn't already have them out and ready. Their sloppiness gave Charlie precious seconds she could use to snap a neck. Lacerate a spine. Crush a windpipe. And open up two femoral arteries.

By the time she again stood in front of the old cat, he'd begun to choke on his own blood.

She didn't say anything to him as he died. What was there to say?

The swinging door between their kitchen and the living room opened and Max walked in. She stopped immediately and looked around until her gaze settled on her sister.

"Need some help with cleanup?" she asked.

Charlie nodded.

"Okay. Let me change my sneakers, though. I just got these Air Jordans." She grinned. "I'd hate to get blood on them right after I got 'em out the box!"

Now . . .

"What?" Max demanded when everyone in the room looked at her. "They were *new* Jordans. You never waste those on a cleanup."

"Shut up, useless badger!" Savta barked at Max.

"Hey!"

"Why didn't you just talk to him?" Savta asked Charlie, ignoring her sister.

"Talk to him about what?"

"You don't even know why he was there!"

"I don't care why he was there. He walked into my house uninvited. He vaguely threatened my family. I have no regrets."

"When someone says they want to talk, you let them talk!"

"If they want to talk, they should make an appointment."

Max snorted a laugh but quickly stopped when Tock's grandmother pinned her with a vicious glare.

"You are a stupid, reckless child!" Savta told Charlie. "And now look what you have done."

Charlie stepped across the room until she stood in front of the older She-badger. She folded her arms over her chest and bluntly told Tock's grandmother, "The last time strangers walked into my house uninvited, just to talk . . . they killed my mother."

Another shocked silence filled the room, this one lasting for more than a minute. Maybe even two. With Charlie and Savta glowering at each other. In that moment, it was as if the entire world was sitting on the tip of a knife.

At least, that's how it felt until Max said, "Awkward *burn,* old lady!"

Mads's aunt barked out a surprised laugh, but she quickly covered her mouth and looked away. Yup, the whole thing was awkward, all right, but at least it broke the tension.

"Look, the deed is done," CeCe Álvarez announced to the room before moving from her seat to sit on the kitchen table. "There's no point in bitching about it. The question is, what happens now?"

"What happens now?" Savta repeated. "Now there's war."

"Oh, my God!" Streep gasped. "We're going to war with *Italy*? But I'm honeymooning there! Ash even arranged lunch with His Holiness!"

"What exactly would you talk to the pope about?" Nelle wanted to know.

Streep's smile was wide. "About his philosophy on love and life and humanity."

"While your mother is stealing shit out of Vatican storage?" Mads guessed.

"No!" Streep snapped. Then she cleared her throat. "That would be my Aunt Trudi and my cousins. What?" she barked into the following silence. "It's not like the Church uses most of that shit anymore!"

Slowly, painfully, Savta put her fingers against her temples, pressing them deep and massaging the tiny muscles before she snarled out, "Master of the Universe, save me from these idiots."

Since Mira Lepstein wasn't exactly known in Israel for her religious zeal, Tock was pretty sure her grandmother was seconds from ordering a drone strike on them all before signing a deal with the de Medicis that would allow them to rule North America, for no other reason than she just didn't want to deal with the aggravation for another second.

Chapter 23

"I would have done the same thing if someone walked into our kitchen uninvited," Keane admitted to his brothers.

Tock had moved quickly, getting her grandmother out of the kitchen and taking her someplace they could talk privately. Not that Shay blamed her. Tock's grandmother looked ready to go on a murderous rampage.

Mads's aunt and her friends had followed them out, leaving the rest of the group to eat Charlie's baked goods and chat with one another.

"You would have done the same thing if someone looked at you wrong," Finn told his brother.

"That's true. I don't like when people look at me wrong."

Now that there were empty seats at the round kitchen table, Streep patted a spot next to her, motioning for Shay to join them. Not a problem. He'd already finished the platter of Danish he'd grabbed earlier, but he was still hungry.

He sat down next to Streep and grabbed several of the cinnamon buns before his brothers could eat them all. She leaned over and said in what had to be the loudest whisper he'd ever heard, "How did it go last night with Tock?"

"Fine." He shrugged while devouring the first bun he put in his mouth. Then added as he reached for another, "I'm in love with her."

Keane threw his arms in the air. "What is *wrong* with you?" He glanced at Finn. "And you." Then he tossed in, "No offense, Mads."

Mads, who hadn't been paying even a little bit of attention, replied, "Huh?"

"We're tigers," Keane went on. "We're supposed to be exploring the world! Fucking every woman that comes along! Not falling in love after just one hump."

"What are you talking about?" Finn asked. "You haven't been on a date in six years."

"It's been *two*."

"Two *years*?" Max stared right at Keane. "How do you go two years?"

"I have a hand," he shot back. "And I've just put a short moratorium on dating right now because women get so moody when—"

"You ignore them?" Shay guessed.

"I've got things to do! I've got a kid to raise—"

"Dani's not your kid."

"—a football team to manage—"

Finn shook his head. "You're not the manager."

"—a brother to get into college—"

"Has anyone seen him?"

"I got a text from him," Finn said, holding up his phone. "He's alive."

"—and a family to keep safe."

"Which is why we're all on wolf territory! Where we could be murdered in our sleep and no one would know."

"Shut up, Finn. And what are you doing?"

Nelle had placed herself behind Keane, arms around his neck, her phone right in front of them.

"I need a picture of the two of us. I just lied to a guy and told him I have a terrifying Russian boyfriend who will kill him if he comes near me. You don't mind, do you?"

"As a matter of fact—"

"There! Posted. Thanks!"

"Why would they try to kill you guys?" Stevie asked, and everyone focused on the Malone brothers. "I mean, I get us. Charlie killed their patriarch and Max helped clean it up. But what does that have to do with you three?"

"The loving bond between all of us?" Streep asked.

"No. That can't be it."

Tock had never seen her grandmother so agitated. They'd gone to some fancy den with a big wooden desk, leather chairs, and shelves along all the walls filled with old books. But glancing at the titles, all she saw was literature written by old European men that meant nothing to a woman like her.

Tock knew pushing her grandmother to speak was a waste of time, so she let Mira pace and take her time. The badger's mind was turning, trying to figure out where to go from here. But she'd faced more serious enemies before. The woman had faced down Brezhnev. Kissinger. Reagan. Even Mao. Why were some Italian cats freaking her out?

But before Tock could get around to asking that question, the den door opened and Mads walked in with Max, Streep, Nelle, Yoon, Álvarez, and Tracey.

"Why did they try to kill the Malone brothers, too?" Mads asked.

Savta stopped pacing, but she didn't speak. Or even look at them.

"She asked you a question, Lepstein," Mads's aunt pushed. "You should answer her."

Finally, she faced them all and said, "Because they wouldn't stop."

Yoon frowned. "Wouldn't stop what?"

"Looking for who killed their father," Tock guessed.

"Not to be rude," Álvarez said, "but who cares whether they look or not?"

"Their father was CIA."

"So? There are a lot of CIA guys out there. What does one matter to a bunch of Northern Italians?"

Savta walked around to the front of the desk and leaned against it, folding her arms over her chest.

"The de Medici Coalition has always been . . . wiser than most. For decades, maybe even centuries, they've had deals with"—she briefly searched for the right word—"institutions that allowed them to function in the world without worrying about repercussions. In turn, they have provided information that helped these institutions take down other, more well-known criminal organizations."

"Oh, my God!" Yoon exploded. "You knew they were trafficking humans and you guys *let them*?"

Savta held up her hand. "Stop. It was not me. It was not 'you guys.' It was others who did this and allowed it."

"But again," Álvarez interjected, "not to be rude, but so what? So one CIA spook knew what some lions were up to? Who cares?"

"He found out about all this at a time when the old guard had been moved out and a new guard was moving in. More than a few of them unwilling to allow something like that to go on. It's believed that the Malones' father was going to let this new guard know."

"And you let them kill Malone?"

"*I* didn't let them do anything. By the time I heard about any of this, he was dead. Katzenhaus didn't want to blow up their organization by turning cat against cat. And BPC doesn't tell their bears what organizations they can work for. If some bear gets killed in a drive-by, they send flowers to the widow and go about their day. There was nothing left to do but start a war. Something no one wanted. So it was left alone. Except . . ."

"Except?"

"The Malone brothers wouldn't stop looking for the people who killed their father," Mads said.

Savta nodded. "Yes. They still weren't much of a problem because they weren't close to the rest of their family or involved in the government. But then"—she stared hard at Tock and her teammates—"they joined up with *you*."

"And they knew we'd never stop either."

"You are also unaffiliated but still have many contacts. Including me. The mistake, it seems, was for Giuseppe to come here to talk to Charlie MacKilligan on his own. And *you* can stop smirking," she said to Max.

But Max couldn't stop smirking. She even tried, but the smirk stayed on her face.

"What can I say?" Max finally asked. "She's my hero."

Before her grandmother could say something vicious to the honey badger she loathed most of all, Tock said, "You need to go."

Shocked, Savta looked at her. "Emily—"

"You need plausible deniability, Savta. You need to go."

"Whatever you're thinking—"

"We never stop. We never back off. And we never lose with grace."

"The honey badger motto," Rutowski said with an approving nod.

Staring at Tock for a few more seconds, Savta grabbed her purse and sunglasses and stalked out of the room, slamming the door behind her.

Tock then looked at Mads's aunt and her friends, but Rutowski smiled and shrugged. "We're in. Like you, we're also unaffiliated, which really pissed off Reagan . . . and Bush." She smiled at her friends. "Such good times."

Shay sat on a picnic table, watching the dogs sleeping under the summer sun, his daughter in his arms. She'd climbed into his lap to give him a hug and then fell asleep with her head against his chest and her arms and legs tight around his body. He didn't want to wake her from her nap, so he just held her.

And when Tock placed her head against his shoulder, nothing had ever felt so perfect before.

"You okay?" she asked.

"I'm great. You?"

"Good."

"How long do we have to stay here?" he asked.

"Rutowski said you and your brothers could stay as long as you want."

"Tell them thanks, but no thanks." Keane stood in front of them as Finn and Mads came up from behind. "We're going home. I already called Mom. She's coming back. Bringing the aunts. It's time for us to decide where to go from here."

"And where's that?"

"I don't know. But I'm not going to stop until every de Medici is dead."

Shay nodded. "So a thoughtful, rational plan. Good to know."

It took a while to track Charlie down. But only because they never bothered to look up. While everyone else was on the ground floor, she was sitting on the roof of the Van Holtz Hamptons mansion. Just staring.

Everyone worried when Charlie started baking, especially what Max called Charlie's Extreme Baking, when she just baked and baked and baked until she'd driven herself to exhaustion. And there was good reason to be worried about that.

But for Max, the real concern came when all Charlie did was silently stare. No screaming at Max. No worrying about Stevie. No cuddling with Berg. No giving a Van Holtz the finger. Not even thinking about her dogs. Because all she was doing was staring. To Max, that was the most frightening Charlie of all, and Max didn't get frightened.

She sat by her sister, their feet braced against the roof tiles—the only thing holding them up there. Sure, Charlie could have stared from the part of the roof that had been built to hold a large number of people for a party, including chairs, a barbeque, and a wine fridge. But nope. She'd decided to hang out on the steeply sloped part of the roof like an angry bat contemplating the end of the world.

"So what do you want to do?" Max asked her sister. "Anything you say . . . we're in."

"This is normally where I say we run them to ground and we kill them all. But I'm not in the mood to hunt right now. In fact"—she put her arms behind her, propping herself up a bit—"I'm feeling a bit more . . . Max-like, at the moment."

Max grinned. "Really? So you wanna start some shit?"

"I do. And if the de Medicis want a war, I say we give them a war. A badger war."

"Okay," Max replied. "And what's the first step in a badger war?"

Charlie finally looked at her, and the grin she now wore was broad and beautiful.

"First," Charlie said, "we make them bleed."

"Because they already made us bleed?"

"Yes. And now they're gonna bleed, too. Only not just with blood."

Chapter 24

"I know you guys are ready to leave," Charlie said to Keane. "But I'm going to ask you and Nat and the kid to stay here another two days."

Keane faced her. "Why?"

"I have something to do with Max and the rest of them. I'd feel better if Nat and the kid were here, though. But I don't want them here without you guys. Maybe you could also help keep an eye on Stevie? She's still working, trying to figure out the origins of that poison, and it'll take the Group a couple more days to reinforce her lab so she'll be safe."

"Yeah. I can do that. But you need to understand something: Paolo de Medici is *mine*."

"That's fine. Because this shit is just starting."

He glanced off, then nodded. "Okay. We'll stay."

"Good."

"But we're in this together, MacKilligan."

Charlie studied him a moment, before replying, "We're in this together."

She headed back to the house, but his voice stopped her.

"Charlie?"

She faced him again.

"I'm really sorry about your mother."

She took in a shaky, angry breath. "And I'm really sorry about your dad."

They nodded at each other, and Charlie walked out, leaving Keane to continue staring off across the compound, while the

Van Holtz wolves watched him for signs of murderous intent toward their pack.

Max walked up to the bear standing guard at the front gate. "Hi!" she said, smiling at him. She wore a cute, loose summery dress with white high-top Keds, and her hair in two ponytails. She'd just bought the dress and loved it. She liked how it moved around her thighs and knees.

The bear glared down at her and immediately told her to "leave" in Italian. Instead, Max went up on her toes and slammed the blade she'd tucked into the pocket of her dress into his neck, severing the artery.

Another bear came at her from her left. She yanked the blade out of the first bear, dropped to her haunches, and stabbed up and into the thigh of the second. The third, armed with a machine gun, pulled the weapon from his shoulder and aimed it. But Streep attacked him from behind, landing on his upper back. Screeching and stabbing at the man's head, neck, and face, she slammed her knife into the bear over and over. The bear roared, reached back to grab hold of Streep, and threw her off. She hit a nearby tree trunk, her body slamming into it with mighty force. But she rolled off and got back to her feet. Then she charged at the bear again.

Lifting his machine gun, the bear now aimed it at Streep, but Tock grabbed the barrel and snatched the weapon up before placing the muzzle of her own .45 Glock against his temple and pulling the trigger.

Once he went down, she tossed the gun to Mads. Her teammate crouched into a combat position, raised the weapon and, with short, controlled bursts of gunfire, took out the other three bear guards with head shots.

Charlie walked past them all to the entry pad to open the gate. She punched in the code Mads's aunt had obtained for them, and the big gates opened. They each grabbed a body or two and walked inside. Charlie followed, dragging a sack that leaked fluid all the way behind them.

★ ★ ★

The grand double doors that opened into the palatial Northern Italian home of the de Medicis were unlocked. Because who was going to try to sneak into this place knowing the de Medicis lived here? Well, who besides Tock and her teammates? But, of course, they were here for a reason.

The small group stepped onto Italian marble floors and looked at the gilded staircase leading upstairs; vases from Ancient Roman times that were nearly as tall as Tock and antique wooden tables that had been around since the Victorian era dotted the long hallway leading into the heart of the house. It was all a little ostentatious for Tock's tastes but it wasn't tacky. This was Old World money.

They waited for Charlie to come into the house, and then they followed her, avoiding the fluid being left on the floor as she dragged her sack. They reached a large dining room. Charlie walked in, looked around, and nodded. Max and Streep followed Charlie.

Tock and Mads headed upstairs; Nelle went down the hallway. They were in search of dens or offices. Tock found an office on the second floor. She went to the computer. It was all in Italian—a language she could read pretty well, though her pronunciation was terrible. Her Russian was much better.

She used a device Stevie had built for Max a couple of months ago when she was bored. It would find the password for the laptop while Tock and Mads went through all the file cabinets. They pulled out folders that would be helpful and placed them on the desk. By then, Stevie's device got them in to the computer system.

Tock went through the files quickly, finding what she needed. Using a thumb drive, she downloaded the necessary information. While she worked on that, Mads dealt with the standing safe. It was a good safe, but they'd dealt with more secure ones, so it took Mads less than three minutes to get in. She easily found the papers they wanted and removed them.

Looking at her watch, Tock snarled at Mads. Time to go. They grabbed everything they needed and headed down the stairs, meeting Nelle and the others in the dining room. As they worked to finish up, Max abruptly stopped and looked toward the door. Then they all did, because now they heard it, too. Someone speaking in Italian.

Four females dressed in designer everything and the kind of gold jewelry Tock would steal when she needed a quick, but mighty injection of cash from her fence stopped at the open dining room doorway, still gawking at the fluid leaked across the floor from the entrance. One had taken off her big sunglasses, and when she glanced up to look into the dining room, Tock spotted the swollen, black-and-blue side of her face.

The She-lions stared at Tock and her team. The badgers stared back. Neither side spoke. Then, the females simply walked away. They didn't run. Or start using the phones clutched in their hands. They just turned and left.

Charlie took in a deep breath and, more determined than ever, went back to work. In another five minutes they were done.

They started for the doors, but Charlie paused long enough to look at Streep and order, "Put that back."

"But it's—"

"From the Vatican. I know. Put it back anyway."

With a dramatic and rather loud sigh, Streep returned the silver cross to the side table near the door. Then they walked out into the bright sunlight.

They didn't all leave, though. Not yet.

Paolo de Medici walked into his Northern Italian home with his five brothers behind him. His nephews and sons would follow and scurry off to other parts of the house. Anything to avoid a direct confrontation with their fathers.

"What is this?" one of Paolo's brothers asked, staring at the floor. Paolo hadn't noticed the fluid dribbled across his marble. It was sticky and a sickly yellowish brown, with a godawful scent. Even worse, his brown suede Gucci shoes had stepped in it.

Paolo lifted his head and sniffed the air. He smelled death and decay . . . and badgers.

Smirking, curious about what the badgers might have been up to—of course, he now knew he wouldn't have to fire the guards who'd left their post outside the gates; they clearly hadn't left of their own free will—he motioned to his brothers to follow. They silently walked down the hall toward the dining room.

She stood outside the doorway, waiting for them. He knew her. Had seen her picture often enough to know her on sight.

"Maxie MacKilligan, yes?" he asked.

"*Sì!*" she said to him. "And *buongiorno!* But before you say anything else . . . that's the only Italian I know. Except for a few curses." She smiled and he was instantly charmed. How darling she was! He was going to enjoy eating her face off while she screamed.

She put her hands behind her back, shifting her weight from one leg to the other. "We just wanted to say," she began, looking up at him from under her lashes, "how sorry we are about what we did to your dad. We didn't know he was anyone important. But we do understand why you're angry—totally justified, by the way—and we understand how things will be moving forward from now on. I'm sure you understand that, too, right?" There was that smile again. "Anyway, that's all I wanted to say. Have a great day."

She spun around, the skirt of her blood-covered dress billowing a bit as she twirled; then she strolled past the dining room and down the hall.

Paolo started to follow her but froze at the dining room doorway. He could do nothing but gawk for a moment.

Horrified, his brothers pushed past him. All of them roared in bewilderment and anger, but not Paolo. He kept his roars for when he truly needed them. Instead, he let himself briefly marvel at finding a true opponent. No shy house cats or lumbering bears or stupid dogs. He had found someone worthy.

Finally, holding in his excitement so as not to upset his brothers, Paola stepped fully into the dining room and went to the end of the long table where the head of the family sat at all meals.

His father's decomposing body had been placed in the chair designed by a master craftsman: two facing lions cut out of mahogany made up the top of the straight-back seat. The old lion's hands rested on the ornate armrests, his head tilted to the side with his chin resting on his chest; his thick tongue hanging from his mouth; clouded eyes gazing at nothing. Giuseppe was still dressed and, when they quickly searched his pockets, they'd find his wallet and passport. Not even the cash would be missing.

In fact, Paolo realized after quickly glancing around, nothing was stolen. Not even the sixteenth-century cross from the Vatican.

On the table in front of their father were piles of papers. One of his brothers picked a sheet up and gave an angry snarl. He held it up for Paolo to see. It was information on recent product that had come into the country. The bill of lading listed forty-seven "artifacts" from the United States. But if anyone did even a little bit of investigation, they'd realize that no artifacts had come into the port that day. Only full-humans for purchase.

Paolo motioned to his brothers to pick up the papers, but it was too late. Police smashed through the big windows of his dining room. Others kicked down the front doors. They also came in through the back kitchen entrance.

The badgers had contacted the Italian police about them. Had put them on a collision course with armed full-humans. Hoping to get them killed? Maybe. Put in prison for life? Perhaps. Paolo didn't know or care. The evidence of the de Medicis' bad behavior was in stacks of papers around his dead father.

Now this . . . this was more than Paolo could have hoped for.

With guns aimed at them, the police yelled at Paolo and his brothers to put up their hands and get on their knees.

Nothing had to be said between the brothers. No looks had to be passed. No subtle hand movements had to be flashed. Because when it came to living in this world—and whether the honey badgers knew it or not—the de Medicis handled things only one way.

Paolo shifted so fast, the police started shooting without

aiming at anything in particular. He launched himself across the dining room table and into the first full-human man he came to, tearing into his throat and clawing through his protective Kevlar.

By the time he was dragging the man's head across the floor, his brothers had gone after the other police in the room.

Paolo jumped back onto the dining room table and dropped the head from his mouth. He heard more police running down the hall toward the dining room, so he roared. He roared until the She-lions came out of whatever den they'd been hiding in to avoid the males in their life and joined the battle. Tearing and ripping and skinning anything that didn't belong on de Medici land.

Max was near the Range Rover when she heard the lion's roar. She stopped long enough to look back at the house she'd just left. This cat was definitely *not* like his father, who would have just bribed his way out of prison. No. Paolo de Medici would rather cause as much destruction as he could manage just to prove a point to a group of She-badgers with rage issues.

Grinning, Max got into the backseat of the Range Rover and Charlie started driving.

The funny thing was, Max had originally thought it weird that her big sister had insisted on keeping Giuseppe de Medici's body in a twenty-five-foot chest freezer she'd had placed in a storage space in Brooklyn. Because Max had never been a big fan of keeping evidence of their crimes around, she assumed they would just call in some hungry hyenas to help with cleanup, but Charlie had been adamant. The body had to go in storage.

Now, however, Max got it. And loved it.

"Tock," Charlie said from the driver's seat. "Time?"

"We're good."

"I've texted the pilot," Nelle said, tapping on her phone. "The jet will be fueled and ready when we get there."

"You know, Charlie, since we're in Italy anyway, why don't we have a little stopover in—"

"We are *not* going to Vatican City, Streep."

Streep flounced back against her seat, folding her arms over her chest.

"Waste of a perfectly good body dump, if you ask me," the actress complained.

"No one asked you!" they all yelled back.

Chapter 25

As Charlie had suggested, Shay, his brothers, Dani, and Nat had stayed two extra days at the Van Holtz compound. Shay didn't know what Charlie had said to Keane to make him change his mind about that, but Shay was impressed. Not a lot of people were able to get through to his brother. He was hardheaded on and off the field.

When they did finally leave, the Van Holtz adults were a little nicer than they had been when the Malones had first arrived. And Dani actually had wolf pups to say goodbye to, which was nice for her. A couple of the families had even asked to adopt Princess's pups when they reached eight weeks old. A good thing, too, since Shay had been planning to dump them off at a rescue when they were old enough to be separated from their mother. A statement that earned him *that look* from his daughter. The one he hated. As if he'd disappointed her yet again. So, he would see about getting the rest of the pups properly adopted to ensure he didn't keep getting *that look*. At least not until she was firmly in her teens.

At this point, all Shay wanted to do was go home and relax, but as soon they turned onto their street, Keane suddenly hit the brakes.

"What the hell . . . ?" Finn whispered from the front passenger seat.

"What's wrong?" Shay leaned forward, trying to see around his brothers' big heads. But Keane and Finn were already getting out of the SUV. "Stay here," Shay ordered his daughter before he opened his door and slowly eased his way out. Ready to dive into the driver's seat and take the kid away if it became necessary.

Thankfully, it didn't.

"Hello, boys!" one of his uncles called out, motioning for them to come over with a wave of his arm.

The Malone trailers and RVs took up both sides of their street, using up most of the available parking and, for those who'd been parked there before the family had arrived, boxing in the rest.

"What is happening?" Keane asked. But neither Shay nor Finn had an answer for him. The family had never stopped by like this when their father was alive. So it was never expected after he was dead. Seeing them all here was, to put it mildly, very weird.

Keane turned to face his brothers. "Think it's a setup?"

"They're barbequing," Shay pointed out.

"Fresh smoked meats. An easy way to distract us before an ambush."

"Or they're just here for some other non-ambush reason."

"Let's go talk to them," Finn suggested. He started to walk off, realized that Keane wasn't with him, and reached back to grab their brother's arm and yank him forward.

Shay went back to the SUV and opened his door. He leaned in and smiled at his daughter. "Want to meet some of your cousins?"

Her eyes widened. "Yeah!"

"Come on." She unbuckled her seatbelt and scrambled across the seats until she reached him. He lifted her out and together they walked down the street toward their house. Malones called out from where they'd set up lawn chairs and tables for all the food they were cooking.

What the Malones were doing was completely illegal, of course. Blocking driveways and the sidewalk. Blocking most of the actual street itself. His neighbors must be livid. Not that he blamed them.

When Shay reached his brothers, their Uncle Callahan nod-ded at Shay. "And who is this darling little kitty?" he asked, crouching down to eye level with Shay's daughter.

"I'm Dani."

"Well, hello, Dani. I'm your Uncle Cally and this is your Auntie Muriel. She can introduce you to our grandchildren, which would be your cousins. Would you like that?"

"Yes! But first, I need to get my dogs out of the car and into the house."

It was as if Dani had suddenly screamed "*Death to the Irish!*" while swinging a musket. Everyone stopped talking, stopped moving, stopped eating and drinking.

"Dogs . . . ?" Cally repeated.

"Yes. My dogs. My daddy's dogs, actually," she amended.

Cally looked up at Shay. "You have dogs?"

"Yes, my brother has dogs," Keane said, leaning down so he could glower right into their uncle's eyes. "It's absolutely okay for my brother to have dogs."

"It is?" both Dani and Shay asked him.

"It is now," Keane snarled through clenched teeth.

"Why don't we get the dogs, as Dani suggested," Finn of-fered, "and get them settled in the house. We'll be right back. You guys just stay here and do what you've been doing and, um . . . wait for the police!"

"Oh, darlin', they've already been and gone," their Aunt Muriel said.

"They have? And?"

Muriel shrugged. "It's fine."

"It's fine?"

"It's fine."

"Okay." Finn walked back to the SUV and the rest of them followed. They took out the dogs and the puppies and walked them back to the house; everyone watched in disbelief as they moved past.

Once in the house, they put the dogs in Dani's room and left his daughter with them. She had a way of making the puppies and Princess comfortable. The last thing she wanted was her father or uncles involved in that complex process.

Returning to the kitchen, Keane said, "Okay, what is going on? Why are they here?"

"I have no idea," Finn said. "Maybe because of what happened in Manhattan?"

"What if they want something? Money? Our cars?" Keane gasped. "The *dogs*?"

"Okay, you're snapping," Finn warned.

"Then what do you suggest? That we just hand over our organs?"

"How did we get to organs?" Shay asked. "Why would they *want* our organs?"

"It's big business. And we have super organs. Imagine all the full-humans who'd love to get our organs when theirs fail. I'm sure all of them would be willing to pay top dollar for a tiger liver."

"So you think our family came here to steal our livers and sell them to full-humans?"

"It's possible, Finn. And stop looking at me like that. I'm not insane."

"Of course not! This is a completely rational reaction to a visit from our cousins."

"We could just talk to them," Shay suggested.

"All right," Keane said. "But they can't have my kidneys."

Shay nodded at his brother. "That's completely reasonable."

Tock wasn't sure she would ever want to travel commercial again because traveling in one of Nelle's family jets was the best. Fresh food, impeccable service, and tons of legroom. Plus, no one ever took a swing at her or tried to open the emergency doors because they were having visions.

But when they arrived back at the house Charlie had rented on a bear-only street and Tock had put her travel bag down on the floor, she immediately felt disappointed. Which was weird, because simply returning to the States alive and with all four limbs still attached had seemed like a win. Yet at this moment, just standing alone in the middle of the MacKilligan sisters' living room, she didn't feel that way. She felt as if she was missing something.

That's when it hit her: she wanted to see Shay. The fact that she wanted to see anyone after a long flight—yes, even on a private jet—simply because she wanted to spend more time with them was shocking. Usually, Tock just found an empty bed and dropped face-first into it or curled up in a cabinet. Maybe she'd take a nap or have some food delivered. She didn't need to be greeted at an airport terminal with hugs and kisses by family and friends when she returned from far away. Yet, it would have been nice to see Shay at the terminal waiting for her.

Tock pulled out her phone, about to text Shay to see if she could stop by his house later, when a tug on her T-shirt had her turning around and smiling.

"Hi."

"Hi!" Dani grinned up at her and waved, even though they were just standing in the middle of that long, not very wide living room.

"What are you doing here?" Tock asked.

"Daddy wanted to pick you up and bring you to our house."

"Oh, did he?"

"So he texted Mads because he was afraid if he asked you, you'd say no."

"What made him think that?"

She shrugged in reply. "But Mads told him she would drop you off later because she wanted to get in a practice today."

Tock began to rub the back of her neck. That's where all her tension went. "We just got off a long flight. We are *not* practicing today."

"That's what Daddy said you'd say. So he decided to ignore Mads and drive over here with Uncle Finn and me."

"And I'm glad he did."

"Did you have fun on your trip?" Dani asked, eyes so innocent.

"Fun?" *Innocent eyes. Innocent eyes.* "Oh. Yeah. Lots of fun. Fun, fun, fun." Tock grabbed her travel bag and pulled a box out of it, handing it to Dani. "This is for you."

"For me?" She untied the pink ribbon wrapped around the box and lifted the top. Dani's eyes grew wide and her mouth dropped open. Tock was expecting the kid to say something or jump up and down. You know . . . kid stuff. What she didn't expect, though, was the high-pitched squeal that rammed into Tock's sensitive ears like an ice pick.

"*What the hell?*" Charlie screeched from the kitchen. And not even a second later, Shay and Finn ran into the house.

"*What?*" Shay hysterically demanded. "*What's wrong? What's happened?*"

"Look, Daddy!" Dani held the open box high so her father could see. "Look what Tock got me!"

Realizing his daughter was safe, Shay immediately released a breath. He bent over at the waist, resting his hands on his knees. "I thought something . . ."

"Train your child," Finn ordered his brother before going in search of Mads.

"Look, Daddy!" Dani said again, completely ignoring her uncle. "Look! Look! Look!"

"Yes," Shay said, now panting from the spike of adrenaline. "That's gorgeous, baby."

"Put it on me! Put it on me!" Dani ordered Tock.

Tock took the watch out from its packaging. It was pink and sparkled like the sun from all the pink Swarovski crystals she'd added because she knew what the kid liked. She put it on Dani's wrist, tightening it almost to the last lug hole on the band. She wanted the kid to be able to grow into it over time.

"There," Tock said when she was finished. "What do you think?"

There went that high-pitched squeal again. Tock reared away from the kid, worried her ears might start bleeding.

Dani took off running, maybe to show Nat.

"Tell me you didn't pay two hundred and fifty thousa—"

"I didn't. She's too young to appreciate a watch of *this* caliber," Tock said while gesturing to her own pride and joy with her other hand. "I just pulled a watch from the case and had my watchmaker bling it up a little."

"Your watchmaker? The expensive one?"

"Yeah, but Dani's watch wasn't expensive. Besides, a watch is an investment."

"No, it's not."

"It is to me, and it is to your daughter."

"How do you know that?"

The high-pitched squeal started again and Dani, now outside, ran by the living room windows, her arms above her head, waving them wildly.

"Let's just say"—the kid ran by again going the opposite direction. And, yes, still squealing—"it's a good guess."

Shay reached over and took Tock's hand into his. "I missed you," he admitted.

Okay. Finn was probably right, and he was moving too fast, but Shay didn't want to hold back or lie about his feelings just to keep from freaking Tock out. If she really liked him, was comfortable with him, telling her how he felt shouldn't freak her out. And he had no doubt that if she wanted him to back off, she'd tell him that in no uncertain terms.

"I was gone three days," she pointed out.

"I know. But I still missed you."

"I—"

Dani jumped in front of one of the living room windows, still screeching about her new watch. They gazed at his daughter until she ran off into the yard and then looked back at each other.

Tock cleared her throat and finally said, "I missed you, too." She gave a small smile. "I also missed the kid. I have five new notebooks filled with equations for her to work on."

"That's great because she already went through the ones you left for her. She tried to work with Stevie, but Stevie was really busy and when she did try to help Dani, she overwhelmed her, I think."

"Overwhelmed her how?"

"Something about time and space and the probability of as-
teroids crashing into the planet and wiping out all of life as we
know it.

"Oh, my God." Tock closed her eyes. "Yeah. I'll . . . uh . . .
I'll work with Dani."

"Thank you."

They were still holding hands, but Tock intertwined their
fingers. Shay decided to take that as a good sign.

"Did you get home okay after you left the Hamptons?"

"Yeah, but . . ." Shay blew out a breath. That conversation
with the Malones had been interesting. Uncle Cally and the
others never admitted to anything. They never said, "We're
here to do this. Or we're here to do that." They never said,
"We're here to protect you because we feel bad about how
shitty we were to you after your father died." Or even, "We're
vengeful tigers, too, and pissed someone shot at us. We'll get
even together!" Instead, they drank Irish beer, made jokes, and
promised to hang around until, one day, as Shay and his brothers knew, they'd all be gone. Off to torture another street in
another neighborhood.

Their next-door neighbor had stormed out of his house to
complain about all the noise and the strangers on "his" street,
but one roar from Uncle Cally had sent the idiot fleeing back to
his house. They hadn't seen him since. More upsetting was the
interest that a few of his dad's cousins were showing in Shay's
mother. Something Keane, Finn, and Shay weren't going to let
get any further than general flirting. Because . . . just . . . no!
Absolutely not!

Dani had been happy, though, getting to meet her younger
cousins and playing with them. But Tock had been absolutely
right. When Dani had had enough socializing, she walked off.
When a young male cousin tried to follow to keep the fun
going, she slammed him into a wall, told him "No means no,
Michael Patrick!" and returned to her room. The dogs were
the only ones she didn't seem to need time away from.

"But what?" Tock asked.

Telling Tock all that stuff could wait. Instead, he asked, "Would you like to go out to dinner tonight? With me? Just the two of us," he added before she could suggest her friends or Dani, who had been bugging him on the drive over about spending the night with Nat again.

"Do you mean, like, a . . . date?"

Shay grinned. "Yes, Tock. I mean, like, a date. A normal, average dinner date between a Siberian tiger and an African honey badger."

"Israeli-Jamaican honey badger and, yes, I'd love that."

She moved close and wrapped her arms around his chest because she was wearing sneakers and couldn't reach his neck.

Leaning down, Shay kissed her. Nothing, except the birth of his daughter, had ever been so perfect.

When he pulled back, he told her, "I'm glad you're home."

"Me, too."

"Did you have a good trip?"

"Uh . . . yeah. Yeah. Sure. Yeah. Good trip."

Shay gazed down at her and, after letting out a breath, asked, "What did you guys do?"

"No, no." She stepped back and took his hand, tugging him toward the front door. "Not tonight, Shay. Tonight is date night. And we are going to have a nice, normal dinner before the shit storm we started in Italy comes crashing down all around us. Sound good?"

"Yeah, sure." Shay stopped cold. "Wait . . . what?"

"So, Charlie MacKilligan killed Giuseppe de Medici?"

Mira shrugged. "Yes."

How many times did she have to say it to these people? What were they not understanding?

"And she really didn't ask him anything? She just killed him?" the wolf asked again.

"Right."

"In other words, Paolo de Medici is now in charge."

"Right."

"Oh, this just gets fucking better," the house cat snarled.

"And to get all the bad news out now," Mira said, "the two older MacKilligan sisters dragged my granddaughter and her friends to Italy on a private jet."

"Oh, for fuck's sake!"

"Why?" the older Van Holtz asked.

"Don't know yet."

"Great. Just great."

"And I've lost track of Rutowski and her friends."

"In other words," Bayla Ben-Zeev said, "you have no control over your people."

"Those three MacKilligan sisters and Rutowski and her friends are *not* my people, and they are *not* badgers. They're insane rodents, running around, chewing through wires, and burning down the world. And they're dragging my beautiful granddaughter with them!"

"Maybe if you didn't call them rodents, Mira, they'd listen to you more."

"Shut. *Up*. Bayla."

"If the MacKilligans have slipped their leashes," the cat suggested, "perhaps we should have them—"

"Killed?" Bayla asked. "Because that worked out so well the first time."

"That was *not* the first time someone tried to kill the MacKilligans," Mira said with a headshake.

"Not killed. Managed."

"Have you ever tried to lock up a honey badger?" Mira turned to look directly at the cat. "Even Stalin's Siberian gulags couldn't hold them."

"I know of several badgers locked away in full-human prisons," she countered.

"Because they *want* to be there! Either they're hiding from something far worse or they're making money. And, when they've finally gotten what they want or the threat has gone away, those badgers will get themselves out. And the ones who locked them up? They'll wake up one day to find badgers in the walls and one of them pissing in their bed."

"Then what do we do?"

"I'd normally say we should try to reason with them before this gets out of hand."

"There is no reasoning with MacKilligans, Van Holtz."

"Mira," he said, his gaze across his office, "I believe you're right."

The wolf grabbed a remote from his desk and pressed a button, taking the mute off the TV that had been on but mostly ignored since Mira had started talking. They all stared at the footage of the burning home of the de Medici Coalition, which had stood for centuries in Northern Italy. But the burning house wasn't Mira's concern. It was the "number of dead police officers" who had burst into the home to arrest the de Medici brothers moments before the house burned to the ground.

When the news report ended, Van Holtz muted the TV again and the five of them sat in silence for nearly ten minutes until Bayla finally said, "Well, this all took a nasty turn, didn't it, Mira?"

Her fangs sliding out of her gums, Mira said the only thing she could think of in the moment: "Shut. *Up.* Bayla!"

Visit our website at
KensingtonBooks.com
to sign up for our newsletters, read
more from your favorite authors, see
books by series, view reading group
guides, and more!

BOOK CLUB
BETWEEN THE **CHAPTERS**

Become a Part of Our
Between the Chapters Book Club
Community and Join the Conversation

Betweenthechapters.net